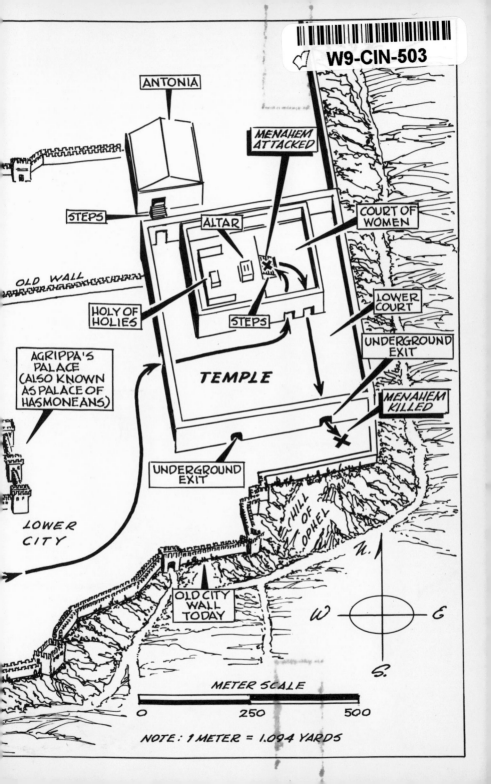

ANTONIA

MENAHEM ATTACKED

STEPS

ALTAR

COURT OF WOMEN

OLD WALL

HOLY OF HOLIES

STEPS

LOWER COURT

UNDERGROUND EXIT

AGRIPPA'S PALACE (ALSO KNOWN AS PALACE OF HASMONEANS)

TEMPLE

MENAHEM KILLED

UNDERGROUND EXIT

LOWER CITY

HILL OF OPHEL

OLD CITY WALL TODAY

N.

W E

S.

METER SCALE

0   250   500

NOTE: 1 METER = 1.094 YARDS

F
G24   Gavron, Daniel.
          The end of days.

F
G24   Gavron, Daniel.
          The end of days.

THE END OF DAYS

THE END OF DAYS

A
novel
of
the Jewish War
against
Rome
66–73 C.E.

by
DANIEL GAVRON

The Jewish Publication Society of America
Philadelphia
5730 · 1970

FOR REUVEN

who fell in the battle for Jerusalem
June 1967

HISTORICAL NOTE

In the first century of the Common Era, when the Roman Empire was at the height of its power, the small country of Judea was the most troublesome of its colonies. Ruled over by procurators of the lower middle class, Judea suffered more than other provinces from the high taxation imposed by Rome. One reason for this was that the procurators, unlike the more aristocratic governors who administered other territories, used their position for personal enrichment. Another reason for the extra burden born by Judea was the heavy tithes and Temple dues levied by the local priestly and aristocratic classes over and above the Roman taxes. Large numbers of peasants were forced to leave the land, and they collected in the towns where they formed a large discontented class.

The Roman Empire was a region of Greek culture, with Roman and local adaptions. The Jews, on the other hand, had fought a fierce, unrelenting struggle for the preservation of their way of life. Their attitude can be summed up by the words of one of their sages: "It is written 'thou shalt meditate therein [in the Law] day and night'—find me an hour that is neither day nor night, and in that hour you may study Greek." The Jewish religion dominated every facet of Jewish national life, and it was religion, rather than social or economic conditions, that fired the revolt.

The war which broke out in 66 C.E. was preceded by a century of intermittent rebellion and a dozen years of complete anarchy. The local populace was not homogeneous, and the Gentiles who inhabited such cities as Caesarea and Scythopolis were hostile to the Jewish cause. Even the Jews themselves were split into dozens of conflicting sects and factions. There was no logic in the revolt of these warring groups against the well-trained soldiers of Rome, but logic had no place in Jewish motivation. For two centuries the Jews had believed that a new era—the End of Days foretold by the prophets—was at hand. They were convinced that God Himself was about to intervene to bring their misery to an end, deliver them from their enemies, and establish His kingdom of righteousness on earth.

It is the contention of this writer that only by trying to grasp the power and intensity of this messianic belief can we hope to understand the story of the Jewish War against Rome.

D. G.

THE END OF DAYS

FLAVIUS SILVA: JANUARY 73 C.E.

And it shall come to pass in the end of days, that the mountain of the Lord's house shall be established as the top of the mountains, and shall be exalted above the hills; and all the nations shall flow unto it.

And many peoples shall go and say: 'Come ye and let us go up to the mountain of the Lord, to the house of the God of Jacob; and He will teach us of His ways, and we will walk in His paths.' For out of Zion shall go forth the law, and the word of the Lord from Jerusalem.

And He shall judge between the nations, and shall decide for many peoples; and they shall beat their swords into ploughshares, and their spears into pruninghooks; nation shall not lift up sword against nation, neither shall they learn war any more.

O house of Jacob, come ye, and let us walk in the light of the Lord.

Isaiah 2. 2–5

L. Flavius Silva Nonius Bassus, seventeenth procurator of Judea, looked out over the craggy brown wasteland of dust and stones. In front of him, sheer and immense, stood the rock, on the summit of which was the fortress. He removed his helmet and wiped his gleaming bald head. For five hours Flavius Silva had encircled the rock, and from each new angle it had looked more inaccessible. For five hours the dark brown cliffs had towered forbiddingly above him. He had seen the dizzying path of the serpent to the east and the supposedly climbable southern flank. Only from the west, where he now stood in his main siege camp, did the summit look almost attainable.

He had inspected all eight camps, the two for the legion and the six smaller ones for the auxiliaries. The camps had been carefully constructed in the classical pattern. He did not wish to expose his soldiers to unnecessary risks. He had been informed that the Jews had an unpleasant habit of attacking even when it made no sense. The camp followers—traders, suppliers, and scavengers—were scattered in a disorderly fashion around the camps; but they were not his concern.

The eight camps covered every possible escape route. Each camp was surrounded by a square rampart, the solidity of which compensated for the shallowness of the surrounding ditches. The gates let into the sides of the ramparts were defended by inward-turning walls. Crossroads divided each camp into four parts, within which the tents of the soldiers were neatly laid out. At the center of each camp was a public square with a platform for the commander.

Silva's own camp was situated to the west of the rock. The procurator had a good view of his task from there—it was from the west that the assault on the fortress would have to be mounted. He contemplated the enormous physical challenge. From his vantage point the procurator could see the defenders carrying water to the summit from the two rows of cisterns in the cliff face. One of the first tasks of the besiegers had been to destroy the aqueducts which fed the cisterns, but the defenders had been left with abundant water.

5

The Roman forces had assembled at Herodium to the south of Jerusalem; from there they had marched through the wild Judean desert to the ruins of Ein Gedi, by the Sea of Salt. Silva had arranged for additional supplies to be sent there from the farmlands around Hebron to the west. At Ein Gedi he had divided his forces into two parts, leading one south along the mountain ridge and sending the other in the same direction along the shore of the sea, both arriving simultaneously at the western and eastern sides of the rock to forestall a possible breakout by the rebels penned up there. As soon as they arrived, the camps were constructed. Silva was worried that the rebels would elude him and begin fighting somewhere else. Unless they could be pinned down and destroyed, there would be no end to the fighting.

The fortress was an irritation, a sore. The war was over, the country defeated; but the fortress remained, an insufferable twenty acres of Jewish sovereignty in the midst of the savage desert. It was a wondrous country, a section of land stripped to its bare elements. The procurator screwed up his eyes against the glare. He replaced his helmet, which afforded him some protection.

Entering his tent, he nodded to the guard and dismissed the two tribunes who had accompanied him on his circuit. He laid his helmet on the rough table, unbuckled his breastplate, and removed his sandals. He longed for a bath, but with water scarce even for drinking, he could not hope for such a wild extravagance. It was not going to be a comfortable campaign.

The tent was constructed like the tents of the soldiers—a circular stone wall above which was pitched a canvas roof supported by a single pole. He lay down on his pallet and folded his arms behind his head.

Silva was of average height, broad-shouldered and athletic. Beneath his prominent nose and thin, hard mouth, he was clean-shaven in the Roman manner. His gray eyes were almost humorous. Although strict, he was not a harsh or stupid disciplinarian and was popular with his soldiers. He was far from being an arrogant man; he had fought in enough different countries to appreciate the different customs and ways of life

6

that made up the Roman Empire. Its diversity was its glory, but diversity did not obviate the need for order.

Order was a quality not possessed by the Jews. The procurator had studied the background of the war and had learned that the rebels in the fortress had not taken any action to relieve the pressure on Jerusalem during the siege because of some factional dispute with the defenders of the capital. He wished to understand the dispute. If he could induce the rebels to surrender, he could save countless lives and a small fortune in supplies. But to offer surrender terms he had to know what they valued.

He lay on his back thinking, trying to understand what it was that made a tiny community hold out in that awful spot for so long. If he could understand what had induced them to seize the fortress seven years previously, he might have a better idea of how to fight them now.

BOOK I

MENAHEM: 66 C.E.

Meanwhile some of those most anxious for war, made a united attack on a fort called Masada, captured it by stealth, and exterminated the Roman garrison, putting one of their own in its place.

Flavius Josephus, *The Jewish War*

1

Eleazar, the son of Jair, was awake. While his eyes took note of the stars in the sky, his right hand moved instinctively to his head, feeling that the rough linen skullcap was in its place. His lips moved in prayer: *"I give thanks to Thee O Lord this day."*

He sat up, reaching for his waterskin and poured a few of the precious drops over his hands. *"Blessed art Thou O Lord our God, King of the Universe, who has sanctified us by Thy commandments. . . ."*

From where he sat Eleazar could see the rock outlined against the stars. The stars were bright here in the desert, brighter even than in Galilee. It was a long time since Eleazar had looked at the heavens from Galilee. He stood up, hugging his woolen cloak about him, unable to keep out the cold.

He started waking his sleeping companions. The experienced veterans woke silently; even his younger brother Simon made no sound. Then he went and stood apart while his men made ready. One by one they came and stood beside the silent figure of their leader. Old John, with his gnarled frame and matted white beard, who had fought with Eleazar's grandfather, came first, followed by the others down to Simon, merely a boy and seeing his first real action. They stood together in the open and prayed almost silently, their voices not rising above a murmur. When they had finished, they ate some meal and drank a little water.

Eleazar led them in single file down into the valley, walking lightly in his goatskin sandals, careful not to dislodge any rocks. It was still dark and they moved partly by feel, partly by the faint light of the stars. They carried no armor, shields, or bows, but each of the men possessed, in a sheath fastened to his belt, a long sharp knife. Eleazar felt the well-worn bone haft of his dagger, the *sica,* the very name of which sent a shudder through the length and breadth of Judea.

11

So far, the plan had been successful, thought Eleazar. God willing, they would capture the fortress that day; but that was only the start. The road that lay ahead was a long one. The Almighty could doubtless fulfill His purpose unaided, but He chose to work through mankind. It was the glorious destiny of Israel to be the particular instrument of the Lord. For what other purpose did he, Eleazar ben Jair, draw breath? Why else did he eat and drink?

Menahem's plan had been a good one, the product of many years of experience. Most of the rebels had wanted to strike as soon as the first disturbances had broken out in Jerusalem, but they had been overruled. The time had not yet come, Menahem had said. Eleazar thought of this as he led his men silently along the narrow desert track through the rock-strewn valley.

"Eleazar knows the fortress," Menahem had said. "He and I were there during the time of Agrippa, and he has been in the region for the past five years. There cannot be another man in the country who knows that desert as Eleazar knows it." Eleazar smiled in the darkness—the old man had spoken the truth.

Though a child of Galilee, he had come to regard Idumea and southern Judea as his home. He knew every track and every water hole. Although the desert could be traversed entirely in one day, there were places where a man might wander interminably without finding his way, places where a man might perish of thirst. The Idumeans grazed their sheep and goats there, and where the water supply was sufficient had built a few permanent hamlets; but someone unfamiliar with the region could walk for days without seeing any sign of habitation. To the east, where the high plateau descended sharply into the basin of the Sea of Salt, the land was bare, and in that rocky wilderness no man lived. For the past six months Menahem had demanded a wide variety of information about this region, but his reasons had emerged only a week previously.

The men followed Eleazar silently as he led them in the darkness along a track that most of them, experienced guerrilla fighters though they were, would have found difficult in daylight. Old John, following closely behind his leader, tried to control his breathing. As he tried to keep up with the slight figure in front of him, he reflected that he was growing old for this sort of activity. Also a Galilean, he had often enough scaled sheer cliffs in his native region while escaping from forces sent out to capture him. As an experienced rock climber he had insisted on accompanying Eleazar, whom he had served as deputy for the past five years. Menahem had remonstrated with him, but old John had refused to heed him. "If you can scale the cliffs south of the spring of Sekaka and north of Ein Gedi, Rabbi," he had declared, "I can certainly traverse a few hundred feet of aqueduct to the cisterns." Here in the dark, his breath beginning to wheeze, he felt less confident.

John had been an outlaw for sixty years, since the time when as a boy of ten he had carried messages during the great revolt of Judah ben Hezekiah of Galilee. In that revolt his father and mother had lost their lives; John had lived with the rebels ever since. In all that time there had been only one short period of four years when he had not been fighting, raiding, or fleeing. That was during the reign of the first Agrippa, when the patriotic bands had become almost respectable.

John had played his part in training the large bands of irregulars in the desert, which were to supplement the king's own troops on the day of revolt; but that day had not come. It had not been the appointed time, as the great revolt of Judah had not been, nor the unsuccessful attempt of Judah's sons, Jacob and Simon. Now, he thought, is the appointed time. It has to be! With difficulty he controlled his breathing as he crept after Eleazar.

Simon ben Jair walked at the rear of the column. He felt elated, for he was to fight. At last his brother had given way —Eleazar the thinker! He thought of his elder brother almost with scorn, admiring the middle brother, Judah, far more; but as he struggled to keep pace with the man in front of him, Simon had to admit to a grudging admiration for his philosophical brother. When the need arose, Eleazar could become very much the man of action. He was finding it difficult enough to

13

follow the man in front of him; he could not imagine how Eleazar was finding his way in the starlight that was no light. For the hundredth time he felt the new wooden haft of his *sica,* which he was wearing for the first time.

Among the youngsters who lived with the Sicarii outlaw band commanded by his brother, Simon excelled. Fighting with a wooden dagger, he could disarm any of the others inside a minute. But today would be different; today he would be fighting fully armed soldiers. His stomach felt weak when he thought about it, but he forced himself on. Then the hair on the back of his neck crawled suddenly with fear, as he felt the man in front signaling him to stop.

Eleazar stopped; they had arrived at the dam. Belting up his cloak so that it would not impede his progress, he started to crawl along the aqueduct. The first few hundred feet were easy enough and not very high from the ground, but then the valley floor dropped away steeply as the waterway approached the cliff face.

Arriving at the cliff, he turned left along the channel which had been cut into the side of the face. Rising to his feet, he stood erect with his back to the rough surface of the rock. Slowly, inch by inch, he started to edge his way along. The first signs of dawn were appearing. The sun would rise on the far side of the rock in less than half an hour, and although they were on the western side of the rock, which would be in shadow, Eleazar began to wonder whether they would reach their objective in time. As soon as it became light, they could be observed from the defense tower above the aqueduct. He tried to move faster, praying that he would not dislodge any loose scree. He could hear old John behind him, his breath coming in short gasps.

The dark brown crags of the surrounding desert were emerging through the morning mist. Eleazar could see that he was coming to the end of the channel. There were some six hundred feet of aqueduct to negotiate before reaching the cisterns. He hoped that the marvelous structure would hold their weight. He swung out into space, and then he was sitting astride the aqueduct, pushing himself along as quickly as he

14

could, tearing his hands on the rough rock as he moved forward. Once he looked down into the abyss below, but then hurriedly returned his gaze to the channel in front of him, marveling at the miraculous construction of a waterway in that place.

He hurried his men along the narrow ledge to the cisterns. The sun was already rising on the far side of the rock and he knew that at sunrise the slaves would come down from the summit for water, carrying their heavy earthenware pitchers.

2

Some dozen miles to the north of where Eleazar and his men waited, Absalom, second-in-command of the Sicarii rebels, lay in the rocky defile of a gorge. He knew that he had several hours of waiting ahead of him, so he was pleased that his men still slept. The auxiliary cohort of the enemy was starting out well before sunrise from Herodium, which lay to the south of Jerusalem; the day would be well advanced before they arrived at the head of the gorge, which led tortuously down to the village of Ein Gedi. Although Absalom's task was the most difficult, it might in the end prove to be superfluous. The fortress should be theirs that day, whereas the soldiers were likely to sleep the night at Ein Gedi before continuing on their way the following morning; but Menahem had been adamant that nothing should be left to chance. At the meeting, Absalom had protested that no cohort would carry out a march like that over such difficult terrain.

"Is it impossible, Absalom?" Menahem had demanded.

"No. Not impossible," he had been forced to admit.

"Then we shall assume it can be done," the old man replied. "I want to cover every contingency."

He had attended personally to every detail, down to the murder of the cohort's Idumean guide and his replacement by Eleazar's brother Judah. Absalom compressed his thick lips when he thought of Judah ben Jair. The young man had a heavy responsibility; it was unlikely that he would survive the day. Once the auxiliary force discovered it had been led into a trap, the soldiers would fall on their treacherous guide; yet Menahem had not hesitated to assign this suicidal role to his own nephew.

Absalom stood up and stretched. He was an enormous man with smooth olive skin and a small, pointed beard. No knife had ever touched Absalom's face, but his blue-black beard and mustache gave the impression of being partly shaven and neatly trimmed. His great chest and powerfully muscled limbs were almost free of hair. He was said to be part Idumean, but he had spent the past few years of his life in the hills of Samaria. Absalom had always been glad to accept the hardest tasks, and Samaria, with its swarming Greek colonies and ambiguous Samaritans, was the most dangerous region in Judea for the outlaws. His band, most of whom were with him now, was a small one.

He started to rouse his men. It was early yet, but Menahem had been insistent that nothing should be left to chance. Just north of where the hundred and fifty men slept wrapped in cloaks, the gorge forked. A troop coming south would not be able to distinguish which of the two tracks led down to the village of Ein Gedi. That was where Judah's task began. On the previous day Absalom's men had flattened down the false path and strewn rocks over the genuine track; but it really depended on Judah.

Absalom's force was divided into two sections. The larger group lay in concealment on either side of the track. Once the whole cohort had entered the canyon, it would be their task to block the way out. They would attempt to build a rock barrier to hinder the egress of the auxiliaries, but Absalom doubted whether they would have much time for its construction. Within minutes they would have to fight—the barrier blocking the entrance to the canyon would be a human one. The remainder of the force would be positioned on the cliffs above the gorge; from there they would shoot arrows and roll down large boulders on the enemy below. Absalom ran his fingers through his sparse black beard and thought about Judah; it all depended on Judah.

16

3

Some dozen miles to the south of Herodium, Judah ben Jair walked with an easy stride alongside the mounted commander of the auxiliary cohort. He was a dark, sullen young man, taller and broader than his elder brother, Eleazar. Judah was a natural guerrilla fighter, completely relaxed, nerveless and sure of himself. On the previous evening he had killed the Idumean peasant who was to have guided the cohort. It had been simple enough. Judah knew how to kill swiftly and silently, and the other had offered no resistance. He had disposed of the body in an unused water hole, and then, completely unarmed, he had walked up to the gates of Herodium, wearing his victim's dirty cotton tunic.

"Where is Eli?" the captain had asked in his rough, Sebastian-accented Aramaic.

"Eli is sick with the fever," Judah had replied. After five years in the south he spoke like an Idumean. "They sent me in his place."

"Do you know the route to the fortress?"

"I could lead you there in the dark," he had smiled. The captain had looked at him shrewdly.

"You may well have to," he had replied. "We are making no stops on the way."

"You are marching to the fortress in one day?" asked Judah in surprise. "Without staying the night at Ein Gedi?"

"Would you say it was impossible, Idumean?"

"Impossible? No, not impossible; but not easy."

"These are troubled times," the captain had replied. "I want my troop inside the fortress as quickly as possible. We shall start before sunrise. I hope your coreligionists are not going to cause us trouble on the way." He looked searchingly at Judah again, but the latter remained expressionless.

Judah and the captain were slightly ahead of the standard-bearer. When he glanced back at the standard, Judah could not help smiling at the way the Sebastians aped their Roman masters, the tiny cohort comparing itself to the mighty legion. Yet as he regarded the small cavalry troop followed by the main body of infantry and slaves, he thought that they were not to be underestimated. Though not as heavily armed as legionaries, they were more mobile and they looked like experienced fighters. Possibly this very cohort had hunted Absalom in the hills of Samaria. Judah pictured the big man's satisfaction on seeing that the force was Sebastian. That was something that even Menahem's intelligence had not known. Not for the first time Judah wondered whether his uncle's plan would really work. It seemed perfect; but was it not too complicated, with its numerous small details? It was a good plan though, there was no doubt about that.

4

It was indeed a good plan, reflected Menahem ben Judah, leader of the Sicarii, as he marched along the shore of the Sea of Salt. He was not leading the column; that would have been foolhardy. No auxiliary cohort, even in Judea, would be led by a man with a long gray beard. Menahem was hidden away in the ranks. His force, four hundred strong, was fully armed in local auxiliary style. A detachment of cavalry led the column. They were armed with swords and light shields and wore breastplates. The infantry carried spears and wore helmets. Several score of bowmen were concealed in the inner ranks.

In a few minutes the first signs of daybreak were due, and the sun would rise within half an hour. To the left of the marching column lay the oily gray surface of the Sea of Salt; to the right towered the cliffs, which plunged sharply from the desert plateau down to the valley. Ahead of them the cliff face was split by two transverse fissures, and on the summit of the section of rock set apart by these cracks stood the fortress of Masada, the most impregnable fastness in all Judea.

A week previously Menahem ben Judah had unfolded his plan. He had summoned his rebel leaders from Samaria, Judea, and Idumea to the community of Sekaka, which was situated on the northwestern shore of the Sea of Salt. The Sons of Zadok, who lived, worked, and studied there in the wilder-

18

ness, allowed the Sicarii to come and go as they pleased. Sekaka was a good cover for the Sicarii. The authorities would never think of looking for the rebels among the scholars of the pious community of the Sons.

By the time they had arrived, it was night. Sitting in a goatskin tent, before a rough wooden table lit by oil lamps, Menahem had outlined his plans to the Sicarii leaders.

The situation they faced was not unpromising from their point of view. Since the death of the first Agrippa and the reestablishment of direct Roman rule, some twenty years previously, Judea had been restless. New taxes were constantly levied. There was a tax for each member of the family, for each building, hut, or shed, for each animal, each plot of vegetables. When they traveled, the people had to pay tolls on the roads; and when produce was transported from one region to another, it was heavily excised. The publicans collected the taxes from the farmers and peasants and passed on the proceeds to the regional administrators, who were responsible to the procurator; at each stage, the individual in question deducted his commission. The publicans were expected to collect a fixed amount, so whatever they could squeeze out of the people over and above that amount was theirs.

On top of the crushing burden of Roman taxes, the people were expected to pay Temple dues and tithes for the priests. The priests were a wealthy class, and the richer priests robbed their poorer colleagues. There was starvation on the land. The smallholder was forced to sell out to the large landowner, resulting in an increasing flow of destitutes to the cities, where they lived on charity and theft. These people were eagerly receptive to messages of freedom and to prophecies of the messianic age. Rebel activity increased.

Foremost among the revolutionary groups was that led by Menahem ben Judah, with a tradition of rebellion going back to before Herod's time. Originally a Galilean movement, the Sicarii had been operating in Judea for more than twenty years. A dozen years previously, Menahem had increased the pressure of outlaw activity by sending groups of assassins to strike against the Romans and their Jewish aristocratic and

19

priestly allies. It was from this action that his band received its name. They were called the Sicarii, after their favorite weapon, the long dagger or *sica*.

In the past year the political situation had become increasingly unstable. Some months before, an imperial decision had resulted in control of the administration of Caesarea passing from Jewish hands into those of their Syrian-Greek co-citizens. Pleased by their success, the latter started a series of provocations against the Jewish inhabitants of the town. The ensuing riots were savagely suppressed, and the Jews suffered considerably. These events inflamed the rest of Judea, where the Jews were a majority; but instead of restoring order and calming the situation, the incumbent procurator, Gessius Florus, chose to provoke the Jews further by having a large sum of money withdrawn from the Temple treasury.

Outside the Temple in Jerusalem, a couple of young wits expressed their derision by sarcastically passing around collection boxes in aid of the procurator. Enraged by this insult, Florus marched to Jerusalem with a detachment of soldiers, to be met by jeering crowds. The Jewish leaders of the city, although embarrassed by the mob's behavior, were not able to deliver the ringleaders to the procurator. Florus responded to the situation by sending his troops to plunder certain quarters of the city; as a result, several hundred people lost their lives. He also ordered a number of people, including some Jews who were Roman citizens, to be scourged and crucified.

The full-scale riot that subsequently broke out was calmed by the priests, who even succeeded in persuading the populace to make a gesture of goodwill by going out to greet the two cohorts of soldiers called up as reinforcements by Florus. The response of the soldiers to this conciliatory gesture on the part of the Jews was to draw their swords and drive the crowd back into the city amid great slaughter. Now nothing could prevent the Jews from fighting back, unarmed though they were. Pelting the Romans with rocks and paving stones, they gained possession of the Temple and cut it off from the Antonia fortress, which normally controlled it, by destroying the connecting galleries and staircase.

20

Florus was forced to withdraw, but Agrippa II, the Jewish king who ruled over some of the northern territories and who administered the Temple, arrived in the city and managed to restore the situation. In an eloquent speech he pointed out the futility of revolt against Rome; he persuaded the people to rebuild the staircase to the Antonia and to collect taxes for the Romans. For the time being, a direct clash had been averted.

The Sicarii leaders had discussed these events, sitting in the lamplight at Sekaka. Menahem sat at the head of the table. To his right sat his deputy, the dark, powerful Absalom. His nephew Eleazar, slight and wiry, sat on his left, and the other leaders sat around the table, only partly visible in the dim light. Absalom had been in a mood of exasperation.

"How many opportunities do we have to lose?" he had demanded. "Have you joined the Sons of Zadok, Menahem, that you sit here waiting and waiting?" His dark, full-lipped face was flushed with wine and his sparse, blue-black beard was disordered by his feverish fingers. Menahem ben Judah had looked him straight in the eye. He was almost as large a man as Absalom, still powerful despite his age, with broad shoulders and a deep chest. His noble head was framed by a halo of thick gray hair, and a vast fan-shaped gray beard spread over his chest. His wide-set, dark brown eyes looked calmly out from their deep sockets beneath his wide brow. His high-bridged nose was covered with a network of tiny red and blue veins, and though his face was heavily lined, his mouth was still firm. He sat at ease, his deep musical voice quiet and reasonable.

"Restraint, Absalom. We must show restraint," he had replied. "We must choose the right time to act."

"When is the right time?" the other had demanded. "Three chances in the last week and you ignored them all!" He ticked off the points with his heavy forefinger: "One, when Florus first arrived in Jerusalem. The mob was ready to fight even then. Two, when his troops plundered the city and they crucified the Roman citizens. Three, when the relief cohorts set

21

on the crowd which had come to greet them. We would not have dared to dream of a chance like that; the mob had taken over the city. There is no limit to what we might have achieved."

Menahem's voice was eager as he replied, "You admit then, Absalom, that the third chance was the best chance, a better opportunity for revolt than either of the previous two instances?"

"I said so," admitted the latter.

"And yet," pursued Menahem, "you wanted to attack at once, as soon as Florus entered the city. We might have thrown everything away on that first occasion, or the second or third." Absalom looked less sure of himself, and the old man continued. "Seventy years ago, in the last year of Herod's reign, a golden eagle was erected above the Temple gate. Naturally the people were enraged by such sacrilege; but the rebellion which followed was quelled immediately and its two leaders burned to death.

"Judah of Galilee, my father, was as appalled by Herod's action as any man; but he waited. He did not take precipitate action. When he finally moved, he launched a revolt that lasted months and he lived to fight another day. After that he waited a decade before striking again. But his next rebellion continued for two years—all Galilee was up in arms and the people talk of the great revolt of Judah even today." The old man's face was animated as he spoke of these events and his deep voice thrilled at the story he was telling.

"We have not been impatient," claimed Absalom. "There have been a dozen occasions during the past year when we might have attacked. Our men will become demoralized from sitting still. Why do we wait?" The old man tried to stop his deputy with a gesture, but Absalom continued. "I understand the Sons here at Sekaka. They are waiting for the Almighty; but since when have we believed that the Lord intended us to wait? We have always believed in fighting, that each day the enemy remains in our country is an insult to God Himself."

"I will tell you for what I am waiting," replied the old man. "I too believe that the time has arrived to strike and to strike

22

fast; but I want to succeed." He struck a huge gnarled fist on the table so that the oil lamps jumped. One was extinguished and a thin line of black smoke curled upward. "My grandfather Hezekiah fought tenaciously; my father, Judah, was among the greatest of our heroes; my brothers, Jacob and Simon, struggled until their last breaths. All of them fought!" His voice sank to a whisper: "All of them failed." The silence that followed was broken by the old leader's shout: "I want to succeed!"

"Faith in the Lord—" began Absalom, but the old man cut him off.

"Did Hezekiah lack faith? Was Judah an unbeliever? Were Jacob and Simon not pious men? Without the Lord's help we can do nothing; but that does not mean that He will do everything for us."

"What are you waiting for, then?" asked Joab, one of the commanders. "A sign?" Joab was short but very thickset. His reddish hair and beard hinted at priestly stock, though he disclaimed any connection. The ruddy skin of his face and arms was covered with a mass of small brown freckles, which stood out against his skin in moments of excitement. His short stature had accustomed him to looking up at people, though not to giving way to them. When he spoke in his clipped manner, his beard jutted truculantly toward the person he was addressing. Even among the Sicarii, his bravery was a legend.

"Are we waiting for a sign?" he repeated.

"Not a sign." Menahem brushed the query impatiently aside. "I agree with Absalom that there have been enough signs. What we need is a stronghold, a base which belongs to us, a place we can call home. We need a center from which we can direct our attacks, a refuge to which we can retreat if necessary, where we can assemble our forces and store our equipment.

"If we are going to achieve more than the sporadic raids of the past few years, we need something more substantial than our caches in the villages, our scattered cells and groups of supporters in the cities. You wish to know why we are waiting? We are awaiting a chance to capture our stronghold."

"What is wrong with here?" asked Absalom.

23

"Sekaka is not ours," was the reply. "It is true that we have something in common with the Sons of Zadok, despite their aloofness and the strictness of their doctrines. I believe that the day will come when we and they will stand together in the armies of the Lord. But that day has not yet arrived, and meanwhile Sekaka is theirs."

There was silence in the tent. Eleazar leaned forward and lit the lamp that had been extinguished. In the brighter light he could see the faces of the leaders, tense with anticipation; they were leaning forward, their eyes on Menahem. They knew that the old fox had a plan, and that their rebellion was moving into a new phase. A dozen years previously he had called them to Sekaka to launch the *sica* raids; now he had called them again. In the intervening years the leaders, each busy in his own area, had scarcely seen each other. And all the while the tension in Judea had been increasing. Absalom broke the silence.

"Where do you propose to find this stronghold?" he asked. "For my part I cannot see what is wrong with Jerusalem. It was good enough for David the King."

Menahem joined in the laughter. "I have nothing against Jerusalem, I assure you," he replied. "But it is premature to talk about Jerusalem. We have many rivals there: the aristocrats, that new slave leader bar Giora, ben Simon's Zealots; it is not so simple. I hope that Jerusalem will be ours before the year is out." There was a gasp of surprise from the assembled leaders. "But first we need a base from which to attack."

"Where, then?" asked Joab.

The old man looked silently around the table, regarding each of them in turn. He was enjoying himself. "Which would you say is the strongest fortress in Judea?" The question hung in the air.

"Masada!" Eleazar spoke instinctively. Menahem smiled and nodded amid the exclamations of surprise.

"I should rather take Jerusalem than Masada," Absalom laughed.

"Masada can be taken, though," Menahem insisted.

"How?" demanded Eleazar. He did not often speak; but it

was clear that his interest had been aroused. "It is an impossible task, Menahem; you know that. There are only two approaches, and both of them are well guarded. A couple of dozen good soldiers could hold it forever. The garrison there is a full cohort."

"Those gates could never be forced," agreed old John. "Not even at night." The old warrior's voice was thin and reedy, though once it had been a deep voice, and the chest it came from had been broad and muscular. The old man with his matted white beard was still tough and wiry, but his fighting days were over.

"Not at night, John, my old comrade-in-arms. Not at night or in secret."

"How, then?" Joab's red beard pointed straight at his leader.

"Openly, in broad daylight," replied Menahem. "I propose to march directly along the shore of the Sea of Salt from a point south of Ein Gedi."

"Have you taken leave of your senses?" demanded Absalom.

"Listen," he replied. "Hear me out." The murmur died down and he was able to continue. "One week from now the garrison at Masada is to be relieved. A cohort will march south from Herodium and replace the Masada cohort, which will return to Herodium. My information is that it will take the easternmost of the three routes from Herodium to Ein Gedi. Probably it will spend the night at Ein Gedi and continue to the fortress the following morning. Probably but not definitely. They know that we are active in Idumea and they may well attempt the march in one day. Part of our forces will cut off that cohort north of Ein Gedi; the main body of our force will replace it."

"That is preposterous," said Absalom. "We could never pass as auxiliaries; we might as well pretend to be the Twelfth Legion from Antioch. I will dress up as Cestius Gallus!"

Menahem did not join in the laughter this time. He turned to Eleazar. "Tell them about the store that lies beneath the fortress of the kings of Judea south of Hebron, beneath the ruins where none now dwell."

"That is our weapons store," explained Eleazar. "We have

25

concentrated there all the equipment captured in the last five years. There must be nearly four hundred suits of armor and weapons. It is enough to equip part of a cohort certainly." He looked doubtful. "We could never assemble there, though; we could not supply the men. It is a wilderness today. The water supply is insufficient for a large force."

"You will assemble fifty men, Eleazar," said Menahem. He had stopped acting, and he spoke briefly and to the point. "You will acquire some horses and a troop of camels from the Nabateans. Is that possible?"

"Gold will buy anything."

"We have not been plundering all these years to enrich ourselves," replied the old man. "You will transport the equipment from the store to a point south of Ein Gedi. The main force will assemble here at Sekaka, armed only with knives. Unencumbered, we can reach Ein Gedi along the shore of the Sea of Salt. There are two difficult stretches: one just south of the spring of Sekaka, the second just north of Ein Gedi; but we can scale those cliffs. Two miles south of Ein Gedi we shall meet up with Eleazar and equip ourselves in a fashion appropriate to an auxiliary cohort. We have enough equipment to deceive a garrison on the summit of Masada into believing that we are a genuine cohort. Eleazar has confirmed that they do not maintain a garrison at the eastern foot of the rock.

"That, in brief, is the plan." He paused. "I must admit that I would be happier if we could arrange for some diversion to distract the garrison at the crucial time. I was hoping, Eleazar, that you might have an idea. Could a lightly armed group penetrate somewhere?"

Eleazar considered. He was a man of deceptively light build, his wiry frame far stronger than it looked. His thin, sensitive face was framed by dark brown hair and a beard of the same color. His brown eyes were surprisingly soft; he looked more like a scholar than a bandit.

"I do have an idea," he said at last. "I have often thought of ways to penetrate the fortress. The idea has fascinated me for a long time, though I never really solved the problem. But I once had an idea that might work together with this idea of

26

yours, Menahem. The point is this: there are actually three gates at Masada, though very few people know of the third one. I have to explain about Masada." The other leaders were leaning forward attentively. Eleazar spoke in quiet, measured tones, as if explaining a point of law rather than discussing a military situation.

The rock of Masada, he explained, rose a thousand feet above the Sea of Salt and was unapproachable from all sides, though to the west one could ascend to within three hundred feet of the summit. Steep cliffs all around led up to a plateau about twenty acres in extent. Herod had surrounded the entire plateau with a casemate wall, fortified by towers at regular intervals. Gates were let into the wall on the eastern and western sides, at the top of paths which led up the cliff faces. The path from the east was particularly arduous and took more than an hour to climb. It was possible, though difficult, to climb the rock on both the northern and southern sides; but once up, there would be no way of penetrating the wall.

Herod had constructed a number of buildings on the plateau, most of them concentrated in the northern sector. Down the northern cliff face, on three levels, he had constructed his private palace, a wondrous hanging villa, projecting out over the abyss. To the south of the palace was a large Roman bath-house and a vast complex of storerooms. Further south in the center of the plateau was a building which served as officers' quarters. About halfway along the western casemate was the largest single building of the fortress, a two-story royal palace, which served as the fortress's administrative center. Further south there were a number of buildings where guests and relatives of Herod had lived.

"I would say that the key to controlling the fortress lies in the two palaces, northern and western, though of course the eastern and southern casemates also contain towers," Eleazar continued. He paused and looked at the faces of his companions. Satisfied that he was holding their interest despite the detailed nature of his description, he continued. "As I said earlier, there is a third entrance. The third gate, the water gate, is simpler than the other two; it does not have to be fortified in the normal way as it is not accessible from the outside."

When Herod had built up Masada, explained Eleazar, he had aimed to make the fortress self-sufficient. His own wife and family had managed to hold out there against the soldiers of his rival, Archelaus, when the two of them were fighting for the Judean throne. They had been on the point of surrendering because of thirst, when rain fell and filled the cisterns which at that time had existed on the summit.

"It was a miracle, I suppose," said Eleazar with a smile. "But miracles were not good enough for Herod. He wanted to be certain, so he created an independent water system. I think it must be one of the most brilliant ever devised."

Two dams had been constructed, he reported. One across the northern wadi and the second across the valley to the west, which encircled the southern foot of the rock. Each dam fed water into an aqueduct leading to a channel cut in the cliff. The northern aqueduct led to a row of cisterns some four hundred feet below the summit; the western aqueduct fed a row of cisterns some hundred feet above them. Each cistern was a vast cavern carved out of the rock by hand, and once they were full, the fortress was supplied with enough water to last through the summer. Slaves carried the water in pitchers from the cisterns to the summit up a special path which penetrated the fortress via the water gate, just south of the northern palace.

"A special tower below the palace guards the water system," concluded Eleazar. "But at night a party could make its way along the western waterway to the top row of cisterns. It would be a difficult crossing in the dark. But a group, if each man carried only a *sica*, could reach the cisterns, and I could lead them there."

Menahem ben Judah had been pleased with his nephew. Since the time of his grandfather Hezekiah, a member of that warrior's family had led the outlaw band. From a group of rebels, Judah of Galilee had formed a national movement, which he bequeathed to his sons; but since his time, the move-

28

ment had not achieved dominance equivalent to that of the patriotic movement. Judah had been a rabbi and Menahem too was a teacher. There was a tradition in their family of descent from the line of David, through Sheshbazzar the prince. But Menahem had no aspirations to a crown. Were he to attain some measure of national dominance, his aim would be to ensure that the rightful Zadokite high priest was restored to his office in the Temple at Jerusalem. Priests had ruled Judah for centuries; the age of kings was past.

Menahem sighed as he marched along the shore of the Sea of Salt, his thoughts eons away from the column of soldiers in which he moved. Surely the appointed time had come! When had the land been more desolate? When had the rule of the foreigner been more oppressive? The Sons of Zadok were sure that the time was imminent, but they would not hasten it. They were not prepared to sink to the level of sordid strategic calculations, at least not at the present time. The Bursar of the community, the only member with whom Menahem had personal contact, had hinted that a change of mind might be on the way, but that would doubtless take time.

The Sicarii and the Sons of Zadok possessed a common heritage, that of the Pious Ones, the group which had fought at the side of the Maccabees two centuries before. The Pious Ones had parted company from the Maccabees when the latter had refused to recognize Jakim, the restored high priest of the Zadokite line. The final rupture had occurred when Jonathan the Maccabee himself assumed the title of high priest.

The Sicarii and the Sons of Zadok followed the tradition of the Pious Ones, but they were separate streams of development. United they had been, and one day they would unite again, of that Menahem was sure. On that day, the success of the revolt was assured. The communities of the Sons, scattered throughout the towns and villages of Judea, would form the perfect complement to the Sicarii cells and groups.

Menahem was not so sure about the other patriotic factions. Galilee worried him least of all, although he had not been active in Galilee for two decades. He was sure that the Galileans would rally to the son of Judah and grandson of Heze-

29

kiah. It was the Judean factions that worried him. Ben Simon would surely be unwilling to place his Zealots under the command of another. He had formed an alliance with the aristocratic faction, which Menahem distrusted. The old man pursed his lips as he thought of that alliance; he did not like it. The aristocrats were worse than the Romans—it was an aristocrat who had crucified his two brothers. The stopping of the imperial sacrifice by the captain of the Temple guard did not mean that he could be trusted. The captain was one of the priestly clique. His own father, the false high priest Hananiah, called himself by his Greek name: Ananias. A high priest of the Temple of God called Ananias! The so-called war party of the aristocrats and priests was quite capable of leading the people on to revolt and turning traitor at the last moment.

There was another group which had come recently to the fore, led by the son of a convert. He sensed in Simon bar Giora, the young slave leader, a kindred spirit; but sympathy would not decide anything. Power would decide, power and the hand of God.

The rock of Masada towered ahead, distinctly visible through the morning mist. It looked unassailable, as if only a bird could attain its summit. In twenty minutes' time it would be sunrise, and by then they should be more than halfway up the path of the serpent. Menahem wondered how Eleazar was faring on the far side of the rock. Shortly after sunrise his nephew would engage the enemy, and thirty men armed with daggers were no match for a fully armed garrison cohort.

"At this time of the year," Eleazar had explained, "they are using the upper row of cisterns. They only use the lower ones in late autumn if necessary. A detachment of slaves carries water daily from the time of the last rains. They work just after sunrise and before sunset, when the air is cooler. We have observed the operation frequently from a distance."

The sun was rising fast, revealing the magnificent bleak panorama of the valley of the Sea of Salt, brushing the surrounding pink hills with gold. The sea was a murky gray, striped with muddy yellow in the shallows. A stiff breeze scuffed the surface with tiny wavelets, topped with occasional flecks of white. Across the water the gray-blue mountains of Moab were half hidden by clouds. The mist of the early morning was dispersing, and the pale yellow sun gained strength with every minute that passed. The cavalry and baggage train had been left at the foot of the rock. The infantry column wound its way silently up the mountainside, slowly drawing nearer to the eastern gate of the fortress.

The garrison made no hostile move toward them. They had sufficient equipment to resemble a genuine cohort, and relief was expected. The advance party stretched out some thirty yards in front of Menahem, and the rest of the column spread out more than a hundred yards behind him. The entire force would take almost a quarter of an hour to pass into the fortress. Menahem hoped that they would be able to penetrate in sufficient strength to hold the gate.

5

When the beam of light came though the mouth of the cistern, Eleazar knew that the sun had risen on the far side of the rock. He signaled to his men to be ready. Within a few minutes, the water party with its armed escort would descend from the summit, each man carrying an empty earthenware pitcher. His men were crouched on the steps which led down into the large, plastered cavern. Not for the first time, Eleazar marveled at the size of the cisterns, carved out of the rock by human hands. He could see clearly now in the dim light that penetrated the echoing cavern, but anyone entering from daylight into the dim interior would be temporarily blinded.

"Try to prevent them from falling into the water," Eleazar had instructed his men. "We do not want to foul our own supply. Try to save the jars too; we shall be needing them."

Eleazar had suggested to Menahem that the slaves be spared and won over, that only their guards be killed; but Menahem had said that the risk was too great. Slaves could not be converted in two minutes, he pointed out. One false move, even without malice, and the whole plan would be ruined.

31

"But these men are our brothers," Eleazar had protested. "They are Jewish peasants and farmers like ourselves. They are not priests or landowners; the slaves are the ones for whom we are fighting this war!"

"We cannot afford sentiment!" Absalom's dark face was set ruthlessly.

"Menahem," Eleazar had pleaded. "These are our people; to kill them will be a sin against the Almighty!"

Menahem had sat there without speaking, his florid face framed by his long gray hair and beard. His wide forehead was wrinkled with lines of worry and his prominent brows were drawn together in a frown.

"It is not easy to sit in the seat of judgment," he had replied finally. "Justice is the Lord's, but sometimes it falls to a man to decide who is to live and who is to die. In war many innocent perish. Shall we then not make war? How many lives have been lost since our illustrious ancestor Hezekiah took to the hills? How many more have died since the Pious Ones joined with the Maccabees to root out the cancer of Hellenism from Israel? How much blood has flown in Judea over the past two centuries? Has there ever been a time of peace, a time without fighting and killing?

"The Lord, blessed be His name, is angry with us and He has caused us to suffer greatly for our wickedness; but we must fight and so bring the day of the Lord nearer. No one is more aware than I am of the tragedy of killing those who should be our friends and who are our brothers; but if we are not prepared to fight this war, then let us put aside our arms now. Let us go to Jerusalem and lick the feet of our Roman masters, or retire here to Sekaka with the Sons of Zadok."

Eleazar had not been able to answer, but now as he waited in the cavern he was afraid. As usual, it was victory he feared rather than defeat; he was afraid of what he might do to others, rather than of what others might do to him. He looked at the lined walls of the cistern, seeing clearly the water levels of past years. It had been a dry year, and nearly a dozen steps were above the water, although it was early in the summer and only small quantities of water had been drawn. After a wet winter, reflected Eleazar, their plan might not have been feasible. At certain points where the plaster had worn away, he could see the chisel marks made by the slaves who had hollowed out the cistern.

Suddenly, outside Eleazar heard the scuffling sound of footsteps approaching along the ledge, and a rough voice swore in camp Latin. He stiffened and felt a sickness in the pit of his stomach. The fifteen men in the cavern froze and held their breath. The beam of light was cut off as a bulky figure momentarily filled the entrance and then began to descend the steps, a large jar under his arm. The bearded slave groped blindly in the gloom.

Eleazar sprang forward, his left hand seizing the slave's throat, while his right hand plunged his *sica* upward under the man's ribs. The man's face showed surprise and then pain, but Eleazar's left hand did not relax its grip, and the long dagger plunged in deeply a second time. One of the other rebels caught the pitcher, a third sprang at the slave who now entered. There was no time to lose. Eleazar made for the opening and his men followed him out onto the narrow ledge. Further along he could see that old John's group had emerged from another cistern, cutting off the thirty slaves and their six guards from the summit.

On the narrow ledge over the yawning gulf a desperate battle was joined. Eleazar jumped for the nearest guard, knocking him over—but not before the man had drawn his short sword. The soldier regained his feet, and Eleazar held the man's wrist with his left hand, striking with his *sica;* but the knife would not penetrate the strong breastplate. The two men fell and rolled on the ledge, each trying to force the other into the abyss.

All the men were engaged now. Several of the slaves had been killed, but the soldiers were putting up tough resistance. Simon, Eleazar's youngest brother, climbed down the cliff and worked his way along beneath the ledge to the spot where old John was locked in a struggle with one of the guards. In his

33

"TEMPLE ISRAEL"

training he had learned just where to make the incision that hamstrings a man, but in the heat of battle, hanging hundreds of feet above the ravine, he slashed blindly and furiously. At last he struck a lucky blow and the guard fell screaming into space.

Eleazar, momentarily disengaged from his assailant, looked up toward the fortress, wondering whether the sound of the fight would be heard. By now they should be busy observing Menahem's group on the other side of the rock. Menahem would be some two hundred feet from the summit by this time.

While he was thinking, Eleazar was climbing the cliff above the ledge to gain an advantage over his opponent. Lacking the brute force of a larger man such as Absalom, he was nevertheless quick and cunning. He noticed a soldier stamping on the hands of one of his men, who appeared to have fallen from the ledge. With a shock he noticed that the hands were those of his brother Simon. Impulsively he threw himself at his brother's assailant, knocking the man off balance. The soldier lurched backward, grabbing the front of Eleazar's tunic and dragging him from the ledge; but Eleazar slashed at the grasping hand with his dagger, simultaneously forcing himself backward and bracing his legs against the side of the rock. The man fell.

The struggle was almost over. The soldiers were all dead and the Sicarii were dispatching the last of the slaves. One of these, a big man with a spade-shaped, dark brown beard, stepped toward Eleazar:

"Brother," said the man, "you are our brother. ..."

Eleazar did not allow himself to think. He sprang at the man, striking out with his knife. The man was elderly and stout. Eleazar knew his blow had not been mortal. He struck again, but the slave twisted around and the blow glanced off his ribs. A further blow made a deep cut in his back, tearing his tunic and revealing the ritual fringes and blue threads of his undergarment. The slave would not die! Eleazar gave a sob as he lunged once more, catching hold of the dark brown beard. He plunged his *sica* into the slave's throat. At last the man

34

crumpled dead at his feet. Eleazar stood limply, his dagger loose in the hand that hung by his side. He was gasping for breath. As he looked down at his fallen adversary, his lips moved.

'Speak unto the children of Israel, and bid them that they make them throughout their generations fringes in the corners of their garments, and that they put with the fringe of each corner a thread of blue. And it shall be unto you for a fringe, that ye may look upon it, and remember all the commandments of the Lord, and do them. ...'

One of the surviving slaves, tall and thin, with hollow cheeks and deep black eyes, had watched the foregoing drama and understood what lay in store for him. Taking advantage of Eleazar's paralysis, he edged toward old John and sprang at the old man, his long, thin arms entwining the old body. Eleazar looked up, but he barely had time to see the expression of terror in old John's face before the two bodies, locked together, plunged to their deaths below. There was a cry of horror from the rebels, and the remainder of the slaves were hastily dispatched.

With an effort of will, Eleazar banished all thought of old John, who had fought with his grandfather, and of the slave he had killed. Acting as though in a dream, he organized his men. The youngest of his band, those with the least obvious beards, stripped the soldiers and dressed in their armor, while the remainder of the group changed clothes with those slaves who had not fallen from the ledge. Eleazar did not allow himself to remain still. He helped to lay out the bodies in the entrance to the first cistern. The sun was climbing fast, but their side of the rock was still in the shadows. The breeze which blew off the Sea of Salt was deflected onto them by the opposite cliff. It was still cool.

When all was ready, the men started up the narrow path in single file, carrying the large earthenware pitchers on their shoulders. Not more than ten minutes had passed since the water-carrying detail had descended from the summit of the rock.

Only in the desert does the sun possess that peculiar burning
quality a few minutes after sunrise, thought Menahem. His
brow was already moist. He was some two hundred feet below
the summit; within five minutes the first of his men should be
through the eastern gate. Menahem hoped that at least fifty of
them would have penetrated the fortress before the garrison
realized what was happening. That would be sufficient to hold
the gate long enough for the remainder of them to enter. They
were climbing now, scrambling up the rough shale. Menahem's florid face was showing signs of strain, but his still-
powerful body climbed swiftly and confidently.

Even at this time, he found himself looking down into the
valley and across the bitter sea. The mountains of Moab, from
which the great leader Moses had looked into the Promised
Land he would never enter, were still partly obscured by a
blue haze, but the stark outlines of the nearby desert stood out
with greater prominence. How puny and insignificant was the
battle about to be joined among the purple-brown flint, the
glaring yellow sandstone, and blinding white salt flats of that
bleak and terrible landscape.

Yet the Almighty, blessed be His name forever and ever,
who had created the searing magnificence of the Judean desert, who had made the rocks, the hills, the cliffs, the sea, who
filled the heavens and the earth with His awesome majesty,
did not scorn to concern Himself with every tiny, insignificant
facet of His stupendous creation. The tiny specks on this bleak
panorama were acting out His drama that day. He would
watch over the battle and decide the victor; He would elect
who was to live and who to die. If they were to lose that day,
reflected Menahem, so be it; it was part of the infinite purpose
of the Lord. If, on the other hand, they were to win, what glory
to have participated in God's victory, what a privilege to be
His chosen instruments to wreak His vengeance!

The sunlight came off the rocks in a blinding, white-hot
glare. Only an occasional withered shrub was visible in the
whole landscape. The old man screwed up his eyes against the

brightness, and thought of Galilee. Even Galilee would be turning brown by this time of the year, but at least in Galilee there were a few green trees and shrubs to relieve the eyes. Here in the desert there were no trees—just the rocks, dust, and sky, and the glimmering oily surface of the strange sea by whose shores the Almighty had once rained down fire and brimstone on the sinners of Sodom and Gomorrah. This desert of wild beauty was a vivid example of the power, the majesty, and the anger of the ever-living God of Abraham.

As he thought of these things, the old man was filled with a glowing pride and assurance that victory would be theirs, that the appointed time was at hand when he, Menahem the son of Judah, son of Hezekiah of the seed of David, would lead the armies of the Lord to cleanse the Holy Land of all vestiges of the foreign intruder.

He could see the leading men approaching the gate, but then his view was obstructed as he climbed up under the overhang. He thought he could hear sounds of fighting, but he was not sure. He concentrated every effort of will on ascending the last few feet as quickly as possible. Oblivious now to the heat, he knew only one thing: he had to reach the gate to fight with his men. He pulled himself up and worked his way along the ledge. A group of men, he saw, were struggling around the gate. Too early, he thought; there could not have been more than twenty inside. At the gate, Menahem found his way blocked by a burly auxiliary captain. The old rebel drew his sword, taking the measure of the captain, who was grouping his men to drive a wedge between Menahem and his advance guard. Many of his men pressed about him, and a backward glance showed the remainder scrambling up the cliff, in complete disregard of the sickening drop one thousand feet into the ravine below. Menahem raised his sword high above his head.

"Their roaring shall be like a lion," he thundered in a deep and terrible voice, *"yea, they shall roar and lay hold of the prey!"* He charged forward, his long gray hair streaming behind him. He parried the soldier's thrust with his shield and brought his heavy sword down between his opponent's neck

37

and shoulder. The chain mail stopped the sword, but the blow broke the auxiliary's collarbone, forcing him to drop his own sword. In that moment, Menahem struck out with his heavy metal shield, knocking his enemy off balance. He was on him instantly, cutting and thrusting, finally succeeding in pushing the steel into his opponent's mouth and through the back of the neck.

The Sicarii swarmed into the fortress. The gate was breached, but groups of the defenders were attacking from several directions. The eastern gate was slightly lower than the rest of the summit, putting the Sicarii at a disadvantage. While Menahem closed up with the advance party to defend the gate, the later arrivals began working their way northward along the eastern wall. They had to fight every yard, but eventually the whole force entered the fortress.

The natural instinct of the attackers was to fight their way inward, toward the center of the plateau; but Menahem constantly directed them northward along the wall to the northern palace, the key to Masada. In a reversal of normal Sicarii tactics, the leaders endeavored to concentrate their men in large groups, for inside the fortress it was the soldiers who knew their ground and the rebels who were subject to surprise attacks and stratagems. As they fought their way through the storerooms, it became increasingly difficult to keep the men together. Menahem noticed that a colleague on his right, a veteran of many campaigns, was having difficulties. A thrust from a long auxiliary spear had wounded him in the right leg. Two soldiers were beating him to his knees. Menahem forced his way through the mass of fighting men toward his companion.

"Back, get back!" the man screamed a warning. Then he was down. The old leader continued to press toward him, but as he reached the wounded man, two spears found their mark in the beaten rebel's stomach. There was no hope for the mortally wounded man, and Menahem found himself menaced by the bloody spears. A third soldier joined the two already advancing on him; a quick glance behind showed him that he was trapped. He parried their feints with his shield, but the soldiers were not hurried—five feet of spear separated each of them from the old warrior. They backed Menahem into a corner, completely isolating him. Then, miraculously, the corner gave way as he felt a narrow opening where none had been suspected. He found himself in a narrow storeroom, but as he looked around he saw that he was now entirely trapped, for there was no exit. The two soldiers followed him into the room, a long narrow chamber containing rows of shelves laden with provisions. A row of large jars lined the walls. The third soldier advanced through the narrow doorway, and behind him Menahem could see the tip of a fourth spear.

The old rebel dropped his shield, which fell with a clang on the stone floor. The soldiers' eyes dropped momentarily and the old man hurled his sword at the nearest one. The hilt hit the man in the stomach, winding him. Menahem whirled about and heaved one of the enormous jars lining the wall into the air, throwing it at the group of soldiers. Two of the men were knocked off balance and the third thrust back against the wall. The jar collided with the corner of the entrance, shattering and splashing the whole area with olive oil. The two soldiers struggled to regain their footing, but slid about in the greasy mud. A second jar followed the first, flying through the narrow opening. Menahem seized a spear from one of the dazed soldiers, charged the doorway, driving back the fourth soldier who was regaining his feet, and rejoined the general melee.

Slowly they fought their way northward. Several Sicarii and a great number of the defenders had fallen. They had passed through the stores, and most of the attackers found themselves in an open space outside the northern palace. The entrance over to the right was heavily guarded, and a line of soldiers faced the Sicarii along the high wall. The soldiers pelted the rebels, forcing them backward. Other soldiers advanced from the stores. They were surrounded. Behind them to the left was a large bathhouse where they could still retreat, but once inside, Menahem knew they would be really trapped. The old man deployed his force in a circular defensive formation. Sicarii bowmen brought down some of the soldiers on the palace wall, but the rebels were hard pressed.

39

Over to the right by the gate Menahem could see Joab, his red beard jutting incongruously from his auxiliary helmet, leading his men against the defenders; but the long spears of the soldiers kept the attackers at bay. The latter were unaccustomed to fighting with heavy equipment and had thrown their weapons away, preferring to fight with their daggers; but they were finding it difficult to approach their adversaries.

Then all at once, one, three, five, a dozen men fell forward from the northern palace wall. Eleazar's fighters had taken them unexpectedly from the rear. With a roar, Menahem's force charged forward, most of them pouring through the gate, but many straight over the high wall, which they scaled with the assistance of their friends above. The soldiers in the palace were bewildered, set on as they were from all directions. The other soldiers hastily retreated back through the stores. The Sicarii fought through the palace with a ruthless fury, cutting down the confused soldiers as they slipped about in their own blood on the mosaic floors. Blood too splashed on the delicate wall frescos.

Once in control of the upper story, Eleazar led his men down the winding staircase to the central terrace. Two soldiers found hiding there behind the ornate columns were picked up bodily and thrown over the edge. A group of slaves, cowering by the outer wall, were captured and sent up the stairs under guard. The attackers swarmed down the second staircase to the lower level, where they found a party of slaves guarded by a dozen soldiers. The smashed bodies of the two soldiers hurled from above lay in the center of the courtyard. The soldiers laid down their arms and came forward to surrender. They were seized by the rebels and swung over into the ravine, hundreds of feet below, their screams fading as they dropped into the abyss.

At a brief conference, Menahem now determined the tactics for the assault of his second objective, the western palace. Eleazar's group was reinforced and sent along the casemate wall to attack the western gate by the palace. Another group of rebels began to prize out one of the large roof beams of the northern palace. Menahem turned to his men:

"Where is Simon the son of Nottos?"

A slim young man stepped forward, dark-complexioned with a curved Semitic nose and dark eyes. The child of a Greek mercenary father and an Idumean mother, he moved with the natural grace of the latter.

"Here I am, Rabbi." Menahem had some machines brought forward for his inspection. The young man looked at them with interest, feeling the wooden parts and leather thongs.

"Do you know how to use these?" demanded the old man.

"Yes," was the reply. "These are only light weapons and very simple."

"Who else knows the machines?" Menahem looked around.

"Simple catapults and quick-loaders," bar Nottos added. Several men stepped forward and began examining the machines.

When the roof beam had been removed, Menahem led his force to the southeastern gate of the western palace. As they approached the massive two-story building, a rain of missiles descended on them, forcing them some distance from the wall. Menahem now directed bar Nottos to keep up a general barrage at the soldiers on the walls of the palace, while the bowmen concentrated with greater accuracy on the area above the gate itself. Under cover of this assault, the party with the roof beam advanced and began to batter at the gate. Simultaneously, Eleazar and his group were engaged with the defenders on the western side of the palace. They were in retreat, and the soldiers emerged from the walls and drove them back.

Meanwhile, with the defenders concentrating on the assaults to the southeast and west, Joab led a picked group of Sicarii to the northern wall. His men carried strong ropes tipped with iron hooks. Several times the defenders drove the batterer back from the south gate. Eleazar's men were retreating down the steep path outside the summit to the white rock below. Joab's group swung their ropes; the iron hooks grappled the upper walls of the palace, slipping at first on the hard flint but eventually taking hold. Quickly the men climbed the ropes and silently penetrated the upper floor, overwhelming

41

the soldiers there before they fully realized what was happening.

Although heavily outnumbered, they managed to fight their way down the stairs to the lower level, where they opened the main gate to their comrades outside. For some minutes there was fierce hand-to-hand fighting in the passages around the central hall, but the Sicarii were superior at close quarters with their deadly knives. The battle quickly became a massacre, as the defending soldiers were cut down in large numbers. The attackers now poured out of the palace and through the gate in the western casemate, thus attacking Eleazar's adversaries in the rear. Many of these surrendered only to be coldly cut down or thrust off the narrow path into the valley below. Within half an hour, not a live soldier remained in the palace. Cowering in fright, the silent, miserable slaves were herded into the main forecourt and placed under guard.

The sun was high now, and the heat was intense. The morning breeze off the Sea of Salt had turned into an oven-hot wind, the east desert wind of early summer. It blew strongly, filling the air with dust, suffocating the men, and sucking every vestige of liquid from their bodies. After fighting continuously for several hours, the rebels were at last able to pause. Large quantities of water were drawn from the cistern under the palace, a vast chamber hollowed out of the rock and plastered throughout. Only now were the wounded treated and moved from the burning heat into the shade. Wounds were bound up and water poured down parched throats.

Menahem was everywhere at once, talking to the wounded, outlining further plans, showing remarkable energy for a man of his age. He was filled with a surging exaltation which entirely banished tiredness. He felt a growing conviction that the appointed time had indeed arrived. At Masada they had food and water for thousands of men; with Masada as a stepping-stone to Jerusalem, how could they fail?

A speck appeared in the sky, followed by a second, and then a third. Soon the sky was filled with vultures, swooping overhead, drawn by the scent of carnage. The huge beige birds

42

swept majestically over the plateau, their off-white wings edged in black. They glided down into the western valley where many of the dead had fallen. The bodies of the dead Sicarii were already being prepared for burial and a party of men were dispatched to the valley to bring up the bodies of the rebels who had fallen there.

7

Absalom lay in the shadow of a large rock, looking down the gorge. The sun was high, and even in the shade it was becoming unbearably hot. The cliff face opposite reflected the glare of direct sunlight, which pervaded the canyon, throwing the minor crevices into relief and casting purple shadows against the pink-brown flint. There was an abundance of vegetation in the valley, which was watered by an underground stream. Shrubs and creepers were much in evidence; juicy shoots peeped out from among the rocks. From where he lay, Absalom could see his men lining the cliff top above the false trail. He decided to make his final inspection. He scaled the cliff quickly, moving lightly for so large a man—the stones were hot to the touch. His deputy, Nahum, a powerful, red-faced man, helped him up the last few feet. Nahum was unusually fair; his hair and beard were tawny yellow, burned almost white in places. His widely spaced pale gray eyes were prominent in the brick red of his complexion.

"I could see your men from below," complained Absalom, his olive skin and black hair contrasting with his companion's fair complexion.

"It does not matter," replied Nahum. "Look." He gave a birdlike whistle. At once the empty cliff top was alive with men, who emerged from hiding, rolling forward boulders, carrying rocks in their cloaks, fitting arrows to their bows. Absalom was impressed.

"Excellent, Nahum," he said. "From now on, though, keep them hidden until they are needed. The soldiers may not arrive for some time, but they could be here at any time." Nahum waved his men back out of sight, and with a final word of farewell Absalom slipped over the edge of the cliff and began to descend.

The hundred and fifty men lay motionless in the baking heat. Several minutes passed, a quarter of an hour. It seemed as though they had been lying there forever. A sound further up the gorge pricked each man into a state of alertness. The sound of stones being dislodged came nearer. Despite the dryness of the air Absalom felt the sweat trickling down his face. He did not even move his hand to wipe it.

Then, tense as he was, he was forced to smile. Tripping daintily along the floor of the canyon came a herd of some fifty wild goats, their long curved horns proudly erect. They began to crop at the juicy shoots that grew along the wadi. The goats would provide excellent cover and warning, thought Absalom. The animals spread out, picking fastidiously at the vegetation. Here and there one would climb onto a ledge after an inviting piece of greenery. They climbed nimbly and quickly.

Suddenly Absalom was aware of a violent movement to his right, and there was the start of a scream, quickly muffled to a groan as the man bit his lower lip until it bled. The rebel was writhing in agony on the ground, holding his sandaled foot. With a curse, Absalom sprang toward the man, his anger changing to sympathy when he saw a scorpion crawling unhurriedly away from its victim. Abaslom picked up a rock and crushed the small, yellow, armored creature. He untied a small leather bottle from his belt and held it to the man's blue lips. The rebel's teeth were tightly clenched with pain, and the sticky red wine dripped down over his beard. Absalom allowed him only a small amount of the strong wine in the heat, supplementing the drink with water from his larger waterskin.

Then all at once the goats were up the sides of the valley, pouring up the cliff, and the cohort, led by half a century of cavalry, was advancing down the gorge. The soldiers paused at the fork, and Absalom could see the tall, dark Judah ben Jair gesticulating. The commander seemed to argue with him for a minute, while Absalom held his breath. At last the officer shrugged and the column started to follow Judah into the right fork of the wadi. The narrowness of the path forced the column of horsemen to proceed in single file.

Absalom suppressed a gasp of surprise as the standard came into view; it was a Sebastian troop. Somehow he had been sure they would be Caesareans. None of the men looked familiar to him, which was strange, until he realized that they had probably been on garrison duty in Idumea for a number of years. The infantry looked exhausted, as well they might after such a march. Loaded down with equipment, they had made remarkable time on foot from Herodium.

Absalom lay waiting, as still as the rocks around him. The last soldier passed into the wadi, but still the big man made no move. He calculated that it would be at least five minutes before the auxiliary commander realized that the track led nowhere; they should be allowed to enter as far into the wadi as possible. Finally Absalom stood up and waved his men forward. The time had come. He thought of Judah, who would die in the next five minutes, and of Menahem and Eleazar at Masada. He wondered whether the fortress was theirs. Menahem had been right about the cohort—unless Absalom stopped them, they would be at Masada that day.

While he was thinking, he was rolling a large boulder across the entrance to the wadi. Many of his men were engaged in similar tasks to impede the egress of the cohort. They had been working for two minutes when the auxiliary horsemen charged them; it was the cohort's rear guard. With a roar, the cavalry troop rushed the rebels, making as much noise as possible in order to warn their comrades. The groups closed with each other, the Sicarii having the advantage of numbers for the time being. Absalom and his men surrounded the soldiers, fighting savagely with their knives. Some of them got down on their knees to hamstring the horses. Several of them seized rocks as weapons. In three minutes the cavalry troop was annihilated and several horses were captured. But the rebels had lost five men and had failed to blockade the valley.

Then everything seemed to happen at once. The canyon became alive, full of running figures. The low birdlike whistle of Nahum was barely discernable, but missiles of every shape and size started to rain down from the cliff top on the running

45

soldiers below. The first group of auxiliaries was smashed apart by a vast boulder that came crashing down the cliff. Several of the men were bowled over and two were pinned under the rock. One of them was killed outright; the second, with the whole lower part of his body pinned under the boulder, screamed in agony, a red froth at his mouth.

Seizing arms from the fallen rear guard, Absalom and his men stationed themselves across the entrance to the canyon. The cohort had been stampeded by the rain of missiles from above, the horses trampling their own men. Nahum's bowmen were at work and the air was filled with arrows. At the mouth of the canyon the battle raged fiercely. Absalom and his men were being slowly forced back by the headlong rush. Soldiers were climbing the sides of the valley in an attempt to outflank the Sicarii. They were starting to get the better of the rebels by sheer weight of numbers, and because of this they were beginning to respond to the desperate commands of their captain. Absalom could see his men falling on all sides. The initial shock over, the soldiers' training was starting to tell. The struggling mass of men had moved further down the gorge out of the range of the barrage from above, so Nahum's men started descending the cliff to take the soldiers in the rear.

Losses had been heavy on both sides, and Absalom felt sure that the cohort had lost sufficient men to prevent its proceeding to Masada. He began to maneuver his men up the steep sides of the valley, thus thinning out the force which blocked the egress of the soldiers. Seeing their opportunity, the soldiers broke through the Sicarii line, whereupon Absalom reversed his men and led them back up the valley to join Nahum's men. Too late, the auxiliaries wheeled about. The rebels were retreating swiftly up the cliff face, where the armored soldiers could not follow.

8

The burning heat of the day had given way to the cool of the desert evening. The late afternoon light possessed a luminous quality, brushing the harsh rocks and steep-sided valleys with fire, contrasting with the vivid blue of the Sea of Salt. The mountains of Moab on its far shore, until now concealed by haze or dust, stood out strongly in mauve—the details of their canyons and gullies etched in gray and black. The salt flats, pink from the setting sun, set off the reddish brown of the hills and rocks of the upper plateau. The wind had dropped, and on the summit of Masada sounds were clear and distinct over the whole of its twenty acres.

After the fall of the western palace, the remainder of the fortress had been quickly captured. The garrison had been wiped out, but most of the slaves had survived. Some of the younger ones were enthusiastic about joining the rebel cause, though the majority of the older ones were reluctant to break with the familiar pattern of their lives. Six hours after the conquest of the fortress, Absalom had appeared with the remainder of his force. Of his original hundred and fifty, only sixty-five remained, bringing Sicarii losses to nearly two hundred, more than one-third of their actively mobilized fighters. The bodies of the fallen had been buried in caves in the side of the rock, and the wounded had been treated. Now, the living had assembled in one of the casemates of the northwestern wall facing Jerusalem for evening prayers and mourning.

"Behold, bless ye the Lord, all ye servants of the Lord, who stand in the house of the Lord in the nights. Lift up your hands toward the sanctuary and bless ye the Lord. The Lord bless thee out of Zion; even He that made the heaven and the earth.

"The Lord of hosts is with us; the God of Jacob is our stronghold: Selah. . . ."

Eleazar ben Jair was thinking of the events of the day. He was not conscious of their triumph; he was obsessed with thoughts of the slave who would not die, who had worn a fringed garment just as he wore one. The man had come forward with love and he had answered him with hate. He, son of the pious Jair, who had declared violence to be a crime against the Lord. Jair had died in a riot when Cumanus was procurator, and Eleazar had gone to learn the way of the sword with his uncle. He had learned it so well that when a Jew called him brother, he had cut him down without hesitation. No such problems tormented his brothers—for them it had been a great day. Eleazar had heard Judah's story from his own lips.

He had been angry with his uncle for sending Judah to apparently certain death, but the nerveless, catlike Judah had never felt a moment of fear. When his treachery to the cohort had been discovered, he had broken the neck of the nearest soldier with his bare hands and used the man's dead body as a shield until he had been able to scale the cliff and make his escape. Judah had no regrets, nor did Simon. Neither had Joab, Absalom, nor Menahem. But Eleazar could not forget. He thought too of old John, of the terrified expression on the old man's face as he lost his balance and plunged into the abyss. The old man had lived with death for sixty years; but in the evening of his life he had not wanted to die and had cried out silently, begging the Lord to spare him.

"Blessed art Thou, O Lord our God, King of the Universe, who at Thy word bringest on the evening twilight," the prayers continued, *"with wisdom openeth the gates of the heavens, and with understanding changes times and variest the seasons, and arranges the stars in their watches in the sky according to Thy will."*

The color of the sky deepened to russet as the sun disappeared behind the western hills; the sound of prayer filled the surrounding valleys in the absolute silence of the desert evening.

"May His great name be sanctified in the world that is to be created anew where He will quicken the dead and raise them up into life eternal; will rebuild the city of Jerusalem ... and will uproot all alien worship from the earth and restore the worship of the true God. O may the Holy One, blessed be He, reign in His glory during your life and during your days. ..."

Menahem's powerful melodious voice seemed to fill the vastness of space as he led the prayers. Atop the steep-sided rock fortress, under the flaming sky, his prayers were touched by destiny. Worship concluded, Menahem addressed his men.

"My loyal sons," he began, "the Almighty, blessed be His name, has allowed us to participate in one of the most glorious

48

days in history; we have captured the stronghold of Masada. Here we have arms, equipment, food, and drink. If we wished we could hold at bay all the legions of Rome; but this will not be our purpose. Today saw far more than the mere capture of a fortress: Masada is but a stage on the way to Jerusalem. It means many things to our movement. No more fleeing, no more skulking in caves, ruins, and rude huts, no more sleeping each night in a different bed. Tonight for the first time in a hundred and twenty years, for the first time since my grandfather Hezekiah began his fight against oppression, we can lay down our heads in peace, knowing that we are at home. Here at Masada we are on nobody's sufferance; no one is offering us charity; none risk their lives to give us shelter. Here we are masters of our own fate.

"Hezekiah fought bravely until he was murdered by that traitor Herod. Judah, my father, led two great revolts; he died believing in his mission. My dear brothers, Jacob and Simon, held aloft the torch of Judah only to be struck down by the dastardly Tiberius Alexander—that Jew who is more Roman than the Romans!"

The old man's voice faltered with emotion, but he continued. "My father taught that we should submit only to God —to God and to no one else. He called anyone paying taxes to Rome a coward! We have tried to live up to those high ideals; we have endeavored to fight for our freedom. My father died fifty-eight years ago and we have been fighting ever since." Menahem dropped his voice, he was speaking scarcely above a whisper, but every word cut incisively through the cool night air.

"Today we lost some of the bravest of our fighters. Old John, who carried messages for my father when I was a child, who fought with us for sixty years, is dead, and my heart aches with the loss. Shall we be worthy of his sacrifice? To us has been given a task not given to Hezekiah, nor to Judah nor to the Pious Ones who fought with the Maccabees. We had not then suffered enough, but now the cup of our misery has truly overflowed. The land groans under the heel of the oppressor. Peasants and farmers slave from dawn to dusk to enrich their masters; the poor starve; our Temple is violated by false priests and guarded by uncircumcised soldiers. For more than two hundred years the people of Judea have been fighting— fighting the kings of Greece, fighting the Hasmoneans, fighting the Herods, and now fighting the Kittim. The time has come: that time presaged by the pagan prophet Balaam, when he spoke to Balak, the time foretold by Isaiah, by Micah, and by Daniel." Menahem's message thundered across the twilit wastes. "The End of Days is at hand!"

His listeners were spellbound; not a soul moved.

"Today we saw the initial skirmishing of the great war whereby God's rule on earth will be truly established. *Hark! one calleth: 'Clear ye in the wilderness the way of the Lord, Make plain in the desert a highway for our God. . . .'"*

Menahem drew himself up to his full commanding height as he faced his men. Flanked by his commanders—the mighty Absalom, the slight and brooding Eleazar, the stocky, red-bearded Joab, the dark, youthful Judah, all of them clad in simple linen garments—he stood there, his fine head framed by his impressive gray mane and beard.

"In a short while we march to Jerusalem." A flash of white teeth showed briefly in the blue-black of Absalom's beard, signaling the big man's satisfaction. "True priests shall perform the rites in the Temple of the Lord. I, Menahem the son of Judah, son of Hezekiah, have spoken!"

9

The fiercest summer heat was over, and high up in the hills, the air was cool. They had moved out of the red-brown flint rocks of Idumea into the pale limestone of Judea; within an hour they would be able to see Jerusalem, at present obscured by the bulbous-topped white mountain of Herodium. There were still two cohorts garrisoned there, but they had not moved since the revolt in the capital and Menahem expected no trouble from them.

The hills of Judea were gentle and rounded after the harsh crags of the Idumean plateau; the sky was paler and the sun lacked that savage burning quality. Clumps of grass enabled sheep and goats to graze on the hillsides all year round, and an occasional large tree caught the eye. To the east, a shimmering glimpse of pale blue was all that could be seen of the Sea of Salt.

Menahem rode a large black mare purchased from the Nabateans—a beautiful animal with a long, silky mane and tail. Eleazar and Joab rode beside him on chestnut-colored horses. Menahem reined up his animal, turning aside to let the rest of the column ride past. He looked up and down the line of men marching three abreast. They were armed in the manner of light auxiliaries, with helmets, breastplates, spears, and shields from the extensive Masada armory. After them came the camel train, the same one that had carried their equipment to Ein Gedi. They were followed by the bowmen without armor, clad in leather jerkins and armed only with light bows and the long, curved knives which Menahem's band had made famous. After the bowmen came more pack animals, mules brought by the Judean and Samarian rebel groups. A detachment of infantry brought up the rear.

Menahem looked at them with pride. No outlaw band had ever been so well equipped; it was an army, three cohorts strong. He would match it against any force in Judea. The men did not march as legionaries, nor did they have the discipline of an auxiliary detachment. But each was a seasoned guerrilla, a fighter of many years' standing. They could move with speed and flexibility. They could penetrate territory where no normal force would dare to venture and could fight in numerous different ways. In a pitched battle they might not be a match for regular soldiers; but at a word from their commander, the fifteen hundred men could instantly break up into groups of ten or twenty, each group able to operate independently, each knowing its particular role and technique.

The old man dug his heels into the flanks of his mare and cantered up the column, his tousled gray hair streaming behind him. In less than an hour he would see the Temple, the sun glinting on its golden roofs and spires and reflecting from its marble walls. Menahem was overjoyed. After a lifetime of

51

struggle he was marching to Jerusalem at the head of a Jewish army; surely the day of the Lord was at hand!

The four months since the capture of Masada had been busy ones. Almost at once Menahem had sent a large force under Absalom and Judah ben Jair to the capital to look after Sicarii interests there. The main body of the movement had been concentrated at Masada. From Judea, Samaria, Perea, and Idumea, the rebels had come with their families; farmers and peasants sympathetic to the Sicarii had streamed southward to the stone fastness. The major part of the garrison slaves had joined the community, which had grown to some three thousand. Living space had become scarce. The palaces were filled and the newcomers divided up the main rooms into smaller units; extra rooms were added on the sides of buildings. Soon even these had proved inadequate, and the families began to move into the casemates of the outer wall, dividing the larger casemates into small rooms, living one family to a room. And still they had continued coming. They brought domestic animals and other supplies with them. Incredibly they managed to drag sheep, goats, and even cows up the twisting, steep slopes, until the central part of the plateau came to resemble a vast marketplace.

All through the burning heat of the desert summer the community had grown, while the situation in Judea and particularly in Jerusalem developed swiftly. Since Absalom's departure for the capital, Menahem had received constant word by courier of happenings there. He learned that the Temple captain's action in ceasing the daily sacrifice in honor of the Roman emperor had been carried out in the teeth of vociferous opposition from the peace party, including the captain's own father, the high priest Hananiah. The city had become divided into two parts, with the rebels holding the eastern lower city, including the Temple Mount, and the loyalists holding the western upper city. The majority of the city's population continued to go about their normal business without committing themselves to either group.

Among the war party there were four clearly defined

groups. At the head of the revolt was the aristocratic priestly group of the Temple captain, drawn chiefly from the younger section of the priesthood, the landed gentry, and the merchant class; but the other rebel groups looked on them with suspicion. Ben Simon was the leader of the second group, a Zealot band that had been active in the region between Jerusalem and the seacoast, plundering the caravans to Joppa from the capital. Simon bar Giora, the gigantic son of a converted Jew from Gerasa, east of Galilee, led a fast-growing gang of former slaves, which made up the third group. Absalom and his Sicarii, who had penetrated the city in disguise during the wood-gathering festival at the Temple, were the fourth group. Since their arrival the war party had increased in strength and had started to penetrate the western part of the city.

Before he saw the city, Menahem saw the smoke.

"Burning, burning..." the word passed down the column of Sicarii. Something in the Holy City was burning; and then they saw the city high above them with the sun glinting on the golden roofs of the gleaming white Temple of God. Behind the Temple, a building was on fire. It was the Antonia fortress. They stopped, spellbound by the sight of the city of David, fascinated by the flames and the smoke, not knowing whether to be joyous or afraid.

10

Menahem had descended from his horse to enter the city on foot. A troop of cavalry left the Dung Gate in a cloud of dust and rode toward them. As the horsemen drew nearer, they could see that they were led by a tall, dark, young man with curly black hair and a sparse beard.

"Judah!" Eleazar was the first to recognize his brother, as the young horseman thundered up at the head of his troop. Springing to the ground, Judah went first to embrace his uncle.

"We are waiting," he informed Menahem. He raised his voice, addressing the whole column: "The city awaits you!"

The walls near the gate were lined with cheering Sicarii,

53

thrilled by the sight of their well-equipped comrades. The baggage animals, they noted, carried yet more arms. There was no doubt that the Sicarii had become the dominant party in Jerusalem.

The high, vaulted chamber was built on large sandstone blocks; narrow windows were set high up into the walls, on which hung a few drapes. The furnishings were severe; a heavy wooden table surrounded by sturdy benches filled the center of the room. Absalom brought wine and Menahem made the blessing: *"Blessed are Thou, O Lord our God, King of the World, who created the fruit of the vine."* The two men drank, sitting at either side of the table, their elbows resting on its rough surface. The old man looked shrewdly at his second-in-command.

"Why here, Absalom?" he asked.

"The aristocratic party is in the Temple," replied the big man. "Here in the lower city we are in the center of things. We did not want to use Ophel, as it is so near to the Temple. It is still secret; we can never know when we might need it."

"Good, Absalom, good," the old man approved. "Never trust anybody, least of all one of our aristocrats!"

"I have no intention whatsoever of trusting them," confided Absalom. "It was our arrival which prevented them from taking over the rebellion completely. As you know," he continued, "we entered the city as wood gatherers for the Temple festival. The Temple captain was about to order the arrest of ben Simon and bar Giora—there is no love lost between those three. Most of ben Simon's men are in the western hills, and bar Giora is only starting to make his mark. He has a large mob, but they have not been together long. Had a struggle ensued, the Temple captain would have been able to cope with the situation. But of course the peace party would have been the real victors; you know that."

Absalom narrated simply, with a minimum of detail. The western quarter of the city had been mostly overrun by the rebel groups, leaving the peace party in possession only of Herod's palace, including its three defense towers. They had

54

also held the Antonia until that day, when they had succeeded in setting fire to it. The palaces of Agrippa and Berenice and the house of the high priest had also been destroyed. Most importantly, they had fired the records office, that vast complex of offices which housed the bonds of the moneylenders, leases, contracts, and most of the financial documents of Judea. With its destruction, all evidence of debts and other financial transactions had disappeared.

"As you can imagine, Menahem, the Temple captain was livid with rage. He realized it was more of a blow against him and his friends than against Rome, but of course there was nothing he could do about it. It has shown him that we shall not be satisfied merely to sweep away the rule of Rome without dealing with injustices nearer home."

Judah, Eleazar, and Joab took their places around the table. The atmosphere in the city was tense, Judah reported. The people feared a clash between Menahem and the Temple captain; but in fact he thought that this was unlikely. A messenger from the captain had informed him unofficially that the latter was prepared to offer the chairmanship of the war council to Menahem that evening.

"What of the Sanhedrin?" asked Menahem.

"For the time being, the Sanhedrin is nearly defunct," answered Absalom. "They are hopelessly split about the revolt, though of course the majority are appeasers. For all that, I am sure that the Temple captain can force anything he wishes on them."

"It does not do to underrate the Sanhedrin," mused Menahem. "They had already degenerated in Hezekiah's day. They wanted to censure Herod for his murder, but he was able to ignore them. Yet the Sanhedrin still exists. It has an amazing way of reviving just when it seems to be finished. We shall have to take the Sanhedrin into consideration. However, the real question is what are we to do about the Temple captain? I take it he is too strong to be attacked directly?"

"I think a direct confrontation would be inadvisable at the present time," said the big man. "We shall have to be ready

55

for anything, though; you know we cannot trust these people."

"It seems to me," interjected Joab, his beard jutting aggressively, "that this fighting between Jew and Jew should cease." Joab had been a prosperous farmer before the large landowners had forced him to abandon his trade. He was no lover of the aristocracy, but his background was more comfortable than that of most of his colleagues, and on social questions he tended to be less extreme.

"The aristocrats are not to be trusted," reaffirmed Absalom.

"And yet, Absalom," stated Menahem, "although I agree with you, as you know, I feel Joab's approach is a healthy one. I do not see any reason against cooperating with the other groups. We are the strongest now. I think we can afford to be conciliatory, particularly in view of Judah's report."

"I am not surprised by what Judah tells us," said Absalom, "but what is the motive behind the Temple captain's offer? Today we captured the Antonia. The next task, the seige of Herod's palace with its three towers, is a far harder one."

"What lies behind your words?" asked the old man.

"I mean that the others are quite willing to let us take over at this juncture because they think that we shall fail," explained Absalom.

"I see." Menahem thought for a while. "Well, it does not matter," he said at length. "I did not expect that they would offer us the leadership through love; but it is a good opportunity. It seems to me that if we prosecute the battle successfully, we can consolidate our position. It is better than having to fight for the leadership."

"I agree with that," affirmed Eleazar. "The important fact is that we shall gain the leadership without a struggle—it is a marvelous opportunity."

"I do not trust them!" Absalom was still suspicious.

"Nor do I," agreed the old man. "Now let us hear about the military situation."

When the revolt broke out, explained Absalom, there had been two Caesarean cohorts in the city, brought up as reinforcements by the procurator, as well as the normal Antonia garrison. These forces had been subsequently strengthened by

56

Agrippa's three thousand cavalry. The Antonia garrison had been destroyed, but most of the Caesareans were shut up in Herod's palace with the cavalry and many Jerusalem peace partisans.

"What other troops are there in the vicinity?" asked Joab.

"The nearest is the garrison at Herodium, which you passed today," was the reply. "There are large garrisons in Caesarea and Sebaste, and small detachments, usually of cohort strength, in every fortress in the country. Of course," he smiled, "Masada is an exception; but Macherus on the eastern shore of the Sea of Salt has two cohorts defending it. These garrisons have one thing in common: none of them have made any move."

"Do you think they will remain immobilized?" asked Joab.

"It seems likely," replied Absalom. "The country is up in arms, and a small force is in danger of being massacred if it leaves the shelter of its fortress. It is almost certain that they will wait for the arrival of the legions."

The legions! The word brought a chill into the room. The Roman legions were overwhelmingly equipped and trained to perfection. Since they had smashed the phalanx of the Seleucids more than a century earlier, no force in the world had been able to resist the legions. So far, the Jewish rebels had proved themselves more than a match for the outnumbered auxiliaries, who were stationed in the colony. But the legions were a different matter. Eleazar brought the meeting back to the immediate issue.

"It seems," he remarked, "that we have some time before the arrival of the governor of Syria. Let us concentrate on the question of the palace of Herod."

"It is an exceptionally difficult building to capture," said Absalom.

"More difficult than Masada?" Joab's beard pointed aggressively at him.

"Our essential weapon at Masada was surprise; we do not have that here." Absalom scratched his sparse black beard. "It is a larger building than any on Masada. The siege weapons we captured there are only of the lightest variety. If we succeed

57

we will be in control of the city, but the task is no easy one."

"From what you have told us," said Menahem, "it seems that more than half the defenders are Jews—I refer to Agrippa's soldiers and the peace partisans. If we could drive a wedge between them and the cohorts, I think we could weaken them considerably. Is there some way to conveying messages to the defenders?"

"They are effectively sealed in," replied Absalom. "We might possibly think of some way."

"We also need a plan of attack," insisted Joab.

11

The dim light from the earthenware oil lamps scarcely penetrated to the high, vaulted ceiling of the Sicarii headquarters. A dozen men sat around the rough table, their faces illuminated by the soft glow. It was the seventh meeting of the war council since Menahem ben Judah had become commander of the rebel forces in Jerusalem. Despite his position, Menahem was commander only in name. The forces under his command were still fragmented and owed loyalty to their individual commanders.

The first meeting had been a success. Menahem had declined the chairmanship of the council, stating that he was satisfied with the position of commander in the field. He had proposed that the Temple captain continue to preside over staff discussions, which should be held every two days. The gesture had been well received. His proposal for regular meetings was accepted. He felt that constant meetings would increase the natural drive toward unity. However, since that original meeting twelve days previously, there had been no military advance; and although Menahem's leadership had not been openly challenged, critical voices had been raised.

A parley with the representatives of the besieged forces had been successfully arranged. At the meeting, the Jewish peace party delegates had been vociferous in their affirmations that they would not abandon their auxiliary colleagues; but their leader, Costobar, a cousin of King Agrippa, had remarked in

Hebrew, which the soldiers did not understand, that a good number of the Jews were in favor of surrender—but it would take time. Menahem had been delighted with the news, feeling sure that the defeatist faction would demoralize the others.

After several days, though, when the rebel attacks had failed to make any impression on the besieged, there was no sign of this demoralization. On the contrary, it was the undisciplined rebels who were becoming discouraged; there was talk of the approach of Cestius Gallus, governor of Syria, with the Twelfth Legion from Antioch. Time was against Menahem. If the palace was not captured soon, his leadership could not survive.

For the first half hour, the seventh meeting was indistinguishable from the previous six; each faction leader felt compelled to reiterate the contribution of his own group to the cause of the revolt.

"We decided to add our forces to those opposing Roman rule when Gessius Florus saw fit to crucify Jewish Roman citizens of the Equestrian Order," the Temple captain started, in much the same words he had used previously. He was a young, handsome man of fair complexion, his hair and beard the fair russet color of priestly stock and worn long. His gray eyes were alert and his features regular and well shaped. Tall and slim, he paced back and forth in front of the table with an athletic stride, talking in a relaxed and confident manner. He wore elegant armor, the silver-plated scales molded to the shape of his body.

"We then realized," he continued, "that there was no difference between Jew and Jew. Many of you think, I know, that we made the discovery rather late." He paused, looking challengingly at the other leaders, but there was no interruption. "Maybe you were right. I know that we priests and landowners were satisfied with Roman rule. I would point out that Rome is tolerant of our ways in a manner that Greece never was; but we have perceived that we were wrong. Rome must be opposed, or at least Florus must be resisted. It is a national struggle now—the whole Jewish nation against Rome. Too many of the previous revolts were civil wars, with the rebels fighting their fellow Jews."

Absalom rose, as if to interrupt, but at a sign from Menahem he resumed his seat.

"We have decided to end this factionalism," the aristocrat continued. "It was our decision to withdraw the Temple sacrifice in honor of the emperor that launched this war. We have seen rioting and murder before; but our action is a ringing affirmation that Judea rejects the rule of Rome!"

Ben Simon was short and stocky, not unlike Joab in build. His dark brown face was scarred and heavily lined, in contrast to the youthful elegance of the Temple captain. Partial baldness emphasized the height of his forehead. His small black eyes were constantly on the move, taking in every word or gesture. His dark brown beard was clipped short and his thick arms were covered with hair. He was simply dressed in linen trousers and a leather sleeveless tunic.

"While you sat at ease with your Roman friends, Temple Captain, we were fighting them," he began. "We have been fighting the enemy for more than a dozen years. We certainly have no intention of handing over power to men who proved to be traitors in the past." The captain of the Temple guard studied his fingernails. "It was our group which prevented the atrocity of the Caesarean cohorts from turning into a full-scale massacre," claimed ben Simon. "We led the people of Jerusalem in fighting back. We fought with sticks and rocks and our bare hands, with the paving stones of white marble that our beloved King Agrippa donated to the city." The last words were spoken with a rough irony. "We started this revolt," he concluded. "We started it and we shall carry it on until the end, whatever that end might be. It is indeed a national war, and it is our Zealots that represent the nation!"

"It is not merely a national war," contradicted Simon bar Giora in his deep voice. His Aramaic was rough and untutored. He spoke haltingly in contrast to the ease of the Temple captain or the confident briefing of ben Simon; but every word was charged with emotion and power. He was a giant of a man, taller than Absalom and even more heavily built. His balding

60

head was small on his enormous shoulders. He wore a full suit of armor, and his helmet rested on the table in front of him, between his muscular forearms. When he spoke, he seemed to grope for words.

"This is more than a national revolt—it is a revolution. A revolution! We have to make changes: we have to change everything." Bar Giora glowered at the Temple captain, who barely concealed his distaste and impatience.

"I am the son of a convert," he continued. "I am new to Judaism; but that does not lessen my devotion to the Jewish nation. My father was a slave!" He allowed the word to penetrate, looking at each of the other leaders in turn. "I do not think there should be slaves anymore. I do not think that our law permits slavery." The Temple captain started to interrupt, but bar Giora waved him silent with a vast hand. "Oh, I know, Temple Captain, that you can quote me the Law. I am a simple man. I do not know as much as you do, nor will I ever know as much. You are a priest and I am the son of a slave. But I do know this: God made man in His image!" He looked around the table once more, resting his gaze finally on the young captain.

"Is the Lord supposed to be a slave?" he demanded. "It is the meaning of the Law that I seek, not the details. I ask myself and I ask all of you: Was God intended to be a slave? Can something created in His image be intended for slavery?

"Rome is the summit of the world and the world is founded on slavery. That is why the world is sick. We must destroy Rome and the evil things for which she stands; but we must also wipe out evil wherever we see it. We must free the slaves! This is a mighty war of oppressed against oppressors. The people will rise not only against Rome, but against their treacherous local masters also!"

Menahem, as usual, spoke last and he was no more concise than the previous speakers. He recalled that his grandfather Hezekiah had opposed Herod's tyranny when the latter was merely governor of Galilee, and that he had been hanged for his pains. He recounted the glorious deeds of his father, Judah of Galilee. He assured Simon bar Giora that Judah had been well aware of the social aspects of the rebellion and had been at particular pains to oppose taxation, the chief instrument of oppression. He dwelt on the fate of his two brothers and described his own years as a guerrilla leader, which had culminated in the capture of Masada and the march to Jerusalem. He concluded: "The time foretold by the prophets is come; this is the dawn of a new age. We shall make a new covenant with the Almighty!"

"We had better capture the palace of Herod first," remarked the Temple captain dryly. Absalom sprang to his feet, his dark face flushed with anger. But Menahem placed a restraining hand on his wrist.

"I hope that by tomorrow, Temple Captain, you will be satisfied on that point." The old man spoke calmly, though he too was trembling.

"Tomorrow?" asked ben Simon, passing his stubby-fingered hand over his bald head. "Why tomorrow? We have been sitting outside that wall for twelve days; why should tomorrow be different?"

"You will see," promised Menahem, with difficulty keeping his temper under control.

"These meetings are for the purpose of discussion and information," said the Temple captain. "Or so I understood," he continued with heavy sarcasm. "I hardly think there is much point in continuing with them if Menahem ben Judah insists on keeping his unique strategy to himself."

The old man's florid face flushed with anger and his hand combed nervously through his full gray beard, but his voice was still controlled.

"I repeat what I said—you will see tomorrow."

"We cannot wait forever," said the Temple captain. "Even Cestius Gallus can hardly continue to prevaricate. I understand that by next week he will be on the move."

"You seem remarkably well informed of the governor's intentions." Now Menahem's tone was sweet.

The captain raised an eyebrow fastidiously. "And you, Rabbi, are not so informed?"

"The people are becoming impatient," rumbled bar Giora.

"If you cannot achieve results, Menahem, make way for some-one who can!"

Absalom's tone was velvet: "And who might that be?"

"Stop this nonsense!" snapped ben Simon. "Have we no serious problems that you can afford to squabble like children?"

"We are eager to hear your words, ben Simon," said Menahem. "Do not deprive us of your wisdom."

"Events moved fast enough until you arrived," ben Simon was stung to retort. "We captured the upper city and then the Antonia. Since you arrived the situation has stagnated; operations are almost at a standstill. The people are beginning to wonder. . . ."

"Are we being threatened?" Absalom was on his feet again, his hand on the dagger at his belt. Eleazar rose on the other side of Menahem.

The tense silence was broken with studied casualness by the Temple captain. "As though all of us did not know," he drawled, "that there are two hundred armed Sicarii surrounding this building!"

Bar Giora sprang to his feet, his small, dark eyes blazing with anger. "Is this true?" He towered above Menahem. The latter shrugged. "Is this your unity? Is this your trust?"

Ben Simon appeared to be amused. He turned to the Temple captain. "Could it be that our young friend," he indicated the enraged bar Giora, "really did not know? Perhaps he is a better actor than we are?" He changed his tone. "Now listen to me, Menahem ben Judah," he looked straight at the old man. "You have the upper hand now. Your men could cut the rest of us to pieces in less than an hour. But it will not remain that way. The people will decide this war, and the people will decide who is to lead it—not a couple of thousand Sicarii. The sooner you call off your men and explain to them that they are not fighting their fellow Jewish patriots, the better it will be for our cause!"

Menahem motioned to Absalom and Eleazar to be seated. Then he rose and faced his rivals. They sat around the table in the dim light, their faces tense and worried, except for bar

63

Giora, who remained on his feet, his face dark with anger.

"I want unity," began Menahem quietly. "I came to Jerusalem in peace—peace toward you, though not toward Rome; but your intrigues began from the moment I entered the city. You gave me the command because you had no choice and because you hoped that I would fail. You knew well the difficulties of the palace siege. You knew that the governor of Syria was approaching. None of you has done anything to foster unity. You have all been reinforcing your own factions at the expense of our unified effort. None of you has shown any loyalty. You constantly alarm the people with false news of the governor's advance.

"The day that I assumed command, ben Simon, you told a meeting of your men in the lower city that they could expect things to slow down after the senile rabbi took control. You, bar Giora, have canvassed the slaves without restraint. In the still-smoldering ruins of Agrippa's palace, you told them that you were the only one who could safeguard their interests, and they should see to it that you became the next leader. You daily tell your colleagues that you will not suffer an inferior bandit chief to rule over you. Temple Captain, yesterday you told a meeting of priests in the Temple forecourt—"

"Spies!" thundered bar Giora. "We have been spied upon. As he spoke his soft words—"

"I meant what I said," Menahem interrupted him. He spoke with force and authority, silencing even bar Giora. "I will step down if that is the way to achieve unity. If the palace is not ours in two days I will relinquish the command."

"Two days . . ." mused ben Simon. "We have already wasted too many days."

"Have we any choice?" asked the Temple captain cynically. Everybody looked at Simon bar Giora, who was still on his feet, his enormous barrel of a chest heaving, his face set in a scowl. Suddenly his mood changed and he grinned. He pulled at his tangled black beard. He turned back to the table and picked up his helmet, holding it in the crook of his arm.

"Two hundred Sicarii!" He bellowed with laughter. He advanced on Menahem, right hand raised. Absalom stiffened, but bar Giora merely clapped the old man on the back in a friendly manner. "Maybe you are the right man for commander of the Jews," he remarked as he turned and strode from the room.

Ben Simon now rose and looked at Menahem. "Remember my words, Rabbi," he said. He addressed the old man with the term of respect. "You were the first of us and you know how we feel about you. Your father failed to beat the Romans, but he never failed the people. Judah of Galilee had no need to set spies, or surround his staff meetings with two hundred armed men!"

Ben Simon and his men left the room, followed by the Temple captain, who did not speak. The Sicarii leaders were left alone. Menahem rested his head on his hands, looking glumly down at the table in front of him. Absalom turned to Judah, who had just entered.

"Any progress?" he asked.

"We are obstructed by a large flint," was the reply. "It is worse than anything we have come across so far."

"Make a detour."

"There is a limit to the number of detours we can make," replied Judah. Eleazar frowned, his lean scholar's face lined beyond his years.

"We have not much more time," he said.

"I will come, Judah," said Absalom. Judah nodded and sat down. The large man put his arm around Menahem's shoulders. "Tomorrow we shall take the palace," he stated. "You will be in control then; the people will hail you, Menahem. You will see."

"I have lived a long time, Absalom," replied the old man. "For too much of that time I have been fighting my own people. Why can they never trust us? Why do we always have to fight each other? Why are we incapable of uniting?"

"The worst is over, Uncle." Eleazar spoke with some conviction. "Tomorrow we shall capture the palace. Tonight I meet with John from the Sons of Zadok. The Master has authorized the mobilizing of the Sons in our behalf. We cannot have Sekaka as a base, but the cells up and down the country will be for us. It is what you wanted, Menahem."

65

"But what of the Priest?" the old man demanded petulantly. He turned on Absalom and Eleazar in a sudden fury, an exasperated old man's rage. "Do you think this a mere rebellion? I tell you that it is the appointed time. The Priest of Sekaka is the last surviving member of the house of Zadok, the legitimate high priest of all Israel!"

"You must have patience, my uncle," said Eleazar. "You have always known how to wait. It is not for us to decide when the Priest will come to the Temple. Meanwhile, we have much with which to occupy ourselves. Tomorrow you will establish your position as commander. The city will be ours. The Sons are with us; news from Galilee is also encouraging. Developments are going our way, the Lord is with us."

"How can the Lord be with us when we are devouring each other?"

"We must devour those who would devour us," replied Absalom.

"Where did I go wrong?" asked the old leader. "Why do they not trust me?"

"They fear you," was the reply. "They have feared us since the assassinations, since they started to call us the Sicarii. Our policy was bound to incur hatred and fear."

The old man shook his gray mane. He rose from the table, swaying slightly on his feet. "One has these doubts," he said, almost to himself. "We seem so near and yet so far away." Eleazar and Judah helped the old man to the door and Judah took him to his quarters.

Eleazar wore a worried expression as he faced Absalom. "He will be well in the morning," said the latter. "He is only tired. Once we have taken the palace, he will be on top of the world!"

"He is an old man," Eleazar pointed out. "There is a limit to his resilience." He changed the subject: "Was it really necessary to surround the meeting?"

"Was it necessary to place spies?" asked Absalom. "You heard for yourself."

"I do not know." Eleazar scratched his head. "Do you think it really helped? People always plot and grumble; our spies did not change that. They just make the people more suspicious of us."

"One day, Eleazar, you will be our leader," said Absalom earnestly. "Menahem is an old man, as you said. A leader should never trust anybody. Put your faith in God, Eleazar, and in Him alone!"

12

Bar Nottos and Simon ben Jair were working with two others in the tunnel. It was hot and the sweat poured from their bare bodies. The torches flared, lighting the narrow shaft with a yellow glare. Where they were working the shaft had been widened to enable them to dig around the rock which was preventing their advance. Here it was possible to stand, though the air was thick with smoke and stank of human bodies.

Simon felt exhausted as he finished his twenty-minute shift. He had been swinging the heavy pick until it seemed to weigh a ton. Each time it hit the rock, fire ran down his arms from his smarting hands; his fingers were stiff and sore. With every swing he felt himself falling, closing his eyes and swaying on his feet; but he clenched his teeth and somehow continued. He struck the rock and again fire poured down his arms. The past few hours had been the worst of all.

Previously they had dug through earth and small rocks; the dust had filled the tunnel, catching in the back of his throat, forming a grit around the red rims of his eyes. He had coughed a dry hacking cough. But they had made progress. The tunnel had advanced and they had been able to feel themselves edging slowly forward. During the past day, however, they had not advanced at all—the vast flint rock had barred their way. There seemed no end to it. They had tried to burrow beneath it and had dug to either side without finding the edge. So for two hours they had attacked the flint itself, hoping that the unceasing battering of the iron would splinter it in the end.

The team working in the tunnel was a small one. It had to be if the secret was to be kept. As the tunnel advanced, they propped up the ceiling with wooden balks under the direction of Nahum. The blond slave had worked in the Nabatean copper mines of the Aravah before escaping northward to join the Sicarii, and he knew all about shoring up tunnels. When he swung his pick, it was with an easy rhythm that enabled him to work tirelessly for hours on end.

"Easy, boy, easy," he would say to Simon or to Judah. "Let the pick work for you; it is your slave, not the other way around." Simon learned to relax; but Judah, obstinate and sullen, had continued to pour out all his vigor and strength in every blow.

Simon allowed the pick to fall from his hands and leaned back against the rough wall of the shaft. Bar Nottos gave him a sign that their shift was finished. He noticed with surprise that Absalom had entered the tunnel with Judah and Nahum. Absalom was stripped to the waist, his smooth olive skin almost hairless. He lifted the heavy hammer and hefted it in his enormous hands. The others stood back as he swung. The great lump of iron smashed into the rock with amazing force. Again he swung, a long easy swing, the powerful muscles rippling under his smooth skin, his calves, thighs, and shoulders tensed as the hammer crashed against the rock.

After a dozen such blows he paused, resting the head of the hammer on the ground. His great body glistened, his broad chest heaved. He shut his eyes, wiping them with the back of his hand. A bead of sweat formed at the end of his sparse, pointed beard and dropped into the dust. He nodded to Nahum, only slightly smaller than himself, his fair hair lit up in the glare of the torches.

Simon and bar Nottos worked their way back along the tunnel, crawling much of the way and bending double in other places. They emerged gulping the cool night air of Jerusalem, finding it incredibly sweet and fresh. They were quickly covered with woolen cloaks to prevent their being chilled.

Absalom and Nahum were working their third shift, hitting the rock alternately. The dark giant continued to use his hammer; Nahum worked with a pick. Absalom swung, Nahum struck, Absalom, Nahum, Absalom, Nahum, each gave the other strength and rhythm until they felt that there was nothing but the two of them, following each other instinctively, gasping for breath. Each spurred on the other with his blows, neither of them conscious of the filthy, smoke-laden air which they breathed, nor of anything save the necessity of continuing to smash and swing. It was as if pure spirit were driving them on, discovering extra reserves of strength and increasing the power of the blows. Absalom could scarcely lower his hammer before Nahum's pick hit the rock, and the pick barely avoided being struck by the renewed blow of the hammer.

Judah and the others looked on incredulously, simply not believing that the two men could continue pouring out so much power. There was no pause in the tempo of their blows. On the contrary, the speed at which strike followed strike appeared actually to increase. Finally Nahum let his pick drop on the floor of the tunnel. He stood there, his chest covered with matted blond hair stained dark with sweat. Absalom cast down his hammer. His almost-black body streamed with moisture; each rib was clearly defined as he sucked air into his lungs.

It was Judah who noticed the crack.

"Look!" he cried, darting forward. "You have done it!" He seized a flaming torch from its bracket in the wall of the shaft and held it near the surface of the flint; a thin line showed where the rock had been split. Within minutes, Nahum was expertly prizing his pick into the crack, and an hour later they were digging through the usual mixture of sandstone, earth, and chalk. As they dug, a constant stream of earth and rubble was passed back along the shaft. The mouth of the tunnel emerged in the midst of the Sicarii advanced positions by the outer buildings of what had been Agrippa's palace. In the ruins of these buildings the earth was concealed.

Early in the morning, as the first light of day was appearing outside the tunnel, Nahum gave a cry of joy—they had broken through to the main sewage drain of Herod's palace. The smell was almost unbearable, but they enlarged the opening and plunged through the filth. Some yards further up they struck off sideways again, propping up the shaft as before. By mid-morning they were beneath the palace wall, and before the evening a dozen massive wooden balks were the only support for the foundations of a large section of that wall.

The Sicarii had brought with them from the Sea of Salt large lumps of oily black pitch, which they had fished out of the heavy water. They melted down the asphalt in large caldrons and smeared it on the balks holding up the palace wall until they were entirely impregnated with it.

13

In contrast to the close-packed houses of the lower city, the buildings of the upper city were well spaced. The outer buildings of Agrippa's palace, where the Sicarii had established their base, approached to within a hundred yards of Herod's palace, where the loyalists were holding out. In the morning Menahem sent word to the other leaders to send support to the Sicarii base for the final attack. Prompted partly by curiosity, the three rival leaders came at the head of detachments of their forces, flanking the Sicarii, who had drawn up in readiness for battle.

As the sun rose, Menahem, his gray hair and beard blown awry by the wind, led the rebel fighters in prayer. The men had turned from the palace to face the Temple, clearly visible above the ruins of Agrippa's palace to the east. The golden roofs reflected the morning light as they bound their frontlets to their foreheads and arms.

There had been no staff meeting on the previous evening. Tension had grown in the city as the self-imposed deadline given by Menahem neared. The Sicarii leader would be relinquishing the command unless the palace fell, and the people were worried about the anarchy that was liable to follow. Despite the mysterious activity in the Sicarii camp, there had been no visible progress toward the capture of the palace, which looked as invulnerable as ever.

The trumpets sounded faintly from the Temple, signaling

the commencement of morning prayers. Mounted on his black mare, Menahem presented an impressive figure in the early morning sun. When the trumpets from the Temple had ceased, he raised his arm and the trumpets of the Sicarii answered with the signal for advance. The rebels moved forward toward the palace in extended line formation.

To their right the attackers could see the gigantic towers of Hippicus, Phasael, and Mariamne, built by Herod and named after the people he loved most. The palace in front of them, though lower than the towers, was nonetheless formidable. It was a building of great beauty, surpassed in Jerusalem only by the Temple itself. Its walls, massively constructed from stones of various hues, were topped at regular intervals with ornate towers, decorative but strong. Behind the walls, not visible to the advancing rebels, were fine colonnades and spacious courtyards with fountains and green lawns.

A rain of missiles poured down on the attackers, who answered with a powerful and varied volley. Bar Nottos, freed from the tunnel at last, was operating a small battery of light catapults and quick-loaders; the remainder of the Sicarii and ben Simon's Zealots loosed volley after volley of light arrows from their bows, and bar Giora's men hurled rocks and stones from their slings.

Twenty yards in front of the rebel forces and twenty feet below the defenders of the palace, Judah ben Jair stood ready in the tunnel, a flaming torch in his hand. He could hear nothing of the sounds of battle that raged above him, but his men were stationed at intervals along the shaft. His youngest brother, Simon, stood some ten yards away.

"Now, Judah!" shouted the boy. "Fire!" He at once began to move down the tunnel. Judah allowed his brother to enter the sewer drain, and then plunged his torch at the nearest pitch-coated balk. The asphalt flared up with an almost explosive force, and Judah, coughing and choking, stumbled into the sewer and on down the shaft to the fresh air.

Emerging from the tunnel mouth, Judah saw that the battle was raging fiercely. A two-way rain of missiles hurtled back and forth between defender and attacker. The defenders were waiting in the towers and on top of the walls with jars of hot oil and large rocks with which to assault any who came too near. Judah watched the section of wall in front of the Sicarii camp. He was the first to notice the barely perceptible movement of the stone blocks. A few seconds later, the defenders themselves must have felt something, for they began to move back out of sight and to vacate the tower above that section. Within less than a minute the whole section of wall was denuded. The clamor of battle gradually died; there was silence over the whole area. The defenders on other sections of the wall as well as the attackers were staring transfixed, as the huge bonded stones began to shift and the masonry to crumble. The tower lurched to one side.

Suddenly, with a rumble as of thunder, the whole section of the palace wall collapsed, and from below, the flames came licking upward. There was silence again, which continued for several seconds after the dust had started to clear. Then there came a wild, exultant burst of cheering from the Sicarii, in which the other troops gradually joined, swelling the sound into a mad, joyful roar from thousands of throats. Quick to sense the popular mood, Simon bar Giora, towering above his fellows, pointed his sword at Menahem, who, bemused in the hour of his triumph, sat wordlessly on his black mare.

"Menahem!" he thundered in his mighty voice.

"Menahem, Menahem!" came the answering roar of the entire rebel army.

Spurred on by the acclaim, the old leader urged his mare forward, leading the rebel force to the breach in the wall. Skirting the pit where the pitch-coated balks were still burning fiercely, he pulled up with a shock at the foot of a second wall. It seemed that the defenders had somehow guessed at the Sicarii plan—perhaps the wall had shifted during the tunneling—and they had constructed a temporary inner wall that was clearly weaker than the original wall.

Realizing that all might be lost if they did not hold the initiative, Absalom signaled to the men to continue their advance. They swarmed up the wall, clawing for handholds on the rough stone. They were now within range of the heavy boulders and oil, and their casualties were heavy. Several were crushed beneath the huge rocks; others screamed in agony as their skins were flayed by the burning, viscous liquid. But the battle-maddened Sicarii were not to be deterred as they hurled themselves forward with increased fury. Bar Giora and ben Simon were well to the fore, leading their men in assault after assault. Three times the rebels almost succeeded in mounting the wall, only to be thrown back by the defenders.

Then—just at the moment when Absalom, whose left arm had been crushed by a boulder, was about to order the retreat —a tall pole surmounted by a piece of white cotton material was raised above the wall.

The negotiations lasted for ten minutes. Half an hour later, the Jews and King Agrippa's auxiliaries marched out of the palace, leaving the Caesareans alone within. They were at once surrounded by a jubilant mob of rebels, who escorted them to their camps in various parts of the lower city.

14

At the meeting of the war council that evening, a new atmosphere was evident. Menahem took the chair. Absalom, his left arm in a sling, sat at his right, Eleazar and Joab at his left.

That day Jerusalem had gone wild with joy. Wherever the story of the defection from the palace had spread, people had poured out into the streets to celebrate. The story of the undermining of the palace wall was told and retold; Menahem was hailed as a second Joshua. Peace party sympathizers had kept silent. Most of them remained in their own homes, while several began quietly to leave the city. The feeling was all in favor of war now, and Menahem was the hero of Jerusalem and unchallenged leader of the rebellion.

Absalom began with a brief report of events subsequent to the Jewish withdrawal from the palace. He alluded to the fact that it had been Menahem's plan from the first to secure this defection, pointing out that the long-term strategy, as much as the physical tactic of undermining the wall, had been responsible for their success. He reported that the auxiliaries defending the palace, after being deserted by their Jewish allies, had fled to the three towers of Hippicus, Phasael, and Mariamne. A number of them had been killed in the retreat from the palace; the remainder was said to be thinking of negotiating a surrender.

Eleazar's report of his meeting with the Bursar of the Sons of Zadok followed. The Master of the pious sect had ruled that its members were free to join the revolt. Most of the Sons were expected to rally to the cause. John, leader of the militant section of the movement, was admitted to the council and took his place among the rebel commanders.

The meeting was about to proceed with a further briefing from Absalom, when Judah ben Jair entered and conferred hastily with his uncle in whispers. He then spoke to Absalom in a low voice. Absalom nodded his approval, and a group of six men entered the room. They were stocky, bearded, and disheveled men, streaked with sweat and covered with dirt; they stood dazzled even by the soft lamplight.

"What message do you bring from Galilee?" asked Menahem.

One of the men stepped forward, taking a scroll of parchment from his tunic. The meeting waited tensely for the message, each of the leaders craning forward to look at the men from the north. The Galileans were the most numerous of the rebels and their decision was crucial. The man unrolled his scroll and read:

"John ben Levi of Gischala greets his fellow Galilean, the son of Judah of Galilee." The message was in Hebrew, the man's accent characteristic of his region. "Since the days of Hezekiah of blessed memory, the people of Galilee have been in the forefront of the struggle against the foreign enemy. Judah of Galilee led two mighty revolts against Rome; his sons Jacob and Simon gave their lives for the cause. It is therefore especially fitting that the sole surviving son of Judah should lead the rebellion—the final and successful rebellion—against the Romans.

"John ben Levi of Gischala recognizes Menahem the son of

Judah, grandson of Hezekiah, of the seed of David, continuing the glorious tradition of the Pious Ones, as his commander. Hail Menahem, captain of the armies of Israel!"

As usual, quick to sense the appropriate moment, Simon bar Giora was on his feet, the voice emerging from his splendid chest, deep and impressive despite his rough, halting speech.

"I and my followers recognize Menahem ben Judah as commander-in-chief of the Judean forces!"

Ben Simon followed him, and the Temple captain made a similar declaration. Throughout the proceedings Menahem sat in silence. Moved though he had been by the Galilean declaration, it was of Sekaka that he thought. He wondered how much influence the Master had on the Priest. Eleazar had promised to arrange a meeting between him and the Master, but there were other matters to be attended to first.

Menahem could not understand the situation at Sekaka. If the Sons were allowed to participate in the revolt, they must believe the new age had arrived. That being so, why did the Priest hang back? The Sons' doctrines were complicated; they seemed to cut themselves off deliberately from the rest of the nation. An example of this was their calendar, based on the movements of the sun instead of those of the moon. They were not prepared to compromise on it. They considered it the true calendar. Menahem, though a pious Pharisee all his life, was prepared to accept the calendar if the Priest ruled on it.

The important thing was to install the Priest in the Temple, the legitimate high priest descended from the pure line of the house of Zadok. He would be the first man worthy to fill that exalted office since the days of Simon the Just, and Menahem was increasingly certain that he was none other than the Messiah of Aaron, the priestly Messiah who was to rule Israel at the End of Days!

While Menahem was lost in his thoughts, Absalom was proceeding with the meeting. He informed the assembled leaders that the rebel army was to be reorganized. Independent forces, he explained, were to be abolished; groups that had existed up to the present were to be liquidated and merged into a single Judean army, its divisions based on careful consid-

erations of regional and strategic factors. The rebel commanders would have important positions; but there was no question
of their retaining their personal forces.

As soon as Absalom finished speaking, the storm broke. The
stocky ben Simon was the first to give his opinion, his small,
dark eyes flashing angrily as he spoke.

"You propose madness, Absalom," he claimed. "My forces
are concentrated in the city and in the hills between here and
the sea. Our men know every inch of the country. We have
fought together for a dozen years and in that time built up a
structure of camps and storage caves in the country, as well as
cells in the towns and villages. We can signal a message to the
coast in half an hour—even at night. The inhabitants of the
region know us personally, they hide us from the soldiers instinctively. My men work together almost without thinking. It
takes years to obtain rapport like that, and you want to break
it up!"

"I am prepared to be entirely frank with you, Rabbi." The
Temple captain addressed Menahem directly, ignoring Absalom. "My followers will not take kindly to your leadership; we
have been enemies too long. Your first assassination victim was
the high priest Jonathan, and you have killed many of our
people since. I, the son of Hananiah the high priest and captain of the Temple guard, have declared my loyalty to you. I
swear to obey you, and my men will obey me. That is the only
way."

Simon bar Giora spoke next. "You are right to want unity,
Absalom," he rumbled in his deep voice. "There must be unity;
but I ask myself what kind of unity? You know that I am not
one to sympathize with the priests and landowners. But what
the Temple captain said has a lot of truth in it. We all lead
special types of groups, the members of which are bound to us
for various reasons. I know how to deal with my men; the
Temple captain knows how to deal with his. We must unite for
war, but there are many dangers in the sort of forced merger
that you want."

It was Eleazar who replied in his quiet scholar's voice, looking mildly at the rival leaders.

76

"You said that there would have to be many changes, bar Giora," he said. "Yet you do not change. You said that the slaves must go free, yet you fear to mix your free men with their former masters. Do you think that this factionalism is going to defeat the legions? The queen of the savage Britons killed sixty thousand Roman soldiers just three years ago; but she was defeated nonetheless, and today Britain is a pacified Roman province. Judea can only defeat Rome if the Jews are as one. A rabble of slaves, aristocrats, peasants, and priests, each fighting their own separate battle for their own special interests, is not going to defeat the greatest power the world has ever seen!"

The discussion continued for several hours; but finally Absalom brought it to an end. "We have made our decision," he stated flatly. "We would rather the union was voluntary. We value your leadership and assistance, but be assured that we shall not flinch from doing what is necessary to ensure the unity of the nation."

15

It was an hour before dawn when Nahum, bar Nottos, and Judah ben Jair brought in the prisoners. One of the men was an impressive figure, tall and broad-shouldered with an imperious carriage. His long hair and beard were probably naturally white, but now they were begrimed and filthy like the rest of him. There was a familiar look about his wide-set gray eyes and regular features. His companion, though resembling him in many ways, was shorter and stouter. Both men, despite their disheveled appearance, had managed to retain their skullcaps.

The Sicarii leaders had sat up all night after the departure of their colleagues, discussing the problems that lay ahead of them, including the danger of civil war. They realized that the other groups were not prepared to accept their plans for a merger of the different forces and would resist its implementation with force if necessary, but they were prepared for an armed struggle if it could not be avoided. There was a feeling that the matter had to be settled finally. They were worn out by the events of the day and the tensions of the meeting, but they looked with interest at the two prisoners.

"What is the meaning of this outrage?" It was the taller of the two who spoke. There was a familiar tone in his drawling voice.

"We found them by the canal," reported Judah. "It seems they had been hiding there since the Jewish surrender. They fled from the soldiers, but they did not wish to join us. They are traitors."

"I know these men!" exclaimed Eleazar.

Menahem was on his feet. He approached the taller man. "Hananiah," he said. "Former high priest of Israel."

"I am still the high priest," replied the other, dignified despite his bedraggled appearance. "It will take a great deal more than a cutthroat bandit chief to depose the servant of the Lord!"

"Do you talk to me of God?" shouted Menahem, stung to anger. "You traitor! Defiler of the holy office you bear! Until now you have been in the palace with the uncircumcised scum who are fighting us, opposed to your own son. You had a chance to repent of your evil. We received all the Jewish defenders with joy and charitable hearts. You could have joined our ranks. Why have you been hiding since the palace fell? There can only be one reason—you intended to go on licking the feet of the foreigner. Have you no shame at all? How dare you continue to oppose the will of God?"

"This war is not the will of God," replied the priest. "You are most presumptuous in invoking the name of the Lord for so questionable a cause. There is no limit to the misery that this struggle will cause. Do you believe that a rabble of bandits and slaves can defeat the Romans? Do you understand what you have started? The whole land will be drenched in blood. Is that God's will?"

"You will keep silent or be silenced forever!" roared Menahem.

"Take care, son of Judah, you will not long survive the murder of the high priest!"

"You are no high priest," said the old man. He spoke more quietly now, but with a cold anger. "There has been no high priest in Israel since Honi was deposed before the revolt of the Pious Ones and the Maccabees. You have no right to speak. The very linking of the holy office with your name is a vile pollution. You and yours are finished forever—a true priest is to reign in Israel!"

Hananiah's lip curled in a sneer. "Menahem ben Judah?" he asked.

"May you be everlastingly damned for such sacrilege! Can I, a leader in battle, a war-scarred rebel, my hands stained with the blood of war, can I fulfill the pure and sacred office? Can I, who am not even a priest, fill the position of high priest?"

In spite of himself Hananiah was impressed. There could be no mistaking the old leader's sincerity. The priest's curiosity was aroused. "Who, then, Menahem ben Judah? Who is worthy?"

"The Priest of the Sons of Light in the community of Sekaka in the wilderness of Judea is the legitimate heir of the Zadokite line."

There was silence. The priest was surprised. He opened his mouth to speak several times, but he was not able to enunciate the words. Finally he said, "So the son of Judah has enrolled in the Sons of Light?"

"Their priest is the true heir," replied Menahem. "We have been close for many years. We both revere the memory of the Pious Ones and recognize their true role in our history. We and they refused to recognize the usurping Maccabees or any other usurpers of the holy office. We are moving closer together. Many of them have joined our revolt. John, their military leader, was at our council this very night."

"What of their calendar?" demanded the priest. "Will you celebrate the feasts on the wrong days and fast at times that the Lord has not appointed?"

"The priests have guided our faith since the time of Aaron," replied the old man. "I am a rebel commander who can trace his lineage to David, a rabbi who has followed the teaching of the sages according to the best of my ability and understand-

79

ing all my life. But I shall not defy the legitimate high priest. If the descendent of Aaron gives his ruling, then I will obey it."

"The people will not be so disposed to obey."

"If he is installed as high priest, the first legitimate holder of the office in two centuries, the people will accept his rulings."

"I do not believe it," replied Hananiah. "But no matter; within a few months all of you will be dead."

"You treacherous swine!" Absalom spoke for the first time. He turned to Menahem, his dark face flushed with anger. "Let us kill him now before his tongue spreads more poison."

"No, Absalom," Menahem contradicted him. "That is not the way. We must behave righteously now. When we had no alternative it was different. Today we have a united Judea." He turned from his deputy and faced the priest. "I am recognized as commander by all the patriotic groups. Your own son, the captain of the Temple guard, swore allegiance to me tonight. John of Gischala sent messengers from Galilee, the Sons of Zadok, bar Giora, the Zealots—all the forces are united. With the Lord's help there is nothing that we cannot achieve."

"There is no unity," claimed the priest.

"Your own son swore—"

"My son?" The priest interrupted him with scornful laughter. "You trust the Temple captain? He does not want war with Rome anymore than I do. From the start, when he ceased the sacrifice in honor of the emperor, he schemed to take over the revolt so that he could bring it to an end at the appropriate time."

"You lie," breathed Menahem; but his face was tired and dispirited. The other was playing cleverly on his doubts and misgivings.

"He tells the truth!" Hezekiah, the priest's brother, spoke for the first time. Menahem did not answer, and Hezekiah continued talking forcefully. He explained that after the provocations of Florus, there had been a split in the Sanhedrin. Some of the priests and landowners had wanted to continue submitting to the procurator, but the younger elements had insisted

80

that a revolt was inevitable. They had argued, therefore, that it was better to join the rebellion and take charge of it, rather than try to oppose it. That way, he pointed out, they realized they would be able to limit the uprising. They wanted Florus replaced by a fair and able procurator. They had feared that if the Zealots, Sicarii, and the other bands led the revolt, it would be uncontrollable. The majority of the Sanhedrin had opposed the idea, but the youthful hotheads, led by the Temple captain, had forced it through.

"Do you really think they agree with your wild schemes for independence, your insane dreams of the Messiah, your ludicrous hope of military victory against Rome? Since when has warfare gained us anything? Jonathan the Maccabee gained more for Judea in half an hour of negotiations than his brother in six years of fighting!"

The doubt was evident on Menahem's face. He was accustomed to the intrigue between rival bandit groups, but he was no match for Hananiah and his brother, masters of sophisticated Temple politics. The priest pressed home his advantage. "The Temple captain is in regular contact with Cestius Gallus, the governor of Syria. The governor has complete intelligence about everything that happens in Judea. He even has my son's estimate on the size of the forces that he will need to crush the revolt, and that estimate takes into consideration the fact that the Temple captain's group will go over to the Roman side. In return for their defection, they will be granted what they want: the recall of Florus. Agrippa managed to convince Cestius Gallus of the need for that.

"You are naive, Menahem ben Judah. You have a certain animal cunning, but you have no real understanding of the world, of how things are managed. If you do not listen to reason, you and many thousands of Jews will be dead before the winter is ended; you and your revolt and your Zadokite priest are doomed!"

"You lie," repeated Menahem. "You are sowing dissension in the army of Judea. We have unity at last; but you eat at our trust with your lies as a worm eats an apple. You have degraded your sacred office and now you betray your people. For more than a hundred years, you and your kind have been betraying the nation. You lick at the heels of your unclean masters and grow fat on the blood of the Jewish peasantry. You pollute the house of God with your presence. You stand in the way of the true high priest of Israel, the Messiah of the house of Aaron. It is not I who will die before the winter. ..." He paused, his eyes staring wildly, beyond reason now—a tired old man who had passed through extremes of emotion and exertion.

Behind him was a lifetime of fighting and running, of slaughter, of single-minded devotion to the cause for which his grandfather, father, and two brothers had given their lives. He had seen moments of triumph and exaltation, felt moods of doubt and the blackest depression. The past few months had been the hardest of all. He had paused on the razor's edge between success and failure a dozen times. He was beside himself with rage and self-doubt.

"Kill them!" he screamed, pointing at Hananiah and his brother. "Kill them! Make an example of them! Show the people of Judea that we are not to be trifled with—kill them!"

"No!" shouted Eleazar and Joab together; but Absalom had already sprung forward, disemboweling the high priest with his dagger, and at the same instant the long knife of Judah ben Jair pierced the throat of the priest's brother.

16

Leading the procession were four men with silver-plated trumpets. Behind them, six abreast, came four rows of armed Sicarii. Then came Menahem ben Judah, walking alone. The old man, with his long gray hair and vast fan of a beard, was an impressive sight. Over his white breeches, he wore an armor tunic, its many scales plated with silver, so that they shimmered in the sun as he moved. A red skullcap rested on his gray mane and a magnificent purple cloak hung from his shoulders. More than a thousand armed men, led by Absalom, followed.

During the two weeks that he had been in Jerusalem, Menahem had not approached the Temple—he had been at war. Now that the war was suspended, he had left his new headquarters in the captured palace of Herod to make his first visit to the house of God. Eleazar and Joab had stayed in the base with half of the Sicarii force. The city had been stunned by the execution—some called it murder—of the high priest. The Temple captain, enraged at the killing of his father, was expected to challenge Menahem.

The other leaders were resentful and suspicious of the Sicarii plan for a merger of their forces. The march to the Temple was a deliberate demonstration of Sicarii power and a challenge to their rivals to oppose them. If there were no move from the other groups, Menahem would know that he was master of Judea. He had no doubts on this score. God had united the people of Judea, and God would use them to drive out the oppressor and establish His kingdom on earth. Once the high priest of Sekaka was installed in the Temple, then all would see that the time for the new covenant had come.

The old leader interrupted his thoughts to observe the crowds lining the route from the palace to the Temple. He was not receiving the rapturous welcome of yesterday. The crowd waited expectantly, neither friendly nor hostile. Menahem felt a tightening in his bowels. Was the day to bring oblivion or triumph, Amos or Isaiah? He turned the opposing images of the two great prophets over in his mind.

Woe unto you that desire the day of the Lord ... the day of the Lord ... is darkness, and not light.... The high places of Isaac shall be desolate, And the sanctuaries of Israel shall be laid waste. ... Surely the darkness is past, thought Menahem. There had been two centuries of darkness, illumined only by brief periods of light. Surely they were now at the start of a new era.... *The rugged shall be made level, And the rough places a plain; And the glory of the Lord shall be revealed, And all flesh shall see it together.*

The tension in the city was rising. Minute by minute it was increasing until it had neared the breaking point. The tension was almost tangible, with a hard, material quality. The crowds were silent, even the murmuring died down as Menahem approached the Temple. He left the spacious upper city, plunging into the narrow alleys of the lower quarters. The column of Sicarii pressed the silent crowds against the walls, as they made their way through the mass toward the house of God.

The Temple. It stood before Menahem, a mountain of gleaming white marble and shimmering gold. The old man felt an uncontrollable surge of emotion; his eyes filled with tears. Here was God's tabernacle: here was Zion, from where the Law would go forth. Had there ever been a building as beautiful as this? In its grandeur, simplicity, and strength, it was surely unmatched. The building towered above him, the marble blocks of its walls and columns so tightly fitted that it was impossible to see where one ended and the other began; the effect was of a construction hewed out of one gigantic block of gleaming stone. The surrounding colonnades were exquisitely proportioned and laid out in a manner which brought every eye to the central focus: the sanctuary where the Lord of Hosts dwelt.

Menahem had not visited the Temple for many years, and now, as he strode beneath its arches, its majesty took his breath away. He was oblivious to the tension which held the city in its vise, deaf to the silent screams of nearly a million people who knew that their fate was to be sealed within minutes. Let the Romans strut about their empire! The God of the universe, who had revealed Himself to the Hebrews in the wilderness, dwelt here in Jerusalem. He had lived here before the Romans existed; He would be here long after they were forgotten. The word passed around the city—upper and lower, east and west—Menahem the son of Judah was at the Temple gates. The fate of Judea hung in the balance.

Menahem had entered the lower court of the Temple, the court of the Gentiles. Unaware of the tension in the crowds that stood around him frozen in silence, he was conscious only of an awesome, all-pervading Presence. *And there shalt thou build an altar unto the Lord thy God, an altar of stones; thou shalt lift up no iron tool upon them. ...* Menahem advanced through the court of the women and began to mount the steps toward the gate of Corinthian bronze. Beyond the gate, through the court of the Israelites, was the altar. One of the

Sicarii approached with a white lamb, perfect in every respect, for the sacrifice. The throng was dense, the Sicarii were hemmed in on all sides. The crowd was still neutral and uncommitted.

Thou shalt lift up no iron tool. Menahem suddenly shook his head. He was in the Temple, approaching the altar, fully armed with his armed followers! Hastily he unbuckled his belt and cast his sword onto the ground. As though hypnotized, his followers did likewise, except for Absalom. His left arm in a sling, the big man grasped his sword with his right hand.

There was a sudden stir in the crowd. The Temple captain was coming through the Corinthian gate from the court of the Israelites. He had with him a large force, all fully armed. Menahem seemed dazed. He staggered slightly, but made no move to pick up his sword or to defend himself.

With a roar of command, Absalom threw himself between his leader and the advancing soldiers of the Temple captain. Many of the Sicarii succeeded in retrieving their weapons, but they were driven back to the lower court where vast crowds were milling around. The advance party of the Sicarii was cut off from the main body of its force. In the crowd were large numbers of the peace party, which had been quiet for several days. As the Sicarii continued to retreat, the peace partisans, who had been organized by the Temple captain, began to pelt them with stones. It was clear now that the Sicarii were on the defensive, and the crowd closed in on them with a vengeful roar. The hero had become the villain, the victor of the palace had become the base murderer of the high priest!

The action of the mob had temporarily isolated the Sicarii from the forces of the Temple captain. Absalom quickly realized what had happened—it was too late to regain control; retreat was the only possibility. He seized Nahum by the shoulder and spun him around, speaking closely in his ear to make himself heard above the noise of the mob.

"Return at once to the palace," he yelled. "Tell Eleazar and Joab what has happened. They are to retreat to Masada. The mob has turned against us; we cannot fight the whole population of Jerusalem. Masada is our only hope." He indicated the

85

dazed Menahem, who was apparently unaware of what was happening. "I shall take the rabbi to Ophel; he is in no state to travel and we shall be safe there. We shall join you later. Under no circumstances are you to delay; you must save as much of the force as possible."

Supporting Menahem with his free hand, Absalom managed to slip away under cover of the chaos that still prevailed in the outer courts of the Temple; but they were not unnoticed. A giant of a man, dressed in full armor, his head rather small on his unusually wide shoulders, spotted them. Gathering half a dozen of his followers about him, he quickly set off to follow the two men.

17

The hill of Ophel to the south of the Temple was covered by a network of outbuildings, offices, and storerooms connected with the Temple. Absalom was almost carrying his leader as he staggered through the alley and up to the door of a large grain store, on which he rapped in a certain rhythm. The door was opened just long enough to allow them to stagger over the threshold, and then immediately closed. The storeman took in the situation swiftly and helped Absalom carry the old man down a flight of steps to the cellar below. Propping him in the corner in a sitting position, they moved two large grain jars aside. The man took a knife from his belt and knelt on the floor. He prized up two sections of floorboard, revealing a ladder below. The two men carried Menahem to the opening; when Absalom had descended a few steps, the old man was passed down to him.

The big man eased Menahem onto the rough straw mattress, which lay on the floor at the side of the cellar. Above him the guard replaced the boards. Absalom knew that he would push the grain jars back over the opening and scatter bran and flour on the boards to obliterate all signs of the entrance. After he had taken the ladder away from the hole, Absalom brought the old man a wineskin which he had found on the table, but Menahem would not drink.

They were in the secret Sicarii headquarters, known only to a handful of the top leadership, from which the Sicarii agents had operated in carrying out their assassinations. The only other entrance apart from the one that they had used was a hole that emerged into the steep-sided valley of Kidron. It was from this hole that a faint light filtered into the cellar.

"Drink," Absalom urged the old man. The latter seized him by the shoulders. There was still strength in the old hands, and Absalom winced as the fingers dug into his crushed arm.

"I felt it, Absalom," he whispered in a hoarse voice. "I felt the Presence. I was face to face with the Lord of Hosts as the prophets of old!"

"I know, my rabbi, I know." The big man comforted him, sitting beside him on the pallet, holding his hand. The leader had aged greatly in the past hour. His eyes were listless and he had difficulty in moving the left side of his body. His mind was wandering too.

"You know Galilee, Absalom. Of course now it is brown, but in the spring it is so green—green from the winter rains. How those rains fall in Galilee! It is as if the sky opens. Then afterward, the birds. I could never believe that the Lord had created so many birds. In the morning the noise is deafening. You cannot hear yourself praying, Absalom, did you know that? Cannot hear yourself pray; the birds are praying too loudly." He laughed weakly.

"Absalom, we have won, have we not? I am commander of Judea; John of Gischala hailed me. I knew his father, one of the few good priests. Galilee will save Judea in spite of Judea. John of Gischala and John of the Sons of Zadok and ... and old John whom we lost at Masada. The three Johns, we can trust them, I think." He looked worried for a moment. Beads of sweat stood out on his wide brow.

"Masada, Absalom, we have Masada; they cannot take it. If something goes wrong we can retreat there, as that rogue Herod did. We should not have trusted the son of Hananiah. You were right, Absalom; but I wanted unity—unity as under David the King. You know, of course, of the tradition in our family that we are descended from the line of David through

Sheshbazzar the prince. The time for kings is past; you know that. The high priest is the supreme ruler. The king Messiah is only a war leader; it is the priest, the Messiah of Aaron, who is to rule at the End of Days." He stopped suddenly and looked around him; but his eyes were glazed, as if he saw something very far off. He could not see the cellar and the table and the mattress. An expression of fright and loneliness came over his tired old features.

"My wife. I have not seen my wife for two years. A clever woman—she knows the Law. An admirer of Rabbi Hillel!" He laughed aloud, a dry mirthless cackle. "My brother Jair also was a peaceful man, though he sired three warrior sons. He had friends among the school of Hillel and the Sons of Zadok. Eleazar has something of his father in him, but do not be deceived. He learned of peace, but he knows how to fight. He will be able to cooperate with the Priest better than I could have done. He will be a good leader now that I am going."

"You will be all right, Menahem," declared Absalom. "We shall bring a doctor from Sekaka. He will cure you and then we will take you to Masada. You will lead us again in battle."

"I know well that I am dying," Menahem interrupted him. "There is much still to be done, but it is not for me to do it. The left side of my body is already dead and the rest will go soon. I have accomplished my task, Absalom. Moses was not allowed to enter the Promised Land; Menahem ben Judah is not to lead the armies of Israel in their final battle against the forces of evil." The old man closed his eyes and lay back on the mattress.

Absalom looked at the dying face. Worn out by a lifetime of struggle, the old man was to die unrewarded. His wound throbbed painfully, but the pain in his heart exceeded that in his arm. He had followed Menahem all his life—was everything to end in a cellar under the hill of Ophel? Absalom believed that the revolt was doomed. He felt instinctively that Hananiah and his brother had spoken the truth and that the rebellion was to be betrayed.

"Is victory ours?" the old man asked suddenly.

Absalom lifted him into a sitting position, cradling the old head in his arms. The tears rolled down his dark cheeks. "The armies of Israel will cleanse the land." It was suddenly terribly important to him that Menahem should die content.

There was a noise from above; the boards were being prized open. Absalom was on his feet, drawing his sword. His crushed arm caused him a stab of pain and he felt dizzy. Forcing himself to look, he saw an unfamiliar face in the square opening. The man's legs came through the opening and Absalom hacked at his ankle as he landed. As he ran his assailant through, another opponent was on him. One-handed, Absalom fought with a savage fury. His sword struck the other's shield out of his grasp and a further blow almost severed the man's neck from his body. Swinging around quickly, he then thrust upward, nearly skewering the third man who was descending.

Then, all at once, the dead body of the storehouse guard came hurtling at him through the opening, knocking him off balance. As he staggered backward, fighting a desperate battle against dizziness, pain, and exhaustion, a gigantic figure dropped with surprising lightness into the cellar. Absalom looked grimly at Simon bar Giora.

He managed to smile, his white teeth showing in his blue-black beard. "Welcome, Simon bar Giora, servant of the aristocrats, lapdog of the priests!"

His opponent did not smile as he made his reply: "I hate all tyrants—Jewish as well as Roman!" Then he lunged with his sword. Absalom jumped back, placing himself in front of Menahem's prone form. The two huge men looked at each other warily, each waiting for the other to make a move. It was bar Giora who thrust first. Absalom stepped aside, forgetting his wounded arm, and tried to trap his assailant's sword arm. A wave of pain and nausea engulfed him. Bar Giora slashed powerfully, cutting deep with his sword into Absalom's side. Somehow gathering the last remnants of his strength, the mortally wounded man leaped at his opponent's throat. But bar Giora moved aside and Absalom fell. The giant's next blow smashed his wrist, and the sword fell to the ground.

18

The pulley used for lifting the heavy sacks of grain had been improvised into a rack. The huge, dark, naked body of Absalom lay stretched out beside it. He had died too quickly—but then he had been nearly dead by the time the Temple captain had arrived. Simon bar Giora had left the two captives, one mortally wounded, the other raving and half paralyzed, with the captain. Yes, Absalom had died far too quickly. They would see to it that the old man lasted longer. Menahem lay stretched out, wrists and ankles tied, his old body hanging unsupported in its pale nudity. His head hung backward and his deep-set eyes were clouded and unseeing.

At a signal from the Temple captain, two of the men started to turn the winch that tightened the ropes. The old man screamed in pain, a wordless animal screech. The captain signaled to the men to stop, keeping the body at the same degree of tautness. Menahem screamed and screamed. The young man took the metal bar from the fire; it glowed pale yellow with heat. He gently brushed the soles of the old rabbi's feet with the bar. The aged body arched in agony, and the tone of the screaming reached a new pitch of intensity. At the same time the men at the winch increased the tension. The sound of old joints cracking under the strain was audible beneath the cries of agony. The face of the Temple captain was as hard as granite, his gray eyes cold and unemotional. He brought his face close to the old man's.

"Do you hear me, son of Judah?" he asked. There was no reply. He tried again. "Do you know who I am, Rabbi?" He signaled for the winch to be loosened. Menahem's broken body hung limply between the ropes. The screams had stopped and a quiet whimper was all that emerged from the old lips. The young man bent close again.

"Murderer of the high priest—do you know who your tormentor is?"

The old man's eyes looked at him unseeing; he was beyond comprehension. The Temple captain raged inwardly. The old man might be beyond understanding, but he was not beyond pain! He thrust the metal bar once more into the fire. When it was hot, he signaled to the men to tighten the ropes. He took the glowing bar from the fire. With an instinctive independent life of its own, the broken old body jerked and writhed. Scream after piercing scream rent the air.

Four hours later, Menahem the son of Judah died.

FLAVIUS SILVA: FEBRUARY 73 C.E.

The wall was complete. Flavius Silva regarded it with satisfaction. The task had not been simple. Masada was surrounded with gorges and steep rocks. The plateau to the west was several hundred feet higher than the floor of the valley to the east, where the flourlike bluffs merged with the glaring white salt flats as they led down to the oily blue sea. Yet the wall had been constructed despite these difficulties. Five of the camps were part of the wall and three lay outside it, including the two camps of the legion to the east and west. Now there was not the slightest chance that the Jews could break out.

` For several weeks the procurator had been the victim of an obsession: if the rebels somehow escaped, it would spell the end of his political career. And Silva was ambitious. Today he was the governor of a defeated province in west Asia; tomorrow a promotion; one day maybe a position in the capital itself. Vespasian had become emperor while engaged in the Judean campaign. He and Titus had been awarded triumphs for it.

For some minutes, the procurator allowed himself the luxury of a furious burst of anger against his emperor and that worthy's son Titus. Inwardly, he cursed them long and savagely, grinding his teeth in frustration. They had already celebrated their joint triumph to mark the defeat of Judea. The coins *Iudaea Capta* had already been minted; indeed, they were in circulation among his troops. But Judea was not defeated, far from it. His predecessor, Bassus, had fought several hard battles—at Herodium, at Macherus, and at the Forest of Jardes in the Hebron hills. Judea was far from finished even though the capital had been taken and the Temple destroyed.

Now, no less than three years after the supposed termination of the war, he, Flavius Silva, was left with the hardest task of all—the siege of the impregnable Judean fortress of Masada, defended by the most extreme and fanatical of the rebel groups, the Sicarii. There would be no glory for Silva, no triumph, no tribute. To celebrate, or so much as refer to, the fall of Masada would be tantamount to an admission that *Judea*

95

Capta was a lie and that the emperor was a fraud. He was facing one of the hardest tasks a Roman general had ever had to face, with no prospect of credit for success, whereas failure would lead to ignominy.

Providing his vast force with supplies had been a formidable operation. To obtain food and wood for construction, the slaves had had to traverse the barren desert to the foothills of Hebron. Silva had been obliged to organize a constant stream of supply caravans, which wound their way between Hebron or Herodium and then down to Ein Gedi and Masada. Meanwhile, it had become clear that there was no prospect of starving out the rebels. Though effectively sealed in the fortress, they showed no signs that they wished to surrender. There was no way of avoiding an assault.

The first flood had hit the procurator's camp some two weeks after its construction. The sky tore open with jagged lightning, thunder crashed, and the water poured out of the heavens into the wadis, churning furiously down to the Sea of Salt and carrying all in its path. Two of the camps were swept away and several soldiers were lost. The entire baggage train of the main eastern camp perished. When they had destroyed the aqueducts leading to the rebels' cisterns, the dams had been adapted for their own water supply; but these also were washed away.

Although the destroyed camps were resituated and rebuilt, the next flood had destroyed the wall in four places and once again had swept away the reconstructed dams. As a result, Silva had been forced to send his slaves as far as Ein Gedi to obtain sufficient water. Food supplies were jeopardized, as the caravans were reluctant to set out on the journey to Hebron, a journey lasting several days across some large valleys, with the danger of flooding imminent. The Nabateans demanded high fees for their supply caravans and for the baggage animals they sold the Romans. Normally the expenses of a campaign were defrayed by the loot taken at its conclusion, but there was no wealth left in Judea. No trace of the supposedly hidden

Temple treasure had been discovered, and the Romans had long since stopped believing the story.

Many a procurator had enriched himself in Judea, but Silva would not be one of them. Judea had been bled dry and the Masada campaign was an unusually expensive operation. Silva's only possible gain was the gratitude of his emperor for finishing off the embarrassing and difficult Judean problem. Silva was well aware of the inferiority of many of his predecessors and understood why the revolt against Rome had broken out; but he was far from understanding the course of the war or the real wishes of the Jews. He yearned to understand the spirit which made the Masada rebels continue their resistance when all was lost. He wished to avoid the difficulties of an assault that would have to be completed before the summer, and once more he wondered what he could offer in the way of surrender terms that his opponents would be likely to accept.

Jews became excited over the most insignificant matters, whereas normally big issues were unimportant to them. They were forever disputing among themselves, and each sect was convinced that only its way was the true way. Even among the rebels there were half a dozen different sects, each with its own special reason for fighting the Romans, each with its own beliefs and its own leader. In the fortress, Silva knew, were the Sicarii. What he found more difficult to understand was the distinction between the Sicarii and the other rebel groups. In what way did they differ from the Zealots? And where did the Zealots part company from the Galilean and Idumean rebels? Silva had made a thorough study of the Judean campaign and shared the general opinion that the war would have been even more difficult for the Romans had the Jews not spent so much time and energy fighting among themselves. Why were these rebels continuing to hold out in Masada? What could Silva offer them that would induce their surrender?

The procurator considered some information offered by one of the Jewish slaves. The man had told him that with the Sicarii at Masada were members of the Sons of Zadok, a strange and

97

fanatical sect who had lived by the shore of the Sea of Salt, further to the north. Formerly peaceful, the sect had joined the revolt against Rome because its members believed in the imminent appearance of the Messiah, the eagerly awaited savior of the Jews. Silva wondered if it was their influence that was causing the rebels to hold out in the hope of ultimate salvation.

BOOK II

THE TEACHER: 66 C.E.

And God observed their deeds, that they sought Him with a whole heart, and He raised for them a Teacher of Righteousness to guide them in the way of His heart.

The Damascus Rule: *The Dead Sea Scrolls*

1

Wednesday. The fourth day. The day on which the Lord created the sun. The Priest crawled out of his tent and stood upright, stretching himself to his full height. He did not reflect that it was a strange indignity for the legitimate high priest of Israel to be crawling on his hands and feet in the dust of the desert. Moses the Rabbi, the greatest of all God's prophets, had lived like this, in the wilderness in the days when Israel was pure. Later in the day, perhaps, the Priest would think these thoughts. For the present his mind was empty of everything except the glory of the Lord and His Word.

He felt an overwhelming sense of adoration for the Almighty, who was shortly to bring an end to the dominion of darkness. In an hour the sun—the wonderful light of heaven —would rise, and the dominion of light would last for another day. The sun would rise as it had risen on that fourth day of creation, as it would rise to signal the end of the dominion of Belial in the not-too-distant future. The time was coming near when the Lord would usher in the new age. Was he, the Priest, His chosen instrument?

For a moment he felt a crushing weight of responsibility; his mind was paralyzed with awe as he thought of the salvation of the whole world dependent on him. But this thought was swiftly absorbed by the all-pervading feeling of love, gratitude, and joy in the Almighty God, Creator of heaven and earth, of darkness and light, of Belial and Michael. The Lord would assure the triumph of light over darkness as He did each morning: the day of eternal light would come. It had all been arranged since the beginning of time; yet he, the Priest, had been granted the astounding privilege of obeying God's laws and carrying out His commandments. Born a priest in the direct line of Zadok, who had anointed Solomon the wise, he was of the seed of Aaron, the holiest house in all Israel.

From where he stood, the Priest could see the dark outline of the center. As he remained, wrapped in his cloak, in silent adoration, the first signs of light appeared in the east. A faint russet tinge appeared atop the mountains of Moab on the far side of the Sea of Salt, a narrow line of light which widened slowly, changing to a deep gold, coloring the undersides of the clouds reflected in the dull gray surface of the bitter lake.

The Priest hurried toward the center, where he knew his priestly colleagues were awaiting him for the morning prayers. All over the settlement, the members would be awakening to their daily tasks, silently and respectfully. In the whole village of more than one thousand souls, not a word would be spoken prior to sunrise.

The Priest was a tall man, very tall and slender. His hair and beard were a deep russet red, the color of the Zadokite line. His features were regular and well formed, and his face had that perpetually burned look common to the fairer members of the community, for no oil was allowed on their skin to protect them from the burning desert sun. Beneath his gray woolen cloak, he wore a single garment, a white linen robe which reached to his ankles. A white skullcap contrasted with the rich color of his thick hair. His eyes were pale gray, so pale as to be almost colorless; they gave the impression of being focused on something a great distance away.

Coming through the gate into the courtyard of the center, he washed his hands in the special cistern, and at the same time recited the appropriate blessing. Then he passed into the hall of assembly, where the priests and Levites were awaiting him. Stretching forth his hand, he blessed them and began to lead the prayers:

"At the beginning of the months of the seasons and on the holy days appointed for remembrance in their seasons I will bless Him, with the offering of the lips according to the Precept engraved forever: at the beginning of the years and at the end of their seasons, when their appointed law is fulfilled, on the day decreed by Him. . . ."

The Priest intoned the words in his rich tenor chant, the

words written by the Teacher so many years before. The priests and Levites followed him, totally absorbed in what they were saying:

"With the coming of the day and night I will enter the Covenant of God. And when evening and morning depart, I will recite His decrees...."

Prayers over, the Priest retired to his chamber for meditation, while a Levite began an exposition to the assembled, explaining the Word, as Levites had since the days of Ezra the Scribe.

Wednesday, he explained, the fourth day of the week, was the day on which the Lord had created the sun, thus creating day and night. The year began on a Wednesday and each of the four seasons began on the fourth day. Today was the start of the winter season, on exactly the same day that it had begun the previous year and the year before that. The times and the seasons were as fixed as the Almighty Himself.

Among the defiled and sinful priests of Jerusalem, there existed a different order, an abomination of the Gentiles based on the movements of the moon, that servant of darkness and evil. Because of this they were worshiping on the wrong days and in the wrong way. The order observed by the Sons of Zadok had been revealed to Enoch by the angel Uriel. Enoch had transmitted it to his son Methuselah....

One by one they went out into the desert, each of them carrying a towel. When they had completed their toilet, the Priest led them to the ritual bath. Taking great care to keep himself entirely covered, the Priest removed his loincloth under his robe and entered the water. Holding his robe about him and not exposing even the tiniest part of his body, he immersed himself, gradually lifting the robe free of the water. As he emerged from the pool, he allowed his garment to cover him and replaced his loincloth. The other priests and Levites followed in order of their rank. The cistern, like the others at Sekaka, was fed by a channel that flowed downhill from the dam across the wadi to the west of the settlement. Being flow-

103

ing water, it was pure enough for ritual purposes. After some minutes, all of them completed their immersions and were ready for the next task of the day.

Assembling in the scroll room, each of them washed his hands in special basins which lined the walls. The eldest of the scribes, who had the honor of writing the first word on the first scroll of the day, picked up his reed pen and pronounced a blessing over it. He took a clean piece of parchment, which he had prepared on the previous day. The parchment consisted of cured animal skin, shaved on the hairy side, on which the lines and margins had been ruled with a metal stylus. The Priest offered a prayer, and the scribe, mouthing his own blessing, began to write. When the first letter was done, the scribe washed his hands a second time before completing the word. When the word was completed, the others dispersed to their various tasks.

The work of preparing the scrolls was so holy that in the community only priests and Levites were permitted to participate in it. From the killing of the animal, through skinning, drying, curing, shaving, sewing, ruling, and finally writing, only priestly hands touched the scrolls. Priests and Levites prepared the ink and the reed pens.

The Priest wandered around the room, where the scribes sat at their desks, concentrating with every fiber of their beings on their tasks. There was no talk and the only sound was of breathing. Once it was his unpleasant duty to point out an error to the oldest scribe. The man placed the requisite dots above the erroneous letters, seemingly with reluctance, as if loath to admit he was liable to make mistakes, and then copied out the word correctly. The senior scribe was fifty-nine years old; he would have to retire the following year. The ruling of the Teacher on that was quite clear—no one over the age of sixty could hold a position of responsibility or carry out an important task in the community.

As he supervised the writing, the Priest allowed his mind, for the first time that morning, to clear for personal thoughts. His first reflections were on the Master. After the morning meal, he was to report on the Bursar's meeting in Jerusalem with the rebel leadership. The Priest did not like it. He knew that he had permitted it for fear of defiance, yet he would not admit to himself that he was not totally in control of the community. The Teacher had stated quite unambiguously that the Priest was the supreme authority of the community, but that impudent Levite of a Master had let his power go to his head! He was even reinterpreting the Teacher's message. He must be controlled, yet the Priest feared to convene the council in case the division in the community worsened.

His mind passed with agility over the ambiguities and compromises of his position: he was the priest of the community, the legitimate high priest of Israel, who would administer in the Temple of Jerusalem. His word was law. And yet, even here at Sekaka, he was forced to compromise in order to maintain his authority. The Master's task was to instruct and guide, to accept candidates and to look after the welfare of the members; but the Priest was the head of the community. He resolved to be firm when he met the Master—he would not allow himself to be converted into a ceremonial figurehead! It was in his veins that the blood of Aaron ran; he would make the decisions. If the struggle had begun, he, and no other, was the Messiah!

2

Jacob and Hanan were loading the mules with the great bunches of dates from the palms that clustered around the spring to the south of Sekaka. They hefted the heavy bunches on their shoulders, straining in the heat, before loading them onto the backs of the mules. Despite the dryness of the climate, they were moist with sweat. The work was very hard in the hot sun.

After a few minutes they went and splashed their arms and faces with fresh water from the fast-flowing stream. The sun was high and the glare was unbearable. The breeze off the Sea of Salt was warm and dry; it caressed them like a tongue of flame. Jacob smeared water over his face and neck, but it did not help. In the ovenlike heat of the valley, it dried in less than a minute. His freckled nose was peeling, raw and red. Their dirty linen work clothes were shorter than the robes they wore for meals and study but too long for convenience. The sleeves were cumbersome and hot.

The boys had risen before sunrise and prayed with the others of their rank. They had then donned their work clothes and proceeded silently southward to the farm by the spring, where they would work until the morning meal. The farm, nearly two miles south of Sekaka and nearer to the shore of the Sea of Salt, was situated in the very narrow strip of land between the cliffs of the Judean desert plateau and the sea. The land was well worked there, where the Almighty had caused a spring to gush out of the dry rocks and the desert to burst forth in sudden local greenery. The spring was indeed miraculous in that barren land. The members of the community had tamed the spring, and their farm provided most of their needs at Sekaka as well as pasture for the animals.

Once the bitterness had been washed out of the soil, the earth was fertile, containing as it did the remains of vegetation washed down the wadis by the winter torrents. There was sufficient water at that spot to cleanse the soil, with the result that the crops grew quickly under the stimulus of the hot sun. Bending over their short-handled hoes, many of the youngsters needed all their resolution to continue working. But they dared not admit to weakness, which could be construed as lack of faith.

Jacob and Hanan were pleased to have a job away from the watchful eye of the supervisor. It enabled them to exchange a few words, which was considered an indulgence and therefore was not done in the main group.

"Your nose looks red, Jacob." Hanan was concerned. "It must be painful."

"It is!"

"You should put some olive oil on it."

"You know the rules," replied Jacob.

"You can get dispensation. Why do you not ask one of the council?"

"Perhaps I shall; it hurts a great deal." He looked around furtively to confirm that they were out of earshot of the main party. "Hanan," he said, "have you heard about events in Jerusalem?"

"I have heard something." Hanan was dark-skinned with a strong, sensual face. His dark eyes were set above a short nose and thick lips. When puzzled, which was quite often, he would purse his lips and open his eyes very wide, so that the whites were visible all around the edge, giving him an expression of utter bewilderment. He wore this expression now, as he fanned his face with a flapping sleeve.

"What do you think about it?" persisted Jacob.

Think? What was he supposed to think? Hanan considered the question with care. It was not his job to think. The Priest thought and the Master and all the council members. But the candidates were not required to think—their function was to obey. "What should I think?" he asked his friend.

"You must have an opinion, Hanan. How can you not think? We are awaiting a great event, are we not? We are the chosen ones."

"Yes, the men of the covenant are the sons of light who will triumph over the sons of darkness." Hanan spoke in a monotonous tone, repeating a well-learned lesson.

"It has begun," explained Jacob.

"What has begun?" asked his friend.

"The struggle against the forces of evil. The war against the Kittim. The Romans have been expelled from Jerusalem. We too will have to play our part in the struggle."

Hanan's face showed total incomprehension. Jacob reflected that it was pointless to continue talking. The other was entirely without curiosity.

Jacob knew that the Sons of Zadok had joined the struggle in Jerusalem and that John, one of the leading members of the community, had joined the rebel command. He knew that the Master supported the revolt, whereas the Priest was undecided. Despite the lack of contact between the different strata of the community at Sekaka, news was beginning to reach the members—not because there had been any change in the rigid hierarchy, but because recent developments in Jerusalem had been so momentous that nothing could prevent rumors from

107

spreading. Many of the members at Sekaka, and most of the Sons up and down the country, supported the cause. Recruitment was being organized, with only the inertia of the priests to hinder it.

The contact between the Sicarii and Sekaka was not a new one. Jacob knew that the rebel leader, Menahem ben Judah, though rumored to be of the line of David, followed the tradition of the Pious Ones, as did the Sons, and was more interested in a priestly than a royal restoration. He recognized the Priest and was prepared to accept his authority, something that no other Pharisee had dared to think of.

Jacob realized that he could not interest Hanan in these matters. Hanan was a child of Sekaka, brought up in the community. His parents had been killed in a Jerusalem riot when he was four years old, and he had been brought to the village by the Sea of Salt. Though nearing manhood, his beard was almost nonexistent on his dark, smooth face, in contrast to Jacob's bristly blond beard, which constantly itched in the dry heat of the valley.

Unlike Hanan, Jacob had come to Sekaka as a result of a deliberate choice. When his father's plot of land in the Samarian hills had proved inadequate to support the family, he could have joined the stream of refugees to Jerusalem or one of the other towns and become part of the flotsam that lived on the streets. Or he might have joined one of the patriotic rebel bands. But he had chosen the Sons of Zadok. They seemed to offer the only form of order and logic in his anarchic country. He had found little comfort in the religion practiced by the majority of his fellows, with its endless wrangles and compromises and its lack of guidance with regard to the crisis in the country. Far worse was the Temple establishment, with its arid ceremonial and greedy, corrupt priests. The Sons of Zadok, with their certainty, their strict rules, their sense of purpose, and their abiding faith, seemed to offer a life with some meaning. So it had seemed from the outside, and his first few months in the local cell had been among the most exciting of his life, as he absorbed the philosophy of the movement. When he was accepted for candidacy at Sekaka, his happiness was complete.

He arrived at the village with high expectations but was quickly disappointed. The life, so full of promise, proved to be overformalistic and dull. Once the basic new ideas were understood, the intellectual content was stagnant. There seemed to be no relationship between their ideas and the reality of life in Judea under Roman rule. Cautiously, Jacob had broached these thoughts to a number of his young friends and found that mostly they tended to agree with him. He also discovered that others in the community were worried about the isolation of Sekaka from the rest of Judea and that this concern reached up into the highest echelons of the community.

The unofficial leader of the new group was the Master. His trenchant, pragmatic interpretation of the Teacher's code was starting to challenge the formalized ways of the community. He linked the ancient teachings with the current situation and pressed for action by the Sons of Zadok, including direct participation in the revolt against Rome.

His mind busy, Jacob continued to work with Hanan loading the mules. They worked with the easy movements of young men accustomed to physical labor, conserving their energy and avoiding wasted movements in the terrible heat. When all the mules had been loaded, they started to lead the animals back to Sekaka. The sun was high in the sky, and the cliffs to the west had taken on a curiously flat appearance; across the blue surface of the Sea of Salt, the mountains of Moab were a dull gray curtain. Despite the imminence of winter, the heat from the burning sun was oppressive. The glare was thrown back off the cliffs, reflected from the dusty ground and the winking blue sea. Their eyes hurt with it and the bleak landscape offered them no relief. But when they closed their eyes momentarily, they found themselves staggering off balance. Beneath their garments they were sweating, but any perspiration on their exposed skin was immediately sucked dry. It took them more than an hour to lead the line of animals along the shore and then climb to the plateau where the settlement was situated.

The candidates filed through the bath room, where they stripped and immersed themselves, washing the sweat and dust from their bodies. They exchanged their working tunics for clean white robes and proceeded to their special dining hall. When all the candidates had entered, the duty priest made the blessing.

Loaves for each person had been placed on the tables, and the cooks now circulated, ladling out oatmeal onto rough earthenware platters. A small quantity of vegetables completed the frugal meal. Although ravenous from their morning's work, the youngsters were careful not to let their hunger appear too obvious or to betray a lack of self-control. There was no talk during the meal except for the routine blessings of the Priest and the responses. Each and every meal in the community was a sacred event, a rehearsal of that final meal which was to usher in the new age. The penalty for speaking during a meal could be half rations for twelve days, which was no slight punishment in the harsh conditions at Sekaka.

Jacob looked speculatively around the dining hall at the faces of the other candidates. There were some two hundred of them, of which more than half worked down near the spring. The others worked around the settlement on building, maintenance, cooking, and cleaning. The Many, those members of the sect who had studied for three years but who had not yet attained full membership, ate separately from the candidates. The members of the council, the highest body, ate alone. Seating was always according to rank and position, and each one knew his place.

Jacob considered the serious features of ben Levi, a fellow candidate of Levite stock, whose rank would entitle him to an elevated position in the community when he reached the appropriate age and enlightenment. Ben Levi always wore the same serious expression, never smiling or joking, even when the candidates were alone together without supervision. Jacob respected his intelligence and wondered what he thought of the dispute that existed beneath the community's surface tranquillity. Continuing his review of the faces around the long wooden tables, he wondered at their variation. The stocky, brown-haired Galileans contrasted with the tall, russet-headed priests and Levites, the dark-skinned Idumeans with the fairer inhabitants of Samaria. Yet all of them had been born into God's elect, and all had joined the virtuous remnant whose purpose it was to preserve the way of righteousness pending the dawning of the age of virtue.

3

Two men stood together on the settlement watchtower, looking northward over the plateau. From the tower they could see down to the shore of the Sea of Salt below. One of the men was talking, gesticulating with his short arms. He was a small man, unusually fat for a member of the Sons of Zadok. His light brown beard ringed his plump red face, and there was a bald patch appearing beneath his curly hair. The malicious whispered that the Bursar did not observe the frugal diet of the community, that he used his trips to Jerusalem on settlement business as an opportunity to supplement the oatmeal, bread, and vegetables with fare more tasty and exotic; but this was totally untrue. Though stout and jovial by nature, the Bursar was a pious and devoted member of the movement. He needed reserves of faith for his dealings with outsiders and had to resist temptations not normally suffered by the others.

Sekaka could not be entirely self-supporting. It sold cotton cloth and dates, and bought weapons, tools, fruit, and certain wines, as well as additional food. The communities of the Sons in the various parts of the country contributed taxes to Sekaka and tithes for the priests.

"That is what I heard, Master," affirmed the Bursar. "We were clear of the gates of the city only a few minutes before they were forcibly closed."

"Whose soldiers closed them?" demanded the other.

"How can one tell?" The Bursar shrugged his plump shoulders, turning his palms upward in a gesture of hopelessness. "There is such a mixture of uniforms in the city. They are all wearing plundered auxiliary armor. The Sicarii distributed a quantity of what they captured—the Temple detachments have been wearing it for years. They are all Jews: beards, fringed garments protruding, heads covered. From a distance it is impossible to distinguish the groups, unless one chances to recognize one of the leaders."

"And you did not see a leader you knew?" persisted the Master.

"I have already told you I did not," replied the other.

The Master frowned. He was a gaunt, powerful man with flashing eyes in a deeply lined red-brown face, framed by iron gray beard and hair. He was the opposite of the Bursar in appearance: hard where the latter was soft, thin instead of fat, stern where the other was jovial. Although the Priest was the supreme head of the community, the Master was really in control. It was he who admitted the new members and instructed the veterans; he administered the affairs of the village.

When the Master had arranged for the Bursar to meet with the Sicarii, the Priest had objected; but he had not been able to show his disapproval. He could convene the council, but the majority of the council members had been appointed by the Master. The Master was a domineering personality, and during the past dozen years he had started to change the dedicated but ineffectual dreamers of the Sons of Zadok into a powerful national movement. Now he regarded the plump figure of the Bursar with the utmost severity, his prominent brows drawn together in a deep frown. His voice was harsh.

"You had just left the city when the gates were closed. Then what happened?"

"We wished to get clear of the city," replied the Bursar. "We did not wait, nor did I send anyone back to investigate; but we continued on our way as quickly as possible. There was a fearful noise in the city—it was clear that fighting had broken out. We were frightened and proceeded with all possible speed. As the noise receded, we felt more secure. But shortly afterward we heard the noise of horses. There is no cover there and we could not hide. The horsemen were Sicarii, led by Eleazar ben Jair's young brother Judah. They did not stop for long. Judah informed me that Menahem ben Judah had been attacked in the Temple and that the whole city was in an uproar. The Sicarii had suffered a reverse and were retiring to Masada in

112

small groups. He did not seem too upset. He grinned and said to me, 'Do not worry, Bursar. The Teacher warned that we would lose the first round. You see I still remember my lessons.' The impudence—he was only with us a few months and the worst pupil we ever had! He then said another curious thing: 'The way is clear for the high priest.' He said that quite seriously and then galloped off with his men."

"I do not understand at all," confessed the Master. He was still frowning. "When you met with Eleazar, the city was under Sicarii control. How could the situation have changed in so short a time?"

"You know the intrigues between the rebel groups," replied the Bursar. "The population as a whole was not deeply committed. They are liable to sudden changes of mood." He shrugged. "I am as mystified as you. We shall have to await developments. What about the situation here? What did the Priest say?"

The Master shrugged, his stern face taking on an almost humorous expression. "We became involved in one of those interminable theological discussions in which a mere Levite can never be a match for a priest. He quoted the Teacher and I quoted the Teacher; we threw his words at each other until we were exhausted. I cannot possibly recount the argument— it was so involved that I cannot remember it myself. We went around in a complete circle several times. I must admit that it was a thoroughly futile argument because we were starting from different premises.

"I pointed out to him that the war had started and that Menahem and the Sicarii, who dominated Jerusalem, were waiting for him to take up his office in the Temple. I informed him that the Sicarii were prepared to accept his rulings. The Teacher forecast that there would be a mass joining of the community in the last days; I indicated that current developments amounted to just that. The Almighty had acted through mankind in the past, I told him, and that if we believed that the time had come to fight, it could only be the Lord who gave us that belief."

"What was his reply to that?" the Bursar was curious; he

113

looked on the Priest with awe and had never before heard from the Master an account of one of their arguments.

"He reminded me that the Teacher had prophesied a forty-year war, during which the righteous priests were to occupy the Temple after seven years."

"That is true," conceded the Bursar.

"I replied that the Teacher had prophesied that such a war was to take place forty years after his own death and that he had been dead three times that period, so that the numbers were not meant to be taken literally. I also asked him how the four thousand members of our movement were to provide the number of troops needed for the final war. Naturally, he said the Lord would provide."

The Master raised his hands in a gesture of hopelessness. Then he turned and looked compellingly at the Bursar. "I believe in the Teacher's message," he declared. "What he taught has come to pass. The events of the past years and months vindicate him. The Priest can be installed in the Temple if only he will agree. If the dominant factions of Jerusalem accept him, that is as if they had joined the community. We are a tiny sect, a mere four thousand members; but through Mena-hem ben Judah we can dominate the nation!"

The Bursar was impressed; the Master was not given to statements of conviction, which were not appropriate to his austere ironic character.

"I am bothered by something, though," confessed the stout man.

"What is that?"

"If the Priest is the Messiah, why does he not lead us? Why do we attempt to lead him!"

"I too have considered that," admitted the Master. "The Messiah of Aaron is a priest. He is the high priest who will preside over the community at the End of Days. I do not recall that high priests were inspired figures—righteous, yes, but not inspired. Not even Aaron; Moses was the Lawgiver." He paused, and for the first time looked almost abashed. Then he looked the Bursar in the eye and continued: "I do not want to fall into the sin of egotism, but I believe that I am the instrument of the Lord. I must lead the community into the national rebellion and the Priest to the high priesthood in Jerusalem!"

"What of the other Messiah?"

"The king-Messiah is part of an earlier tradition, but there have been no kings in Israel worthy of the name for centuries. The very institution runs counter to our most ancient beliefs. Curiously, there is a legend in Menahem's family that they are of the seed of David—you know the constant occurrence of the name Judah: David was of the tribe of Judah. Some of his simpler followers make much of it, but Menahem himself does not set much store by it. There are more than eighteen generations between Sheshbazzar the prince and Hezekiah, and only the Levite and priestly lines can be certain of their heritage over so long a period. However, Menahem is a warrior leader and as good a candidate as any for the second Messiah. He will certainly fill the role."

4

Eleazar ben Jair was in a state of complete exhaustion, but he forced himself to keep moving. In the hot desert sun it would have meant death to lie down—he was losing blood from a neck wound. Most of his party were wounded and several had been killed. The majority of the Sicarii had fled directly southward to Ein Gedi via Herodium. But Eleazar's group had deliberately drawn the pursuit northward, knowing that the men of the Temple captain would assume they were making for Samaria, where the Sicarii under Absalom had been active. After the clash with their rivals, Eleazar's amazing knowledge of the Judean desert had enabled them to double back on their tracks and make for Sekaka, where he knew they would be sheltered. From there they would be able to go south along the shore of the Sea of Salt.

The Bursar was still standing with the Master on the watchtower of the community building, when he spotted a group of people to the north. The figures were tiny and indistinct, but it was clear they were approaching the settlement. As they came nearer, they could see that they were not drawn up in regular formation, though the sun glinting on their helmets and armor indicated that they were soldiers of some sort. They were clearly in distress and many of them were walking with some difficulty. The two men looked at one another.

"This is the sequel to your story, Bursar," said the Master. "You had better arrange for them to stay with the families."

"I will make the necessary arrangements at once," was the reply. The Bursar moved quickly for a stout man. In a minute, the Master saw him striding purposefully across the plain to the family tents in the northeastern part of the plateau.

Although the community at Sekaka was in some ways organized as if its members were celibate, nearly all the adults were married. Wives and children were not full members of the community and lived some distance from the center, only approaching on special occasions. It was not an easy life for the women, many of whom left the desert village to return to a larger town. The family was an appendage of the member rather than the central social framework of his life. The men would not visit their families for weeks on end as they remained in the center engaged in prayer and contemplation. Those who wished to maintain ritual purity would not see their wives at all. Despite their low position in the community, the women were important to Sekaka: they ensured its continuity. The priestly and Levite families in particular required heirs. The leader of the women's community was the wife of the Priest; she would bear the heir to the Zadokite line. She was a simple woman, chaste and unpretentious, as were they all. She organized the caring for Eleazar's group. The men were taken and laid down. Their wounds were cleaned and bound. They were washed and dressed in soft, clean robes. Most of them were asleep long before the ministrations of the gentle women had been completed.

When Eleazar awoke, he lay still in the open door of the tent where he had been carried. He was dressed in a simple, clean garment; his tunic, soaked in sweat and blood, had been stripped off him. He felt the rough linen with his fingers. The feel reminded him vividly of his youth, of the peaceful commu-

116

nity where he had worked and prayed in the oppressively peaceful environment of the valley of the Sea of Salt. He recalled the iron routine of rising, working, praying, eating. The silence and contemplation, the teaching and study, the sense of unreality, as though Sekaka were some place outside the normal boundaries of society.

5

Sixteen years previously, when Cumanus was procurator of Judea, Eleazar's father had been crushed to death in a Temple riot caused by the obscene gesture of an auxiliary soldier. As the pious Jair had lost his wife in childbirth less than a year previously, the children had been left on their own in the turbulent city. Eleazar had been fourteen years old at the time and Judah nine. Together they fled from the city, carrying their baby brother, Simon, with them. Once clear of Jerusalem they made for Galilee in the north of the country, where their uncle Menahem ben Judah led a rebel band. They had been forced to beg for food, to lie and steal; but somehow they had kept alive, and at last they arrived in Galilee and were taken to the outlaw center.

The boys had been well cared for by their uncle's wife, Rivka. But after a year Menahem had sent them to the community of Sekaka, the center of the Sons of Zadok by the shores of the Sea of Salt. The baby had remained with the outlaws, but Menahem had felt that Sekaka would offer a better education to the older boys than the uncertain life of his band. Judah had not been able to settle down in the community. His excitable temperament was not suited to the quiet, contemplative life and the rigorous study, and after a few months he returned to his uncle.

Eleazar had remained; he had learned quickly. He enjoyed the routine of life at Sekaka. He worked hard at his tasks and was fascinated by the expositions of the Levites. The unchanging formality of the life gave him a sense of security he had lacked since the shock of his father's death. His father had instilled in him a love of law and learning, and he felt at home

117

in a community where piety was so highly valued. He worked hard too at the physical labor, and when the time came for the morning meal, he found a sublime pleasure in immersing himself in the cool water and putting on his clean garments. The silent meal was no strain for him as it was for some of the children. He felt no urge to talk and was content to eat his simple meal slowly and silently.

At first he had been terrified by the harsh cliffs and dry wastes of the valley of the Sea of Salt. The hard sunlight dazzled him and the emptiness depressed him. The awesome silence frightened him; the grotesque canyons and rocks were something alien and strange, symbolizing man's sinfulness and God's anger. He could feel the hostile presence of the terrible and jealous God of his forefathers in the location of the destruction of the cities of the plain. The hot desert wind was God's breath; the clear brightness of the air was the piercing gaze of the Almighty; the sheer cliffs, lifeless and empty, were monuments to His fearful anger.

But gradually, as he came to know the countryside, all that changed. The desert ceased to be the avenue of God's anger and became the place of His revelation. The emptiness represented the basic simplicity of the one God. The bright sunlight came to mean cleanliness and sanctity; the hot wind was the warmth of the lifeblood itself.

Eleazar discovered too that the desert was far from lifeless. The Lord provided even in this place. There were many insects and reptiles and even rabbits and deer. Around the spring, which lay to the south of the settlement, there was a profusion of wild life and vegetation. The wild goat, with his magnificent curved horns, was there in abundance.

The boy came to understand why it was that the Sons of Zadok had their center in the wilderness. Their life and aspirations were personified by the Almighty Himself in His creation there. They had returned to the simple ascetic desert life, to the way of Moses, the pure, clean, hard, righteous way. They rejected the fat of rams, the opulence of the cities. In the wilderness Israel had found God, and in the wilderness she was finding Him anew.

118

Every minute of the day had its appropriate activity. Each week had its routine, as did each month, each year, and each season; all were fixed and unchanging. The life had its severe logic far simpler than the religion of the rabbis, with its interminable discussions and disputes. There was no Hillel and no Shammai, only the Law of Moses and its interpretation by the Teacher. Out of the chaos of his life, Eleazar found absolute certainty and he was comforted by it.

History itself took on a new dimension as he learned it anew through the lips of the priests and Levites, the teachers of Sekaka. The Law and the other holy books took on fresh meanings as he read the interpretations and explanations of the Teacher. The story of the sect was told in fables, in parables and interpretations of the Scriptures; it came in hints, anecdotes, and quotations, gradually piecing itself together. When he prayed and sang songs of praise, he learned. The picture formed, blurred, and formed again in his mind ever more strongly, as the collective memory of the community poured into the mold of his brain. The wonderful purpose of the Almighty was revealed, His charge to Israel, His task for the community. From the day of creation His actions had set in motion a train of events, the furious climax of which was due at any time. Eleazar himself might be privileged to play a part in it!

Immersed in the teachings of the Sons of Zadok, Eleazar began to perceive a pattern in life. He began to understand why there was so much misery, evil, and death, why he had lost his mother and his father, why Judea was oppressed by foreign rule, why there had been two centuries of almost uninterrupted bloodletting. As against this, the way of the Lord was clear, and all he had to do—all he could possibly do—was follow.

From the time of their first covenant with the Lord, Eleazar learned, the people of Israel had strayed from His way many times. Their misdemeanors had culminated in idolatry and immorality, which resulted in their near destruction by the Babylonians, mightiest of God's instruments. Their nationhood obliterated, they were driven from their country; yet they survived, for the mercy of the Lord was infinite. A pitiful remnant returned to Judah and slowly started to piece together their shattered identity. Ezra the Scribe and Nehemiah restored the law and the Levites expounded it to the people: Judah lived again.

With the passing of the years came a cunning new enemy, who wooed the people of God with idols, myths, nakedness, and sensuality. Again Israel strayed, attracted by the new philosophy; they fell to the new Greek gods as they had fallen to Baal, Astarte, and the Golden Calf. They aped Greek customs, wore the new clothes, wrestled naked in the gymnasia, and lay with boys and animals. Even the Temple of the Lord, administered by a high priest who was not of the Aaronic line, was not immune to the new curse. The first of a long line of wicked priests defiled the Temple and profaned the house of God. The pious few, who had always existed in Israel, who had refused to dance around the Golden Calf or to succumb to Baal, these Pious Ones fled into the wilderness, the clean, pure, hard desert, where Israel had found God before.

They had been pursued by the ungodly and slain by them. But a new leader had arisen among the Jews. He was called the Maccabee, and the Pious Ones of the desert rallied to his cause. The Maccabee struck back against Israel's oppressors, dealing powerful blows in the cause of the Almighty. In an age of turbulance and infamy, his struggle brought comfort to the hearts of the righteous. The wicked king of the Greeks died and his son restored that which his father had taken away. The Temple was cleansed and purified; Jakim of the line of Aaron was high priest in Israel and the Pious Ones rejoiced.

But the Maccabee was not satisfied, wishing to continue the struggle until the heathen was driven from the land, the uncircumcised from the city of God. The Maccabee was killed in battle and his younger brother Jonathan took command of the rebels. High Priest Jakim betrayed the Pious Ones who had supported him and ordered the execution of sixty of their men.

Friendless and deserted, the Pious Ones again fled to the wilderness, blindly groping for the way of God, which had

somehow eluded them. Jakim died and Jonathan the Maccabee was forced to retreat across the Jordan, while the heathen
Greeks still ruled Judah. Not without reason was Jonathan
called the fox; cunning and ruthless, he plotted his advance
with daring and imagination. The Greek Empire was breaking
up; and rival hands grasped for power. Jonathan returned to
Judah and set up his center at Michmash. Since the death of
Jakim, there was no high priest, and with the Maccabee name
behind him and his faithful henchmen still with him, Jonathan
was the only power in the land. As rival princes bid for his
support, he waited.

Jonathan knew exactly why he was waiting; he knew what
he desired. The Pious Ones also waited but for what they did
not know. In their simple camp by the shores of the Sea of Salt
they lived, uncertain and afraid, until they heard the shattering news: Jonathan the Maccabee was high priest in Israel!
Stunned and horrified, they reeled from the shock. Jonathan,
the warrior brigand, the battle-scarred fighter, had been appointed to the most sacred office in the land, an office whose
incumbent from time immemorial had been from the line of
Aaron, who had been a man perfect and without blemish, pure
in every respect. The original defilement had been imposed by
heathen invaders, but—though appointed by a foreign ruler—
Jonathan was no foreign imposition; he was the Maccabee, a
leader of national redemption, loved and admired by the people of Judah.

Almost insane with anger and frustration, the Pious Ones
brooded in their desert retreat; the sky had fallen on them and
the Lord showed them no way ahead. And then the Teacher
came to them. None could remember the actual occasion of his
arrival. In those terrible days after the sin of the Maccabee,
they had lived as if in a bad dream, hardly making the transi-
tion from day to night. But the Teacher was with them, behav-
ing as if he had been with them always. They did not know
where he had come from, but all felt the warmth of his presence. He was a lamp in the darkness. He was tall, very tall and
very thin. His soft beard and hair bore the russet color of the
priestly line. He wore simple white garments and a white

skullcap. Though clearly a priest, he dressed as a simple shepherd. His eyes were very pale gray and when he talked they seemed to be focused on a distant object. His voice was soft; but when he spoke, all hurried to do his bidding.

The Teacher led them to live in humility and respect for one another, holding their goods in common. They pooled all their possessions and there was enough for all. Their prayer and contemplation was supplemented by other activities. They utilized the spring to the south for cultivation, working the land and raising livestock. They built themselves a center of stone, with a hall for prayer, rooms for learning, and baths fed by a channel leading from a dam built across the wadi to the west. Under the guidance of the Teacher, the restless group of half-mad hermits took on the shape of a purposeful community. The priestly members began to perform tasks befitting their rank. They cured parchment and prepared to write the Law under the Teacher's direction.

The Teacher taught them the Law of Moses. The holy books were revived as he explained their relevance for the present times, showing how the stories and prophecies of old contained hidden meanings for current developments. He taught them how to live and how to pray, restoring their belief and conviction. He reintroduced the ancient calendar of Enoch and laid down a strict code of conduct for the community. In every age, he explained, there had been a small group of righteous men for whose sake the Lord spared mankind. The Pious Ones were the righteous of the current era; moreover, they were the righteous remnant for all time!

The day was fast approaching when the Almighty would make a new covenant with His people, a renewal and final version of the covenants with Abraham and Moses. The tribulations through which they had passed were the preliminaries for the creation of the kingdom of God foretold by the prophets. The community was none other than that of the sons of light, who were to triumph over the forces of darkness at the End of Days!

Although the personality of the Teacher remained an

enigma, his identity became known. He was none other than the son of Honi, the high priest murdered by the original usurper who had profaned the Temple. He was the legitimate heir of the Zadokite line, the high priest of Israel!

Their lives were bound up in this message: *that they may abstain from all evil and hold fast to all good; that they may practice truth, righteousness and justice upon earth and no longer stubbornly follow a sinful heart ... they shall separate from the congregation of the men of falsehood and shall unite with respect to the Law and possessions under the authority of the Sons of Zakok, the priests who keep the covenant. ...*

The Teacher wrote hymns of praise and taught them how to celebrate the festivals, isolated as they were from their Temple—which was to be restored to them. He revealed that the community was part of the Almighty's purpose; they were to prepare for His kingdom. From the priests of the community would come the Messiah of Aaron. *The Sons of Zadok are the elect of Israel, the men called by name who shall stand at the End of Days.*

Thus inspired, the community at Sekaka by the Sea of Salt grew and prospered. Strong in their belief, they worked and prayed and sang praises to the Lord. They no longer regarded Jonathan the Maccabee with their former air of fear and bewilderment. He was now clearly designated: *the Wicked Priest who was called by the name of truth when he first appeared.*

Many observant Jews who had supported the Maccabees in their revolt were nevertheless horrified at their usurpation of the high priesthood. Since the time of Solomon, the high priest had been a member of the Zadokite family and more recently Joshua ben Sira had given voice to popular feeling when he had expressed the hope that the holy office would never leave the family of Simon the Just. Hitherto there had been no alternative to the Maccabees; now the community of Sekaka offered hope to righteous Jews, many of whom flocked to join it. The first signs of the division between the Hasmonean family and the people—which was to develop into an open rift later on—appeared.

Jonathan took severe measures against his rivals. Pointing

123

out that a Greek garrison still occupied Jerusalem, he maintained that opposition in time of war was treason. But he could not dampen the Zadokite fever that was sweeping the nation; so there came the day when the Maccabee resolved to deal with the trouble at its source.

It was on a Friday in late summer that he rode down to the Sea of Salt at the head of a troop of cavalry. In the bleak wilderness, the soldiers in their plumed helmets and armor, their splendid horses decorated with finely embroidered saddles, presented an opulent picture. The Maccabee himself was unarmed, but his soldiers bristled with pikes and javelins. After they had descended the road to Jericho, they wheeled about toward the south, thundering along the shores of the Sea of Salt to Sekaka, the focus of opposition to the Jewish ruler.

The day chosen by Jonathan for his show of force was the Day of Atonement as observed by the Sons of Zadok, according to their special calendar. For any Jew, the Day of Atonement was the holiest day of the year, a day of fasting and penitence, a day of prostration before the Lord's power. But for the Sons of Zadok, the day had acquired a special significance. As the last of the righteous, they had on their shoulders the sins of the whole world and the accumulated wrongdoings of the entire people. Abject before God, they beseeched His forgiveness for their unworthy selves.

Since the previous evening, not one morsel of food or drop of moisture had passed the lips of anyone in the desert community. The day was one of uninterrupted prayer and adoration, of confessing sins and asking forgiveness. The members, dressed in their newest white robes, were assembled in the hall. The Teacher was officiating in person and the climax of the day had approached—when it was the duty of the high priest to prostrate himself before his Maker—as the Maccabee rode up leading his soldiers.

All over Judea, the personal cavalry force of the Maccabee drew the gaze of crowds by its impressive and striking appearance. In the empty valley of the Sea of Salt, their appearance was bizarre and incredible—and yet the arrival of the soldiers

124

did not interrupt the ceremony for the slightest moment. The Teacher did not look up from his scroll. In spite of himself Jonathan was impressed, and he waited for completion of the prayer before ordering his soldiers to move in and arrest the Teacher. The members watched in horror as the uncouth soldiers laid hands on their Priest on this holiest of holy days, but the Teacher signaled to them to continue and allowed himself to be led out to confront the Maccabee.

Jonathan, although short in stature, cut an impressive figure —his powerful, wiry body at ease in its armor, a short brown beard framing his scarred and deeply lined face. There were streaks of gray in his hair, and the lines around his eyes told of the years of strain under which he had lived. His black eyes were like small beads, deep-set and cunning; they flickered everywhere, missing no detail. The Teacher towered above Jonathan, but in contrast to the virile warrior, his presence lacked physicality. Clad in his simple white robe, he was almost unreal. His russet beard was flecked with white and his pale gray eyes were focused on eternity. When he spoke, his voice was elusive. It seemed to sound inside the heads of his listeners. "You add to your already grievous sins by disturbing the holy ceremonies!"

"Today is no holy day," snapped Jonathan. "What is the meaning of the ceremony we witnessed? Prostration takes place only on the Day of Atonement, and in the Temple of God in Jerusalem."

"Today is the Day of Atonement, Maccabee, according to the true accounting; and in the event of the Temple being defiled by the ungodly, we have no choice but to—"

"You forget yourself," Jonathan cut him short. "The Temple was cleansed by my brother, Judah the Maccabee."

"It has been profaned once more by a high priest not of the line of Aaron."

"You accepted the traitor Jakim! Who more than my family is responsible for restoring the nation?"

"That you were called in the name of righteousness only makes your crime the more heinous. You above all should have known better!"

"God gave me the high priesthood. Only a priest can rule Judea and I am the one who must rule."

"You are cursing yourself with such sacrilege," said the Teacher almost sadly. "You are canceling your former valor; you will come to a violent end at the hands of your enemies —" He never completed the sentence. Jonathan, pale with fright, gave a signal and the soldiers closed in on him.

The Teacher was imprisoned among criminals and degenerates but otherwise was not harmed. Jonathan feared to lay hands on him. But as the Maccabee increasingly dealt with kings and princes and engaged in conspiracies involving thrones and positions of real power, he found himself growing more contemptuous of the potential threat from a few dreaming madmen in the desert.

After a year the Teacher was released and permitted to return to Sekaka. A short while later Jonathan died in the manner prophesied by the Teacher. Simon, his brother, succeeded him. He also would not harm the community, but he strengthened his authority in the face of possible challenges by forcing the people to legalize the Maccabean high priesthood and by dealing summarily with any kind of opposition.

When in due course the Teacher died, his memory lived on in his beliefs, his writings, his deeds, and his personality—and in the collective memory of the community. The Sons of Zadok clashed many times with subsequent rulers. The cynically ruthless John Hyrcanus and the crazed Jannai persecuted them. But then came a period when they were not disturbed; even the mad Herod let them be. Gradually the prophecies of the Teacher came to pass as all Israel groaned under the foreign yoke; the time was drawing nearer when the community would come into its own to lead the forces of righteousness against the prince of evil. Then Sekaka was destroyed by an earthquake, forcing its people to flee for several years; but eventually they returned to their home by the Sea of Salt and rebuilt the center.

There was always a priest of the holy line of Zadok as head of the community, and the people believed that there would come a generation when their priest would emerge as the Messiah of Aaron. As the oppression in the land worsened, the community grew, for more and more people sought salvation. The Teacher had been priest and guardian, teacher and manager. But with the growth of the community—a contingency anticipated by him—a more elaborate structure was needed. The Priest remained at the head of the community and led in matters of ritual and religion; but a Levite Master instructed the members and examined the candidates.

When Eleazar arrived at Sekaka, the Master, a powerful personality, had already established his authority there after only three years in office. Although the young boy did not meet the Master in his early years, he was greatly under the leader's influence. The children were cared for by the women in their tents in the northwestern part of the plateau. Their religious instruction was the task of the junior priests and Levites. The Master was a distant, rather frightening figure.

The young man continued to absorb the ideas of the community. He came to believe that he would witness cataclysmic events: from that wilderness where God had manifested Himself to His people, He would emerge again to ensure their triumph at the end of time.

When the time for Eleazar's candidacy arrived, he sat trembling before the gaunt, forbidding Master. But the Levite's voice was kindly and solicitous. He asked the boy about his life at Sekaka, his ideas on the lessons he had learned, his feelings about the future; and he was well pleased with the answers he received.

Eleazar was judged suitable and therefore able to undergo a further period of training. He would have to undertake to obey the Law of Moses, as revealed and explained by the Teacher, no matter what terrors lay ahead. After a further period, he would be allowed into meetings of the community, but only as an observer with no right to speak. Later still, he would be allowed into the purity of the Many, an especially pure ritual meal prepared with the greatest strictness.

Eleazar did not flinch from the austere life that stretched

ahead of him, but anticipated with joy a life dedicated to the Almighty. He worked uncomplainingly in the kitchens where the food was prepared and in the unbearable heat of the bakery and at the pottery kiln. When not doing his tasks, he could be found in the center, poring over a scroll, praying, singing, learning, and thinking. The Master developed a particular affection for Eleazar. He was impressed by the boy's unaffected humility, his genuine curiosity, and his intense desire to immerse himself in the life of the community. For this reason the shock, when it came, was all the more brutal.

Eleazar ben Jair tried unsuccessfully to mask his emotion as he sat across the rough wooden table from the Master. He was deathly pale and felt drained of all feeling. His life, so laboriously fashioned anew after his father's death, was shattered again.

"I wish to be of the Sons of Zadok," he said.

"Each of us has his own role to play," replied the Master. "Your task is among your own people. Menahem is of your blood; if he calls for you, I cannot refuse him. The Sicarii too are fulfilling God's purpose in their way. It is not for us to choose how we are to be used."

"I feel I want to belong to this community," insisted the boy. "If the Lord has put such a feeling into my heart, surely I have the right to defy my uncle?"

"Listen carefully, Eleazar," said the Master. "The time of the final battle between the forces of light and darkness draws near. The people of Judea are oppressed as never before. The double burden of Roman taxes and priestly tithes has passed tolerable limits. Rebellion will break out—this week, next month, next year—I do not know exactly when. The Sons will join the rebel cause; you will be there, Eleazar, a man who knows the Sons of Zadok, at the center of rebel power!

"That is the task the Lord has for you; that is the purpose for which Menahem sent you to us. You will be the one who will bring us together. Without the rebels we have no power; without us the rebel cause is an empty one. Together we shall succeed. Every man has his own special role. Do not forget what you have learned here with us."

"I will never forget," pledged the youth. "I will endeavor to carry out God's purpose, if my task is that which you claim. But I shall live for the day when I can return to Sekaka and live out my life in prayer and study!"

Those had been the last words that Eleazar had spoken to the Master. He had never returned. In the years that followed, turbulent, active years, he had often thought of Sekaka and of the life he had been forced to abandon. Although he became a rebel leader, one of the most dangerous men in Judea, he had retained much of the identity he had developed in the community by the Sea of Salt.

6

As Eleazar climbed the steps that led to the roof of the watchtower, he found that his memories of the Master were muddled with his earliest memories of his uncle Menahem, and his thoughts of the Teacher mingled with memories of his own father. He was lightheaded from loss of blood, which only added to the dreamlike quality of the scene, as he stepped out onto the platform. The Master had aged considerably. He came forward and took both of Eleazar's hands. He was even more gaunt than he had been, and his hair and beard were iron gray. His grip was firm and his eyes sought Eleazar's as if trying to read their expression. He looked uncertain, and a little anxious.

Eleazar knew that he had not developed spiritually since leaving Sekaka; there had been little time for study or contemplation, yet the simple fact of his being a war leader had elevated him in the eyes of his former mentor. The Sons of Zadok could work out the time and purpose of the final war; they might forecast the length of each phase and prophesy how God would intervene. They might prognosticate on the number and identity of the saved, the nature of the final banquet, and the social order of the kingdom of God. But they knew that in the actual fighting, they would play a comparatively minor role. In this decisive period of war, Eleazar ex-

129

ceeded the Master in importance. He realized this with a shock before being greeted by the older man.

"Welcome, Eleazar," the Master said at last, infusing real warmth in his salutation. "How are you feeling now?"

"I am well rested, thank you, Master; our gratitude is—"

The Master waved his words aside with something of his old authority. "It is nothing. Please do not speak of it. You are welcome to remain here as long as you wish. I do not know what plans you may have." He was diffident.

"We have suffered a reverse: we are retiring to Masada."

"I hear so," replied the Master. "I found it difficult to credit."

"We killed Hananiah, the high priest, and his brother Hezekiah!"

"How did this happen?" The Master was entirely aghast at the news. Eleazar recounted briefly the developments of the previous two days.

"Joab and I tried to stop them," he concluded. "But you know how Menahem is about treachery. They played on his fears most skillfully, until he was half crazed with fury and doubt. The next day he marched to the Temple and they attacked him there."

"Is there no limit to their abominations?" The Master struck his fist into his palm. "An attack in the house of God!" He continued, "However, I still do not see how he lost his dominance so swiftly."

"There was no real unity," confessed Eleazar. "Intrigues were being carried on all the time we were in Jerusalem. The other leaders were jealous of our success; they were suspicious and frightened of Menahem. They did not want to merge their groups into one army. They were only too pleased to attack us."

"What happened afterward?"

"I do not know exactly," admitted Eleazar. "Nahum came with orders that we were to retreat to Masada, and that Absalom and Menahem were in hiding and would follow later. I took the road to Samaria with the largest group, to draw off the pursuit. Then we descended the Jericho road and doubled back." He looked at the older man with some concern. "We do not wish to involve you at this time."

"We know how to deal with this situation; you are not to worry," said the Master emphatically. "Now I understand the Bursar's story," he said quietly, almost to himself. He explained to Eleazar how the Bursar had met his brother Judah. "Well," he continued, "I cannot feel regret for the death of that old scoundrel Hananiah or that of his scheming brother; but I wonder whether it was advisable."

"It was madness," admitted Eleazar. He added bluntly, "The old man lost his reason. He has been under a great strain recently, but we can still count on him. He will retrieve the situation for sure. He has remarkable resilience." As he spoke, Eleazar felt his confidence returning. Menahem had survived worse setbacks before. They had Masada and they could hold it against the world, if need be. From Masada they would advance again, when the time was ripe.

The clouds were gathering above Moab, their bellies bright gold in the late afternoon sun. The Master looked at his former pupil, seeing before him a young man of slight build, scholarly and sensitive in his simple white robe, his face lined with worry, the strain evident in the expression in his eyes.

"Eleazar, I do not know," he confessed. "For the first time in my life I must admit that I am uncertain. If life has any meaning, if faith has any meaning, then the time has come: all the signs are favorable, except for this latest news of your reverse."

"A mere setback," replied Eleazar, his confidence growing. "We shall regroup at Masada. Menahem will have a plan."

As he spoke the last sentence, he was looking over the Master's shoulder at the stretch of plateau to the north. The sun was setting behind the Judean bluffs and the whole area was dyed crimson. In the gathering dusk he could just make out a group of figures coming south.

Bar Nottos was at the last stages of exhaustion, as were his men. Eleazar and the master had descended from the tower to meet the new arrivals. The tired rebel walked slowly, dragging

131

his sandaled feet in the dust. He did not greet Eleazar and seemed to be trying to avoid his eyes.

"Greetings, bar Nottos," said Eleazar, embracing him. "From where have you come?"

"From the city," replied the young man.

"When did you leave?"

"Ours was the last party to leave; we had to fight our way out. There were heavy losses."

"So all the Sicarii have left Jerusalem?" Eleazar was relieved.

"No."

"Why? Were some trapped, unable to break out?"

"Judah your brother returned to the city."

Eleazar felt a sudden shock. "Why did he return?" he demanded. "Had he taken leave of his senses?"

"He returned for the body of your uncle Menahem ben Judah!"

Somehow Eleazar retained his balance as the ground lurched violently beneath him; he flung out his arms to steady himself. Bar Nottos' words, hollow and unreal, echoed and reechoed in his head.

Bar Nottos continued: "We do not know where—nobody knows where it happened; but the news is around the city. They took him and Absalom and tortured them for several hours. Absalom also is dead."

"No ... no ... there is some mistake. Almighty God, no!" The words escaped from Eleazar as he stood with the valley of the Sea of Salt reeling about him. He turned toward the Master, but saw on his face only bafflement and fear. He looked into the heavens, but there was no comfort there.

"Dear God, make him wrong," he whispered. "Let it not have happened."

As the day died, hope died in the heart of Eleazar the son of Jair.

FLAVIUS SILVA: MARCH 73 C.E.

Winter was turning into spring, the wild, gusty spring of the Judean desert. Silva had been facing the rock for three months and still there had not been so much as a skirmish between his soldiers and the defenders. Week after week the Roman forces had faced nothing more formidable than the vagaries of the Judean climate. The Jewish commander was staying his hand. The Roman continued his preparations for the assault methodically, endeavoring not to show his irritation at his opponent's tactics.

At Macherus, on the eastern shore of the Sea of Salt, his predecessor, Bassus, had faced a problem similar to that of Masada. Silva had visited the site and had wondered at the effrontery with which Bassus had defied and altered nature itself by filling a whole ravine to facilitate the approach of his army.

What had been accomplished at Macherus could be carried out at Masada also, he had concluded, difficult as the task was. He quickly decided where his ramp was to be constructed. The nearest point to the summit of Masada was a white rock two hundred yards from his main western camp. From there to the summit was a matter of some four hundred feet. Huge balks of wood were brought from the hills of Hebron. Ruined villages as far away as Ein Gedi were pillaged for their roof beams. Every piece of wood that could be found in Idumea was dragged or carried to the camp at the western foot of Masada. The wood was used to contain the earth and rocks which were dug out of the vicinity of the white rock. The whole slave force and large numbers of the soldiers were mobilized for the task. Thousands of them toiled all day long, carrying basket after basket of fill.

The days stretched to weeks, and the weeks to months, as the stupendous job continued without respite. Gradually the vast ramp started to take shape; still the defenders made no move. Masada did not fall, but the land crept up to the walls of Masada. The earth ramp dominated the valley, covering the

135

remains of the aqueduct that had conveyed water from the western dam to the upper cisterns.

A bare minimum of men guarded the eight camps and the wall, which snaked its way through the valleys and gorges around Masada. Slaves fell ill and men died from exhaustion or in accidents, but these incidents did not halt the advance. As the burning desert winds came and went, Silva ordered a three-hour pause in the middle of the day, during which the soldiers and slaves sweated under the canvas roofs of their stone-walled tents. The procurator was an economical man and by Roman standards a humane one. He did not want unnecessary waste or loss of life.

When it was finished, the giant mound of earth, rock, and wood, its sides sloping steeply from the knife edge of its summit, pointed like a dagger at the heart of the Sicarii stronghold. Silva was proud of his achievement; he knew that no other force in the world would have so much as contemplated such a task, let alone achieved it. In this waterless waste it was little short of a miracle. Yet as he surveyed the ramp, wall, and camps, his economical mind could not but reflect on the enormous cost of destroying less than a thousand human beings. Week after week, the caravans bringing food toiled across the plateau from the Hebron hills with grain and olives and inadequate quantities of livestock. The water was hauled daily from Ein Gedi; despite the strict rationing, there never seemed to be enough.

As he contemplated the next stage of his plan, the building of a siege tower on the ramp, the procurator once again considered what he knew of his enemy. Why had the Sicarii never assisted the other rebels? Even when the capital was in danger, they had made no move. Silva knew that there had been a bitter quarrel, that Menahem ben Judah, a Sicarii and first leader of the revolt in Jerusalem, had been murdered by rival factions and that his followers had been forced to flee to Masada. They had waited at Masada for nearly seven years.

The present leader was Menahem's nephew Eleazar ben Jair, who had taken over on the death of his uncle. He must control the fortress with an iron discipline, reflected the Ro-

136

man. No young hotheads had tried breaking out to attack the besieging forces. Eleazar was evidently in complete control of the fortress, but Silva knew from his questioning of the Jewish slaves and his studies of the Judean campaign that it had not always been thus.

Simon bar Giora, leader of the Jewish forces in the final battle for Jerusalem, had sought refuge in the fortress in the early stages of the war. He had tried unsuccessfully to force a more active policy on Eleazar and had led away more than half the garrison who agreed with him. Simon was dead now, strangled at the triumph in Rome; but maybe some of his sympathizers remained. Could he offer terms that would once more split the defenders into hostile factions? the procurator wondered. He doubted it; the issues that had divided them once were dead now. It might be valuable to learn more about that incident, though. He decided to continue his questioning of the Jewish slaves.

BOOK III

SIMON: 67 C.E.

Simon, son of Gioras, collected a large band of revolutionaries and gave himself up to pillage. . . . When a force was sent against him by Ananus and the magistrates, he fled with his followers to the bandits at Masada, and there till the death of Ananus and his other enemies, he remained.

Flavius Josephus, *The Jewish War*

1

Rain had been falling for three days, a raw, cold rain that chilled to the bone. The sky was gray-black and heavy, occasionally split open by a jagged crack of lightning, followed by the rumble of thunder. The visibility was poor, the mountains of Moab invisible and even the gray mass of the Sea of Salt only barely discernable through the mist below. To the north and west the wadis were full, the water tumbling in frothy brown torrents. Both dams had overflowed, but not before many thousands of gallons of fresh water had flowed along the aqueducts and channels, filling both rows of cisterns.

On the summit of the rock, the water had gathered in several places, much of it draining into the various pits and cisterns of the surface. The beasts huddled miserably in their pens under the inadequate shelters. The people remained in their rooms, the men together with their families, crowding around their cooking fires in the hollowed earthen ovens. When they ventured out to collect wood, tearing down the roofs of the Herodian buildings, now empty of habitation, the wind whipped the freezing rain into their faces, instantly soaking their woolen cloaks, which became heavy and clammy, gripping their bodies in an icy grasp.

In his room next to the stores, Nahum threw some more wood on the fire. It flared up, blackening the red panels of the fresco on the plastered walls. His two light-haired, dark-skinned boys fought on the straw that he had spread for warmth on the mosaic floor. Nahum joined in with the boys, and they fought playfully, both children wrestling their broad-shouldered blond father. Nahum caught David, who was seven, and threw him over his shoulder, allowing him to land gently on the hard floor. Uri, aged five and a half, was busily strangling his father from behind. But he soon followed his brother over the broad back of his father, by which time David was on the attack once more.

"Leave your father alone!" their mother told them. Leah was as dark as her husband was fair, a plump, comfortable woman. She was nursing a third boy at her ample breast, rocking the five-month-old baby as he sucked. The fat, bald little infant sucked greedily, trying to stuff as much of the nipple as he could into his mouth. His dimpled hands rested on the brown skin of his mother's bosom, as if he was trying to squeeze out that extra bit of nourishment.

"You are getting them excited," she complained to her husband.

"Nonsense," he replied. "It gives them something to do and keeps them warm. Just listen to that rain out there!" They all listened and they could hear the splash of water on the muddy surface outside the door.

"That is enough of fighting," insisted the woman.

"No, Mummy, no!" cried the boys.

"Yes. That is enough. You are unsettling the baby."

Nahum laughed. "Nothing would unsettle him! I do not believe he even knows we are here."

"Well, you are unsettling me," replied the woman.

"Oh, Mummy, just when we were enjoying ourselves!" David's lower lip protruded in a pout that was sometimes a prelude to tears.

"Have you read your portion of the Law?" demanded their mother.

"Yes I have—three times." He turned appealingly to Nahum.

"That is correct," confirmed his father. "He read it very well too."

"The rabbi says you must study all day," said the woman.

"But we cannot read all the time!" complained David.

"You must not expect too much of them," agreed Nahum.

"Very well then," the mother relented, "tell them a story."

"Story, story!" shouted the children. They were sitting astride their father as he lay in the straw.

"Get up off your father now," snapped Leah.

"It is perfectly all right," said Nahum. "I am quite comfortable."

142

"How can you tell them a story while they are sitting on you?"

"Who is telling the story?" demanded the man.

"Daniel and the lions," shouted Uri.

"Noah. . . ."

"David the King. . . ." The ideas exploded from the mouths of the children. Nahum scratched his almost-white blond beard.

"We must agree on a story," he said.

"He always wants Daniel and the lions," complained David.

"We have not had Daniel for ages," retorted Uri. "Yesterday was David the King. I want Daniel and the lions. It is not fair; it is my turn today."

"There is somebody at the door," Leah broke into the argument. Nahum rose, gently tumbling his sons onto the ground, and went to the door of the room. He came back shaking his head.

"Somebody needs flour," he told his wife.

"They should come at the proper time," she insisted.

"I cannot refuse somebody on a day like this!"

"It is most inconsiderate," complained Leah. "They have plenty of time in the morning without coming to drag you out on a day like this!"

"That is why I am here," said Nahum over his shoulder as he left, pulling a heavy cloak about him. "I will not be very long," he shouted to the children. "Behave yourselves and I will tell you the story when I return."

Eleazar ben Jair sat at a table in his room on the lowest tier of the northern palace, poring over a scroll. Leader of the community, he was also its rabbi, as his uncle Menahem and grandfather Judah had been before him. During the past few hectic years of his life as a bandit chief, he had not devoted any time to study. But now, isolated a thousand feet above the desert, he had found the opportunity for the first time since his days at Sekaka. Since the start of the rains, few people ventured out. Only a rudimentary watch was posted, for the Roman forces could not approach in the rain; even the other

143

rebel groups could not arrive in the vicinity of the fortress while the torrents raged and frothed at its base. Eleazar silently reproached himself for thinking of military matters while sitting before a scroll of the Law.

In the corner, watching Eleazar, sat a young woman. Her skin was the color of dark honey and her black hair was bound in a single plait that hung down her back. Her large, dark eyes, upward sloping, were covered by long lashes. Her features were small but finely cut, the teeth startlingly white, like a row of tiny pearls in her dusky face. The slightness of her build and delicacy of her hands and feet contributed to her air of vulnerability. Dressed simply in a single linen garment reaching to her feet, over which she wore a thick woolen cloak, she looked like a young child. She shivered slightly and the gooseflesh appeared on her long slender neck. Eleazar looked up, sensitive to her every movement.

"Hagar?"

"Yes?

"Are you cold?"

"A little; it does not matter." Her voice was soft and low, with a slightly guttural Idumean pronunciation.

"I will finish soon."

"It is all right."

"I have to study."

"Of course!" A smile of great sweetness lit up her face. She regarded her husband affectionately. The forehead above his sensitive scholar's face was creased in a frown of concentration. As he sat there before his scroll, it was hard to identify him with the active figure of a guerrilla leader. His finger traced the words over the page as he read, and he looked as if he had been studying and praying all his life. His hands did not look capable of wielding weapons.

Hagar rose and put some pieces of wood carefully into the earth fireplace, maintaining the heat but conserving the wood. She rested the earthenware cooking pot over the hole in the top of the structure, where the flames could lick at its conical base, and began to stir the gruel with a wooden spoon. She tasted the food and then threw in a pinch of salt. As she busied

144

herself with the preparations, she thought about the enigma of her husband, Eleazar, and his Sicarii movement. Everyone in Judea knew that the Sicarii were a gang of cutthroats, indeed their very name was a boast that this was so; even the ignorant daughter of an Idumean peasant knew that. Yet Eleazar, the leader, was studious and gentle, a follower of the Law, a true rabbi; and the other members were ordinary pious Jews.

Even among the leaders, violence and brutality were not in evidence. Joab, with his bristling red beard, looked fierce enough, but there was humor in his green eyes. When the others teased him about his three daughters and his failure to beget a son, his laughter rang out. His small, aggressive wife ruled him strictly. Nahum with his three sons was like an overgrown boy himself; he was good-natured and free of malice. The young bar Nottos sulked occasionally, but everyone at Masada knew that his moods were the result of the vagaries of his romance with the daughter of Joab.

Only Judah, Eleazar's brother, fitted the part of a fanatic. Hagar shivered as she thought of Judah. Morose and sullen, he spent his days brooding, his glowering expression unchanged even for his mirthless snarl of a grin. She could imagine Judah as an assassin. At this very moment, when the whole community was indoors huddling over its fires, Judah was standing out in the rain. If she went to the door she would be able to see him, his tall, lean form hunched in his soaking cloak, oblivious of the rain and cold, gazing northward toward Jerusalem.

Judah did not feel the cold; but he did take note of the rain and the streaming desert, reflecting on the contrast with the parched dusty region of the summer months. The whole area seemed to be running with water. It was difficult to conjure up the picture of the desert in its normal state, when the ground was cracked with drought, the dry dust filled the burning air, and a man could wander for a day without locating a drop of water. Could this be the same rock they had captured less than a year previously?

He bore very little resemblance to his elder brother. His face was broad and coarse, his expression shallow, and his dark

145

eyes angry. He was as senseless to wet and cold, heat and drought, as he was to fear and pain. Judah ben Jair was a hard man. He had inherited none of the gentleness and piety of his father. He only remembered that his father had died because of his gentleness, and he despised it. Named after his grandfather Judah of Galilee, he possessed the nerveless courage of his illustrious forebear, with none of his depth and learning.

When he had arrived at his uncle's camp in Galilee, after the death of his father, he had been entrusted to the care of the women, whereas Eleazar was old enough to mingle with the men. On his return from Sekaka, his aunt Rivka, the wife of Menahem, had continued to look after him. Judah had resented her attentions. Unable to bear children of her own, Rivka had lavished on the two orphans, Judah and Simon, the love she had never been able to give; but Judah felt strangled by it. Her failure to bear children had given Rivka a great respect for human life and had turned her into a paradox: a lover of peace in a rebel group. Judah had turned from her and her ways, finding satisfaction in the violent life of the revolutionary band.

The past few months of inactivity at Masada had not suited Judah's temperament. Since Menahem's death the Sicarii had made no move. Secure in their fastness, amply supplied and armed, they had not ventured far from their base. Gradually they had become used to the idea of existence without their leader. Slowly life was returning to normal, and the group was regaining its confidence and identity. More wives and families had arrived at the fortress, and the community thrived. Several of the wives, including Rivka, had become widows; but others had been reunited with their husbands for the first time in many years. And so the community waited, building its strength for the future.

But Judah did not like waiting. Restless and frustrated, he longed to break out of the fortress, which he was coming to regard as a prison. He was not happy unless in action. The daring raid into the capital to bring out the body of his uncle for burial at Masada had suited his taste. He was a brilliant tactician, but he lacked the ability to take a long-term view.

Raging inwardly, Judah stood on the lowest terrace of the northern palace, his tall, dark, lightly bearded figure wrapped in his sodden cloak. The rain ran down over his tight black curls and his broad dark face. It was while he was standing there that he saw them—a bedraggled group spread out in a long line, the end of which disappeared into the swirling mist and rain. Judah's first reaction was to marvel that they had managed to arrive in the vicinity in such weather. They must have started out in fine weather, only to be caught in the storms. They looked miserable in the rain with no shelter. He could see men and women but few children and almost no baggage animals. They were obviously members of some outlaw band, but their identity remained unknown until suddenly Judah caught sight of their leaders; a giant of a man, his curiously small head set atop unusually broad and powerful shoulders, he towered above his fellows. Excited by the prospect of some activity at last, Judah went in out of the rain to tell his brother.

2

Simon bar Giora was wondering what to do until the rain stopped; there was no way of approaching the rock during the downpour. As soon as it was possible to approach, he intended to seek admittance to the Sicarii stronghold. He was in flight from the high priest and the aristocratic cabal that had seized control of the revolt, that same element that had turned on Menahem ben Judah. Surely the Sicarii would receive him as an ally—he had not killed Menahem and he was certain that no one knew that it was he who had captured the old leader.

The journey through Idumea had not been easy. They were already in the vicinity of Masada when the rain had started. The violence of the sudden flood had taken them by surprise. The torrent had come roaring down the canyon, sweeping away a third of his force and almost the entire baggage train. They had looked on in incredulous horror as the huge foaming brown wave descended on them, helpless against its fury as it swept all before it. The survivors were those who had managed to scramble up the sides of the gorge, out of the reach of the stream.

For three days the two groups of survivors had regarded each other from either side of the foaming wadi, until, with the ceasing of the rain, the stream had vanished almost as quickly as it had appeared and they had been able to struggle across the mud to reunite. Now they stood in the rain before Masada, and there they would have to remain until the weather permitted them to ask the Sicarii for permission to enter.

The day after Menahem had died in Jerusalem, the garrisons of the towers of Phasael, Hippicus, and Mariamne had surrendered. Deserted by their Jewish allies, they had accepted the terms of safe-conduct offered them and marched out unarmed. Drunk with his new power, the Temple captain had ordered the massacre of the soldiers, who were cut down to the last man. On the same day the Greeks of Caesarea attacked their Jewish neighbors, killing large numbers of them. All over Judea, and even in Syria and Alexandria, fighting broke out between Jew and Gentile. In the Jewish areas, the Gentiles were massacred; in the Hellenistic cities, the Jewish minorities were exterminated.

Meanwhile the Twelfth Legion from Antioch and several thousand picked men from other legions, supported by a host of auxiliaries and led by the governor of Syria in person, marched southward, meeting no resistance from Galilee to Caesarea. By the time the Roman force arrived in Lydda before the Judean foothills, the small villages were deserted by the Jews, who had gone up to their capital for the late harvest festival of Succot. The overcrowded city was apprehensive. They had seized Jerusalem from auxiliary soldiers, but now they were called upon to face the legions. As the Romans advanced, the capital prepared to withstand a siege.

It was the wild, impulsive rabble of Simon bar Giora that had the effrontery to make the first attack. Pouring out of the city in a wild, undisciplined rush, they took the rear guard of the attacking force by surprise, killing numbers of troops and cap-

148

turing a part of the baggage train. The Jews were jubilant, for it showed that the legions consisted of men who could be attacked and killed. The feeling of dread eased, and the preparations for the siege were carried out with increasing confidence.

When he saw the Jews preparing the defenses of the city, Cestius Gallus, the governor of Syria, hesitated to press on with his plans for attack. Jerusalem was a supremely defensible city—cut off on all sides by ravines and protected by stone walls of remarkable size and strength. The Jews were undisciplined, but the Romans had already felt the strength of their fanaticism and their impulsive fighting ability. The reduction of Jerusalem would take several months, and the winter rains might come at any time, cutting the Romans off from their supply lines and severing their communications with the rest of the country.

Taking all these factors into consideration, the Roman commander made his decision: he gave the order for retreat—and the Jews went mad with joy. For months they had dreaded the day when the Roman legions would encamp before their city. They had known that the reality of their strength and power would swiftly dissipate the euphoria generated by their initial victories. Yet the legions had been harried and attacked, and now they were raising the siege like the Assyrians of old. Truly was the Lord working miracles for His people!

In vain Simon bar Giora had tried to rally his forces for an attack on the retreating enemy, but his men were literally drunk with their success. As the heroes of the capital, they had been wined and dined wherever they went. The force of bar Giora's personality could dominate the wild group of slaves for only limited periods; now they were scattered all over the city.

Instead, it was the veteran Zealots of ben Simon who followed the retreating Romans. Joined by their colleagues in the Jerusalem hills, they were kept in constant touch with the army's progress from their various bases and outpost in the corridor out of Jerusalem. Cleverly they began to harry the retreating Romans, leaving them alone in the open country, assaulting them violently whenever they were forced to pass through the valleys. When they arrived in the valley of Beth Horon, scene of the famous Maccabee victory of two centuries previously, ben Simon attacked in full strength and the Romans were routed. By abandoning his baggage train and all his equipment, Cestius Gallus saved most of his men; but for the first time, the country was able to see the mighty Twelfth Legion in headlong, ignominious flight!

The war party was the only party in the country now, and the people hastened to join the rebel cause. While the discontent which had provoked the rebellion had been real enough, it was only now that the majority of the population began to envisage the possibility of success. The Jerusalem aristocracy, threatened with complete isolation, rallied to the party of the Temple captain, which set about organizing the defense of the country. Hanan, the new high priest, assumed the command of Jerusalem and appointed regional commanders for the other parts of Judea: Joseph ben Matthew for Galilee, John of the Sons of Zadok for the central region, and the brother of the Temple captain for Idumea.

With the retreat of the Sicarii, the other rebel factions were edged out of the leadership of the revolt. Simon bar Giora, now leader of a group which had disintegrated, was ignored entirely, his key role in previous events forgotten. Ben Simon managed to remain in the city with his highly disciplined followers, and he kept hold of the booty his men had captured at Beth Horon. Despite the machinations of the aristocratic party, he remained an important factor in the city.

Bar Giora fled southward, taking with him only a few of his trusted friends. He set about the task of gathering another force. He freed the slaves on country estates throughout Judea and the garrison slaves of Herodium and other outposts. In a matter of months he had collected a larger force than before, and there were even some among the aristocracy who were attracted by his virile leadership and sense of mission. His band was a mixed company: Jews and Gentiles, slaves and soldiers, dancing girls and whores—an undisciplined, riotous, free-living, free-loving band, which rampaged its way through southern Judea, sleeping every night at a new place.

When Hanan, the high priest, sent out a detachment from Jerusalem to put a stop to their activities, bar Giora's mob was quickly put to flight. Once again Simon bar Giora withdrew southward, but this time he had learned his lesson. His ability to raise a large band was not enough; he needed a core of well-trained fighters to hold his group together. It was not long before he realized where the solution to his problems lay, and he led the remains of his band across the desert to Masada.

It never occurred to Simon that the Sicarii would not be amenable to his persuasion. He knew that they might be suspicious of him initially, but he was confident that they would see the logic of his position. Together, he and the Sicarii could wrest the leadership of Judea from the priests and aristocrats, turning the rebellion into a revolution.

Beside the white rock to the west of Masada, bar Giora's party had succeeded in erecting a rudimentary shelter, a tent of the sort used by the nomadic Arabs. At first the rain dripped through the coarse weave of the camel hair; but as the rough cloth became uniformly moist, the warp contracted and no more water penetrated. Less than a hundred remained of the five thousand commanded by Simon bar Giora only one month previously. A couple of hundred more were scattered around the country. As he crouched in the shelter waiting for the rain to stop, Simon bar Giora knew that he had reached the lowest ebb of his fortunes.

3

Within minutes of Judah's sighting of the bar Giora group, the Sicarii leaders were assembled in Eleazar's room in the northern palace. Joab, Nahum, and bar Nottos had joined Eleazar and his brothers around the rough table. In the corner, away from the men, sat Rivka, widow of Menahem ben Judah. Rivka had been beautiful once and she was still impressive. Her fine dark eyes blazed from her pale, high-boned face, and her white hair was still thick. Despite the unpopularity of her

151

views, Rivka was granted a certain deference as the widow of the dead leader.

"I do not like it!" It was Judah who spoke first. "I do not trust that man."

"We do not know what brings him here," said Joab. "It seems likely that he quarreled with the other leaders—otherwise he would not have come."

"Unless it is a trap," replied Judah.

"He would not come to Masada in this weather to lead us into a trap," retorted Joab. "He would hardly expect to draw us out now."

"None of them are to be trusted!" insisted Judah. "Where were they when we were attacked? Where were they when Menahem was murdered?"

"Bar Giora's men may have been lying around drunk," suggested Joab. "It was quite normal for them. I did not see any of them around at the time and the Temple captain probably took advantage of that. Possibly he even arranged to have the drink provided."

"That is only supposition," Judah pointed out.

"It is a fact, though, that they were not anywhere to be seen," confirmed Nahum.

"Bar Giora was active enough afterward," said Judah. "It was his group that made the first attack on the legion. He must have remained on good terms with the leadership, and that is enough to condemn him in my eyes."

"The question is what attitude to adopt toward him now," stated Eleazar. "We are faced with the immediate problem of whether to admit him or not."

"It depends on why he is here," suggested Joab. "If he has fallen out with the leadership, then he is naturally our ally."

"I do not agree," said Judah. "If he was friendly with them after Menahem's murder, he is our enemy. The fact that they threw him out later is irrelevant."

"We do not even know what he intends to propose," said Joab. "I think we have to hear him before we can make any decision."

"I am not sure that we should even listen to him," replied

152

Eleazar. "He is a dangerous man who certainly knows how to talk. He might be dangerous for our community."

"If he is in need of help, he should receive it!" All heads turned to the corner; it was Rivka who had spoken.

"Your views, Aunt, while most admirable, are hardly practical at the present time." Judah spoke with a heavy sarcasm.

"If they seek shelter, we should not refuse them," repeated the old woman stubbornly.

"I must confess that I fear this man," stated Eleazar. "I fear what he might do to us. He is cunning and ambitious and men are drawn to him. We must build up our strength and wait for the appropriate time. Premature action would be folly, and there is no knowing where bar Giora might lead us. My whole instinct is to avoid too deep an involvement with him. If he needs shelter, he should only be granted it on a temporary basis."

"I think we are being unfair," said Joab. "Bar Giora is a brave man; he supported us admirably in the attack on the palace. He could be a great asset to our movement. One day we will emerge from our retreat, and then he could be useful to us."

"I do not trust him," said bar Nottos. "I do not trust any of them. They were all against Menahem in Jerusalem. Menahem wanted power for the Lord, but they all wanted it for themselves. I saw them."

"It is a sin to turn away someone who needs shelter," affirmed Rivka.

"I say we should attack them," countered Judah. "We can wipe them out now. In a few more days there might be a far larger force."

"I have a suggestion," said Nahum. He scratched his blond beard and looked anxiously around the faces of his colleagues. "We can be careful without being hostile. It would be a shame to lose the opportunity to gain more adherents; consolidation is our basic reason for being here. On the other hand, we should not allow him to become a threat to our security in any way at all.

"You all know that the only way into the northern part of the fortress is through my gateway. If we transfer the arms store from the western palace, the northern section will be unassailable. We can let Simon into Masada, but only into the southern section." There was silence for several minutes as the leaders thought over the implications of this suggestion.

"I admit the idea attracts me, Nahum," confessed Eleazar. "I fear bar Giora, but I am loath to turn him away—it seems a coward's solution. Your plan, on the other hand, combines prudence and charity."

"We cannot deal with our uncle's murderer!" protested Judah.

"That is ridiculous," snapped Eleazar. "We have no evidence whatsoever for such a supposition."

"He was active in the revolt after Menahem's death."

"So were we," said Nahum. "The struggle had to be continued. We have also continued in our own way."

"If we fear bar Giora, we shall achieve nothing," said Joab. "We must take care, but if we are going to fear each little group of a hundred souls who arrive, we are not capable of continuing the revolt. Prudence does not mean cowardice!"

"I think we will allow Nahum to transfer the arms," decided Eleazar. "I am curious to hear what bar Giora has to say. I feel instinctively that we should block our ears against this man— he means danger—but I am curious. Joab is right: we are far stronger than he is. We have absolutely nothing to fear. We are naturally defensive and suspicious after what happened in the capital, but we must conquer that in ourselves if we are to resume Menahem's task."

4

Simon bar Giora mounted the stairs to the upper story of the western palace, where he had his room. He had inspected the guards under the command of his deputy Malachi. His other commander, ben Josiah, was already asleep. On the following day he was to journey northward to collect what he could of the scattered remains of the slave army. Bar Giora had accepted the terms which the Sicarii had offered him; there had been no alternative. He was quite satisfied and did not object

154

to his being confined to the southern part of the summit. He conceded the right of the Sicarii to view him with suspicion. He himself was not entirely trusting, and for that reason he had posted guards at every entrance to the palace. He arrived at the top step and entered his room.

An oil lamp was burning beside the low couch. Miriam stood up as he entered, allowing the robe to fall from her perfect body. Miriam had not been brought up as a Jewess; she was as shameless as a Greek. Her figure was full and mature, and her dusky skin shone in the soft glow of the lamp. The smooth muscles of her thighs and stomach rippled as she moved toward him. The large man was overwhelmed by the sudden rush of physical desire. His large hands gripped her shoulders, and he buried his face in the smooth, hard groove between her neck and collarbone. Her hands moved with swift expertise over his body, unbuckling his armor and removing his undergarments, until they stood naked by the couch, limbs entwined. He forced her toward the couch, but she resisted him with her strong dancer's body, before giving way and drawing him down beside her.

Her hands moved over his body until, unable to prevent himself, he cried out. She responded with a low laugh of satisfaction, moving herself against him.

When they were sated, Miriam slept with her head on Simon's great chest, her legs entwined with his, one hand resting on his powerful shoulder. The man lay awake thinking. He only slept for some four hours a night, this son of a slave from Gerasa. He was filled with a grateful wonder for the ecstasy of love, for the sweet strength of his mate's body, and for her sensuous tricks; but he knew that nakedness and lust were sinful.

Miriam had been sold to the theater in Scythopolis by the Greek family which had murdered and dispossessed her own. Even as a young girl, she had possessed a figure of unusual beauty, with a fullness of breast and hip, which left her with a slim, sinuous waist, and long, straight, beautifully curved arms and legs. Her skin, smooth and flawless, was the color of tawny wine. Her almost angular face was not pretty—it possessed a quality of hardness. Her black eyes were angry and her mouth was full and sensual.

Theater was perhaps too grand a word for the disreputable house where Miriam performed; her dancing and that of her companions was more lewd than artistic. The dancers were in a happier situation than the other slaves since they had baths and clean clothes and decent food; but they were expected to perform duties over and above their public ones. Miriam had been the owner's favorite, which did not mean that he used her exclusively—he shared her with favored friends and clients, boasting of her qualities. She grew up with hatred, and the men who came to watch her and lie with her found a disturbing excitement in her fiery hatred, in her total lack of tenderness.

During the period of anarchy which followed the revolt in Jerusalem, anti-Jewish riots were as common in Scythopolis as in the other Greek cities; but later the Jewish bands from the countryside came in night raids to exact retribution. One night a wild horde of rebels had arrived at the barricaded villa of the theater owner. They threw firebrands at the house and set it on fire, slaughtering all who tried to flee. Simon bar Giora had started to enter through the smashed front door, when an elderly matron had emerged, white-faced, her plump frame shaking with fear. As she sank down on her knees before him, begging for mercy, a savage, dark-eyed girl had flung herself on the old woman from behind. Before Simon had been able to move, the old lady was dead, and the wild girl was weeping and holding his hand in a grip so tight it seemed she would never let go.

Early in life Miriam had lost the capacity for love; but she was capable of gratitude, and her ability to please men, for which she was so well equipped, had been highly developed. She was assured and confident, delighting in the youth and virility of her new master.

Simon bar Giora had never known his mother. He remembered his father as a broken old man, working another's fields

156

and praying to an invisible God who would one day send His Messiah to redeem the world. A portion of their miserable rations was always set aside for tithes for the priests, although the men who came to collect their pitiful contributions looked anything but poor.

"Our priests are worse than the Romans!" the young Simon had declared once.

His father had been scandalized. "My son, this is for God's work and for His holy Temple."

"If our God is just," the boy had replied, "He would not want us to starve ourselves to pay for His Temple."

"It is not for you to question the ways of the Lord, Simon."

"I do not question the ways of the Lord, Father; it is the ways of the priests that I question!"

Simon had been a large child and his father's owner had treated him well, seeing in the boy a good investment. But Simon had known that he would never be a slave. His father had converted to the Jewish religion as a slave and from it he had found comfort; but the young Simon had grown up with an idea of the dignity of man, and he could not reconcile slavery with the idea that man had been created in God's image.

While his father had lived, the boy remained loyally by his side, helping the old man with his tasks. When the old man had prayed with the other Jewish slaves, turning toward Jerusalem, Simon had prayed with him. But the night after the burial of his father, he had fled to the bandits, who lived in the mountain caves. Throughout his youth he moved from band to band, being no one's man but his own. He never stayed long in one place. His only companion was a lad named ben Josiah—the son of a fellow slave of his father's—who had deserted with him.

As he grew to his vast size and strength, the germ of the idea that had first come to him as a child developed in his mind: there must be no slaves! He was a simple man, not capable of grasping complicated ideas; but he was tenacious and dogged. He did not allow the idea to leave him—the slaves must be set free; the priests are worse than the Romans; God would

157

not wish us to starve to pay for His Temple!

Wherever he lived, whatever his group, Simon was always the strongest, the quickest, the bravest. But he could not find what he sought. He began to talk as well as fight, and despite his lack of scholarship, he talked well. He talked simply and straight from the heart. Wherever he appeared he drew crowds of slaves and peasants, many of whom afterward joined his group. He knew nothing of organization, of strategy and planning; he knew merely how to talk, how to lead, and how to fight.

It was an undisciplined rabble, with nothing in common except an impulsive devotion to their giant leader, that Simon bar Giora had led to Jerusalem to participate in the revolt; but instinctively he was feeling his way forward. Out of the intrigues between the different rebel groups he could yet emerge as leader, for he was the only one sufficiently adaptable to change his tactics to meet the needs of the day. His greatest disadvantage, the lack of a coherent religious philosophy, was also his greatest asset. With only a few simple general ideas, he was not bound by rigid adherence to a previously forecast plan of action.

Only ben Josiah, his deputy, had remained with him for more than a short time, for Simon shed friends as easily as he acquired them. Ben Josiah, who had fled with him the night after his father's funeral, was a slave and the son of a slave and understood little of religion, though he called himself a Jew. In his mind there was one fixed idea: he had to follow his giant leader, to protect him and fight at his side.

Malachi, Simon's other commander, was quite different. Slender where ben Josiah was broad, temperamental where the slave was stolid, Malachi, an aristocrat, was also a convert, but of a different sort from Simon and his friend. He was driven to expiate the guilt of his past, a past that had betrayed his people for generations.

"The lot of the slave is degrading," he would explain. "But the owner of slaves is a traitor to mankind and to God. He daily despises the image of the Almighty. We must liberate the slave owner no less than the slave!

158

"Once all Israel were slaves, and because of this we have laws for their protection. We are worse than the Gentiles, for they do not know it is wrong. But we were slaves in Egypt. Our laws do not go to the heart of the matter, which is the ownership of one human being by another."

Simon would listen to the young aristocrat attentively. Many of the ideas were beyond his comprehension, but he had a talent for catching a telling phrase and storing it for future use. Unfortunately, Malachi had not yet joined them in the time of the revolt in Jerusalem. Simon often reflected that the young scholar would have been useful in those early days. He could still be useful, though; he could discuss matters of doctrine and belief with Eleazar, matters too complicated for the big leader.

As Simon lay thinking, Miriam stirred beside him. Her body was smooth and warm with sleep. He ran his hand down her strong back and her body arched against his, groping for him instinctively in her sleep. She began to slide over him, her eyes still closed, lips parted, her breath quickening, her hands strong yet soft, doing their wonderfully mysterious work. Instinct took control of his enormous frame and he rolled over on top of her, forcing himself inside her. He drove in again and again, until her strong white teeth bit savagely into his shoulder. Finally bar Giora slept, and Miriam, his woman, slept by his side.

5

Eleazar ben Jair was easier in his mind than bar Giora. He had seen the size of the slave group and its pitiful lack of equipment, and he had ceased worrying. If bar Giora was to prove a threat, it would not be for some time. Even Judah had conceded that an attack on the slave group would be tantamount to murder. It was only a few months since the broken remnants of the Sicarii had struggled leaderless to their fortress. Seeing Simon's group reminded Eleazar of how far they had come since then. Now they were a united, organized community, confident and well-armed, waiting for the opportune time to emerge and play their part. They could afford to wait, reflected Eleazar. He would like to watch developments. As yet it was too early to be sure whether the revolt was indeed the start of the final battle or a mere incident set off by human impulsiveness.

Eleazar lay beside his wife in comfortable intimacy. He ran his finger down the girlish profile of her face, tracing the outline of her delicate features. Her body was small and slender, almost fragile, with soft bones as delicate as a bird's. His two hands could nearly encircle her waist. He could not see her smile in the dark, but his finger traced the curve of her lips, and he kissed her gently on the mouth, his tongue feeling the tiny, shapely teeth.

Hagar was overcome by desire for her husband. She loved his gentleness and suffered with him at the cruelty and violence of his world. Circumstances had forced Eleazar into the role of a ruthless guerrilla leader; but she knew that the real man was the one who had entered the community of the Sons of Zadok in his youth, the gentle pious rabbi. She accepted his absorption in his task, which often caused him to ignore her; she understood that he had dedicated his life to serving the Almighty and to carrying out His purpose—which meant that she, his wife, was merely of secondary interest to him. It would not be true to say that she was free of resentment, but her overwhelming feeling was one of gratitude at being granted a husband such as Eleazar.

Hagar had been born in a small Idumean village only twenty miles from where she now lay. Her people were shepherds, wandering with their flocks of sheep and goats to look for pasture. Her village was built of simple stone houses and possessed a number of water holes. For much of the year, the flocks found nourishment on the surrounding hillsides and notably in the wadis, where the moisture caused the growth of shoots and grasses; but during the long, dry summer, the villagers would pitch their tents in the hills south of Hebron, where there was more water, and the grass, though dry and yellow, grew all year round. They grew crops in the spring, damming

160

the wadis and trapping the runoff water. Even in the summer the dew was heavy, and considerable amounts of water were collected. On those years when the winter rains were plentiful, the desert exploded into color with endless varieties of wild flowers. The villagers would gather the flowers to make perfume, though their modest industry was in no way comparable to that of Ein Gedi, where the water flowed all year.

When Eleazar had led his band in Idumea, he had come frequently to the village, with its curious small stone dwellings, the doors and windows shaped like narrow slits to keep out the sun and wind and dust, and the courtyards built up for the same reason. His band never plundered the small villages, and therefore they were welcome everywhere; there was not a village in Idumea which would refuse to hide them from the Roman or Jewish authorities. When they succeeded in attacking a caravan, or raiding Hebron or one of the larger towns, they would bring grain and oil to the poverty-stricken hamlets of southern Judea.

The people of Hagar's village were third-generation Jews, converted in the reign of Jannai. The tradition said that after the third generation, converts became real Jews, and the good King Agrippa had been acclaimed as "brother" in the Temple by the Jews of Jerusalem. Eleazar would come and eat at the table of Hagar's father. Sometimes he was preoccupied, his forehead creased with frowns and his eyes far away; but at other times he would look at the slender, dark girl who modestly busied herself with the cooking pots, her scarf held in her teeth covering the lower half of her face, revealing only her dark, orblike eyes. When she walked, carrying a jar on her head in the fashion of the desert people, it was with a remarkable grace, her slender frame upright, her hips moving almost imperceptibly. Once the scarf had fallen from her mouth, revealing a smile of dazzling sweetness. Eleazar had hastily turned his attention to her father, but his regard for her grew. She was always nearby when he visited, and he visited with increasing frequency.

One day he had passed through the village with fifty men and a train of camels loaded with strange, unfamiliar bundles,

161

and then he did not appear for several months; Hagar heard there had been fighting in the Roman fortress above the Sea of Salt. When he came again, he looked older, and his brown hair and beard were streaked with gray. There was pain in his eyes and the creases on his forehead were permanent; but he was still Eleazar the son of Jair, the rabbi who came armed but who sat at the table to study the Law with her father.

This time he had come and asked her father for his daughter's hand in marriage. He had brought a ring, a simple band of gold, which he had slipped onto her finger during a brief ceremony. There had been no feast, for the land was troubled and it was not a time for feasting; but the feast had been in Hagar's heart, as they sat at her father's table in his small stone house.

Eleazar had taken her to the fortress, where she had lived in the strange northern palace built by the mad king Herod. She kept house for her husband, for although he was the leader of the community, he would have no servants. She watched him as he studied the Law, teaching himself so that he could teach others.

She would sit in the shade of the vast rock which towered above her to the summit, and in the cool breeze she would look north across the bleak plain, where the red soil and flint rock merged with the strange chalk formations surrounding the Sea of Salt. She watched the sea, its blue changing color with the seasons and the time of the day. She would look north to the splash of green that was Ein Gedi, west to the direction of her father's home on the high Judean plateau, or east to the purple mountains of Moab across the sea. South of Moab lay Edom, where her own people had originated, when Esau had sold Jacob his birthright for the *adom* which gave his descendents their name—Adomites or Edomites. Now the Edomites had returned to reclaim their birthright as Idumeans, and the family of Antipater had stolen back that which had been stolen from them. Later the mad Herod had ruled with an iron hand for thirty years, and the well-loved Agrippa for a mere four. Esau and Jacob had reunited—the two peoples could live as one.

162

In the mornings Hagar could hardly make out the land of Moab, but as the day wore on, its mountains were revealed in a misty blue that merged with the sky. As the sun slipped slowly over the desert of Judea, the mountains became increasingly visible, until in the afternoon they stood out in harsh magnificence, the purple shadows of their cliffs contrasting with the mauve of the more distant summits.

Autumn had passed and winter came, with rain falling from an angry sky. The wadis around the rock frothed and seethed, and the waterways flowed with water, filling the cisterns. The wonderful creations of Herod's engineers directed the water into the rock, into its secret pools and pockets, into its gigantic man-made cisterns. The rock was like a great sponge as it sucked up the water which fell from the sky.

Hagar lay beside her husband, her slender arms around him. She kissed him and he returned her affection; they lay in the dark and caressed each other gently and lovingly. She thought that she was going to burst with joy and happiness. When they finally came together with unbelievable sweetness, their love was heightened by the knowledge that they were creating a new life in their union.

6

The morning prayers had ended; but Eleazar remained in the large section of the northwestern casemate, which faced Jerusalem. The same room had been used for prayer since the evening service on the day the fortress was captured. The Roman garrison had used the room as a stable; but it had been used for prayer during the time of Agrippa, Eleazar recalled. The Sicarii had decided to rebuild the place as a synagogue. They were putting in a new floor and constructing stone benches around the walls. Stones were being carried up from the central tier of the northern palace for the purpose; the men sweated, dragging the heavy blocks of flint up the winding stairway. Typically, the weather had changed suddenly and had become mild. The workers were red-faced with their effort in the heat. For a time Eleazar helped them push the heavy rocks into place, before leaving them to visit the center of the plateau, where Joab was working.

In the middle of the plateau there was a large but shallow pool where the rain had collected, and on the slopes surrounding it Joab had planted vegetables. The rains had benefited the crop, and the green shoots were already visible; but the weeds too had flourished and the workers were having to spend many hours of backbreaking toil to keep them under control.

Joab had joined the Sicarii party comparatively late in life. He had been a small-scale but prosperous farmer in a village not far from Jerusalem. Gradually the taxes and the tithes had reduced his living, for there was no room for the small farmer in the Roman colony of Judea. Increasingly the peasants and the smallholders were forced off the land for the benefit of the large estates. Rather than join the general aimless drift to Jerusalem, Joab had joined the Sicarii.

Although a devout Jew, he had for many years regarded the outlaw groups as criminals and troublemakers; but finally he was forced to acknowledge the rightness of their cause. He had become an underground leader of outstanding bravery— his name, Joab, had taken the place of his real name in recognition of this. But he was happiest when ploughing, weeding, or working in some activity connected with growing food. At Masada he was back in his natural element, and he seemed to be achieving remarkable results.

Joab waved a cheery greeting to Eleazar as the latter approached from the synagogue. He indicated the western palace, where bar Giora's followers were housed, with a sideways movement of the head and raised his fiery eyebrows.

"They have not stirred yet," Eleazar answered the unasked question.

"I can believe that they are exhausted," said Joab. "It is a wonder they arrived at all."

"They have posted sentries," Eleazar told him in an undertone.

"Very sensible," said the other. "He cannot afford to take any chances, but we can behave normally. We must simply

164

continue our daily activities as though nothing had happened. The men have already been too confined during the rain."

"I agree," said Eleazar. "Nothing could be worse than to allow our two groups to brood in idleness. Keep an eye on the palace, though."

Eleazar continued his tour of duty. On the eastern casemate, some of the newer families who had arrived before the rain were continuing with the preparation of their living quarters, dividing the sections into small rooms and constructing ovens of earth. To the south of the vegetable plots were the pens for the livestock, supervised by Rivka, Menahem's widow. A number of young women, among them Hagar, were milking the goats. Hagar worked efficiently, her dainty hands stroking the milk from the swollen teats with a practiced rhythm.

"I hope we can graze the animals before too long," said Rivka.

"It should be possible in the spring," he suggested. "It is only the weather that prevents us. There is no threat from the Romans or from the other groups."

"I am more worried about internal sabotage," remarked the old woman ominously.

"Bar Giora?" Eleazar was surprised. "I thought you were in favor of granting them shelter!"

"Nonsense!" Rivka made an angry gesture with her hand, as if brushing off a troublesome fly. "I am not talking of bar Giora. I leave the childish war nonsense to the men. I am concerned with Nahum bar Eleazar!"

"What about Nahum?" asked her nephew, feigning innocence.

"You know well, my boy—his obstinate refusal to give me enough food for the animals puts the whole livestock section in jeopardy."

"He must look after the interests of the stores; it is his task to see that we use as little as possible."

"It is not his job to talk nonsense," countered the woman. "He tells me that the humans must be supplied first and only then the animals. How can the humans eat if the animals do

165

not? From where shall we obtain milk? How will we have meat for the Sabbath meal?"

"The humans also complain of shortages," replied Eleazar. "We do not know how long we shall be here. We must conserve the supplies as long as possible and avoid indulgence."

"Nonsense, I say again," insisted Rivka. "There are three enormous storerooms stuffed with pulse—"

"Pulse is a most important food," he interrupted her. "Joab explained to us that it is very nourishing."

"There is no doubt," insisted the old woman, "that the animals should receive more than they are getting at present."

"I will speak to Nahum, Aunt," Eleazar promised her. He smiled at his wife, who had been listening to the conversation with ill-concealed amusement, and set off immediately for the stores.

As he approached the stores, Eleazar could hear the sounds of an argument. A shrill voice shouted, "Your wife does not manage with one small jar for the whole week. She receives a jar each day, while my family starves!"

"Everyone receives the same," answered Nahum good-naturedly. "You are most welcome to come to our home and see for yourself."

"I do not need to," retorted the woman. "It is obvious that if you are in charge here you will give her more. My husband would do the same, it is natural; but at least give me enough for my family's needs."

Eleazar approached, unnoticed by the disputants. He stood silently, watching the argument. The woman was one of the newer arrivals, a thin, sharp-faced girl prematurely aged by too much childbearing. Her nose stood out like a beak, and there were lines around her mouth as if she were permanently sucking a lemon. She presented somewhat of a contrast to the jovial, open-faced Nahum, his brick-red face framed by his bleached blond hair and beard. Nahum's easy temperament was ideally suited to his job as storeman, which was one of the hardest and most responsible in the community. Few of the women could resist his banter and his ready smile, and even the men were charmed by his openness and honesty. Though attempting to dissuade the families from withdrawing too much, he ensured that each family had a minimum of necessities.

Supplies could be bought for money or vouchers. Only very few of the arrivals at Masada possessed any money; but those who could were expected to buy their supplies until their money ran out. Vouchers of sherds marked with ink were issued against livestock or other items of value brought to the community. The destitute were simply issued free vouchers. In this way no one was allowed to starve; but the voucher system helped to ensure against hoarding or excessive withdrawals. In a general way, supplies were issued according to the size of the family. In return, the able-bodied members of the family were expected to work, stand guard, and perform any communal duties asked of them. Records of each family's original contributions were kept to enable a fair assessment of their rights in the event that they chose to leave later. The system fell far short of the rigid communalism that Eleazar had grown up with at Sekaka, but it was better suited to Masada.

"My dear lady, I promise you that we receive our weekly portion of oil like any other family!" Nahum clasped his hands together in a gesture of mock sincerity.

"This is a serious matter," snapped the woman, unamused. Eleazar decided to intervene.

"What is the trouble?" he inquired. The woman spun around.

"Rabbi, I do not mind how much he takes for himself—anyone would do the same; but I must have enough."

"She received the normal ration," said Nahum. "She does not understand that if I distribute too much we shall run out of oil, and then where shall we be?"

"What is your name?" Eleazar asked the woman. His voice was grave and considerate.

"Naomi, Rabbi, the wife of Yoezer." Toward Eleazar the woman had adopted an effusive attitude, which did not suit her.

"When did you arrive in our community?"

"Before the rains."

"We all receive the same here, according to the size of our families. Your jar is a large one because you have a large family. I receive far less myself. You must make it last, as we all do. Now bring your jar and Nahum will let you have some more." The woman looked doubtful and uncertain. "Where is your jar?" asked Eleazar. "You cannot receive supplies without containers—you know that."

"The jar is broken, Rabbi," confessed the woman. "One of the children knocked it over. There are so many of us."

"Why did you not tell me?" demanded Nahum.

"You never get your rights by telling the truth," complained the woman. "You cannot tell me—only those who know how to make a fuss get what they want."

"Not here!" said Eleazar decisively. "We live differently here. We do not give in to bullying, and everyone receives their just requirements. You will be given a new jar full of oil."

"That is correct," affirmed Nahum.

"What shall I pay with?" The woman was incredulous.

"You need not pay. Take care in the future to conserve everything. The food belongs to all of us. I believe your husband is working with Joab."

"Yes, Rabbi, he works with the red beard." She was eager to please.

"Well, if they are successful, we should have fresh vegetables in the spring. The children will have priority with regard to the fresh food as they do with milk."

"Yes, Rabbi; thank you, Rabbi."

"Do not thank me, Naomi," replied Eleazar gently. "You are entitled to your share if you have come to join us. If you think there is something unfair, your husband can mention it at the weekly meeting."

"Yes, Rabbi." The woman's thin face softened and she smiled at Eleazar before leaving.

"In half an hour I will have a new jar ready for you," Nahum told her. He turned to Eleazar. "She has no sense of humor, that one," he complained.

"You cannot use your market-day chaff on all of them, Nahum. Some of them are not amused. I know Hagar loves it, but that does not mean that they all do."

"How was I to know that she had spilled the cursed oil?" he asked.

"You were not to know," admitted Eleazar. "But you might have guessed. She was so eager to justify herself and to accuse others that you might have guessed at a guilty conscience."

"I am afraid that I do not possess your understanding."

"Oh, it is a matter of experience mostly. I grew up at Sekaka, so I have seen a good deal of communal living. Of course, among the Sons of Zadok that woman could have been most severely punished for the aspersions she cast on your character."

"It would be a good idea to introduce a few more of their ideas here!"

Eleazar laughed and shook his head. "We could never organize life here as they did. The Sons of Zadok are a highly dedicated and specialized group. There is nothing special about our community, though. We are just an ordinary group of people who happen to believe in freedom. You heard what that woman said—you only obtain your rights by making a noise. That is the bitter lesson that life has taught her. We have to make her understand that it is different here. We are lucky to have supplies enough for years. The real test will come if we do run short, and of course it is your business to see that we do not."

"We can continue to live here for years, thanks to old man Herod," said Nahum, scratching his blond beard. "With the livestock and the fresh vegetables, the prospect is limitless."

"I want to have the herds grazing outside in the spring," said Eleazar. "But I want us to remain self-sufficient on the summit, if need be."

"I am sure it is possible," affirmed the other.

"That brings me to the problem of the animals," said Eleazar.

"Problem?" asked Nahum in a puzzled manner.

Eleazar laughed and prodded him in the stomach with his forefinger. "You know perfectly well what I am speaking about, you rogue," chuckled Eleazar. "I promised the old girl that I would have a word with you."

169

"She is an old witch!" stated Nahum. "I have more trouble with her beasts than I have with the humans."

"I think that we are lucky to have her," said Eleazar.

Nahum shook his blond head. "I am never too sure whether or not we are," he confessed.

"She is wonderful with the animals," Eleazar pointed out. "None of the men has her feeling for the beasts. How many women could organize the care of the livestock on such a scale?"

"Why cannot each family look after its own animals as usual?"

"It is not practical here. There is not enough space and they would fall off the edge all the time. They are safer penned up in the center."

"That is true, I suppose," conceded Nahum. "We really ought to do something similar for the children. I am terrified that some of them are going to fall."

"It is certainly not a suitable location in which to bring up children," said Eleazar. "I do not see an easy answer to the problem. The families would never agree to part with them as at Sekaka. Eternal vigilance is the answer, but that is one of those things that is a lot easier to say than to carry out."

"What did Herod do, I wonder," mused Nahum.

"He had hundreds of servants to do the watching," replied Eleazar. "Anyway, I doubt if it worried him very much. If they fell off Masada, it would save him the job of killing them later on!"

"He was certainly a raving lunatic," said Nahum. "Yet no one but a lunatic could have created all this." His gesture took in the summit of the rock, its wall, towers, palaces, villas and storerooms, the bathhouse and the cisterns.

"It was a mad extravagance," agreed Eleazar. "The ways of the Lord are strange. Who knows whether it was His purpose to cause the murderer of Hezekiah of Galilee to build this fortress so that Hezekiah's grandson could capture it more than a century later."

As he returned to his own quarters, Eleazar thought about his two brothers. He had inspected the guards, commanded by

Judah, and visited his younger brother, Simon, who was organizing the water detail. The water-carrying was sheer drudgery, but Eleazar was determined to maintain it regularly. It was the only way to ensure the summit was always left with an adequate reserve. Simon had taken on the responsibility with pride, and his young team worked with enthusiasm and persistence. The path from the lower cisterns to the summit was steep and narrow, and the jars were heavy; but they were not daunted.

Something had happened to Judah during the time Eleazar was at Sekaka. In retrospect Eleazar blamed himself for not remaining with his younger brothers. But he had been young at the time, and he had felt that his responsibility had ended when he had delivered them safe and sound to his uncle. There had been a barrier between him and Judah. Judah had despised Eleazar's scholastic temperament, Eleazar had been alarmed at Judah's lack of learning. An attempt to convince his brother of the value of study, coupled with a reminder of the nature of their late father, had led to a violent argument between them. With Simon, Eleazar had managed to retain some rapport, though the youngster followed Judah in all things. Since the capture of Masada, their relationship had even improved, for Simon had seen with his own eyes the evidence of Eleazar's fighting prowess and leadership. Simon still loved him but Judah hated him, and Eleazar was forced to admit to himself that he could not bring himself to like Judah. There was a hard, alien quality about the boy which had not been evident in Menahem nor even in the ruthless Absalom—a total lack of fear, an assurance in battle that almost amounted to enjoyment. Judah seemed fulfilled in fighting. It was hard to remember that he was a son of Jair.

It was afternoon. The purple shadows deepened on the mountains of Moab and the sky was a luminous yellow. A cool breeze blew, which some of the younger members of the community enjoyed as they sat out in the open air. Most of the families were in their own homes, prior to going to the synagogue for evening prayers.

Nahum was tumbling with his boys in the straw which covered the cold mosaic floor of his room by the stores.

"How tall were the elephants that the Greeks brought against Judah the Maccabee?" Uri asked his father. "As tall as you?"

David roared with laughter, amused at his younger brother's naiveté. "Much bigger, Uri. Elephants are much bigger than Daddy. They are bigger than camels, even!"

"Bigger than camels, Daddy?" Uri was not convinced. David laughed again.

"David is quite right," confirmed Nahum. "They are as tall as this room!"

"As tall as the room?" Uri's question ended in an excited screech.

"Yes, really."

"I never in my life saw anything so big!" exclaimed the five-year-old. Nahum and David laughed together, but then David turned seriously to his father.

"Were the Maccabees good people, Daddy?" he asked.

"Of course they were good—they were great heroes of our people."

"Rachel told me that only Matthew and Judah were good. She said that Jonathan and Simon were bad because they became priests."

"It is difficult to explain, David. They were all good; but Jonathan and Simon made mistakes later on. Nobody is perfect; even David the King was a very wicked man sometimes."

Uri was bored by all the talk. "Let us play Maccabees, Daddy, come on," he suggested. "You be the elephant, I will be the Greek, Lys ... Lys—"

"Lysias," said his father.

"Lysias, yes. David can be Eleazar," said Uri generously.

"Could our Eleazar kill an elephant?" asked David.

"I expect that he could," replied Nahum, "But he would have more sense than to try. Eleazar the Maccabee was very brave and strong, but he was not really very clever."

"Why not?" demanded David.

"He wanted to show that elephants could be killed like any other animal, because the Jews were frightened of them. But

172

as it turned out, he himself was killed as well as the elephant, and the people were even more frightened at losing a Maccabee."

"Come on now, David," interjected Uri. "If we do not start, I am not going to be Lysias." Nahum went down on his hands and knees and maneuvered about for some minutes with his youngest son on his back. Uri sat astride his father, excitedly waiting for his brother to attack.

Joab sat at his table peering at a scroll in the dim light of an oil lamp. He was not a good student, but he was conscientious. He would sit for hours in front of a piece of parchment, but his thoughts tended to wander. His vivid red hair and beard had become streaked with gray during the past year. He looked over to the earthen oven, where his wife, Sarah, was preparing the evening meal, assisted by Shifra, their eldest daughter. His wife was a small, slender woman, prematurely gray, with a delicate face and soft brown eyes. Her appearance was deceptive, for she was a woman of strong character. Her angularity was not repeated in her daughter, a striking red-haired girl who already possessed a well-rounded body. Freckles covered most of her face and arms, and her green eyes had rust flecks in them.

Her two younger sisters were playing with a weaving loom in the corner. They were smaller editions of Shifra, though their hair was not quite so vivid a color. At that moment they were laughing a great deal about something.

"What are you doing, you two?" Shifra's voice contained a note of exasperation.

"It does not matter." Sarah's voice was calm. "They cannot do any harm."

"You underestimate them, Mother!" She strode over to her younger sisters. "What are you giggling about?"

"Nothing, Shifra," replied Rachel, aged eleven. Her last word ended in a snicker, and the two girls shrieked hysterically.

"Come on, tell me what you are giggling about!"

"Leave them alone, Shifra," said her mother. "They are only

173

young and stupid; you were like that once."

"I could not have been; I do not believe it."

"Bar Nottos, bar Nottos, Simon bar Nottos!" the two younger girls chanted and collapsed again, giggling. Shifra seized Rachel's hair and pulled it hard. The latter gave a squeal of pain.

"Why me?" she squealed plaintively.

"You are the elder; Deborah only learns from you."

"Let go!" shouted Rachel. "You are horrible." Her sister released the hair reluctantly. "Oh, my head aches now," she exclaimed.

"It will teach you not to interfere in matters that do not concern you."

"Ooh—matters that do not concern you." Rachel wrinkled her face, trying to imitate her sister. She and Deborah burst out in a fit of renewed giggles. Shifra advanced on her again and Rachel ran behind her father.

"Now stop it this minute, girls. Stop it I say!" Joab was singularly inept at dealing with his three daughters. He could lead a guerrilla raid more effectively than anyone in Judea, but he was incapable of imposing the most rudimentary discipline on the three girls.

Rachel clung to her father for protection. "Help, Daddy," she laughed breathlessly. "Keep that wildcat away from me!"

"She started it, Daddy," complained Shifra, almost in tears from frustration.

"I did not!"

"Yes, you did!"

"No!"

"Liar!"

"I only said Simon bar Nottos," Rachel giggled. "What is wrong with saying Simon bar Nottos? I shall say it if I want to."

Joab opened and closed his mouth ineffectually. "Er, I think ... that is, Rachel, I think. ..."

"Simon bar Nottos, Simon bar Nottos!"

"Please, Rachel. Have you read your portion of the Law today?" Joab asked desperately. Shifra was edging around the

table toward Rachel, and Joab was trying to hold them apart.
"That is enough!" The command was like the lash of a whip.
Sarah had decided that matters had gone far enough. She
bundled her protesting younger daughters from the room.
Shifra was in tears. "They are driving me crazy," she com-
plained.

"Do not mind them, love." Sarah's voice was soft, very different from that of a moment before. "They are merely young
girls; you were the same."

"I could not have been so beastly," she laughed, wet-eyed.

There was a knock on the door and Eleazar entered. Joab
stood up to greet him.

"Welcome, Eleazar, you have come to share our evening
meal?"

"No. I have only come for a moment. I wanted to know what
you thought about the first day."

"To tell you the truth," said Joab, "I had forgotten all about
Simon bar Giora. I think that is a good sign."

"Yes, I think we were overly suspicious," said Eleazar. "Of
course we must remain on our guard."

"Certainly," agreed Joab. "But I maintain that his joining us
is a positive development."

"We shall see," replied Eleazar. "His attitude is certainly
friendly; but I find myself concerned about him."

"In what way?" asked Joab.

"A way I find difficult to define," admitted Eleazar.

7

Judah grinned with satisfaction as he looked down from the
cliffs at the prosperous village of Ein Gedi, busy with its preparations for Passover. The little figures below strode about self-
importantly, making ready to celebrate the liberation of the
Israelites from slavery. There will be a liberation, thought
Judah. They would find out soon enough. He breathed deeply,
as untroubled by the heat as he had been by the cold three
months before.

The unsuspecting village was entirely surrounded. Judah

175

was situated in the cliffs to the west, Eleazar had worked his way around through the hills to the north, Joab was advancing along the ridge from the south, and bar Giora was approaching northward along the shore of the Sea of Salt. Judah was glad to be in action again—he had fretted too long at Masada. He needed excitement. He was not content to study like Eleazar, or work like Joab, or organize like Nahum. Fighting was his life; it had been so ever since he could remember. Rivka thought that bloodshed was evil; Eleazar regarded it as a painful necessity; even for bar Giora, fighting was merely a means to obtain what he wanted. But Judah liked fighting. Battle was for him a sublime experience.

Bar Nottos approached silently.

"Is everyone in position?" Judah asked him.

"Yes."

"Are you certain they can all make the descent?"

"Quite sure; it is easier than it looks."

"You are taking into consideration the fact that we are carrying arms?"

"Yes."

"And that we have to descend with the greatest speed to ensure that we do not arrive too late?"

"Too late for what?"

"For the battle."

"I thought that our task was to cut off their retreat."

"Our task is to attack that nest of collaborators and smite them with all our force!" Judah felt himself becoming angry.

Joab had been the first to arrive at his position, as his route was the most direct. He looked across at the village, a green patch in the dun-colored expanse of desert, the little farms clustered around the various water channels. From where he lay the waterfall was invisible, but he had seen it enough times to be able to imagine it gushing down into the pool ringed by cool, green fronds. He took a small sip from his waterskin.

Joab was not entirely happy about the attack. He did not like the idea of assaulting a defenseless Jewish village, whose inhabitants included women and children. Although Judah was

176

always urging action, he reflected, it had been bar Giora who had maneuvered them into the present position. It was true that Ein Gedi was contemptible. The villagers had played no part in the revolt, but had continued their daily lives as if nothing had happened. They had ploughed their fields, harvested their crops, including the famous flowers, and distilled their perfumes. Prices had risen because of the revolt and the difficulties of transport; but the villagers of Ein Gedi had taken advantage of the rise in prices to raise them still further, profiting from the struggle of their countrymen without making any sacrifice themselves. They were certainly contemptible, but that was a long way from saying that every man, woman, and child in the village was fit only to be slaughtered. He agreed with bar Giora that the slaves should be freed, but he did not agree that to facilitate this a full-scale attack was needed.

Joab could see the fields clearly from where he lay in the shade to the south of the village. It had taken the work of generations of farmers to create this miracle in the wilderness; Joab especially could appreciate that. Family after family had inherited the land and the water rights to the crystal stream. They had worked hard to improve the land and its yield. No other grapes in Judea were as sweet as those from the vines of Ein Gedi; nor was there any perfume to compare with that produced from the exotic flowers which flourished in this unusual region, where hot sun and water existed in abundance. It had taken generations to create, but it could all be destroyed in a few hours. Joab removed his helmet and felt better; it was oppressively hot. His men were in their positions, waiting for dusk.

Simon bar Giora saw the issue simply: the village was an abomination. It had not lifted a finger to aid the revolt, and it was based on slavery. Slaves had built the water conduits and dug the irrigation channels. Slaves built the fires, collected the fuel, harvested the flowers, and stirred the caldrons which created the wealth of that jewel in the desert. They had to be liberated, and their enslavers destroyed. Passover, the festival of freedom and liberation of the slaves, would this year see the

177

freeing of yet another group of degraded human beings. The attack on Ein Gedi would also be an important stage in the development of the revolution; the Masada power base would be extended northward. It was bar Giora's plan to expand it gradually westward, too, throughout Idumea and into southern Judea, until the whole of the southern part of the country was under the dominance of the united Sicarii-slave group at Masada.

The progress of the legions through the north of the country had caused him to discount Galilee as a factor for the present; but once the south was in his hands, he could strike at the capital. As he marched west toward Ein Gedi from the Sea of Salt, his commanders, Malachi and ben Josiah, by his side, bar Giora looked with pride at his company. They were fewer in number than most of the groups he had led recently, but superior in training and equipment. He and Eleazar were a natural alliance: together they would advance toward the liberation of Judea.

As bar Giora's group moved to take up their positions only a few hundred yards from the village, the wind dropped. All morning it had been blowing steadily from the east—a hot, dry wind from the mountains of Moab across the Sea of Salt, caressing them with its breath of fire. Now the air was oppressively still; the clouds in the sky were motionless. The sun beat down, a hard, tangible bar of glaring heat. Beneath his tunic, Simon's big body ran with sweat. He spat in the dust, trying to rid his mouth of the bitter taste of the Sea of Salt carried to them by the wind.

Malachi was positioned to the left of bar Giora, his thin face set in determination, his sparse brown beard damp with perspiration. Ben Josiah, solid and firm, was over on the right. All around them, concealed in the shrubs and stunted trees, were the men who would make up the nucleus of the future Judean army. Bar Giora thought ahead to possible alliances with the Parthians and the Nabateans; there was no limit to what he might achieve.

Eleazar had led his party up the canyon to the west of the

village and around to the north. In view of the difficulty of the climb, his brother Simon had brought the other half of their group separately along the same route an hour later. Eleazar's men were lightly armed like Judah's to facilitate climbing; Joab and bar Giora, who had the more direct approaches, led the heavily armed men.

Ein Gedi had to be neutralized, Eleazar had decided. The village was a loyalist stronghold that straddled all the main routes between Jerusalem and Masada. It was true that hitherto it had given no trouble and that the Sicarii had always managed to avoid passing close enough to make contact; but if the Romans or even the Jewish central authorities in Jerusalem decided to attack Masada, Ein Gedi would be the base for launching the assault. Eleazar had not accepted the argument of the bar Giora group that it was their duty to liberate the Ein Gedi slaves. There were no slaves at Masada, and since the time of Judah the Sicarii movement had opposed slavery; but liberating the slaves of Ein Gedi came very low on Eleazar's list of priorities. However, he had been persuaded that the attack was necessary to safeguard the security of his community. As he waited for darkness, Eleazar reflected that his real reasons for deciding to proceed were perhaps more complicated. His apprehensions concerning the bar Giora group had proved to be justified, but not in a manner that he could have predicted.

8

Simon bar Giora and his group had been quickly absorbed into the Masada community. His deputy ben Josiah had collected an additional two hundred of the former band and brought them back to the rock. The newcomers contributed their skills to the community. A kiln was built for firing clay jars locally, and a group of leather workers started up a tannery, turning out leather for every purpose from scrolls to sandals. Several of the women were skilled with livestock and reinforced Rivka's team. Within a short time the new group was entirely submerged, and its members indistinguishable from the others.

The prohibition on arms and admittance to the northern palace complex was quickly rescinded as it had become an anachronism. There was no point, concluded Eleazar, in maintaining a proportion of the defending force permanently underequipped.

Bar Giora became one of the commanders, deferring in all things to the leader. Never by word or gesture did he challenge Eleazar's authority. Malachi, the former aristocrat, would take an active part in the study circle, often disputing with Eleazar, or notably with Rivka, on points of law; but Simon confined himself to asking questions. He was learning in his customary manner, absorbing the feel and the sound of the Sicarii ideal, without comprehending every detail.

Almost despite himself, though, he began to collect a following. Simply by being who he was, he drew people to him. Judah was attracted to him despite his former hostility, and he began to talk to him, urging on him the need for action; but he was given no encouragment. With the Roman advance through Galilee and the civil strife in Jerusalem, the stream of fugitives to Masada increased, until the new arrivals outnumbered the Sicarii and slaves together.

A carpet of golden and purple flowers on the summit of Masada heralded the spring, and the desert burst into life as the winter rains took effect. The camels stood out with unwonted clarity against the suddenly green hills, and the sheep grazed in the surrounding area. The closed-in feeling of the winter months had lessened with the enlargement of the community, and now it disappeared altogether. There was no action in southern Judea; but as they heard about events in the rest of the country, the desire to participate grew once more.

Eleazar shied away from precipitate action. He had before him constantly the lesson of Menahem ben Judah and his premature advance on the capital, leading to its disastrous result. For Eleazar the issues were larger than simply fighting the Romans. Like his uncle before him, he was convinced that the final battle between good and evil was due; he wanted to be certain before he moved, but the certainty he sought would not come.

On the other hand, bar Giora knew exactly what he wanted. He had a logical plan of action, which led from Masada via Ein Gedi to Idumea, and from there to southern Judea and the capital itself. His ambitious ideas appealed to many, even among the Sicarii veterans. They had fought all their lives for Judean independence and were now ready to offer their loyalty to a man who showed them a plan for its attainment. Judah was becoming open in his scorn for his elder brother, and Simon ben Jair, though loyal to Eleazar, found himself increasingly impatient with the latter's inaction. The defection of Judah did not surprise the Sicarii leader, but that of his younger brother pained him deeply. To Eleazar, Simon was still a child, and he felt like a father toward him.

It was Judah who gave open expression to the rift in the community.

"We are tired of waiting!" he stated at the weekly meeting. "Menahem also made us wait; but then we knew why we waited. When the time came we marched to Jerusalem."

"Menahem is dead," replied Eleazar. "He was my uncle too, and I loved him no less than you; but the Lord allowed him to die. I do not know the reason. Perhaps he did not wait long enough."

"What are we waiting for now?" demanded Judah. "For the Messiah? For some priest in Sekaka who does not know what to do himself?"

"The priest of the Sons of Zadok is the legitimate high priest of Israel; do you dare mock him?"

"Who do you belong to, Brother—the Sicarii or the Sons of Zadok?"

"To both!" Eleazar's answer produced a shocked silence. He continued, "Menahem wanted me to bring unity to our movements. We are both heirs of the Pious Ones. Menahem accepted the Priest of Sekaka and rejected claims to a messiahship based on his rumored descent from Sheshbazzar the prince. I do not know whether Menahem was mistaken or not, but I do know this: Menahem's only wish was to carry out the purpose of the Almighty. He did not knowingly confuse his own ambitions with this desire. I can only strive to do the same."

181

The dispute had raged late into the night, and all eyes had focused on the huge man who sat next to Eleazar, his small head resting on his hand. He stroked his balding pate and pulled at his unruly black beard, while all waited for him to speak. Finally, Eleazar turned to him in exasperation.

"What does Simon bar Giora think?" he demanded. "Why does he sit in silence while his followers question my authority?"

"There is no dispute between us, Rabbi," answered the big man. "I am a novice in rebellion; you are the grandson of Judah of Galilee. I pray to Almighty God only with difficulty; you are a learned teacher. You know about the kingdom of God which is to be set up on earth, but I know nothing of this. I agreed to follow you, and that is my only wish. But I suggest that we must regain the leadership of the revolt so treacherously stolen from the rightful leader, Menahem.

"We both made mistakes on the last occasion. You relied on too small a group; I relied on numbers, but mine was an untrained mob. Both of us can learn from our mistakes. The priests and aristocrats will not outwit us a second time!"

"What is your proposal?" Eleazar was tired after sleepless nights of worry.

"Galilee is falling," commenced the slave leader. "Even Placidus is nearly unopposed. Can you envisage what will happen when Vespasian arrives with the legions? Galilee is lost and I ask myself why.

"Are the Galileans not patriots and fighters? Was Judah of Galilee not a Galilean, and Hezekiah his father? How many of your Sicarii are from there? I myself am from Gerasa to the east of Galilee and I know the people; I know John ben Levi and I know he is no coward. Why then is Galilee not resisting? The answer is simple: treachery. Not straightforward treason, but a treachery so devious as to be almost imperceptible. Joseph is the commander in Galilee, appointed by the central authorities in Jerusalem. He spends more time intriguing against John than preparing for defense. The same thing is happening all over Judea—you heard what happened in the attack on Ashkelon. Traitors command Jerusalem, men who are ready to sell out to Rome as soon as they receive the right price. I admit that I was wrong in Jerusalem; but I have learned my lesson. All the true patriots must now unite to drive the traitors from the capital!

"The first step is to control the south. We must extend our power northward. We have to advance gradually, step by step. Our first move should be to wipe out Ein Gedi, that loyalist stronghold only a few miles away. We have let them be too long. Slavery exists there on our doorstep to this very day. Passover is upon us; let this Passover be memorable for the freeing of another group of slaves!"

"I do not believe that your plan is a wise one," replied Eleazar. "Ein Gedi's slaves are no concern of ours. Our main task is the war against Rome, not adding to the civil war that is already raging among the Jews."

"You must see the connection," exclaimed Malachi. "When you destroy slavery, you undermine the power of Rome, which rests on slavery. The whole empire could be up in arms."

"We are concerned with Judea, not the empire," said Eleazar. "It is difficult enough to manage our force here, let alone lead an uprising of the whole empire. I do not want us to become diffuse or our group to become unwieldy. Our movement is the instrument of the Lord; it must remain a sharp instrument!"

"I said I had learned my lesson," said the big man, "and I have. But have you learned yours, Eleazar? My overinflated group was as vulnerable as your small elite, but together we can conquer Judea."

The discussion continued for more than an hour. It was the shrewd Malachi, not unlike Eleazar in build and manner, who brought forth the clinching argument.

"To defend Masada," he said, "we must attack Ein Gedi."

"Why are you so late, my love?" Hagar's voice was sleepy when Eleazar returned from the fateful meeting in the early hours of the morning. Her husband shivered as he climbed in beside her. He was tense with worry. "You are so cold!" exclaimed the girl, folding her soft, warm arms and legs about him.

He buried his face in her neck and took her in his arms; but the chill would not leave him and he continued to shiver.

"What is wrong, my husband?"

"We have decided to go to war again." He told her of the meeting and of the decision, of the way the discussion had developed. "I was convinced by Malachi's argument, but I do not think that was the real reason," Eleazar admitted. "It is true that Ein Gedi is a threat to us. It is a loyalist village, and all the routes from Jerusalem to us lead through Ein Gedi. But the real reason is that the men are becoming impatient. Before Simon came, they had no alternative; now they have—there is no avoiding the fact."

As he spoke the tension eased out of him; slowly he relaxed into the soft warmth of her body, and soon he slept. He woke again an hour later and they made love softly and gently. He pressed himself against her small body, seeking her warmth and serenity, finally falling asleep in her arms.

9

Eleazar took his pitch-coated arrow and plunged it into the heart of the fire. It caught fire and flared vividly; fitting it quickly to his bow, he fired it into the air toward the village. The arrow traced its fiery path through the night sky and fell on the thatched roof of one of the houses. Within a minute the roof was ablaze and the night rang with sound. Bar Giora's force was first in the village, according to plan. The big man made straight for the slave quarters, which he was able to find quickly in the confusion. Meanwhile, Judah, who had descended the western cliff in the last hours of daylight in defiance of orders, arrived with his group. More fire arrows had followed Eleazar's, and many of the buildings were burning. Judah's men seized burning brands from the fires and began to set fire to those buildings as yet untouched.

The villagers were taken completely by surprise. There was uproar and total panic as they started to flee in all directions, finding their exit blocked at every turn. With the whole village ablaze, the flames licking skyward into the night sky, the rebel force lost all restraint. The pent-up frustrations of six months' isolation on the rock were released in an orgy of slaughter. Women and children, even the old, were shown no mercy. Families were trapped in their houses while they burned down over them. The rebels were screaming no less than the villagers as they struck about them in blind hatred, destroying all that was in their path.

"Murderers! Bandits! Cowards!" The cry was taken up by the survivors, many of them women. They had to be silenced, and the rebels fell on them, cutting and bludgeoning. The slaves freed by bar Giora joined in the killing, lashing out at their former owners with their iron chains, smashing, cutting, and even strangling their victims. There was no logic in the wanton destruction that followed, but the attack had already taken on a momentum of its own and was beyond all control. The storehouses, which they had come to plunder, also caught fire.

Judah burst open the door of a stone house, using a flaming brand to light his way. He had been in his element, quick and deadly with his long knife, never hesitating. A tall, dignified old woman barred his way. Judah hit her savagely with the hilt of his *sica*, stunning her. She fell to the ground, knocking her head against the wall. She lay on the beaten earth breathing harshly, the blood trickling over her handsome face. Her gown had ripped, revealing still-full thighs. The blood beat behind Judah's eyes, and all at once he was upon her, trying to take her savagely as her children looked on speechlessly. He brutally assaulted her, until with an empty fury he knew his true impotence. Overcome by an anger more violent than any he had ever known, Judah stabbed the woman with his knife, driving the point into her again and again. There were three children, two girls and a boy. The oldest girl could not have been more than nine years old. They started to scream with fear and horror. Judah killed them coldly, efficiently. His brand was still smoldering on the floor, and he picked it up and thrust it into the thatch. The roof caught fire and he watched it from the outside until it collapsed on the scene of his shame.

By the time Eleazar and Joab arrived with their forces, it was all over. A horrible scene met their eyes. Hundreds of bodies lay scattered chaotically in the light from the blazing houses, the dead and the wounded together. Women and children, young and old lay indiscriminately on the ground. They lay at peculiar angles, arms and legs sticking out strangely. Apart from the whimpering of the survivors, there was no noise save the crackling of the burning houses.

10

The hall of the western palace was crowded. The effect of the Ein Gedi raid on those who had participated in it had been profound. For two days there had been no other topic for discussion in the fortress. It quickly became clear to Eleazar that the whole question would have to be thrashed out openly, so that the general feeling about future action could become known. The alternative to an open clash was endless gossip and intrigue. The mood of the people was restless as they sat on the benches around the walls in the light of flaming torches. The crowd murmured angrily as Rivka the widow of Menahem stood up to speak first. Although she knew that her views were unpopular, she stood before them calm and dignified, her voice clear and strong.

"Who are the brave?" she demanded. "Those who thirty years ago stretched out their throats to Pilate, the Roman procurator, inviting him to kill them so that they should not live to see the Temple polluted or those who yesterday slaughtered young children?"

"Silence, woman!"

"Hold your tongue!"

"Will nobody shut the old cow's mouth?"

The cries were angry and indignant. The mood of the assembled people was ugly. Eleazar calmed them, speaking quietly so that they had to quiet down in order to hear him.

"Hear the widow of Menahem," he said. "Everyone has the right to speak."

"I do not claim that Menahem shared my views," continued

the old woman, "anymore than he shared those of his brother Jair, the father of Eleazar, Judah, and Simon. He did not. Menahem disagreed with me—he believed that a just war was possible, that it carried out the purpose of the Lord God. But Menahem would never have countenanced the killing of women and little children, nor the violation of Jewish maidens."

"Menahem organized the *sica* raids," shouted Judah in a sudden fury. "He ordered the murder of tens of his fellow Jews in cold blood!"

"I was always opposed to assassination," replied the widow. "But you cannot compare the killing of carefully selected victims, the punishment of traitors, to the indiscriminate extermination of an entire community."

"I was an assassin!" screamed Judah. "I was taught to murder and believe I was fulfilling God's purpose. I still believe it!"

"You, Judah, a son of Jair?" His aunt paled.

"Forget Jair!" shouted Judah. "What did Jair receive for his piety?"

Rivka indicated her furious nephew with a sweeping gesture of her right hand; but her eyes were on Eleazar. "There is your result, Nephew," she declared. "Hatred only leads to more hatred; destruction causes more destruction. There is no difference between your way and Judah's; my way offers the only real alternative."

"You are wrong, Aunt," replied Eleazar. The private family quarrel riveted the attention of everyone present. "Your way will come about one day, in the Lord's good time. For the present we must fight to win His battles. Love does not win battles, nor drive the oppressor from our holy city. Sometimes refusal to kill can bring about greater evil than the slaughter itself. I used to doubt it when Menahem told me so, but now that I sit where he sat I understand.

"No one regrets yesterday's carnage more than I do, but Ein Gedi had to be destroyed. Left intact, it would have become a base for attacks against us. I value the lives of the villagers of Ein Gedi, but I value our lives more. The Lord bids us smite our oppressors as David and Saul smote the Philistines, as Elijah slew the prophets of Baal, as the Maccabees and the Pious Ones fought the Greeks, as Judah fought the Romans. But each battle should be weighed and considered: Does it further the Lord's purpose? I do not believe that the Lord intends us to slaughter indiscriminately, but neither do I believe that it is His wish to betray our revolution. Our fight is His fight!

"I still do not know whether Menahem was mistaken in his judgment, whether he moved too soon. Imagine Ein Gedi last night magnified a hundred and a thousand times—that is Galilee today and Galilee tomorrow! The country is in flames and the very fabric of our world is in ruins. Can this be anything other than the prelude to the coming of the kingdom of God? But we must not anticipate the Almighty; we must conserve our strength until it is time to fulfill our role in the final battle. God will show us the way, as He has in the past."

When Simon bar Giora spoke, it was a different man from that of the past months, more akin to the Simon who had fought in Jerusalem. Though groping for words as always, his speech rough and untutored, he was confident. He stood there, tall and powerful.

"I know little of signs," he began. "Because of my lack of understanding I bow to the judgment of Eleazar ben Jair on matters of doctrine; but I beg to dispute with him about Ein Gedi. What is so terrible about the attack on that village? A few people were killed, but the suffering they experienced is not a tenth, not a hundredth of what they and their kind have caused over the years. Do you grieve for the death of a few slave owners, men who actually possessed human beings? Save your sympathy, son of Jair, save yours, widow of Menahem, for those who deserve it.

"Much of the killing was done by the slaves we released; will you judge them? You want me to feel sympathy for a few score aristocrats, when for century after century slaves have been oppressed and maltreated, bought and sold? Ein Gedi is a mere incident; many more will perish before this war is over.

"We are the many!" he thundered, raising his voice to a

188

shout. "We are the many: the slaves, the peasants, the ordinary people. The priests and aristocrats can only dominate us if we allow them to. Hezekiah would not bow to Herod, Judah taught that we must submit to God and no one else. Why does the grandson of Judah of Galilee hesitate? Why does the widow of Menahem grieve over the deaths of a few traitors?"

"All human life is precious, Simon," replied Eleazar, his quiet tone a contrast to the other's shouted rhetoric. The crowd had to lean forward and quiet each other to hear what he said. "The Lord has commanded us to grieve even over our enemies. To this day the firstborn of each family fasts for half a day before Passover, to mourn for the death of the Egyptian firstborn—this despite the fact that the Egyptians enslaved us."

"You often mention that man is made in the image of God, bar Giora," said Rivka. Bar Giora had spoken to her also and she did not intend to forfeit the right to answer him. "You ask how one can enslave something made in God's image. Well, I ask another question: How can one kill something made in God's image? How dare you mutilate and destroy that which He has created in His image! I repeat, violence leads to more violence, death creates death. I say we have no right to kill!"

"And I say that we have no right to behave like sacrificial lambs," shouted Malachi, springing to his feet. His thin face twitched nervously as he spoke. Of those present, he alone was from an aristocratic background. His conviction, that of a convert to a cause, was clear in every word that he spoke. "If God gave us lives, we have an obligation to defend them; if He has given us bodies, must we not protect them? Did we start this war? Are we attacking Rome, plundering her temples, debasing her gods, enslaving her people, taxing her citizens, making whores of her women?

"What a monstrous perversion of the truth it is to blame us for the bloodshed. We have not ventured one inch outside our country to enslave another. It is the Romans who have crossed the seas and the continents to make all men pay them tribute. It is the Romans who sit in their capital eating bread baked with corn from Alexandria, adorning themselves with silver from Britain, drinking wines made from the grapes of Gaul, guzzling oil from our olives, clad in cloaks died purple with our shellfish. They kill and plunder, debauch and rape, while mankind labors for their benefit. Who gave them the right to trample on humanity? Who wants their cursed roads, theaters and gymnasia? All we ask for is the right to live our own lives in our own way. Is that too much to request?"

"Once we begin to murder indiscriminately, we become like them," said Joab. "Did the Romans not aid Simon the Maccabee against the tyranny of the Greeks? Roman legions coming to fight the Nabateans on our behalf altered their route so that their standards would not be seen in Jerusalem. Was there ever a people with greater honor? Ask yourself, Malachi: What was it that changed them? I will tell you what I believe. I believe that they did not know where to stop. They are mad now with the sense of their own power because they did not limit their greed and their appetites. We must learn. We must not allow ourselves to lose control of our actions. We must always remember that we are carrying out the purpose of God and not satisfying our own desires.

"Your way, Rivka," he turned to face the old widow, "is the way of righteousness. We must never forget your ideal, and it will be an evil day when there is no Jew in Judea with the message of Rabbi Hillel in his heart. But if all of us carry out Hillel's commands literally, there will not be a single Jew in Judea ten years from now! I never wished to fight, but we do not have any choice. If we do not stand up for ourselves now, we shall never have the opportunity. Is this not what Hillel taught?"

"Hillel meant that we should stand up for truth and justice," interjected Rivka. "He taught that real strength is inner strength. It is the strength of our belief that will ensure our survival—nothing in the world can destroy that!"

"They can destroy us, though," replied Eleazar. "One by one they can destroy us and then what will become of our spirits? No, Rivka, your way is not possible; but that does not mean that there need be no limits to our conduct. I do not accept for a moment that such behavior is inevitable."

"What then do you propose, son of Jair?" asked bar Giora. "Our argument is of interest; there is no real end to it; but what are we to do now? Ein Gedi is destroyed. Are we to go forward on the road to Jerusalem?"

"Ein Gedi was destroyed because it menaced us," answered Eleazar. "We are secure now. I have never said we must remain in Masada forever, but it is for God to decide our future actions. We must not lose faith; we must hold ourselves in continuous readiness to carry out His purpose. It is harder to wait than to fight. Once more we are facing a period that will try the patience of all of us. We must be strong and resolute."

The big man opened his mouth to reply, but he checked himself. For some minutes there was only murmured conversation in the torch-lit hall. Bar Giora exchanged glances with Malachi. It was the latter who finally spoke.

"If that is your decision, Eleazar, we are bound to accept it." he said. "We came to this place to join you and not to offer defiance. Already our groups are as one."

Ben Josiah seemed about to say something, but in the end he remained silent. The discussion ceased. There was an awkward silence. Eleazar felt uncomfortable. He had particularly desired a vigorous, even violent, dispute; but somehow, although it had started well, it had not been allowed to continue. He closed the general meeting with a sense of dissatisfaction.

11

Eleazar stood with Joab and Nahum on the lower terrace of the northern palace, with its fine view of the sweep of the desert to the north and west. The walls of rock plunged steeply a thousand feet into the abyss. To the north glowered heavy black clouds. The sudden bursting green life of spring had disappeared during the long summer; now nothing remained but the dun-colored rocks and brown dust. The weather was warm and humid; one large drop of rain fell on Joab's arm. He held out his hand with the hard and callused palm upward, but no other drops followed the first one. The three men stared tensely northward, their faces tight with worry, the eyes straining in the gathering gloom. Occasionally they glanced at the roughly hewn hills or east to the oily gray surface of the Sea of Salt; but most of the time their gaze was fixed northward. Behind them towered the two upper tiers of the palace; from there too men watched. All around the wall of the fortress they stood and watched. They had been waiting for three days.

"There is no sign of them," Joab said.

"They took only a small supply of food," said Eleazar. "They will return."

"Unless they are killed," suggested Nahum.

"Who will kill them?" asked Eleazar. By way of reply, Nahum shrugged his broad shoulders. "No force south of Jerusalem can oppose them," Eleazar continued, thinking aloud. "The Romans will not move out of Caesarea before the spring and the Jewish forces are fighting each other in Jerusalem, so who is left to oppose bar Giora?"

"If the situation is so ripe, perhaps Simon is correct," suggested Joab. "Maybe with the Romans penned up at the coast and anarchy in the capital, our united force could take over the leadership of the revolt."

Eleazar permitted himself a bitter smile. "Were we united, we would simply be adding yet another faction to the Jerusalem strife," he pointed out. "We would have to start all over again with the intrigues and machinations. I want no part of it. I am sure that is not the way."

"Three days is a long time," said Nahum.

"It is not so long," replied Eleazar. "Tomorrow they will return and then we must decide what to do."

"What are you going to do, Eleazar?" There was anxiety in Joab's question.

"I do not know." Eleazar continued to scan the darkening desert, his face taut.

"They cannot be allowed to stay," said Joab.

"I do not think that they will want to remain," said Nahum. "It is safe enough to move about in Idumea now, with the Romans in Caesarea, Galilee fallen, and the Jews penned up in the capital. They do not need Masada now."

192

"What is it to be?" Joab turned to Eleazar. His gray-streaked red beard jutted out as aggressively as ever.

"Perhaps our men will decide to go with bar Giora."

"Only those who have already gone," replied Joab.

"I do not agree," said Eleazar.

"It depends on the success of the raid," said Nahum. "If it fails, most of the people will come crawling back; but if it succeeds, many may wish to join bar Giora."

"They will not fail," stated Eleazar. "There is nobody to resist them. Most of the fighting men are in Jerusalem." He knew only too well the size and strength of the Idumean hamlets, nomadic camps with a few stone houses added. He shivered in the clammy air.

Nahum rolled over onto his back, holding his youngest son astride his chest. The baby's fat brown legs stood out stiffly, his head wobbling on the thin neck. He gurgled and smiled a one-toothed, bubbly smile, then laughed out loud.

"Fool!" exclaimed Nahum. "What are you so happy about?" The baby laughed uproariously. "Why were you not born a girl?" demanded Nahum. He sat up, holding the fat, soft body, squeezing it gently. He kissed the baby on top of his head, feeling the gentle pulse. Then he kissed the firm cheeks. He lay on his back again and held the baby up at arms' length. The little one lay spread-eagled in the air. "What do you know about anything?" asked his father. "What do you think of the present situation?" The baby replied with a loud belch. "Yes, I think that just about sums it up," agreed his father.

"Story, Daddy, story!" Uri came tumbling into the room, and jumped astride his father's prone form. He gave the baby a half-deliberate knock. The baby started to howl, and Nahum sat up and comforted him. David, who had followed Uri into the room, struck him on the ear, causing him to cry.

"Why did you do that?" demanded Nahum angrily of his eldest son.

"He hit the baby on purpose, I saw him!"

"I did not, I did not, no!" Uri's face was crumpled and red.

"You are a naughty boy, David," shouted Nahum. David

pouted, on the verge of tears, his lower lip stuck out. His eyes were very bright and his young face looked very vulnerable.

"He hit him deliberately; I saw him."

"Now, you are all to stop," shouted Nahum in exasperation. "Stop this instant and I will tell you a story." Uri continued to whimper. "No, Uri, I said at once." Finally there was silence, broken only occasionally by a sniff from Uri.

"Tell us about Simon bar Giora, Daddy," demanded David. "Why did he and the others run away?"

"They did not run away; do not be silly!"

"Where are they then?"

"It is a complicated issue, and you are far too young to understand, David."

"Whose side are you on, Daddy, Simon's or Eleazar's?"

"I am on the side of Simon and Eleazar against the Romans," explained Nahum patiently.

"Why did Simon go away with all those men then?" asked his son. "Why are you posting a double guard around the wall?"

"You promised me a story of David the King," interrupted Uri.

"Be quiet, Uri, I was talking first."

"Evening prayers," exclaimed Nahum in relief. "We must go to the synagogue at once or we shall be late."

Joab returned from evening prayers to find supper spread out on the table, ready to eat. The two younger girls were nowhere to be seen, but Shifra sat at the table staring moodily into space. Her face bore a pained expression. Some weeks previously she had become betrothed to Simon bar Nottos, and bar Nottos had departed with the rebels. Despite her pleas he had left with them, and she did not know when he would return. Shifra had grown to full maturity during the past year. With her fiery red hair and full round body, she presented an arresting contrast to the lean, dark bar Nottos; they were to have been married the following month.

Sarah entered with her two younger daughters, and the family sat down to their evening meal. Joab made the blessing:

194

"Blessed art Thou, O Lord our God, who has brought forth bread from the earth."

The meal was a simple one: gruel made from pulse, flat breadcakes from the communal oven, olives, onions, and a few dates. Food was plentiful in the community, if somewhat austere. They ate unhurriedly.

"Rachel, why are you not eating?" asked her mother.

"I am not hungry," she replied. "Shifra is not eating either —why don't you ask her?"

Sarah ignored the question. "You did not eat lunch either," she told her daughter. She was suddenly suspicious. "Were you playing with David ben Nahum today?"

"Yes. Why not?"

"I knew it," snapped the gray-haired woman. She turned to her husband. "Joab, you must put a stop to this at once!"

"Of course, my dear." Joab spoke firmly.

"Did you hear what I said?" demanded his wife.

"Certainly I did," replied Joab. "You said that I must put a stop to Rachel's not eating."

Sarah was exasperated. "It is not simply that. Please listen. David steals dates from the stores and they sit and guzzle them. Look at her plate; she has not eaten anything. How can she eat after all those dates?"

"It is not true," protested the girl. "I have eaten; it is just that you gave me so much to eat."

"Joab, will you please take a firm line?"

"Of course, Sarah." He turned to Rachel, who wrinkled her nose at him, pouted, and opened her eyes very wide. "You heard what your mother said, Rachel?"

"Yes, Daddy, sweetie!" Deborah began to giggle and Rachel snickered also. Even Shifra permitted herself a smile. Sarah glowered as Joab tried manfully to frown.

"Now listen to me, Rachel," he said. "This eating dates has to stop. They are the property of the community; what right have you and David to take them? Will you stop giggling; do you want a smack?"

"Oh no, Daddy, please!" Mock terror crept into her voice. "I will be a good girl." The two younger ones approached their

195

father. He lifted one of them onto each knee and hugged them to him.

"You are naughty girls, do you know that?"

"Yes, Daddy. Sorry, Daddy." They kissed him on either side of his face. "You are so prickly and scratchy!" exclaimed Deborah.

"Joab, is that what you call being firm?" Sarah had been watching the proceedings with growing impatience. Her husband looked up guiltily.

"They have promised not to do it again and they are sorry."

"Very sorry!" chorused the girls gaily. Sarah gave an angry shrug and started to clear the table. Shifra rose to help her. Joab bent and whispered in his daughters' ears. They jumped down from his knees and started to help their mother and elder sister.

"Now, do not think you can placate me so easily," warned Sarah. "Shifra, you sit down, dear; you look worn out."

Shifra obeyed her mother and sat opposite her father. "Did you see anything this evening?" she asked him.

Joab leaned across the table and took his eldest daughter's hands in his own rough, callused hands. He gave them a reassuring squeeze. "They will return, Shifra."

"How can you be sure?"

"They left their wives here."

"Are they interested in them anymore?"

"Bar Nottos is."

Shifra blinked back her tears and tossed her head. "I am not sure," she said.

"I have known him a long time," said Joab. "He is a very serious young man."

"Why did he go then?"

"Why did they all go?" Joab asked softly, speaking almost as though to himself. "Because the truth of the matter is that we do not know what to do. In the old days we followed Menahem. He always knew what to do—that is why we followed him. There was such certainty about him; yet in the end he was mistaken, I think."

"And Eleazar?" asked the girl.

"Eleazar is different. He is more like one of us. He never really knows what to do until a decision is forced on him. He is not weak; I think in his own way he is stronger than Menahem. It is not weakness that is Eleazar's problem, but intelligence. He sees every side of a problem, understands every point of view. Menahem never saw anyone else's point of view, that is why it was always easy for him to decide. We followed Menahem for his certainty."

"Why do you follow Eleazar?" asked the girl. She was interested now, and her depression had lifted with the conversation.

"Love," replied Joab. "It sounds like a stupid answer—overly simple; but it is the truth. He has an overwhelming affection for all of us, and the feeling is returned. He is far from weak. He is complicated and, I think, very strong. I think he could accomplish what other men could not."

"We are faced with my original question," pointed out Shifra. "Why did the men, including my bar Nottos, follow Simon bar Giora?"

"Bar Giora is sure of himself; he knows exactly what he wants. He is simple and his directness appeals to many. The men are tired of being cooped up here while the whole country goes up in flames: Galilee fell and we made no move; Roman legions are quartered in Caesarea and Sebaste; there is anarchy in the Holy City, and we sit here praying in our synagogue while the Temple itself becomes the scene of armed conflict!

"It is not easy to say why we remain here and do nothing. There are times when I myself doubt the wisdom of our policy. Had bar Giora come out into the open, we could have retained control of the community; but after Ein Gedi he changed his tactics. He had never opposed us openly—he could not do that; but before Ein Gedi he used persuasion. He exerted pressure indirectly and tried to influence us to carry out his plans. He made a show of being subservient, but there was no secret about his views. Since the Ein Gedi raid he pretended to agree with us on everything and he laid his plans in secret.

197

We could not oppose him, for we did not know that there was anything to oppose. You must not blame your betrothed, Shifra. He is a good man; he will return to you."

"Why does all this have to happen, Daddy?" Shifra lifted her face and looked at her father, her vivid green eyes wet with tears. "Why cannot we live our own lives without all this fighting and war and death? How can the Lord be good if He allows this?"

Joab was deeply moved. He came around the table and took his eldest daughter in his arms, holding her head against his chest. He stroked her hair soothingly. "If I could answer that, I should be wiser than any man since the world began," he replied.

Hagar lay on her back, her slim arms folded behind her head, staring up in the dark at the beams of the ceiling. The full moon cast its silvery light into the room. The clouds had cleared. Eleazar lay beside her, his hands resting gently on her swollen belly. The skin moved under his hands, contracting and expanding.

"He is alive," said Eleazar.

"How do you know it is 'he'?" asked Hagar. She stroked her husband's hair with her delicate hand.

"I think it is a boy," replied Eleazar.

"I do not know," said his wife. "It is wonderful to start with a son, but will he have to fight and die?"

"Is the fate of woman better?" asked Eleazar. "The Lord creates life seemingly for death, conflict, and misery. All my life I have seen fighting, mutilation, and destruction; yet there has also been joy and love. There was joy in study and work at Sekaka, in my love for you and yours for me. I love you and I love our baby that we are going to have. I love every part of you, the tiny nails on your hands, your wrists, your neck, your ears. I love you, Hagar; I am sorry if my thoughts are not always with you. I have other responsibilities and cannot always devote to you the attention I would have wished."

"I love you, Eleazar—more than life itself. I love you for your goodness. You are strong, but you hate to use your strength."

198

"Maybe my failure to use it is cowardice."

"No, Eleazar, do not say that!"

"I cannot make up my mind. I cannot decide what has to be done."

"Who can decide in these mad times? Who can understand the purpose of the Almighty?"

"Because I did not decide, they left me. I gave them no leadership, so they went with Simon to ravage Idumea. Your own family might perish because of me."

"All of us may soon lose our lives. How many more months of life are there for Judea? If the Lord is with us, then all will be well, and whatever happens is part of His purpose; if He is not, then we shall all die before the moon has changed many more times. My village lived because you were the commander in Idumea; we owe you our lives, whatever happens now. If they are not killed by Simon's band, they will be killed by the Romans, as we shall all be before long."

"You have been talking to Rivka," Eleazar accused her.

"Yes, I have," she admitted.

"She is wrong," insisted Eleazar. "We must resist tyranny. We cannot love our oppressors. The only way that we can ensure our survival is by fighting. I do not love to fight but there are times when man has no choice. Hagar, you must see that; you must see that I have to fight to protect you and my child."

"Fighting only leads to more fighting," replied the girl. "You were convinced that to defend Masada you had to destroy Ein Gedi. Simon is convinced that he must overrun Idumea, and to safeguard Idumea he must control Jerusalem. Where does it all end, Eleazar?"

"It ends when every Roman soldier has been driven out of Judea," he replied. "That will come about in the Lord's good time. I do know one thing—I shall never allow you to fall into the hands of the enemy alive!"

"What do you mean?" She was suddenly frightened.

"I do not really know," he confessed. "It was just a thought that came to me."

"Why did you think of it?"

199

"I was thinking about Menahem." Eleazar sat up clasping his knees, staring in the moonlight that filtered into the room. "Menahem was an old man, still vigorous, but old. They took his old, wrinkled, gray-haired body and they broke it in pieces and mutilated it. Our own Jews did that. I should have died then with him; we should have fought until not one of us remained alive; but we fled and came here to Masada. I married you and have known love and joy, though my uncle, my own flesh and blood, was tortured to death!"

"You followed his orders," she pointed out.

"Yes," he conceded bitterly, "that is what I tell myself a thousand times a month. I followed his orders; but I am so uncertain that I lost half the force we so carefully built up here!"

"They will return."

"They will return, but Simon will be the leader now. For the first time in a century, the Sicarii have been led into battle by someone not of the blood of Hezekiah."

"Judah and Simon are your brothers; they are of the seed of Hezekiah."

"Judah and Simon deserted me. That is what happened, and it was my fault."

"But you were right," insisted his wife. "There was and is no point in adding yet another faction to the Jewish internal strife, letting the Romans sit in Caesarea and watch us win the war for them."

"I was right," agreed Eleazar. "But I was not sure enough. Had I been certain, far fewer would have left with bar Giora. If I had been more of a leader, he would not have been able to set out at all."

"He never gave you a chance to oppose him. He did not work in the open, but conspired behind your back. Pehaps you were too trusting, but not too weak. Events assisted him too. As you said, it is not easy to sit back and watch developments in the rest of the country from here."

"I was a fool," said Eleazar. "I always knew that he was not to be trusted. But what you say is right—so much has happened in Judea during the past year."

12

It looked like a large force, but that did not worry the defenders. They knew that bar Giora's men could not enter without their permission. The women of the dissidents had been confined to their quarters under guard to prevent the possibility of treachery; but there was no attempt at any ruse by Simon bar Giora. He led his group openly to the western foot of the rock, halting by the white hillock. It took them some time to arrive. They had acquired a number of recruits and a good quantity of booty: camels, mules, goats, and sheep.

Simon himself cut an impressive figure on a large white Arab horse. He was dressed in his outsize suit of chain mail and wore his plumed Roman helmet. As always, he was flanked by Malachi and the sturdy ben Josiah, but on this occasion his new leaders, Judah and Simon ben Jair, were in evidence.

Finally, Simon bar Giora stepped forward and spoke. His rough voice was perfectly audible to the Sicarii waiting on the summit.

"Against whom are you defending the fortress?" His great arm gestured, indicating the guards posted by the gate and along the walls.

"Why do you wish to enter?" asked Eleazar. "You have left, why do you return?"

"Our families are in the fortress; we wish to see them."

"We shall arrange for them to come out to you."

"I wish to talk with you, Eleazar," said bar Giora. "Will you not let us enter in peace?"

"Once before I admitted you in peace, Simon."

"Will you not hear me?" demanded the big man. Eleazar looked at Nahum and Joab. The former shrugged wordlessly, but Joab said, "Let us hear him for the last time; we have nothing to fear on this occasion."

Simon bar Giora brought four others with him to the parley, which was conducted on the lower terrace of the western palace. The weather had improved and there was no sign of the clouds of the previous day. Despite the warmth of the midmorning sun, it was cool on the terrace, where they were sheltered by the towering rock itself. Rivka and Hagar brought the men wine as they sat on the stone benches. It was bar Giora who opened the proceedings.

He began by surveying the events of the past year since his arrival. He related the story of Vespasian's advance through Galilee and the lack of effective resistance there. He spoke of the arrival in Jerusalem of John ben Levi of Gischala with a number of the loyal Galileans, who had managed to reach the capital, outstripping his Roman pursuers only with greatest difficulty. He recounted how the factional fighting between the different rebel groups in Jerusalem had resulted in the final deposition of the aristocratic party and the death of Hanan the high priest.

"It was the obvious time to strike, Eleazar," he declared. "Nearly all the Idumean fighting men were in Jerusalem, where they had been called in to help John's faction. My old enemy, the high priest, was dead. The city was a mass of intrigues and uncertainties. I have been through Idumea now, and it is ours. There is nothing to prevent our marching on Jerusalem. We did not see a single auxiliary or Roman soldier in the three days we have been away. Eleazar, I appeal to you, join us now. Come with us to Jerusalem!"

"You speak in a friendly manner now, bar Giora," replied Eleazar. "But you plotted behind my back. You have split my community and stolen my leaders and men!"

"What we did was not against you, Eleazar; we had to force your hand. There was no other way; but we want you with us —we always did. Since I have lived in Masada I have done nothing but dream of the day when we would march on the capital together!"

"It is possible that you speak the truth, bar Giora," conceded Eleazar. "But you cannot have me on your terms. You want me as a figurehead while you make the decisions."

"If you will not come with us," said bar Giora, "we shall go without you; the time has come to strike. I appeal to you in the memory of your uncle Menahem ben Judah, who died at the hill of Ophel . . . ."

The blood drained from Eleazar's face. Trembling, he rose

to his feet. "Ophel? What do you know of the hill of Ophel, Simon bar Giora?"

"It is common knowledge," the big man looked flustered. "It is common knowledge that Menahem died on the hill of Ophel."

"Common knowledge?" asked Eleazar quietly. "Whose common knowledge?" He looked venomously at his brother. "Judah?"

"No, Eleazar, I swear it; never have I revealed about Ophel to a living soul!" Judah too was pale, staring with horror at bar Giora. "We swore never to reveal the secret. Only seven men knew the hiding place: Absalom, Menahem, Nahum, Joab, you, I, and another who is now dead."

Simon bar Giora shrugged his great shoulders. His tone was conciliatory. "I have always been open with you, Eleazar. It is no secret that I was opposed to Menahem. I told you I had learned my lesson, I followed him to Ophel from the Temple; but I swear—"

Like a cat Eleazar was on him, his deadly *sica* striking for the big man's jugular. Although taken by surprise, bar Giora was quick to defend himself, parrying the blow with his forearm. The knife made a long gash in his left arm. He was on his feet in an instant, drawing his sword. The giant bar Giora was clad in chain mail, but if that slowed him down, it was not evident. His head was bare and he made no attempt to retrieve the helmet he had laid on the bench where he had been sitting. Eleazar was flung backward as bar Giora parried the blow. The others formed a rough circle around the two men.

"Eleazar, Simon, no!" Rivka the widow of Menahem ran forward and would have thrown herself between the combatants had not Joab seized her and held her. Hagar stood petrified, holding her swollen stomach.

The two men encircled each other, neither taking his eyes off the other, the one huge and armored, the other lithe and unencumbered. Simon advanced, cleaving the air with his heavy sword, his small dark eyes riveted on his quick-moving opponent. Eleazar retreated slowly, allowing himself to be driven back to the spiral staircase which led to the upper levels. He ascended three steps backward, then with lightning suddenness he dove at his giant opponent, striking out with his razor-sharp knife. Bar Giora had no time to step aside. He went down on one knee, striking upward with his sword; but Eleazar had dived low and the two men collided. Eleazar's blow glanced off the big man's bald skull, tearing the skin above his right ear. Both men sweated as they picked themselves off the ground, and their breath was coming in short gasps.

Again bar Giora advanced. Eleazar sprang behind a pillar as the slave leader struck; his sword clanged on the sandstone and sliced an inch of plaster from its surface. Tension rose on the lower terrace as the dozen men and two women watched the fray. They remained silent, even Hagar managing to control herself so as not to distract her husband. She held onto Nahum and buried her face in the front of his tunic. Again it was bar Giora who advanced, his superior weight and strength making it impossible for Eleazar to take the initiative. He was again beating Eleazar back, forcing the smaller man into a trap.

On the eastern side of the terrace was a stairway leading down to a small private bath room built by Herod. The steps overlooked the steepest drop on Masada, one thousand feet to the valley floor of the Sea of Salt, and Eleazar was being driven down these steps. Expecting that bar Giora would anticipate his keeping to the western side of the stairs away from the drop, Eleazar slowly worked his way across to the eastern edge. He shifted his feet almost imperceptibly and leaped suddenly. He was on the edge of the abyss, ready to jump upward out of the trap into which he had been forced; but his opponent was quick too. The huge man was over Eleazar with a deadly swing of his heavy sword. Eleazar ducked the blow but was forced to parry with his *sica*. The powerful blow knocked him off balance and he swayed on the edge. Bar Giora's foot struck out with the speed of a snake, kicking Eleazar's support from under him. The son of Jair clawed the air as he fell, and a horrified groan went up from the Sicarii.

As he fell, Eleazar let go of his knife, which fell into space. He twisted wildly in the air, clinging instinctively to life. He fell against the rock and grasped for a hold. His fingernails

204

scratched the rough surface, his body pressing its entire length against the cliff face. He slid sickeningly toward emptiness and then stopped. He was still alive! He lay spread-eagled, maintaining his position by inertness; a sudden movement on his part would mean instant death. His hand gradually slid upward until it grasped a ledge.

Up to this point Eleazar had acted without thought, but now he was filled with self-disgust. For a year he had befriended the murderer of his beloved uncle, and he had pathetically failed to avenge Menahem. He was not fit to live! But he thought of his wife and his unborn child and realized that the will to live was strong.

The watchers of the contest were convinced that they had seen the last of Eleazar ben Jair; but Simon bar Giora, peering over the edge of the precipice, had witnessed Eleazar's miraculous escape. He was exhausted with emotion and effort. In a lifetime of fighting, he could not remember a more exacting experience. Almost paralyzed by inertia, he watched Eleazar's hand moving cautiously until it gripped the ledge two feet below him. He reached down and grasped the man's wrist, pulling upward with his tremendous strength and lifting the Sicarii leader. To the watchers, it seemed as if he plucked Eleazar miraculously out of the air. His immediate thought was to wonder at the lightness of the man who had given him such a hard fight.

13

Eleazar remained alone with his two brothers on the terrace. There was no sign of the struggle that had taken place there half an hour previously. Judah, tall and lean, his broad face topped by strangely boyish black curls, had aged greatly in the past eighteen months. Simon was still a youth, a smaller copy of Judah, yet with something of the quality of his older brother also. His eyes were softer and wider set than Judah's, his beard was still light on his cheeks, and there was an expression of uncertainty on his face. Eleazar had changed in the past hour. He was still pale, as he had been since the moment when

Simon bar Giora had mentioned the hill of Ophel. The three of them avoided each other's eyes, looking northward from the terrace toward Ein Gedi. When Eleazar spoke finally, his voice was low, almost a whisper.

"I have not much to say to you, my brothers, for you are strangers to me. For this, I am to blame. When our dear father died, we fled together and traversed the whole country from Jerusalem to Galilee without separating; but then I allowed us to become divided. I thought that you would be well cared for by Menahem and Rivka and that I would benefit from my studies among the Sons of Zadok. I did not realize that our backgrounds would cut us off from each other.

"You, Judah, have become a complete stranger to me. There is no point in denying it. I do not understand you, nor you me. As for you, Simon, since I returned to the Sicarii, I have not let you out of my sight. I still love you as a brother, but there is a gulf; I wish I knew how to cross it. For more than a hundred years, our group has been led by a member of our family. Judah replaced Hezekiah, Jacob and Simon replaced their father, and Menahem succeeded his brothers. You, Judah, are named after Judah of Galilee and Simon is named after his son Simon, the brother of Menahem. I ask you to stay with me and help me lead the Sicarii.

"You have heard the rumor that we are of royal seed, that from our line, the line of David the King, will come the Messiah of Israel. Like Menahem and Judah before him, I believe that the age of kings has passed; but that does not mean that our tasks are any the less glorious. The Messiah of Aaron, the rightful high priest of Israel, awaits the call. It is our task to escort him to Jerusalem when the time comes. Stay here with your own people, my brothers, and await the Lord's bidding!"

"The time for waiting is long past," replied Judah. "Our task is clear. We must continue the revolt. We must carry on the work of Menahem."

"With Menahem's murderer?"

"You accepted your life back from him willingly enough," replied Judah. "Were Menahem alive today, he would support Simon's plans. For Menahem, Masada was a stepping-stone to power; for you it has become a refuge which you will never leave. You will no more leave Masada to fight the Romans than the Sons of Zadok will leave Sekaka to officiate as righteous priests in the Temple. It is all in your heads and in your hearts. Wars are not won by pious thoughts and wishes, but by action!"

"For you, war has become a way of life, Judah. You see nothing else, and apparently you need nothing else."

"That is the way I grew up, Eleazar; that is what I was taught."

"And you, Simon?" Eleazar turned to his younger brother. Simon looked at Judah and then back to Eleazar again. At first he looked uncertain, and then he seemed to make up his mind.

"I do not know very much about the Law, Eleazar," he said. "I do not understand the purpose of the Almighty. I know that we have always had to fight and that we still have to fight. I lived for the day when I would be old enough to possess my own *sica*. The raid on Masada was the greatest day of my life. I understand that it was a good idea to return to Masada after Menahem's death. It was difficult to recover from that blow; but we have recovered and we are stronger for it because we can rely on ourselves and do not have to rely on him. Once there was only Menahem; now there are you, Joab and Nahum, Judah, Simon bar Giora, Malachi, and ben Josiah—we are ready as never before.

"What are we waiting for? You do not know. You say we have to wait for the Lord, but how are we to know when He is ready? Will the Messiah of Aaron at Sekaka give us a sign? You know well that he will not! Come with us, Eleazar—despite our differences, you are as a father to me. Come with us to Jerusalem!"

"And if I will not come?"

"Then I will go with Judah and Simon bar Giora."

14

It was raining again. The heavy gray clouds hung over the rock, almost obliterating the view of the surrounding desert.

The rain was still light and the wadis only trickled with water. They moved slowly in the raw, damp weather, the mud sticking to their sandals and slowing them down. Joab had descended to bar Giora with a message from Eleazar, inviting the slave leader to remain in the fortress until the rain had stopped. But the big man was impatient to be off.

Simon the son of Giora had arrived in the rain and in the rain he was leaving. He had arrived as a fugitive at the head of less than a hundred ragged followers; he was leaving proudly at the head of a well-equipped army. But he was not a contented man. He had succeeded in winning for himself a large and well-supplied force, but he was leaving with his main aim unfulfilled. The winning over of Judah and Simon ben Jair, with a good number of the Sicarii, did not compensate for his failure to gain the adherence of Eleazar and the senior leadership. He had made a final attempt to persuade Eleazar, offering him the leadership of the group and anything else he desired; but he had been unable to convince the austere leader.

Eleazar had made no attempt to dissuade his followers from joining bar Giora. The younger Sicarii had joined Simon and Judah in following the slave leader; but the senior members, including the leadership, had elected to stay at the fortress. Of the community of three thousand souls, less than a thousand elected to remain.

Bar Giora's force, with its women, children, baggage animals, and flocks, filled the western valley; the thick snake of humans and animals had taken two hours to make the short descent. From the western gate Eleazar was able to distinguish his two brothers, ben Josiah and Malachi, Miriam, and of course Simon bar Giora himself, towering above the multitude. Slowly, like a great beast gathering itself for motion, the party moved off into the rain. Simon looked backward once and raised a huge arm in salute. The Sicarii left the casemate wall and went in out of the rain. Only Eleazar the son of Jair remained, his tears mingling with the downpour.

FLAVIUS SILVA: APRIL 73 C.E.

Flavius Silva looked down on the Jewish fortress from the top of his armored siege tower. The tower was a mighty structure of vast wooden beams covered with heavy iron plates. It stood firmly on great bonded stones, which had been hauled up to the top of the earth ramp. It seemed invincible as it rose above the casemate wall, dominating the fortress.

It was while the slaves and soldiers were struggling to carry the stones into position, painfully edging up the slope with the weight of the rocks pulling them into the abyss, that the defenders had made their first attack. The rebels had poured over the walls and engaged the attackers in fierce hand-to-hand fighting. It had been difficult for the Romans to defend themselves effectively, encumbered as they were by the stones. They were forced to retreat, suffering several losses. Before they made another attempt to move the foundations of the tower into position, Silva arranged for covering fire by a stone-thrower, set up further down the ramp, and a company of auxiliary bowmen. The defenders countered by rolling stones down from the walls onto the stone-thrower of the Romans. Finally, with a combination of covering fire and shielding by heavy infantry, who preceded the slaves with their shields aloft, the stones were placed in position and construction of the tower was begun.

Time after time, the defenders burst out of their fortress and succeeded in toppling the structure; on one occasion they attacked it with firebrands and set it alight. Both sides lost men in these battles, and once more the cream-colored vultures with their black-edged wings gathered in the skies above Judea.

After the enormous work of building the ramp, the construction of the tower was a relatively light task, but the vicious fighting on the narrow edge of the ramp complicated matters for the besiegers. Finally, through dogged persistance and efficient direction and planning, the tower had been erected; Silva stood looking right into the fortress. He had seen the

211

general layout previously from his camp above the summit to the southwest. His close view showed him nothing new. The defenders lived for the most part in small rooms within the casemate wall. The heaviest defenses were concentrated by the western gate, where the siege tower stood; but that did not mean that there was any chance of making a surprise attack from the east, for all entrances, and indeed all parts of the wall, were guarded. Stone-throwers and catapults mounted in the tower managed to keep the defenders off the actual walls; but when an attack was mounted, they counterattacked with great fierceness, and the soldiers were beaten back several times.

It seemed to the Roman commander that he had been directing the attack on Masada all his life. In spite of himself, he was succumbing to a feeling of vindictiveness against the obstinate and illogical defenders, who had forced him to expend so much time and resources. Surely now, with the opposing commander looking into the heart of their defenses, they could be induced to lay down their arms! Not for the first time the Roman tried to fathom the thoughts and reactions of his opponents. He was consumed by an insatiable curiosity, a desire to understand what drove them to act as they did.

Since he had been able to examine Masada at close quarters, Silva had been aware of what seemed to be a separate group within the community there. They wore long white robes instead of short tunics and appeared to be unarmed. A Jewish slave had informed him that they were none other than members of the sect called the Sons of Zadok, of which he had learned earlier in the siege. Their center at Sekaka, farther up the coast of the Sea of Salt, had been razed by Placidus nearly five years previously. It had been rumored at the time that they were the guardians of the missing Temple treasures, but nothing had ever been found. The Sons of Zadok had been reputed to be pacific scholars who lived their communal life by the Sea of Salt in piety and contemplation. But no part of Judea had been immune to the madness of the rebellion against Rome, and the Sons had conducted a stubborn defense of their settlement. Silva had heard that survivors from Sekaka had escaped to Masada; now the evidence of his own eyes supported this.

For some moments he wondered whether the key to surrender might lie in this group; but what he had heard of the battle for Sekaka five years previously did not encourage the procurator to believe that the Sons of Zadok were, in any way, a weak link in the chain of the defenses of Masada.

BOOK IV

THE MASTER: 68 C.E.

. . . On the day of calamity, the sons of light shall battle with the company of darkness amid the shouts of a mighty multitude and the clamour of gods and men, to make manifest the might of God. And it shall be a time of great tribulation for the people which God shall redeem. . . .

The War Rule: *The Dead Sea Scrolls*

1

It was the eve of Shavuot, the Festival of Weeks, which commemorated the giving of the Law to Moses on Mount Sinai. For the Sons of Zadok it was the climax of their year, the day on which new members were admitted to the covenant, and senior members elected to the council of the community. It was the day of the great banquet, a rehearsal of the messianic banquet that would usher in the kingdom of God on earth. One year, maybe this year or next year, the Messiah of Aaron in person would preside over the banquet and usher in the final age. On this day every year, the whole community of Sekaka ate together, and even the candidates were allowed into the Purity of the Many, although not as full participants.

Jacob, Hanan, ben Levi and their friends stood on the threshold of adulthood—they were to be admitted to the covenant. They were taking an important step, for once admitted there was no turning back. There might well be no advance either, for whether they later gained admittance to the inner circle depended on their individual temperaments and abilities. But they were irrevocably members of the Sons of Zadok, bound by their oaths to the way of the Teacher, obligated to follow his doctrines until their deaths. No matter what sufferings lay ahead, they would have to remain steadfast.

They could be expelled for violation of the code and expulsion meant death, for none could survive without the council's jurisdiction once they had sworn to honor it. They could eat no other food save that prepared in purity by the community, yet once expelled they would have no access to it. Penalties for minor infringements of social behavior were harsh, and the life they were to live was far from attractive. Now they could turn back; they could refuse admittance to the covenant. But they did not consider refusal anymore than they would have considered stopping breathing. They looked forward with eagerness to the life of austerity in front of them, for it offered them that most precious thing: certainty in an uncertain world. While the society around them was in a state of flux and turmoil, life at Sekaka, in the silence of the valley of the bitter sea, continued sublime and unchangeable.

The silver sun blazed out of the pale blue sky; the summer heat burned the valley floor. In the largest hall of the center preparations were being made for the great occasion. Sheep had been brought from the farm in the south, including perfectly formed white lambs for ceremonial purposes. Barred from the Temple by the impious, the Sons of Zadok performed their sacrifices by special dispensation of the Priest. At this time, when the Holy City was under siege, when foreign troops were ravaging the nation, when towns and villages were in flames, Sekaka was totally absorbed in the excitement of celebrating Shavuot, the anniversary of the giving of the Law and the prelude to the new age that was dawning.

The members of the community knew that death was approaching. Three months before, when the Romans had swept through Perea, they had seen the dead bodies floating down the Jordan to the Sea of Salt. Yet most of them had not really absorbed the idea that an actual attack on Sekaka was imminent.

The Priest directed the preparations for the festival. He supervised the making of the wine and the food, and the ritual dressing of the animals for sacrifice. They would read that night from newly copied scrolls of the Law. The candidates had been examined a number of times and in a number of ways; only those suitable were allowed to apply for membership.

The Master, though also busy with preparations for the festival, was at the same time working out plans for the defense of Sekaka. He had decided on his strategy and knew exactly what he wanted to do. He too had been examining the young candidates for the past year to decide on their suitability for admission to the covenant. He knew each of them, and they were greatly under his influence.

Had the Priest known that the Master's questions and teaching touched on matters other than pure theology, he would have been horrified. The Master was well aware that the Priest and his colleagues would put up no resistance to the Romans when they arrived at Sekaka, but he was determined that the center be defended. His purpose was not simply to defy the Romans, but the details of his plan had been confided to no one. Shortly, the Master was to reveal his ideas to a trusted few among the candidates. But for the time being he contented himself with seeing to the distribution of arms and ensuring that each of the defenders knew his position and duty.

2

That spring the Roman commander Vespasian had been stirred out of his lethargy by the provocative actions of Simon bar Giora in Idumea. Following his departure from Masada, the giant slave leader had overrun most of Idumea before the Roman had decided that he must be stopped. The soldiers burned their way through the south of the country, leaving a trail of utter destruction. Perea to the east of the Jordan had been ravaged by Placidus, the man who had made the initial advance into Galilee the year before. Attacking and destroying Simon's birthplace of Gerasa, to the east of the Lake of Gennesaret, he swept southward as far as Macherus, the Masada-like fortress on the eastern shore of the Sea of Salt. Bar Giora meanwhile was forced to take refuge in the caves of Idumea.

In Jerusalem the death of the high priest, Hanan, had not resulted in stability. Fighting continued between the Jewish rebel groups: John of Gischala fought his erstwhile allies the Idumeans, and both groups were opposed by ben Simon, the Zealot hero of Beth Horon. Ben Simon, who controlled most of the Temple Mount, had decided, in view of the uncertainties of the situation, to send away for safekeeping some of the vast Temple treasures. After considering carefully the various possibilities, the Zealot leader had decided to send it to the community of the Sons of Zadok. Apart from their respect for Temple property and their feeling that they were in any case

219

the rightful guardians of anything connected with the Temple, the Sons were renowned for their lack of greed. They were less likely than anyone else to steal the property and make use of it for their own ends.

Secretly, at night, the heavily laden mules had made their way down the narrow track which led to the wadi Sekaka. Emerging in the vicinity of the settlement, they had been met by the Bursar and his young assistants, who made haste to hide the treasure. It was concealed in caves and cisterns, buried beneath rocks, and secreted in the foundations of ruined buildings. By the time that it had become impossible for ben Simon to dispatch any more, as he was surrounded on the Temple Mount, the Sons had spirited away a vast quantity of valuable property. The record of the hiding places was written in code and hammered out on sheets of copper. All other records were then destroyed and the copper sheets were rolled and hidden.

There were two clusters of caves in the vicinity of Sekaka. The nearest ones were below the plateau on which the village was situated, in the white sandstone cliffs which led up to the plain. The most distant caves were situated in the brown flint cliffs that rose above the plateau to the west. Scrolls, including the codes, were hidden in both sets of caves; but in the most inaccessible of the higher caves, the Master arranged for the laying in of stores of food and water.

"What are we preparing for, Master?" Jacob had asked.

"You will see," the gaunt, gray-bearded man had replied.

"Are we to live in the caves?" he had persisted.

"You will learn when I decide you shall learn!"

The Roman forces had continued their ravages in Idumean and Perean territory. There had come that dreadful day when the Sea of Salt was a mass of floating dead bodies of Perean Jews killed by the cavalry of Placidus. According to the Law, a person must be buried before sunset on the day of his death, and the young members of the community had labored hard at digging the shallow graves. Although they had known that many of their members were participating in the struggle

220

against the Romans and that John, one of their members, had been among the first commanders of the Jewish forces, the Sons of Zadok at Sekaka had been isolated from the war, as they were from all life outside the valley.

The sight of the dead bodies had changed their attitude. With a chill of fear, they had seen their own ends foreshadowed in the hacked carcasses floating in the bitter sea. The iron routine of their lives still pervaded their thoughts and they forgot themselves in hard work, meditation, and worship; but occasionally they were moved by apprehension and they looked northward with furrowed brows. Yet, though their glimpse of reality had moved them more than any previous experience, they were still for the most part unaware of their peril. The priests were occupied with the question of the Kittim. Were the Romans indeed the Kittim foretold by the Teacher? Was this the final forty-year battle which would wipe out the legions of darkness? Calmly they considered their doctrinal problems as the nation burned around them— in their valley it was still peaceful.

Eleazar was at Masada, not even contemplating a move. Bar Giora, who had marched from Masada the previous winter so full of confidence, was hiding in the Idumean caves. John of Gischala, ben Simon, and the remainder of the rebels were bottled up in Jerusalem. The Roman forces were in Jericho, and there was no one to defend Sekaka save the Sons of Zadok themselves. That night the celebration of the giving of the Law would begin. In all probability, before the celebrations were ended, the sons of light would have to face the children of darkness in real battle.

The Master had sent for Jacob, ben Levi, Hanan, and a dozen of the other candidates. They stood before him grim-faced, wondering what he was about to tell them. That night was to see their induction into the covenant, their first step on the road to salvation. The Master would address them that night; why did he require their presence now?

"I have called you here on the eve of a great event," he began. His voice was quiet and subdued yet still authoritative.

221

"Tonight you will become members of the Sons of Zadok. I will not enlarge on this; tonight you will appreciate the full meaning of this step you are taking, if you do not appreciate it already. But now I have called you here on another matter. You know of the Roman advance through the country. They have destroyed Galilee, Idumea, and Perea. They are at present destroying Judea and soon they will advance on Jerusalem itself. Tonight they are in Jericho; tomorrow they will be here.

"They know that our men have been fighting against them. They know that we sheltered the Sicarii. Above all, they know that we are the guardians of a significant part of the treasures of the Temple. The Romans are greedy; they want that treasure, and you may be sure that they will show us no mercy. Some of us, including those of you whom I have summoned to this meeting, are prepared to defend our village—to the death if need be. The Priest is opposed to this. He wishes us to ignore the enemy, even if we are attacked.

"None of us can be sure whether or not this is the final war spoken of by the Teacher, though with the country so utterly ravaged, one is forced to conclude that it must be. Only one thing is absolutely certain: the war is still in its early stages. There will be far more fear and suffering and bloodshed before it is over. The Teacher spoke of a forty-year war. Whether or not we take his number literally, it is clear that Jerusalem is not going to fall easily and the struggle ahead is long and bitter.

"The question arises: What are we to do? Are we to defend our village to the death and rest content that we have done our duty? Is this to be the end of the glorious destiny of the Sons of Zadok? Or does our main task lie in the future? Have we a further role to play? I am sure you know my answer to these questions!"

The Master had then informed them of exactly what they were to do. At first his words had been greeted with cries of disbelief. Then they had argued with him. But there was no dissuading the Master. He had made up his mind and they were bound to obey.

The whole community had gathered outside the center as the sun was setting. All were dressed in gleaming white garments. They had bathed and purified themselves for the ceremony. Over a thousand of them had assembled under the fiery bowl of the evening sky. Then the Priest, tall and slim, his burnished coppery hair reddened by the setting sun, approached, and the crowd stood back to let him pass. Behind him came the other priests, each of them according to rank and seniority. They walked with an unhurried majestic walk as they entered the building and made for the main assembly hall. There was a low murmur from a thousand pairs of lips as the tall, impressive figure of the Priest passed by the people. None knew him personally, but he was the most revered man in the community, heir to the Zadokite line, rightful high priest of all Israel.

After the priests came the Levites, each one in his place according to his rank. When the last of the priestly members of the community had entered the building, the lay members began to move forward. First came the members of the community court, then the officers of the council, followed by the Many, the members of the covenant, each one in his appropriate place. None tried to jostle, for each of them knew where his correct position was. Only after the members of the covenant had entered were the candidates able to move forward. First came those whose admission to the Many was to take place that night, and now for the first time they had been placed according to rank. Ben Levi, as the senior Levite present, led the candidates in; Jacob and Hanan were farther back in the line. Finally the other candidates, who were to seek admission in the following years, passed in, until the assembly hall was tightly packed with people. The hall was a sea of faces, a mass of gleaming white robes and skullcaps. The Priest too was dressed simply; only a gold-embroidered border to his robe and a scarlet skullcap distinguished him from his fellows. He looked over the congregation, and his pale gray eyes seemed to be looking into a great distance. The mass of people stood motionless.

The Priest began to speak, his voice deep and melodious as he began to conduct the same ceremony that he had been leading now for more than two decades. *"Blessed be the God of Salvation and all His faithfulness."*

"Amen, Amen." The response from a thousand throats was like the rumble of thunder.

The Priest and his colleagues recited the favors of God, depicting His grace and itemizing His favors to His unworthy people Israel. The priests were followed by the Levites, who recounted the iniquities of the children of Israel.

The whole congregation participated, shouting aloud their admissions of guilt: *"We have strayed! We have disobeyed! We and our fathers before us have done wickedly in walking counter to the precepts of truth and righteousness, and God has judged us and our fathers also; but He has bestowed His bountiful mercy on us from everlasting to everlasting!"*

Then again the priests praised the Lord and His righteous followers: *"May He bless you with all good and preserve you from all evil. May He lighten your years with lifegiving wisdom and grant you eternal knowledge! May He raise His merciful face toward you for everlasting bliss!"*

With hatred did the Levites curse the men of evil: *"Be cursed because of all your guilty wickedness! May He deliver you up for torture at the hands of the vengeful avengers! May He visit you with destruction . . . ."*

The ceremony continued in the flowing language, with total communion between man and God. All eyes were on the Priest, the center of the ceremonial, all hearts were filled with love of God and hatred of evil. They warned the hypocrite or the stubborn or the halfhearted:

"He shall be cut off from the midst of the Sons of Light and because he has turned aside from God on account of his idols and his stumbling blocks of sin, his lot shall be among those who are cursed forever."

"Amen, Amen!"

In the cool morning, the members of the community had reassembled and the Master was expounding the Law. Last night the Priest had been the center of the ceremonies; this morning the Master was taking over the instruction. The Priest had presided at the banquet, where each man had sat in his rightful place. The new candidates had been admitted, sprinkled with the purifying water, and then had taken the fearful oaths that would bind them forever to the covenant. Now they sat with the Many, ben Levi among the Levites.

Exposition and instruction had been the task of the Levites since the time of Ezra the Scribe, and even the Priest, who presided over all the sacred ceremonial, was listening to the Master's lesson. For almost two centuries the ceremonies had been carried out in this identical manner, and the various celebrations would continue throughout the day.

The Master's explanation of the Law was in the identical language used by previous Masters on the same occasion, the same language that had been used since the time of the Teacher: *"From the God of knowledge comes all that is and shall be. Before ever they existed He established their whole design, and when, as ordained for them, they come into being, it is in accord with His glorious design that they fulfill their work.*

"He has created men to govern the world and has appointed for him two spirits in which to walk until the time of His visitation, the spirits of truth and falsehood. . . . All the children of righteousness are ruled by the Prince of Light and walk in the ways of light, but the children of darkness are ruled by the Angel of Darkness. . . ."

The Master continued, telling the tale which they all knew by heart, yet holding them with the conviction and sincerity of his voice. The ceremonies of the previous evening and of this morning would be deeply ingrained on their minds. Year after year, the same words had been spoken at the same time and place, in the same way, word for word, unchanging as time itself.

The Master was ending his peroration: *"He knows the reward of their deeds from all eternity. He has allotted them to the children of men that they may know good and evil and that the destiny of all living may be according to the spirit within them at the time of the visitation."*

"Amen, Amen."

Then something happened that made every one of the thousand people present gasp with appalled surprise and disbelief. Had the light of heaven stopped in its course, they could not have been more aghast. The Master had completed his exposition, concluding as he had always concluded, as every Master had always concluded, the words of the Teacher—and he was continuing to speak!

"The visitation: is it now? Are we the ones privileged to participate in this glorious event? I say to you that the time for dreams is past; the kingdom of God is at hand. Never before in all our history has the land known such destruction. And there will be more of it—more death, more burning, more killing! The cup of our suffering will overflow still further; the day of the Lord is darkness!

"Yet this is the preliminary to the rule of righteousness. When the Lord has inflicted on us more than we believed we could bear, and then more—for there is no limit to what we deserve—then and only then will He raise us up. Then He will smite our enemies, then He will—"

The Master never completed his sentence for he was interrupted by the sound of Roman trumpets from the valley below; the attack on Sekaka had begun.

4

The Master felt pain, agonizing, excruciating pain, permeating his whole body. He would not have believed that there could be so much pain. He was stretched out on a wooden frame to which his hands and forearms were bound; a heavy stone was strapped to his chest to hold him in the correct position. His naked body was startlingly white, the whiteness of skin never exposed to the sun. He was deeply distressed by his nakedness, for it was a sin before the Almighty. His back was already a crisscross of angry red weals, but there was no pause in the powerful blows of the whip administered by the brawny Roman centurion. The sharp, knotted leather thongs continued to bite into his skin. Not a sound escaped the Master's lips, not so much as a groan or gasp. He forced his lips into a smile, with difficulty avoiding a grimace. This infuriated the sweating centurion, who increased the power of his strokes, swinging his whole body with the effort. A line of blood appeared on the white skin of the Master's back—the skin was broken. Soon it was broken in several places and the blood splashed onto the Roman, but his assault never faltered.

A sigh went up from the onlookers who were assembled in the courtyard of the center at Sekaka. The surviving members of the community were lined up against the western wall of the yard, guarded by half a dozen legionaries. At the sound of the sigh, a short, stocky man, Placidus, raised his hand, signaling to the centurion to cease his whipping. He strode forward until he faced the white-clad Sons of Zadok. His armor shone in the sun, but he was bareheaded. Placidus looked up and down the line, his bushy brows furrowed.

"Your leader bleeds and suffers," he said, "unnecessarily!" He looked up again and shouted: "Are we Romans known as torturers? Do we do this for pleasure? Soon we shall take your Temple and all its treasures. Does the small quantity that you have hidden warrant such suffering?"

There was no answer; the Sons of Zadok stood gravely and silently in their line.

"I asked a question!" Silence. "I said is it worth your Master's suffering for the sake of a hundredth part of the treasures that we shall take in totality soon?" No word came from the line of survivors. The Roman walked around until he was facing the Master, spread-eagled on the wooden frame. He seized the old man's iron gray hair, and pulled his head up with a jerk, almost breaking his neck. "Is it worth it, I asked?" The Master managed a gentle smile. "Damn you!" The Roman was incensed. Holding the Master's head he struck his face repeatedly, until the nose spurted blood and the teeth fell in the dust at his feet. Again the Master managed to smile, though this time there were gaps in his row of teeth, and the blood dripped from his mouth. Through the red haze of pain, he was thinking of the recent defense of Sekaka. They had not done so badly for a group of pious dreamers!

The plateau on which the settlement was situated was naturally approached by the path from the coastal plain, which led up to the northeast of the center. There was another eastern approach further south; but as he had not anticipated any resistance whatsoever, Placidus had ridden up the main track with two centuries of cavalry.

As soon as they heard the Roman trumpets from the plain below, the various groups had taken up their positions. The first group, numbering some forty youngsters, had rushed for their arms and at once charged out of the center and down the path leading to the plain below to try to prevent the Roman forces from ascending to the plateau. They were totally untrained and unpracticed in warfare, but their sudden wild rush took the Romans, who had been expecting peaceful submission, by surprise. The young warriors fought wildly and blindly, with no thought for their own safety. After an initial retreat, the cavalry charged them, inflicting heavy casualties, but they continued to defend the pass and would not retreat. They fought with knives and stones, javelins and sticks, with bare hands and teeth. The fighting continued until every one of them was dead.

Meanwhile, two other groups had carried out their allotted tasks. A dozen young men, including ben Levi, Jacob, and Hanan, slipped quietly out of the western gate with a large bundle, moving swiftly along the water channel to the cliffs. Before the Romans had reached the plateau, they had disappeared.

The remaining three hundred young men had acted quickly. Herding their elders, including the priests, with unwonted disrespect into the inner chambers of the center, they swiftly barricaded all entrances with balks previously prepared, tearing down beams from the roof to supplement them. The reckless attack of the first group had given them sufficient time to complete the job, and by the time the Romans reached the plateau they were lining the upper walls, ready with missiles of all kinds to hurl down on the approaching cavalry. Two centuries of cavalry were not equipped to lay siege to a fortress, even a weak one, and Placidus was forced to send for reinforcements. The infantry, when they arrived, stormed the center, supported by light machines, and managed to breach the wall; but a stiff rearguard action enabled numbers of fighters to retreat to the strongly built main tower.

The noncombatants, including the older members and the priests who had been closed in the inner chambers, were captured; many of them were at once cut down by the angry attackers. In concentrating their attack on the center, the Romans had ignored the tented camp to the north, where the families lived. Most of the women and children, including the wife of the Priest, tried to escape northward to Jericho; but they were pursued by a detachment of cavalry and eliminated. The siege of the tower continued for a further day until that too fell, and the survivors were taken prisoner.

The Master was barely conscious and he wished that he were not. He felt himself slipping into unconsciousness, but the relief was not allowed him. He was doused with water, which revived him to the savage pain. He forced himself to relax, not even letting himself groan or clench what was left of his teeth. Placidus, the Roman commander, was still speaking.

"Today I chanced to walk in this strange sea of yours," he said to the row of survivors. "I had a small sore on my ankle, where it had rubbed the saddle strap of my horse. I have been a soldier for many years and you can believe me when I say that I know what pain is, but I have never experienced anything as painful as the water of the Sea of Salt on an open wound. Your leader's back is now one large wound!" He indicated the area of raw, red flesh which had been the Master's back. On the right side, the white of a bone showed through. One of the onlookers vomited. "If you will not give me the information for which I ask, we shall take what remains of this man down to the sea!"

This time there was a gasp of horror from the men, but still none spoke. They knew that the Master would wish them to behave thus. They were bound by their oaths, no matter what terrors lay ahead.

229

"And when I have finished with him," continued the Roman, "I will mete out the same treatment to each and every one of you."

Not a word was spoken. The soldiers stood on guard, expressionless and uninterested. The Sons stood silently with heads bowed. Placidus waited in the silence, sure that one of them would break down. When he saw that this was not the case, he gave the necessary orders and the Sons were formed up by the soldiers, who set them walking toward the sea. The Master was untied from the wooden frame and the stone removed from his chest. Unconscious at last, he was laid gently face downward on a stretcher carried by two soldiers. The swaying motion awoke him. His back was one continuous burning pain; but it was a relief to relax on the stretcher, good to be rocked gently rather than to be tied to the wooden frame with a heavy rock attached to his chest.

It was of his youth in the community of the Sons of Zadok that the Master thought now. All his life he had known nothing outside the community. His parents had been members of the first group of thirty families who had returned to the fallen ruins by the Sea of Salt to start rebuilding the center of the Sons of Zadok, which had been destroyed by an earthquake thirty years previously. The young pioneers had returned to the desert full of enthusiasm and ideals, singing praises to the Lord, determined to re-create the spiritual community of the Teacher. The enthusiasm had been quickly burned out of them by the scorching sun and the parched wastes. The days were unbearably hot and the nights afforded little relief. Several died of fever and others left, unable to stand the harsh conditions. Slowly the kernel of the group worked on. They rebuilt the center and reconstructed the water system. They reclaimed the land near the southern spring, creating once again a farm irrigated by its clear water. More died and many left, but always others came. The movement of the Sons of Zadok gave the project its full support, but only a minority of the hardier and more enthusiastic were prepared to leave their towns or villages for the life of the Judean wastes.

230

Over the years the situation improved. The center started to function as of old. The farm started to produce food and fodder for livestock. More members joined them and more hands were available to do the work. It was only after the difficult first years that the young families were able to start having children. Even from the earliest days, the members had spent much of their time in prayer and study. With the growth of the community, they were able to devote an ever-increasing proportion of their time to prayer.

The Master could remember vividly the day that the heir to the Zadokite line had returned to live at Sekaka. The present incumbent had been a mere infant, but the Master had been nine years old. There had been no elaborate ceremonies, just a sincere and overwhelming joy on the part of those who had re-created the village. From that time the village had once again become the center of the Sons of Zadok; cells of the Sons in the towns and villages throughout Judea looked to Sekaka for inspiration and leadership.

The father of the Master, the senior Levite of the community at that time, had been appointed Master, and with the Priest as his mentor, it was his job to administer the community. The Priest, who was a shadowy figure, maintained supreme authority and was leader in all religious matters. The Master was responsible for instruction and administration. Later on, with the growth of the community, a Bursar was elected for purely administrative duties. The community was divided into twelve groups or tribal units like the Israelites of old, and the tribal groups were divided into subgroups numbering ten.

Their life was organized according to the doctrines of the Teacher, with the economy on a strictly communal basis and ceremonial worked out according to the rank and position of the participants. Each member had his own special tasks, from laboring on the farm to teaching or scroll copying. With the success of the community and the worsening situation in Judea, large numbers flocked to join the village, but many were deterred by the strictness of the life. Only a small proportion were suitable and accepted as members.

The Master had been born into the community, not needing to win his place but entering as his birthright. He grew up in the sect and its way of living became instinctive to him. But the Master had a lively, inquiring mind and demanded explanations of everything. He studied deeply and immersed himself in the Law and the writings of the Teacher. It was natural that he should succeed his father as Master of the community. He was spiritually equipped for the task and was of appropriate rank. Increasingly dominant in managing the community's affairs, the Master had aligned the Sons of Zadok with the rebel cause in the teeth of priestly opposition. Yet in the end the Priest was supreme, for the Master was to die and the Priest to live. In giving the Priest his final victory, the Master conquered the latter's apathy. Although he could not tell how the Priest would react, he had ensured that he would be available to play whatever role the Lord assigned him. By now, the Master knew, the Priest would be safely hidden. He could rely on ben Levi, Jacob, and the others to do their duty. Contented, the Master sank down through his agony into unconsciousness.

He was awakened by a tearing, burning pain, sharper than any yet, an unbearable wrenching agony which forced him to the border of madness. As the thongs of the whip had cut into his flesh and flayed his skin to the bone, he had thought that he was experiencing the final limit of pain; but now the former agony was surpassed a hundred times. He felt a maddeningly insistent, searing anguish as his torn body was dipped into the bitter sea, raised and dipped again; but although he thought a scream was being sucked from his flayed body by the unbearable pangs, he remained silent. There was nothing left in the whole universe but this pain—not himself, his body, or his thoughts, not even the Lord God Almighty. Nothing at all beyond this continuous, ever-increasing, all-embracing agony, which somehow continued to match and exceed itself. The Master's mind had gone, though his nerves continued to pass on his excruciating paroxyms; but deep down within him, his iron will continued to suppress his reactions.

He was taken from the sea and laid face downward on his

litter again. The surviving Sons were horrified at the vividly white body of their Master, with its red gash of a back, face and eyes turned into something quite inhuman. Their Master, who had been so human as to contain something of the divine, had been reduced to a primitive bundle of reactions—and yet not entirely. Had the Master made some sound, had he cried out, had he so much as allowed a tiny whimper to escape his lips, it is probable that one or another of the surviving Sons would have broken down; but until he died, a broken, writhing, mindless organism, he remained silent. For five hours, from the first lash of the whip until the final lowering into the Sea of Salt, no sound escaped the lips of what had once been the Master of the Sons of Zadok.

One by one the remaining survivors were tortured to death, but the whereabouts of the treasure was not revealed. Sekaka was utterly destroyed and burned to the ground. A halfhearted attempt at searching for the treasure was initiated, but messengers came to Placidus from Vespasian, who had arrived in Jericho. The Roman commander was eager to return to Caesarea and start his advance on Jerusalem, so the search was called off. Placidus led his troops northward to join up with Vespasian, victorious yet dissatisfied.

5

Jacob looked out of the mouth of the cave. Gingerly he felt his still-peeling nose and scratched his bristly blond beard. There was a steep drop of nearly a hundred feet from where he sat to the valley below. The triangular plateau containing the smoldering ruins of the center was visible to the left of the wadi. Without their rope, they would have been entirely cut off from the outside world in their cave; with it they were well supplied with food and water, and they had no desire for contact with the outside. They were not able to maintain full ritual cleanliness and purity within the cave, but they endeavored to as far as conditions would permit. Jacob reflected that their lot was better than that of the Teacher, when, in his day, he had been flung into prison.

Hanan sat opposite Jacob, grasping his spear tightly in his right hand. He still possessed little understanding or imagination, but his loyalty and tenacity proved a great asset to the group. His dark face was free of expression. In the past year he had become more inscrutable, betraying his emotions less and less. He had obeyed the Master implicitly, never doubting or questioning; now he would obey ben Levi in the same manner.

The cave was too dark for study and too small for any vigorous activity, so there was no alternative to sitting and waiting. It was a difficult period for all of them after the hectic and unprecedented actions of the previous days. Ben Levi, the leader of the group, was still dazed by what had happened. Along with his colleagues he had laid hands on the high priest of Israel, heir to the Aaronic line and possibly the Messiah. As a Levite he was more aware than the laymen of the enormity of such an act. Unless the Master had been right, and they were indeed carrying out the will of God, they had perpetrated a terrible sacrilege. Ben Levi knew the fixed and irrevocable nature of rank and position with regard to Temple office, carried down from the time of Moses and later elaborated in the days of David and Solomon. For laying violent hands on the high priest, as they had done, the punishment could be nothing less than death.

The Priest himself was in a complete state of shock, praying frequently but instinctively, without comprehension or fervor. Almost from the day of his birth, he had fulfilled ceremonial duties and responsibilities. He continued to perform the expression of the ceremonial, even in the cave, but his mind had become feeble. His whole life had been one long preparation for office, for the day when it would be his duty to preside at Sekaka and to come into his inheritance as spiritual leader of the Sons of Zadok in reality as well as in name. He had prepared for the day when the sons of light would fulfill their destiny as the faithful remnant, when they were to direct the final war against the forces of evil. He knew that he might be the Messiah of Aaron, chosen to rule Israel at the End of Days, and this responsibility had constantly weighed on him.

234

Yet when the day of testing had finally come, the decision had been torn from his hands. The time had come for him to act, but he was only allowed to react. The Teacher in his time had suffered violence, had experienced the ordeal of being imprisoned and cast among the unclean; but he had not been physically assaulted by his own people. The Priest had been stunned by the speed and unexpectedness of events; there was a glazed look in his light gray eyes. The boys worried about him, relieved that at least he performed the actions necessary to keep alive. Despite the burden of their guilt, they were still fired with the burning zeal of the Master.

"What happened to the Teacher must not happen to the Priest!" he had said. The Master had outlined his plan when he had called them prior to their joining the covenant. For the past few years, he had explained, it had not been clear to him what the task of Sekaka was to be. He had not been sure how long the settlement could survive. He had wished to canvass the maximum possible support for the rebel cause without sundering the movement of the Sons of Zadok. He had been hopeful always that the pressure of events in the country would jolt the Priest out of his passive ideas and convince him of the need for immediate action.

"Now I know for sure," he continued, "that Sekaka's days are numbered. There can be no doubt that we are to be destroyed. That, it seems, is God's purpose; but the Priest must not die. He must be kept alive until the time of the seventh lot, when the righteous priests are to reoccupy the Temple in Jerusalem. That is the message of the Teacher!"

The assembled candidates had thought over the implications of the Master's words.

"The Priest must flee," stated ben Levi.

"He will never agree to leave," replied the Master.

"What can be done?" asked Jacob.

"He must be made to leave!" was the reply.

"The Priest made to leave? Do you realize what you are saying?" ben Levi had demanded.

"May the Lord help me, I do realize," the Master had replied.

Hitherto the young candidates, who had been preparing the caves under the Master's direction, had believed that his plan was for a general retreat into the hills in the event of attack; now his plan was revealed as infinitely more subtle. The defense of Sekaka was to be conducted with obstinacy and tenacity. Under cover of this defense, the high priest of Israel was to be spirited away. His role was still to be played, even if that of Sekaka was at an end.

"I wish to speak quite clearly," the Master had told them. "You are to take the Priest forcibly, bind him and carry him to the northernmost of our caves. It will be your sacred task to guard him and watch over his welfare. You must see that no harm befalls him."

"How can we possibly carry out such a monstrous act?" asked Jacob. "I do not believe that we could succeed."

"When the Romans attack Sekaka, there will be chaos and panic," replied the Master. "We will defend Sekaka to the last man, and in the turmoil you will be able to carry out your mission."

"I will not run like a coward while you die defending the village!" declared Jacob.

"Nor I!" agreed ben Levi. Several of the other candidates expressed similar sentiments.

The Master looked up and his voice, although quiet, was one that brooked no argument as he replied to them. "It is not for us to question our destiny; each one of us has his appointed task and he will carry it out. You will bow to the dictates of God's purpose, as did the young Eleazar ben Jair when he had to leave our community and return to the Sicarii against his personal wishes. It is not difficult to die for a cause; it is far harder to live for one. The task of those of us who remain to defend the village will be completed in a few days, whereas your mission may continue for many years. I have selected you most carefully for your tenaciousness and reliability. I feel that I can trust you to the end!"

"But the idea of laying violent hands on the high priest is simply unthinkable, Master," declared ben Levi. "I do not understand how you, a Levite, can make such a suggestion."

His dark features had borne an expression of baffled anger.

The Master drew his gray brows into a frown. He looked at the young Levite, concentrating his authority in the glance. "Would you prefer to be an accomplice in his murder, by refusing to accept the chance of saving his life?" he snapped.

Ben Levi was undaunted. "The Priest is a man of absolute ritual purity. He must keep himself free of contact, even the contact of fellow Jews and community members, lest he be defiled. Laying hands on him is tantamount to killing him. He could never officiate as high priest following such an occurrence."

"The Teacher returned."

"The Teacher was not called upon to officiate in the Temple."

"And I tell you, child, that you cannot act within the formal rules," thundered the Master. "These are unusual times and unique events; we have to take unparalleled measures!"

"But our whole life here at Sekaka is based on the inviolability of our laws and regulations, in contrast to the supposed flexibility of the other Jews, which we despise," persisted ben Levi. "You have always taught that others compromise to achieve their ends, but not the Son of Zadok."

"You are right, ben Levi," agreed the Master. "What you say increases not only the enormity of the crime I am asking you to commit, but also its grandeur. It is nothing for a normal Jew to bend a rule; for us it is cataclysmic. There is no doubt at all in my mind that we must do this thing. The village is about to be attacked, but the Priest can be saved. Is this to be the end of our mission, or will there be a continuation?

"Do not ask yourself what the Law is; that is not the question. It is answered before it is asked. Ask yourself rather what the Lord desires of you. I do not know whether this war is the final war prophesied by the Teacher. All I know is that it is the last war for us, for in another day our community will cease to exist. I do not believe that the Teacher founded the covenant two centuries ago so that it could dissipate amid arid legalisms. The fate of the community lies in your hands, and I think the fate of all Israel!"

It had been Hanan who had resolved the deadlock. After sitting in puzzled silence through the dispute, he said, "We must obey the Master, for through him come the commands of the Lord."

When the attack had begun, they had acted instinctively, breaking in on the Priest at the first sound of the Roman trumpets, and gagging and binding him with terrified haste. As the first group had charged out to block the cavalry's approach, the small group had slipped out of the western gate with their sacred cargo. The Priest had been surprisingly heavy, but they had made swift progress to the wadi Sekaka. Afterward it had become more difficult. The ascent to the selected cave was not an easy one even under normal conditions; now, weak with excitement and fear of what they had done, they found it a terrifying experience.

Jacob had forced himself to concentrate on the practical problems of the ascent, the achieving of each step upward, the searching for ledges and handholds. He had forced the nature of the burden he was carrying from his mind, but ben Levi had found himself unable to do so. He was overwhelmed with fear and guilt and awe. Hanan had saved the situation. He climbed like a mountain goat with absolute sureness and no wasted effort. Having determined the correctness of his course of action in obeying the Master, he was beset by no doubts. He seized the inert body of the Priest from the faltering ben Levi and assisted Jacob to carry it to the cave. Jacob could never have made it without him.

Jacob, who had been looking out into the sunlight, found it difficult to accustom his eyes to the gloom of the cave. Gradually his eyes focused on the figure of the Priest, hunched up with his soiled white robes drawn about him, eyes staring vacantly. He was relieved to see the Priest still in a state of shock; he feared the man's awakening, his awful fury. He addressed ben Levi. "I have not seen a soldier for the past two days," he reported. "Surely we could reconnoiter."

"We are not short of supplies," was the reply. "I feel we should wait a little longer."

"I cannot wait!" exclaimed Jacob. "Sekaka was destroyed. I cannot sit here coldly without going to see."

"One impetuous act can destroy all that we have done," said ben Levi. "We remain here until we can be absolutely sure."

It was a command. It had always been inevitable that ben Levi would lead the group, even though Jacob had been the first of the candidates to be singled out by the Master. It was fitting for a Levite to command; Jacob did not resent it.

6

The full moon gave a silvery sheen to the surface of the Sea of Salt. Although the sun had long since set, it was hot. The breeze which blew off the sea was warm and dry. The night gave little relief from the harsh midsummer heat of the valley. The ruins of the center were a burnt-out shell consisting of a few battered walls and the charred remains of the roof beams and furniture. The water channel had been smashed and the cisterns cracked. Most of the water had drained away. The survivors, some fifteen in number, surveyed the ruins speechlessly in the moonlight. The love and care of two centuries had been destroyed in two days. It was their task to ensure that the destruction was neither complete nor final. Slowly, moving almost with reluctance, they gathered their possessions together and began to move southward along the shore of the Sea of Salt.

FLAVIUS SILVA: MAY 73 C.E.

Flavius Silva regarded the three Jewish leaders who stood just outside the western gate a little to the north of the breach in the wall and tried to fathom their reaction to his offer. What could he suggest to these men who were so alien to him? He had not been remiss in his studies. Silva had read all he could about the Jews and Judea; he had some knowledge of their history, customs, and beliefs. He had questioned numerous slaves and prisoners.

But there was always something that eluded him, something outside the plain facts. He wished he could put himself in the position of the enemy commander, but it was impossible. Silva would never have behaved as his opponent had behaved; it was inconceivable that he would ever have allowed himself to arrive at a similar situation. It was a whole attitude, a way of looking at the world, which eluded the Roman. He knew about the featureless, all-powerful God the Jews worshiped, but he could not fathom their belief. He could not understand why, now that they were utterly defeated and their God proved to be weaker than the gods of Rome, they continued to trust and believe in Him.

Silva had served Rome in various parts of the world and appreciated that not all men were motivated by the same ideas. He accepted differences of belief and of values; but the Jews were something entirely alien, so different as to be incomprehensible. He had often enough been surprised and puzzled by his opponents, but he had always understood them once he had been given the opportunity to comprehend the situation more fully.

With the Jews it was different: the more he learned, the more he realized how little he knew. As he became familiar with Judea, the situation, far from becoming clear, became more complicated. The more he saw of the Jews, the less he understood them. They never acted rationally. They did things that no one else would ever do, for reasons which would simply not occur to normal men. They were unpredictable, obstinate, and obtuse. What could they be offered? Life? Life was not the most important thing to them. Wealth? That did not interest them. Position? They did not seem to recognize the concept. They wanted this intangible thing they called freedom, an idea as nebulous as that extraordinary God of theirs. Roman roads, Roman buildings, Greek culture, theaters, amphitheaters, baths—in short, civilization—they rejected. All they wanted was their covenant with their God, even now, when Jerusalem lay in ruins and the house of their God had been burned to the ground!

The leader of the rebels, Eleazar ben Jair, was speaking in reply to Silva's surrender offer. The Sicarii leader was very different from the man Silva had pictured in his imagination. When he had seen him from the tower, inspecting the defenses and directing attacks, he had never suspected that this was the famous son of Jair, fourth-generation guerrilla commander descended from the line of the kings of ancient Israel. He was small and slight, with a scholarly expression on his mild, bearded face. His voice was gentle and slightly hoarse.

When Silva had originally offered a parley, there had been no response; but since then he had brought up the battering ram, and the ram had created conditions for negotiations. The gigantic iron-headed balk that had battered the walls of Jerusalem was still with the Tenth Legion; they had needed four mules to drag it to Masada via Herodium and Ein Gedi. The batterer had been balanced in its rope sling attached to the strong frame of the siege tower, and they had begun to swing it against the wall. The crash of iron on stone filled the whole valley with an awe-inspiring sound; the interval between the crashes shortened and became regular, as the remorseless pounding of the wall began. The defenders had made renewed attacks on the tower, but nothing they could do had been able to stop the inevitable action of the huge battering ram.

The procurator forced himself to concentrate on Eleazar's words. He listened carefully, wondering if he was dreaming, astounded at the lack of reality in the whole situation. In the middle of the bleak wastes were all the trappings of Rome's might. An entire legion, backed by countless auxiliaries, lay encamped about the walls of the enemy stronghold. A mighty ramp topped by a siege tower dominated the fortress whose walls had been breached. All this he saw from where he stood. Some twenty paces from him a gentle, pious man, his thin face framed with a brown beard, flanked by two guerrilla soldiers, read his speech in precise, scholarly tones, whereby, on behalf of less than a thousand people, many of them women and children, he totally rejected Silva's generous surrender terms and pledged that he would fight on to final victory.

BOOK V

ELEAZAR: 73 C.E.

In Judea Bassus had died and the new procurator was Flavius Silva, who, seeing the rest of the country reduced to impotence, and only one fortress still holding out, marched against it with all available forces.

Flavius Josephus, *The Jewish War*

And with the seventh lot, the mighty hand of God shall bring down [the army of Satan and all] the angels of his kingdom . . .

The War Rule: *The Dead Sea Scrolls*

1

Eleazar ben Jair stood in the shade of the rock on his lower terrace at the northern end of the rock of Masada. From where he stood he could see the main camp of the enemy quite clearly over to the west. The smaller auxiliary northern camp was below him, and another, smaller camp stood in front of the main one. He could not fail to notice also the northern and western sections of the encircling wall, and if he turned and looked to the south, he could see a part of the gigantic siege ramp topped by its soaring tower.

There was no escape, Eleazar told himself. There never really had been. From the day that they had attacked Masada under the leadership of Menahem, the final confrontation with Roman power had been inevitable. He felt a reluctant admiration for the Romans and the way they had made the unassailable fortress accessible to them. First, the camps, eight camps all around the rock, sealing off every possible means of egress. As if this were insufficient, they had connected the smaller camps with a wall that entirely circled the rock, a wall which did not give way to hill or steep-sided valley. They had then built the ramp, which covered the western aqueduct. They had constructed it with earth and rocks, strengthened by vast balks of wood dragged miles through the empty desert to besiege the small fortress.

It had been the sheer size of the Roman force that had impressed Eleazar. He had known that there were six thousand troops in a legion and that Silva was advancing on Masada with far more than a legion; but the actual appearance of the soldiers, who filled the area surrounding the rock both east and west, was staggering. They had arrived almost simultaneously at the western foot—approaching over the high Judean plateau—and the eastern foot, along the shore of the Sea of Salt.

First came the scouts, followed by a group of lightly armed auxiliary bowmen. They were followed by a large column of heavily armed soldiers in full armor, bristling with pikes and carrying shields. Following them was a multitude of slaves with shovels and other leveling tools, who cleared the rocks and broadened the paths for the approaching army. Then came the personal baggage of the commanders, Silva's to the west, his deputy's to the east, each guarded by a century of cavalry and followed at once by the commanders in person, escorted by troops of horsemen and pikemen. Following the commanders, the legionary cavalry filed into sight, and some time after them mules dragging or carrying the siege weapons. Some mules were dragging larger wooden logs, and to the west four mules dragged a vast balk with an iron head, the batterer of the Tenth Legion. Behind the siege engines came the other officers with the standards, the eagle of the legion going to the western foot. Trumpeters with their endless brazen fanfares followed the standards, and only then came the main body of the soldiers. The columns seemed to continue interminably as they swung in perfect order into the two valleys, the centurions keeping them in line.

By the time the last of the infantry had arrived, the advance unit of slaves had the camps marked out, so that the main body of slaves who came after the soldiers could assist in building the stone walls and digging the ditches. The various auxiliary brigades followed the legion slaves, arriving as the legionaries were settling into their camps. The rear was brought up by a motley collection of camp followers, scavengers, suppliers, slave dealers, and prostitutes.

Three hours had passed from the time of the appearance of the first bowmen to the arrival of the last straggler, three hours of solid marching humanity to give battle to less than a thousand men, women, and children.

Eleazar remembered vividly the coming of the Romans. They had arrived in the winter. In the months that had followed their arrival, the Lord had seemed to be helping the Sicarii, as the Romans were buffeted by the elements, their camps flooded, their ramp washed away in the foaming brown torrents, their tents ripped to pieces by the howling winds. But they had persisted despite every drawback. For them, as for

250

Eleazar, there had been no alternative. Rome could not tolerate Masada; they had to destroy it promptly and utterly, lest the lie of *Iudaea Capta* be revealed.

So the Tenth Legion and its multitude of slaves had set to work and now the fortress was menaced; the white ramp pointed like a dagger at her and the siege tower stood above the height of the western wall. From their tower the Romans could shoot down into the fortress, menacing the defenders with their quick-loaders and stone-throwers. The round boulders stocked above each camp to repel attack remained unused except in the west. The Romans were placing their faith in the tower and in the huge batterer which worked beneath its cover. They had breached the section of the wall by the tower, but Eleazar had found an ingenious solution to prevent their further penetration.

Eleazar had not been surprised by Silva's offer of surrender terms, though he knew that he could only give one answer. The procurator's whole approach to the siege had combined that essentially Roman mixture of formality and flexibility: the insistence on orthodox camps first and foremost, despite the special conditions; his methodical construction of the wall; his organization of supplies; his refusal to be overawed by the magnitude of the task of approaching the walls towering four hundred feet above him. He had carried out a classical Roman siege—on the face of it unoriginal, yet only a man of great imagination could have carried out an orthodox siege in such conditions. The surrender offer was of a piece with the rest of Silva's conduct. He had nothing to lose and he might save the lives of a number of his soldiers.

Eleazar knew that his answer to Silva had doomed them. They had been living on the summit of the rock for seven years. They had refused all opportunities to leave. Simon bar Giora had always wanted to leave and he had left, as Menahem had left before him. Menahem had died and now Simon too was dead, strangled at Rome in the triumph that celebrated Judea's defeat. The Temple had been destroyed, the land scoured, and shortly this last outpost of resistance would exist no more.

After seven years of war Eleazar could see only the inevitability of Roman power. Intervention by the Almighty simply did not fit the pattern. It was not that such a thing could not happen; but the time was not ripe, the Romans were at the zenith of their power. It was true that their empire would fall one day and that one day the kingdom of God would arrive on earth. But that time had not yet arrived.

Only Rivka the widow of Menahem had dissented from the reply that Eleazar had given the Roman commander.

"If there is a hope of life," Rivka had said, "we should take it. The Almighty has put a momentary kindness into this Roman's heart; let us take advantage of it."

"He has offered us life, not freedom," Joab had pointed out.

"What is freedom?" the old woman had asked. "Freedom is an idea. All of us in this world are slaves to someone or something—even those Romans out there, the lords of the earth. It is only in your heart and in your soul that you can be free. I say that our hearts and our souls can triumph under any conditions that leave us alive."

"Why are you so afraid to die?" asked bar Nottos. "All must die in the end."

"It is not death that I fear," replied the old woman. She stood straight and proud, her white head held aloft, her voice strong and clear. "I fear violence, which is sacrilege against the Lord. He and He alone must decide when this wondrous thing He has granted us called life is to be cut off. It is not for us to mutilate His work!"

"It is His war we are fighting," said Eleazar. "We are His soldiers. It is His purpose that Judea be free, otherwise He would have not put the dream into our hearts. My conscience tells me to fight, and that does not mean to surrender when the situation looks blackest. We must have faith in God and fight on."

Ben Levi had then spoken, his tall, slim figure dominating the assembly. He spoke with an inner certainty that was lacking in the others.

"The Teacher is unambiguous on this point," he stated. "In the seventh lot, the forces of light are to gain their first victory;

the righteous priests will take over the administration of the Temple from the hands of the defiled—"

"Where is your Temple?" interrupted Rivka. "Where is Jerusalem? Where are the unrighteous priests, let alone the righteous ones?"

"The legitimate high priest of Israel, heir to the Zadokite line, is here at Masada. The Messiah of Aaron, destined to rule Israel in the last days, as foretold in the Scriptures and in the writings of the Sons of Zadok, will shortly join the struggle against the Kittim!"

Eleazar had been impressed by ben Levi's sincerity, but he had been unable to believe his message. War was a matter of soldiers and fighting, of strategy and weapons, not an old half-mad priest calling on heavenly legions and waiting for the miraculous intervention of the Almighty Himself.

"That is not the way," Rivka had insisted. "The kingdom of God is here with us in the hearts of each and every one of us, if only we allow ourselves to feel it. The Messiah is the spirit of the Lord which is waiting to be allowed to emerge. It is love that will conquer the world—love for one's neighbor, not hatred and might. We cannot stand against Rome; we have seen that."

She turned to Eleazar and addressed him directly. "Eleazar, I appeal to you: for the sake of the children, accept the Roman's offer. They are young and innocent; they do not understand why you fight. They want to laugh and play and enjoy the warmth of the sun. They have a right to grow up and bear children of their own. Would you condemn them to death in a battle that they have not sought and do not understand?"

"Will it be better for them to live as slaves?" demanded Eleazar. "Should they grow up as chattels of other men to be bought and sold, to live in chains? Should the girls grow up to be whores and the boys to be eaten by animals in the arena?"

"How can it be avoided?" asked Rivka. "It was always inevitable that we would lose. Had you listened to me, you could have prepared the children for their future, you could have instilled in them knowledge and love that nothing could extin-

253

guish. But instead you talk of war and fighting!"

"The things that you say are not inevitable," Eleazar had said. "Your picture of the future is not the only possible one. Death is inevitable but not slavery, violence but not chains. If we surrender now, we betray everything that we have struggled for. We betray Menahem and Absalom and Simon—yes, Simon, for he was our comrade. Above all, we betray God!"

It would not be much longer now. Wherever one looked from the summit of the rock—north, south, east, or west—the wall was there, as were the eight camps. There was no way out. The dry desert wind that blew from Moab left no moisture; it was oppressively hot. Eleazar felt his head aching and his nose blocked. His eyes smarted and the hair on his arms stood away from the skin. The sun was a silver coin in the gray sky. One could not see far into the distance, for a thick haze hung everywhere. At least they had no water problem, unlike the enemy below. Another summer of siege would see their water supply severely curtailed, as the aqueducts had been destroyed; but for the time being they were amply supplied.

Eleazar continued to reflect on his difference of opinion with his aunt. Owned chattels, dependent on their owners for everything, devoid of any rights, could not be expected to live as Jews. Agrippa, the Jewish king, had organized games in his capital of Caesarea Philippi to honor Titus—games in which thousands of Jews had been publicly massacred, eaten by lions, gored by bulls, burned, racked, and tortured. Death in battle was far less terrible than slavery; but Eleazar did not see how they could escape that fate, despite his words to his aunt. Some of the men would be captured before they died, not to say the women and children. Eleazar shuddered as he thought of young virgins like Rachel and Deborah, the daughters of Joab, raped by the victorious soldiers. Even young lads could not be safe from the filthy attentions of the soldiers. He thought of his own son, a mere six years old, and so handsome as to be almost pretty. It must not happen!

They had been moving toward this moment for seven years, but they had always hoped that something might intervene.

254

They had never faced reality, even when the Romans had swept through Galilee, Idumea, and Judea—when the capital itself had fallen. They had felt safe in their fastness. Even with the Roman soldiers in the valley below, sealing off every exit, with the battering ram smashing the very walls of their invincible fortress, they had not felt the immediacy of defeat. Eleazar was forced to admit to himself that there would be no seventh-lot victory; this was the wrong war. Maybe it would be the next war, or maybe the war had already been fought a long time ago. What did time mean in the timeless desert of Sekaka?

Eleazar forced the images on his reluctant mind. He made himself see women and children with laughter in their eyes. He saw their expressions change, their eyes turn cloudy with fear, their mouths gape in surprise and horror. This was the reality; this had happened a thousand times throughout Judea. He saw his brown-skinned, brown-haired son with his mother's eyes, dark with amazement. The thought came to him again: it must not happen!

2

Simon bar Giora had never returned to Masada, even when Vespasian's ruthless advance through Judea and Idumea had forced him into hiding. He and his party had lain hidden in the caves of Pharan as the Roman armies laid waste to the land. With all of Judea subdued, Vespasian had hurried back to Caesarea to prepare his assault on Jerusalem; but on arrival there, he had been informed of the death of the emperor in Rome. Throughout the remainder of the summer and well into autumn, the Romans had remained in Caesarea, awaiting orders from the new authorities in Rome.

With the legions thus immobilized, Simon bar Giora was able to renew his activities. His power grew as he collected more and more adherents from the lawless countryside, merging the diverse elements into a powerful army. Zealot forces had emerged from Jerusalem in an attempt to liquidate the threat of this vast new faction, but they were defeated in battle. Defeating the Idumean forces also, by a combination of intrigue and force, bar Giora sacked Hebron and advanced to the walls of Jerusalem. In an engagement with Zealot forces, Miriam was captured and held hostage; but the slave leader perpetrated such terrible violence on his prisoners that she was hastily returned. The Romans waited in Caesarea and Simon waited outside the walls of Jerusalem.

Within the city the Galileans under John of Gischala fought the Zealots of ben Simon, and both groups fought the Idumeans. After continuing the struggle inconclusively, the Idumeans decided to allow bar Giora into the city in an attempt to alter the balance in their favor. So at last bar Giora achieved the aim for which he had left Masada—but though leader of the dominant faction in Jerusalem, he was far from being in sole control of the capital.

The civil strife in Jerusalem was paralleled by civil war in far-off Rome. After the second claimant to the imperial throne had been installed, the eastern legions decided to proclaim Vespasian as emperor. Controlling as he did the granaries of Alexandria, Vespasian was irresistible, although it was some months before he was able to travel to Rome and consolidate his position. Before leaving the east, the new emperor entrusted the completion of the Judean campaign to his son Titus, who at once proceeded from Alexandria to Caesarea. Spring of the following year saw Titus before the walls of Jerusalem.

The onset of the Roman siege did not halt the vicious factional fighting among the Jews, and it was only after the capture of the two outer walls by the Romans that the defenders finally united against the enemy. By this time the plight of the capital was extreme. Food and water were scarce, and stories of unbelievable horror emerged from the besieged city—of disease, cannibalism, and death. John of Gischala's men defended the Temple Mount, while Simon bar Giora held the upper city. Concentrating his forces against the Temple Mount, Titus attacked in overwhelming strength. His soldiers succeeded in capturing the Antonia fortress, and although the Jews fought with tenacity over every inch of their sacred building, a month later the young general was hailed by his legions in the smoking ruins of what had been the Temple of Jerusalem. A few weeks later the upper city fell and Simon bar Giora was captured.

Titus had traveled the length and breadth of Judea, celebrating the Roman victory with games and gladiatorial contests. The few survivors who had escaped from Jerusalem fled to Herodium, south of Jerusalem, Macherus on the eastern shore of the Sea of Salt, and to Masada. Although some small outposts still remained undefeated, Titus and Vespasian celebrated a joint triumph in Rome, at the end of which the giant figure of the Jewish commander, Simon bar Giora, was brought into the forum. A rope was fastened around his powerful neck and he was savagely beaten with spearshafts as he was pulled by the ever-tightening noose through the city to his death. Thus bar Giora earned from his enemies the recognition he had wanted, though never received, from his own people.

Bassus, a new general, continued the Judean campaign. The following year he captured the remaining Idumean garrison of Herodium and successfully besieged the fortress of Macherus, where a mixed group of Pereans, Zealots, and Galilean survivors still held out. He then proceeded to the forest of Jardes where Judah ben Jair had based himself with three hundred men. Judah had slipped out of the doomed capital via the sewers; but to Eleazar's chagrin he had not returned to Masada, preferring to roam the countryside. Surrounding the forest and cutting down most of the trees, the cavalry of Bassus, the Roman commander, eliminated the last of the roaming bands of Jewish rebels; Judah the brother of Eleazar was killed.

Only Masada remained free. Bassus died and Flavius Silva was appointed procurator of Judea. That was in the winter. By the end of the spring, Masada was surrounded by a wall and eight camps, menaced by the siege tower from the incredible ramp which filled the western valley. Try as they might, the defenders had not been able to destroy the iron-covered tower. They had rolled stones down onto it, but they had bounced harmlessly off into the valley below. They had attacked it directly, only to be beaten back. They had tried to pour boiling oil on the attackers, but the deadly barrage of the stone-throwers and quick-loaders had driven them from the walls. It had become clear to Eleazar that nothing could save his casemate wall from the battering ram, so he had devised an ingenious defense which gave the defenders further respite.

He had ordered his men to dismantle the roofs of some of the larger buildings, taking down the large beams. The balks were carried to the section of wall behind the batterer and lashed to upright posts, forming a containing double wooden wall, which would block further penetration when the outer wall was breached. The space in the middle of the wooden wall was filled with earth and rubble, which was thereupon doused with water, forming mud. In due course the Romans had breached the outer wall and come upon the second wall. The blows from the giant battering ram, which was brought forward, had merely strengthened the wall of mud and wood, compressing it into a harder obstacle. The head of the ram became coated with a layer of mud, which unbalanced and slowed up the machine.

The new wall could be destroyed by fire, but fire was a two-edged weapon. It could never be entirely controlled. Roman siege towers had been burned down before in the course of the war in Judea, and Silva had not wanted to take unnecessary risks. It was characteristic of his conduct of the siege. The same mind that had decided upon circumvalation—building the ramp and tower—had attempted to negotiate surrender rather than risk using fire; but his generous offer had been rejected, and no alternative remained.

3

It was already dark when Nahum and his sons returned from evening prayers and sat down to their supper. The boys were already useful members of the community. David at fifteen could stand guard and run messages, and both of the elder sons helped their father with his duties in the stores. Despite the fluctuations in the size of the community, the stores had remained plentiful, thanks to the abundance of the original supplies and to Nahum's careful husbandry. Joab still managed to grow fresh vegetables on the summit, and Rivka continued to preside over the livestock. Most fugitives that arrived at the fortress brought with them a minimum of supplies. That afternoon David had been working in Simon bar Nottos' water-carrying party, while Nahum had been distributing supplies with Uri. Six-year-old Joseph had generally hindered them in their duties.

Great excitement had been caused in the synagogue by the first appearance of the Priest in more than a year. Since the Sons of Zadok had arrived five years previously, the Priest had lived the life of a recluse. Ben Levi and the others had spoken on his behalf and collected his tithes. He had been accepted as priest of the community, and, at Eleazar's behest, many doctrinal changes had been introduced to bring the community into line with the beliefs of the Sons. But he had seldom appeared and never spoken. As soon as he had entered the synagogue, Nahum caught sight of the tall, arresting figure, with his white hair and beard. His hair had turned that color after the fall of Sekaka. The pale gray eyes might almost have been sightless as they swept the congregation. All eyes had been focused on the Priest, but the prayers had been led by ben Levi as usual.

The family sat around the rough trestle table, eating their simple meal and discussing the Priest.

"It is the first time he has been present for more than a year," said David. "I wonder what it means." The smoke curled up from the oil lamp to the dim rafters of the ceiling. The table was illuminated with a soft glow. Nahum's blond hair and beard were streaked with gray, bleached white in several places. His fair skin had been burned a brick red by the sun.

"I find it very hard to understand the Sons of Zadok," he confessed. His forehead was creased with concentration. "They regard every disaster as a triumph. I suppose you could

259

say that they brought out the Priest to celebrate the imminent destruction of the fortress!"

"Why is it so difficult to understand them?" asked David. He was serious in expression, though his face still bore something of his boyish petulance. "They believe that each new disaster brings us nearer to the final redemption."

"I certainly understand Eleazar better since I have known them," said Nahum. "But that does not mean that I really understand them!"

"What is going to happen now?" asked Uri. At twelve he was old enough to notice his father's concerned expression and his mother's red eyes.

"It is going to be difficult," answered Nahum.

"Will they start throwing the stones again and those metal things?"

"I expect so," replied his father.

"Do you think they will set fire to the inner wall?" asked David.

"Almost certainly," conceded Nahum.

"Would you have surrendered if you were Eleazar?" asked David. Nahum looked at his aging wife, her hair also streaked with gray, her plumpness giving way to wrinkles, a tired and hurt look in her eyes. Then he looked at David, now never to become a man, his olive skin and light hair like that of his brother Uri. Both boys had that petulant look that only age could erase.

"I cannot say," he admitted. "I am glad that it was not my decision. I do not think I could decide something of that sort." He regarded his youngest son, Joseph, born and bred in the fortress, having lived all his short life on the summit of the rock. Joseph had a special place in his affections.

Masada had been a difficult place in which to bring up children. At the age of three and a half, Joseph, a large, fat child with a bright smile and a manner of squinting in the bright sun that made him look thoughtful for a three-year-old, went walking happily over the edge of the cliff. Nahum had heard the child's cry as he fell and ran quickly to the spot where he thought the boy must be. His first shock was when

260

he did not see his son; his second was when he caught sight of him struggling, suspended on a narrow ledge a thousand feet above the valley. Nahum had been paralyzed with terror and trembled violently, with the sweat pouring down his body. Only a week previously a child had fallen to his death from the cruel heights.

It had been fortunate that bar Nottos arrived at that moment, for Nahum had been incapable of action. Not waiting for a rope, the young man had swiftly climbed down the cliff face to where Joseph lay. He sat there with him on the ledge, keeping him from further harm, until Nahum managed to call for help and obtain some ropes. The scene was sharply engraved on Nahum's memory. It was not only the dangerous situation of the child, but his own utter helplessness which had terrified Nahum night after night as he thought and dreamed about the incident.

Nahum had a special feeling for his youngest son, Joseph, snatched as he was from the very jaws of death. His throat ached as he surveyed his family in the lamplight. As a rebel fighter he had faced death many times, but he could not bear to think about the fate of his dear ones at the hands of the victorious Romans. He knew what the Romans did to their prisoners—the ones who died were the lucky ones. Thinking about his family sapped Nahum's determination to defend the fortress and set him to thinking of possible escape. Looking back over the years at Masada, Nahum concluded that they had been among the happiest of his life. There had been quarrels and fighting, but there had always been enough to eat and drink. Even with Judea being destroyed around them, they had contrived to maintain a normal life on the rock.

But like all of them, Nahum had been heading for the day of reckoning—he had known that the day would come since he had fled north from the copper mines of the Aravah. For more than six years he had been able to raise his family in relative tranquillity. He was especially grateful for those years, for he knew now there would be no more of them.

Joab, his red hair and beard speckled with white, paced by

the eastern casemate wall with his son-in-law, bar Nottos. It was dark and the night air was chilly, but the stars were glittering in all their splendor. Of all of them at Masada, bar Nottos, possibly because of the ageless quality of his finely chiseled featured and smooth skin, had changed the least.

"We have so little time, Simon," pleaded Joab. "Do not waste it in these pointless quarrels."

"It is not my fault," claimed the young man. "I am ready to make up with her, but she will not hear of it."

"You know I do not like to interfere in matters that do not concern me," said Joab.

Bar Nottos laid an affectionate hand on the older man's shoulder. "Do not say that, Father," he replied. "You are wonderful to us. Without you I do not think we could have continued to live together."

When bar Nottos had returned from the raid with bar Giora, Shifra had refused to speak to him, despite the fact that he had elected to remain at Masada. It had taken Joab many hours of patient persuasion to bring them together. Soon after their marriage, they had parted after some trivial argument, and once again it was Shifra's father who reconciled them with each other. The birth of their daughter, seven months earlier, had hardly eased matters between them; the placid child was only another source of conflict between them.

With motherhood, Shifra had arrived at blazing, redheaded maturity. Her plumpness had left her, leaving her with a sinuous but full body. Her high-boned, freckled face was arresting without being beautiful, and her green eyes with their rust flecks flashed in her frequent moments of bad temper. There was no lack of attraction between her and bar Nottos, but their fierce love could not always overcome their basic incompatibility. Shifra was hot-tempered and impulsive, liable to explode with anger over a seemingly unimportant matter. Bar Nottos was calm and quiet but he was abnormally stubborn, and once his mind had been made up it could not be altered. He was frequently engulfed by the wave of feeling that overcame him in his wife's company, but he found that his love could be turned to hate almost instantly. Irritated by some-

262

thing in her behavior, he would release a word or phrase of such savage bitterness that its consequences could not be evaded, causing them to separate for weeks at a time. They would live together in an icy politeness and formality, which masked the reality of their cold rage.

The previous evening bar Nottos had been left alone with the child. Bathsheba was a quiet child and would play by herself without demanding attention. On this occasion, bar Nottos had been sitting at the table lost in his thoughts. He had been intensely irritated when his reflections were interrupted by a scream from Shifra, who stood in the doorway.

"There by her hand, look there!" she screeched. His head jerked up in irritation.

"What?" he snapped impatiently.

"By her hand on the floor! Do something, you fool!" Then he had seen it. Crawling slowly in the direction of her plump, white hand was a long yellow scorpion, its tail curved upward ready to strike; he could distinctly see the dark poison behind the barb. It had been the work of a second to jump to his feet, sweep his daughter into his arms, and stamp his tough leather sandal on the creature. He shivered with fright, hugging the plump little body to him. She was safe, praise the Almighty! Angrily, Shifra strode up and seized her daughter.

"Give her to me," she snarled. "You are not fit to look after her!"

"What do you mean?"

"I left her in your care for one minute, and you let her kill herself!"

"It was not my fault," he claimed. "She always plays on the floor. You allow her to play on the floor."

"I watch her."

"Do not be utterly ridiculous. It is impossible to watch her every second. She is all right—that is the most important thing."

"In spite of you. You did your best to murder her!"

"I suppose you think your hysterical screeching saved her?"

Later in the evening when the child was sleeping peacefully, bar Nottos had tried to reopen the argument; but his

263

words had met with no response. Finally in exasperation, he had crossed the room and seized his wife by the shoulders. She was a wildcat, spitting and clawing. They fought wordlessly, the slim, dark man and the flame-haired woman. Finally, not without difficulty, he overpowered her and she bit him, sinking her sharp teeth deeply into his sinewy shoulder. The smooth brown body and the creamy, freckled, white one came together in a silent passion that was totally physical.

"I thought that the quarrel was over last night," explained bar Nottos bitterly, "but apparently I was wrong. I do not know what I can do to end the dispute."

"I will talk to her," promised Joab. "I simply want to know whether you will cooperate."

"Of course I will, Father," was the reply. "You know that I love her!" Now it was the turn of the older man to put his arm around the other's shoulders. They continued to pace silently in the night, each with his own thoughts. Bar Nottos thought of his wife, of how he loved her and how he was infuriated by her.

Joab was afraid; for the first time in his life, he faced the future with abject terror. Even within the warrior community of the Sicarii, where feats of daring were taken for granted, Joab the redhead, named after King David's general, was regarded as outstandingly brave. He had never been known to flinch in battle; but as he paced beneath the desert stars, he wondered for the first time whether he had been right to join the rebel band of Menahem ben Judah.

The stocky commander loved his family deeply. He worshiped his diminutive, gray-haired wife, Sarah, and willingly jumped to obey her orders in a manner so obsequious that it amused the remainder of the community. A strong leader in battle, at home he was dependent entirely on his wife. Sarah kept the most orderly home at Masada, and Joab was humbly grateful for it. He occasionally tempered his wife's severity to his daughters with his own mild tolerance, seeing as little fault in his daughters as he saw in his wife. He ached with anguish over Shifra's marriage, having strong feelings of affection for her husband also. He was always between them, comforting one or the other.

Possibly, he reflected, he interfered too much. Left to themselves, they might have been forced to adapt to each other, whereas they had always known that Joab would smooth the way. Their daughter, Bathsheba, was the most perfect of all God's creatures as far as her grandfather was concerned. He held her on his knee, tickled her, and threw her in the air. She pulled his white-streaked beard and reserved her special smile for him. He rarely lost patience with Deborah and Rachel, his younger daughters. "They are only young girls," he would say. "Young girls are supposed to giggle."

Joab was terrified at the thought of what was going to happen to his family. He saw Bathsheba, her plump bandy legs seized by rough hands, her brains dashed out against a wall; Deborah and Rachel, unready for womanhood, raped by soldier after soldier; Shifra sold into slavery and prostitution; Sarah humiliated; bar Nottos turned into a professional killer —a gladiator; himself. ... Joab did not fear for himself; he would fight until he was killed. His risk was the same each time he went forth to battle. But as he thought of his family, he trembled violently, a cold sweat running down his back. He wanted to vomit.

Eleazar sat with his son while the boy fell asleep. Menahem resembled his mother in looks, with a black-eyed, darkskinned prettiness countered by a mischievous, boyish expression which prevented effeminacy. His thick, light brown hair fell into his eyes, and he was always pushing it aside with his hand. His full lips were slightly parted, revealing the small white teeth. Despite the darkness of his skin, there was color in his cheeks, particularly in sleep. He was gracefully built, with long limbs and loose, easy movements. His laugh was spontaneous and ready, the accompanying smile lighting up his whole face. He spoke slowly and distinctly in a voice that was rather low for his age. He had a sensitive look about him yet also a quality of animal vitality. He looked entirely innocent in sleep as his father bent to kiss the velvet cheek.

265

Eleazar knew only too well what would happen to young boys captured by the Romans. A child as beautiful as the young Menahem had no chance of escaping the male brothels, unless it was for the private boudoir of some old governor or senator. Eleazar ground his teeth. He remembered his son as a round brown baby, bursting out of his skin, helpless at his mother's breast, a totally dependent creature. He remembered him as a vigorous, red-faced toddler with a strong grip and stronger lungs. At that age, Eleazar's departure would be signaled by the crumpling of the young face into an ugly, red, crying mess and his arrival with loud shouts of glee. He would grasp his father's finger tightly with his small hands. His head had been a mass of curls. Before he had learned to talk, the young Menahem would shout gibberish with an enthusiasm that had made his father laugh aloud. As a toddler, he was so solid and vigorous that Eleazar would marvel at such a creature's emerging from the womb of his slim, fragile-looking wife. He resembled his uncle Simon more than anyone.

It was his son's helplessness that Eleazar had loved initially, or possibly it was a feeling of responsibility for something so dependent. When his son's covenant with the Lord had been consecrated, Eleazar had felt a physical pain in his own genitals as the cut was made in the tiny member. During the next stage in his son's development, his father had loved the reflection of his wife that he saw in the child. But then, as the boy developed his own personality, there came the deep and overwhelming love for the child himself.

After the birth of Menahem, Hagar had suffered a number of miscarriages, and it became clear that they would have no more children. For this reason it was especially worrying to them when, in his fourth year, the boy had become ill with a fever. As he lay tossing on his pallet, feverish and pale by turns, seemingly thinner and weaker by the hour, his parents had become almost insane with worry. Ben Levi treated him, for the Sons of Zadok were knowledgeable about medicine; but despite the constant administering of potions and herbs, he could not say whether the boy would recover.

They had taken turns sitting by him, wiping his hot brow

with damp cloths. The child looked ever more weak and help-less. Eleazar became like a man demented. He prayed unceas-ingly to God for the life of his child, but the face became thinner and the eyes larger and darker. The body was warm and damp, burning with heat; his cheeks were flushed. It seemed to Eleazar as if the child were burning away, like wood consumed by fire. For days they sat by him, powerless to do anything to save the helpless little person who depended on them so totally, whose eyes, through all their suffering, looked on them with such trust.

When the boy had awakened one day, weaker and thinner but without the fever, his father had broken down entirely, weeping with tears of joy and gratitude. He gave thanks to the Almighty with all his heart.

Watching him sleep, Eleazar felt that some of the vulnerabil-ity of his son had returned. He was no longer the self-assured red-faced toddler, shouting his gibberish; but he was older and more aware, sensitive and capable of being hurt. When moved, his lower lip would tremble and his black eyes moisten. He was a bright child and could already read fluently. When he was listening to the surrender terms, the thought had fleetingly crossed Eleazar's mind to offer the surrender of Masada for the freedom of his son; but such an idea would betray the boy. He sat there in the shadows by his son's pallet and his mind wan-dered into the past as it had so often during the past weeks. He recalled sitting on the knee of his uncle Menahem, while his father was still alive. Menahem had told him of the deeds of Hezekiah and Judah, for his father, Jair, would tell no tales of death and violence. He must have been the same age as his son was now when he had first heard the story of Hezekiah.

"Hezekiah was the first of us," the rough-bearded man had explained. Menahem's beard and hair had been brown then. He was strong and quick, and although he knew of his father's disapproval of Menahem's activities, Eleazar had thought his uncle the most wonderful person in the world.

"Hezekiah was called a bandit," the rebel leader had con-tinued, "but the father of Judah of Galilee was no mere cutthroat—he was a patriot, fighting for his people's rights. He and his followers refused to accept the Roman takeover, which the country's supposed leaders were arranging. They were the successors of the Pious Ones who had supported the Maccabees. They did plunder and steal, but only to keep themselves alive. Their aim was freedom and independence for Judea.

"Hezekiah carried out many bold exploits before he was captured and executed by the Idumean turncoat Herod. Herod had to face the Sanhedrin for that; but it was weak already, composed of a number of tired, frightened old men. They were no match for Herod. You do not think, though, that Herod would have been challenged for the murder of a mere bandit leader, do you? No, Hezekiah was recognized as a patriotic leader.

"After the death of Hezekiah, the movement continued under Judah. The rebels lived in caves in the mountains of Galilee, and after the Romans had made him a king, Herod pursued them again. The caves were unapproachable to those who did not know the mountain paths, but Herod was a clever rascal. He lowered his soldiers by ropes from above. Once they wiped out a whole cave community in that way. The community leader on that occasion did a remarkably heroic thing. ..."

The young Eleazar had listened spellbound to the stories of his uncle Menahem. Now the adult Eleazar watched his son, the young Menahem, sleeping; and the old Menahem was dead.

Menahem had always hoped that Eleazar would serve as the link between the Sicarii and the Sons of Zadok; Eleazar knew the Sons and knew their ways. When the party of fugitives had arrived at Masada after the fall of Sekaka, he had felt no hesitation about admitting them. They had arrived with their Priest and their dreams of grandeur.

Eleazar, on the other hand, had come to realize that the group at Masada could not influence events in Judea. For many years Eleazar had anticipated the historical moment when the Sons of Zadok and the Sicarii would combine, not merely in a military alliance, but in a united movement which would include the piety of the Sons and the valor of the Sicarii; the Pious Ones would live again and the land would be liberated. He had visualized a gigantic ceremony in the Temple to celebrate the unification of the independence movements under a united religious and secular authority. Ruled by the legitimate high priest, led by the master strategist Menahem ben Judah, organized by the Master into a tightly knit, strictly observant community, the fellowship of light would vanquish the forces of darkness and evil.

The actual union of the tattered remnants of the two movements on an isolated rock in the middle of the wilderness proved to Eleazar, deep within himself, that his dream was not to be. Nevertheless, he proclaimed the Priest as religious leader of Masada, introduced the Zadokite calendar, and formally divided the community into twelve units which represented the twelve tribes. The Sons took control of the religious life of the community, though the Priest himself remained in half-mad seclusion. Tithes were collected for the Priest, and jars for his portion were marked in the stores. Study of the works of the Teacher was introduced and his commentaries were used in the study of the Law.

Eleazar cooperated fully with ben Levi, who led the Sons in the name of the Priest. The Pharisiac community of the Sicarii was smoothly transformed into a group of the Sons of Zadok; but, though Rivka resisted all the changes fiercely, the alterations were on a purely superficial level. The new community lacked the inner fire of the community at Sekaka; the atmosphere was more relaxed.

In theory the doctrines of the Teacher ruled; but in practice a mixture of customs and beliefs was evident in the life of the fortress. Eleazar clearly saw that his was not the harsh, sure, divine community of his vision and grew increasingly certain that this was not the prophesied time. Although his doubts were felt even before the survivors of the Sons of Zadok arrived in Masada, it was not until he gave his reply to the Roman commander, Flavius Silva, that Eleazar the son of Jair realized that final and absolute defeat was at hand.

4

The Sons of Zadok were convinced more than ever before that they were witnessing the dawning of the new age. The destruction through which the land was passing strengthened, rather than weakened, this conviction. With every step in the ravaging of Judea they became more certain. The very events which had convinced Eleazar of the futility of the rebel cause served only to raise their enthusiasm. The siege of the Holy City caused excitement and jubiliation; the destruction of the Temple brought them to fever pitch. It was happening according to the words of the Teacher and the prophecies of old— first the destruction, then the redemption; first the casting down, then the raising up. With Judea in flames, the house of God in ruins, the land a waste and the heathen victorious, the people of Israel had indeed come to the lowest ebb of their fortunes, from which they would rise to unparalleled heights of glory.

Some two dozen survivors from Sekaka, led by ben Levi and Jacob, had arrived at Masada five years previously, carrying with them some of their scrolls and little else. They had been the only survivors of a community of more than a thousand souls. They made up in conviction for what they lacked in numbers. The mission entrusted to him by the Master had transformed ben Levi. Gone was his former scholarly superciliousness. His purpose in life was now clear to him, and he was proud to take up the obligations of his lineage.

The Sons needed his leadership. The Priest was still badly shaken. He spoke to no one, prayed formally, and spent his whole day in apparent contemplation. He ate unthinkingly, enough for his basic needs but no more. The expression in his pale gray eyes was vacant. He lived the life of a recluse, only rarely venturing from his room in the casemate wall by the synagogue. Ben Levi made all the decisions in his name. Despite the adoption by the entire community of many of the Sons' tenets, the group remained apart from the others, eating together and living an entirely communal life among themselves.

Ben Levi's outward appearance had also changed. He was still the scholarly aristocrat with refined features and the thick russet beard and hair which indicated his family background; but his looks had matured. His face bore a determined expression and his mouth was set in firm lines. He looked directly at whomever he addressed, and few could resist the authority in his glance. Like the other Sekaka survivors, he lived celibately. At the time of Sekaka's fall, the young members had not arrived at the age where they could be betrothed. Now they were of an age, but as they felt the struggle with the forces of evil was entering the critical stage, they wished to remain in perpetual ritual purity, which prevented the possibility of any contact with women.

The Sons of Zadok had been in a perpetual state of excitement for some weeks, fully expecting the first victory of the forces of righteousness now that the seventh lot was due. The seventh lot was the year of release, and from that time on, the tide of battle was to be turned. At any time, they felt, the Lord would intervene to start a series of events which would quickly culminate in their advance to Jerusalem. They were well aware that the struggle was merely in its initial stages, but the vital fact was that the forces of light were about to win their first victory.

Ben Levi knew that he had not convinced Eleazar of the correctness of his belief, despite that leader's extensive knowledge of the writings of the Teacher. He was in fact rather amused at the naiveté of the Sicarii leader, who put greater faith in weapons, tactics, and fighting men than in the power and presence of the Lord. The prophet Isaiah had illustrated forthcoming events with an account from ancient history: *Then shall Asshur fall with the sword, not of man, And the sword, not of men, shall devour him. . . .*

Jacob had approached ben Levi on the question of the lack of faith among the Sicarii. "Surely all of us here should believe," he claimed. "Why do they not see the truth?"

271

"They do not have our training and background," replied the Levite. "We grew up at Sekaka. You cannot expect them as adults to learn in a few years that which we imbibed as children over the entire span of our lives."

"But they are not prepared," protested Jacob. "They are not ready!" With his brick-red skin and pale blond hair, bleached white in places by the sun, Jacob resembled a younger, smaller Nahum. Together with ben Levi he led the small community of the Sons at Masada. Hanan, despite his early lack of interest, had proved a loyal member of the group. The Master had spoken on that fateful day five years previously, and Hanan, dark and serious, pursing his thick lips in puzzlement, had obeyed. He had followed ben Levi ever since.

While the fearless and experienced Sicarii—with a tradition of fighting going back for a century and a half—looked to the morrow with apprehension and terror as they thought of the fate of their dear ones, the scholars of the Sons of Zadok, inexperienced in war, faced the future calmly in the serene knowledge that Almighty God was about to award them a decisive and miraculous, if not final, victory.

5

The Roman attack was not long in coming. The heavily armed legionaries swarmed up the knife edge of the ramp. From positions on the western gate and from the rooms to the south of the ramp, the defenders sent their large boulders crashing down toward the enemy. Most of the rocks were deflected by the sloping sides of the dam and fell ineffectively into the valley below.

Bar Nottos was stationed with his machines behind the earth wall. Until the Romans were in position, they kept up a barrage of missiles at the tower; but once the soldiers had manned their posts on the solid framework, the superior weight of the Roman engines soon scattered the defending group, forcing them to retreat out of the angle of the attacker's fire north and south along the casemate wall. Out of range of the Roman engines behind the western gate, a party of archers

272

rained a hail of arrows on the enemy. Some of the soldiers on the ramp were hit, but the armored tower was unaffected by the volleys.

The dull thud of the giant batterer against the earthen wall told the defenders that Silva had decided to make one further attempt to penetrate the fortress before resorting to fire. When it had battered the casemate wall previously, the noise of the ram's heavy iron head on the flint rocks had resounded with an explosive crash audible all over the summit. The endless rhythmic pounding had been as demoralizing to the defenders as the damage caused to the wall. Now the muffled thump was equally demoralizing to the attackers.

Eleazar had not wasted any time since he had rejected the surrender terms. All through the night, party after party of the defenders had been packing the earth tighter, reinforcing the balks and damping down the dust. The ram continued to swing, the wooden beams splintered and occasionally broke; but the blows only packed the wall tighter and strengthened it. Once again the monstrous iron head began to acquire its shell of mud, upsetting the battering ram's balance. The rhythm slowed and gradually came to a halt. In the silence that followed, a ragged cheer broke forth from the defenders, followed by a stream of jeering insults:

"What has happened to the mighty Roman machine?"

"Where is your ram, Silva?"

"Where is the ram?"

"It has turned into a sheep!"

The last pleasantry was greeted with a roar of laughter, and a volley of obscenities on the subject of Silva's supposed impotence followed. Provoked by the insults, a party of soldiers emerged from the tower in order to dislodge the mud from the head of the batterer. A group of defenders swarmed over the wall to attack them and a fierce hand-to-hand fight was joined. The Sicarii found it difficult to penetrate the thick protective armor of the soldiers, while the latter, defending themselves from the narrow base of the platform, found their adversaries too mobile to be effectively stopped. The fighting continued as the Roman soldiers turned their attention to the wall, trying

273

to break it up with their javelins, swords, and even bare hands. The defenders were reinforced and the skirmish grew into a fierce battle. Joab led his group out of the western gate in an attack on the tower. The soldiers in the tower, distracted by the disturbance directly in front of them, though unable to use their machines for fear of hitting their own men, did not notice the new attack until Joab and a dozen of his men had ascended the massive stone supports and had started to hack away at the base of the tower with hand axes.

When the soldiers attacked them, they used the axes as weapons but were forced back by the long javelins of their adversaries. Finally, Joab was left by himself at the base of the tower, bravely slashing at the menacing pikes and contriving to strike a few blows at the tower in between defending himself. Finally, he was forced to leap from the rock platform to the ramp below, from where he managed to scramble up the steep side to the safety of the western gate.

Meanwhile, the fighting raged fiercely on the wall. When it became clear that they could not advance, the soldiers withdrew into the tower, where the defenders could not follow. As soon as they were inside, their companions opened up a deadly barrage from their stone-throwers and quick-loaders, driving the Sicarii back over the wall. Many of the defenders fell under the deadly hail of stone and metal.

One of the young defenders had been hit in the leg with a rock. Alive, he lay among the dead, writhing in agony. All at once a swarthy, thick-set figure was scrambling over the wall. It was Yoezer, of Joab's group. He jumped down beside the wounded boy and gathered him in his arms. As he climbed back over the wall into the fortress, an iron bolt from one of the quick-loaders in the tower took him from behind, penetrating deeply in the region of his right lung. He pitched forward on top of the boy he had rescued. In the shelter of the wall, the defenders moved quickly to aid the stricken men. Apart from his broken leg, the boy was all right; but Yoezer was gravely wounded. His thin-faced wife, that same woman who had argued with Nahum over the supplies, was by his side, weeping, cradling his dark head on her lap. The man's tangled beard was covered with a pink froth that emerged from his mouth, and his nose streamed crimson. He opened and closed his mouth several times in an effort to speak to his wife. His tongue moved slightly but no sound emerged. He managed to nod his head twice, and then he shut his eyes; his tense body relaxed and he was dead. The woman's eyes brimmed with tears and she began to sob, her whole frame shaking. Eleazar knelt beside her, his eyes full of pain at her distress.

"What will become of me?" she demanded. "What will become of the children?"

"We shall look after you," Eleazar told her. "You and the children will be cared for. Yoezer will not be forgotten." The woman nodded dumbly; she started to sway backward and forward, praying.

Several fires had been lit in the valley below, outside the gates of the camps. It was some half an hour after the failure of the batterer that the soldiers began to run up the ramp with burning brands of wood in their hands. A gentle but steady breeze blew from the southwest, deflected off the cliff face opposite. Eleazar, standing by the western gate, exchanged glances with Nahum and Joab. The message in their eyes was the same: this was the end. Nahum directed volley after volley of arrows at the advancing line of soldiers, but few arrows penetrated their heavy armor. The first group of attackers threw their brands at the base of the wood and earth wall. The defenders climbed over the wall and, seizing the flaming pieces in their bare hands, threw them clear. A deadly barrage from the tower cut many of them down, but they continued their task until all the brands had been extinguished or thrown clear.

In the face of the shower of stone, metal, and fire directed against them, the defenders did not flinch. They wound strips of wet cloth around their hands and destroyed each threat of fire as it appeared. Eleazar had moved to the wall and was playing his part in fighting the flames. Sweating, his hands covered with raw blisters, Eleazar noted with amazement that ben Levi, Jacob, and the rest of the Sons of Zadok were fighting the fire alongside the Sicarii. They had always assured Eleazar that they would fight when the time came, but hitherto they had not taken any active role in the defense of the fortress. After half an hour of continuous attempts to set the wall afire, the Romans were forced to retire and replenish their brands. The wind continued to blow steadily. Ben Levi had a look of triumph in his eyes as he addressed Eleazar.

"Do you know what day this is?" he demanded.

"I have lost my accounting of days," confessed the Sicarii leader.

"This is the seventh lot! Seven years ago, by the proper calendar, you captured Masada: the participation of the Lord God can be expected at any instant!" Eleazar, his hands smarting with pain, his face smeared with ash and blackened from the fire, could only gape at the young Levite. "We must pray," continued ben Levi. He raised his voice: "Pray, all of you; pray to the Lord God Almighty for deliverance, that He may deliver us with His hand!" The Sons of Zadok stood together and raised their voices in prayer. At the same time the firebrands started coming again at the wood and earth wall, the last defense of Masada against the Roman besiegers.

"Pray!" shouted ben Levi again. "Pray, all of you!" The Sons of Zadok turned their backs on the siege tower and faced northwest to Jerusalem, praying. Standing in the midst of the battle, begrimed from their recent fire fighting, robes belted up for easy movement, they were an incongruous sight in the midst of the battle.

The soldiers altered their tactics, running forward to place their brands by the wall instead of throwing them. The Sicarii struggled ferociously to prevent them, but aided by the steady wind from the southwest and the dryness of the air, the uprights ignited and the wall was on fire. There was an exultant scream of triumph from the soldiers in the tower, who had been crazy with frustration at their earlier lack of success. They were answered by a groan of dismay, unwittingly forced from the throats of the defenders. The praying of the Sons of Zadok increased in volume, but their entreaties were soon drowned out by the crackling of the burning wall. Smoke

276

poured into the sky and the flames licked toward the stricken fortress.

Eleazar stood with Nahum and Joab behind the earth wall, where they had concentrated the main body of Sicarii, ready to defend the breach that the fire would shortly make. All three of them were dirty and disheveled, covered with burns and smears of ash. The dominant expression on their faces was one of utter weariness. Eleazar felt the tiredness of a heavy weight that seemed to paralyze his limbs. He forced himself to move, but his legs were as lead, his head was light, and there was a singing in his ears. For a moment he seemed to be a great distance away, and then he returned to his position by the wall as he felt the hot breath of the flames on his face. Some of the wall had already fallen, and through the blaze the invincible siege tower was clearly discernable. Suddenly, as they stood there waiting for the end, the wind changed. One minute the wall was blazing and the fire roaring inward to consume the fortress; the next minute a sudden powerful gust came blowing from behind them, screaming across the summit of the rock, churning up clouds of dust.

6

Before the unbelieving eyes of the defenders, the massive sheet of flame, which seconds before had been menacing them, seemed to leap forward, as if directed by them, at the Roman siege tower. The Romans, who had been slowly advancing toward the wall to be ready to invade the fortress at the first opportunity, fled back toward their tower. But some dozen of them were consumed in the sheet of orange flame. The wind continued to blow from the northeast, and a roar of triumph, exultant yet still incredulous, broke from the throats of the defenders as they saw that the tower was in flames. The noise in the tower was phenomenal, a mixture of panic, anger, and surprise. From the back of the structure soldiers poured out onto the stone platform and then down the ramp in utter confusion. The defenders clambered up onto the casemate wall to watch the incredible sight.

His tiredness gone, Eleazar stood on the casemate to the north of the still-burning earthen wall. Nahum was at the western gate below him, directing his bowmen to shoot at the retreating soldiers. Joab stood by Eleazar. The two of them knew that if the tower burned down, they would have at least two weeks respite. Then, as the hair stood up on the back of his neck, Eleazar saw a tall, white-robed figure standing by the gap in the earth wall, seemingly oblivious to the flames. There could be no mistaking that figure—the Priest, legitimate heir to the high priesthood of the Temple of God, descendant of Aaron, whom some considered to be the Messiah, was praying by the wall of the fortress of Masada at the onset of the seventh lot. The fire struck inexorably at the Roman tower. The words of the Priest were audible despite the noise of the wind and the crackling of the fire. He did not appear to be speaking loudly; rather, the words sounded as if each man heard them in his own head.

"O God of Israel, who is like Thee in heaven or on earth?
"Who accomplishes deeds and mighty works like Thine?"

Eleazar gasped in amazement, remembering the words. The Priest continued:

"Truly the battle is Thine! Their bodies are crushed by the might of Thy hand and there is no man to bury them.

"Thou didst deliver Goliath of Gath, the mighty warrior, into the hands of David Thy servant, because in place of the sword and in place of the spear he put his trust in Thy great Name; for Thine is the battle."

Ben Levi was beside Eleazar, wild-eyed in triumph. He seized the leader by the shoulder and pointed to the figure of the Priest outlined against the flames. The latter had stopped praying and was standing silently, swaying.

"Then the High Priest shall rise with his brethren," quoted ben Levi. Eleazar recognized the quotation, as he had the prayers, as being from the doctrine of the Teacher. *"...with his brethren and the Levites and all the men of the army and he shall recite aloud the prayer in time of war of the rule concerning this time...."* It was as if the breath of God were truly breathing fire on the company of darkness. Eleazar no

278

longer heard ben Levi; but the words of the Teacher continued to echo in his mind: *He shall go forward to strengthen the hearts of the fighting men, speaking he shall say. . . .*

The Priest was speaking again, although Eleazar could not be sure where his own memory ceased and the actual words of the Priest started: *"Be strong and valiant; be warriors! Fear not! Do not be fearful, fear them not! Be brave and strong for the battle of God . . . against all the host of Satan."*

Ben Levi was filled with a wild and surging exultation—before his very eyes the Lord was smiting the enemy; the last days had arrived and the kingdom of God dated from this very hour. His secret doubts vanished; he felt a sublime joy in the fulfillment of his vision. The Priest continued to pray in his remarkably penetrating voice. He had been saved for this hour —a silent recluse for five years suddenly emerging to fulfill the purpose of the Almighty, the ever-living, all-pervading, eternally present God of Israel.

"For the God of Israel has called out the sword against all the nations and He will do mighty deeds by the saints of His people."

Standing next to ben Levi on the casemate wall, regarding the incredible scene before him, Eleazar felt his reason slipping. Was it possible after all that ben Levi was right? Was it conceivable that they had not misjudged the time, that Menahem had indeed been prompted by the spirit of the Lord when, seven years previously, he had attacked the fortress of Masada? Was this the breath of God that rained down fire on the enemy? The Romans had retreated in disarray on the brink of victory. If they advanced at once, the Sicarii might break the Roman lines. If they could break through the ring of Silva, the whole of Judea was wide open to them. It was unbelievable, yet was it less than the miracles that God had always wrought for His people? Was anything beyond the power of the Almighty? Eleazar raised his eyes to look again at the Priest, prior to giving the order to advance.

The tall figure in white appeared taller than ever. His voice rose: *"He will pay their reward with burning. . . ."*

At Eleazar's side ben Levi raised a delicate, ornately deco-

279

rated silver trumpet to his lips; he blew a sharp blast. The wind veered suddenly, as suddenly as it had changed just ten minutes earlier, and within one minute the sheet of flame came roaring back toward the fortress, consuming the strangely insubstantial figure of the Priest, and with it their hopes.

For some time the defenders made renewed attempts to extinguish the fire that was burning down the inner wall. They tried pouring water on the flames, but the blaze was too strong. They attempted to smother the fire with earth, but the wind blew most of it away. Meanwhile, the Romans contrived to control their blaze. The tower had not caught so thoroughly as it had seemed earlier, although it suffered some damage, and the fire was quickly extinguished.

It was evening and the crimson sunset matched the color of the flames. The wind dropped but the wall continued to burn. Eleazar watched the Romans retire to their camps. It was clear that the attack would be left until the morning. It was typical of Silva's carefulness not to waste men in a night attack or to endanger them from the still-burning fire.

Thoughts and memories crowded into Eleazar's mind. He remembered the first attack on Masada, the advance on Jerusalem, the retreat to Sekaka, the seven years at the fortress. He thought of the End of Days, which was not at hand and of the Teacher, the Master, and the Priest. He thought of God, the Lord God Almighty, whose ways were beyond the understanding of men. Even the privileged and learned Sons of Zadok had not been able to understand His actions, His reasons, His terrible vengeance and anger. He thought of the thousands of Jews who had lost their lives since they had sat in the goatskin tent at Sekaka, planning to surprise the Masada garrison. He thought of the fate of his community, of his family and his friends, and of their families, and of the dreadful things that were to happen to all of them. He thought of Menahem and of his brothers, Simon and Judah, of bar Giora and Judah of Galilee, of Hezekiah. Again he saw his wife and child facing a fate too horrible to imagine, and he thought, It must not happen! Then all at once he knew exactly what he had to do.

280

7

Torches flamed in the wall sockets in the courtyard of the western palace. The fire had spread to some of the western casemate rooms, and the night sky outside was red with flames. Apart from the few guarding the western wall, most of the men were assembled in the courtyard. Eleazar looked at the familiar faces, some two hundred in number, straining toward him, waiting to hear what he had to say. Seven years previously the community had venerated Menahem ben Judah, looking on him as a prophet, infallible and unapproachable. Five years before, the people had worshiped the dashing figure of Simon bar Giora, swept away by his oratory, dazzled by his mercurial personality. But for five years there had been no one to challenge the authority of the son of Jair. Many of those present had not known the earlier leaders, for they had arrived during the past five years. They had lived at peace and Eleazar had been their rabbi. The terrible events which occurred in the country at large had affected them only indirectly. Only in the past months, since the arrival of Silva, had the community once again been brought face to face with reality. Once again Eleazar had changed his role—this time, from rabbi to military leader. But he was revered more than a mere commander would have been.

He stood before his community, and Joab and Nahum stood with him; they had been together for a long time. A few faces stood out with particular prominence. He noticed bar Nottos, one of his original commanders; Rivka, his aunt, was one of the few women present; and he saw ben Levi and Jacob of the Sons of Zadok. He still wore his begrimed tunic, and his face and arms were smeared with the ash from the fire. The torches flared, throwing flickering shadows on the rough flint wall.

Eleazar searched his heart for the right words, and when he spoke in his soft, slightly hoarse voice, he spoke plainly without any orator's tricks: "The wall is burning. In the morning it will be gone, and then there is nothing to stop the Romans from entering the fortress except ourselves. We are well supplied with weapons, and I would say we have some of the best fighting men that Judea has ever possessed. I have no doubt that we could hold the Romans for many hours; but there is far more than a legion out there, and I would be lying if I did not admit that ultimately they must prevail. Even if each one of us succeeds in killing ten soldiers, there will be many thousands more ready to attack us. The Tenth Legion is no mere auxiliary force; its soldiers are among the best in the empire.

"Were we here on our own, we fighters, defending the fortress in the normal way, I would say that we should fight on to the last drop of our blood. We should defend the breach in the wall, then the casemate, storerooms, palaces, bath rooms —every inch of the summit. But we are not alone, as you know. Masada is not an ordinary fortress; it is a village. We have women, children, babes, and old folks. It is true that these often suffer in war when victorious troops sack and destroy villages, but here the families will be in the field of battle. If tomorrow we let Masada become a battlefield, we will be making warriors out of infants and soldiers out of old women; we have no right to do that! So we cannot continue to fight and we cannot surrender. What else is there left for us to do?

"We have come a long way together, you and I. It is seven long years since we captured this fortress from the auxiliary garrison, and six and a half years since we fled here from Jerusalem. Five and a half years have passed since Simon bar Giora marched away with more than half the community to become leader of the revolt in Jerusalem. Five years ago Sekaka fell and the survivors came here to establish the covenant at Masada. Tonight, when the fire struck at the enemy and the legitimate heir to the Aaronic line stood in the front of the battle after the years of his voluntary seclusion, I believed for a moment that Menahem had been right and that the End of Days was at hand, that the Priest was the Messiah of Aaron, and that I, may the Lord forgive me, had been called upon to play the role of the Messiah of Israel.

"The fire turned about, the Priest is dead, and our fortress is open to the sons of darkness. The time for the kingdom of God has not come. This might be the seventh year of the war, but this is not the final war. I thought that our cup of suffering was full, but I erred—it must be filled yet more. Who are we to judge? Can we assess the amount of suffering that must be inflicted on us before we can triumph? No. Only the Lord God, Creator of heaven and earth can decide. This then is the end for us. It is not to be our destiny to participate as we had believed in the kingdom of God on earth; but we should feel privileged to have participated in this preliminary stage of the struggle. We are blessed indeed that we have been able to carry out the work of the Lord, praised be His glorious name forever and ever. We should never feel a moment's regret, for to regret that which we have done would be sacrilege.

"We cannot reproach ourselves for our actions, for we never really had any choice in the matter. Each step that we took was inevitable and in turn determined the next development. We, descendents of the Pious Ones, of Hezekiah and Judah, had no choice but to revolt against the Romans. Our cause was just; we never sought to dominate Rome nor anyone else. It is not the will of God that has allowed the Romans to enslave the world, but the evil of Belial. These forces are the forces of darkness. Submission to Rome is submission to evil, and therefore acceptance of Roman rule is not obedience to the Almighty, but, on the contrary, defiance of His holy name. This is not the appointed time, but that does not mean that our struggle is an unjust one. We know that the forces of righteousness must suffer many defeats until the dawning of their day of triumph, so do not weep, my people. Rejoice that you have been permitted to carry out a tiny part of the infinite purpose of the Almighty!"

Ben Levi's thoughts were in a turmoil. For the first time in a number of years he was faced with his own uncertainty. As he had raised to his lips the silver trumpet, so carefully guarded for the occasion, he had been certain that he was announcing the kingdom of God; but now he was unsure. Was the Priest's death a mere preliminary to his reappearance at the End of Days as the Messiah? Were they all to die now in order to rise again? Was that the meaning of all he had learned and believed? He could not absorb Eleazar's words; he was too

283

full of his own thoughts. Ben Levi could not abandon hope. He had to reinterpret events, to understand them anew. He looked at Jacob, his redness accentuated in the flames, and at the dark sensual features of Hanan. What were they thinking? He had led them for five years; had he let them down?

"We have until the morning," Eleazar was saying. "The Romans will not attack before dawn, so we have more than seven hours to do that which has to be done. Since it became clear that the fortress would be captured, one thought has occupied my mind. I have thought of my family, of my wife and son. I have thought also of your families, of your wives and children and parents. I have thought of what will happen to them when the Romans finally overrun the fortress. We should harbor no illusions regarding the treatment that our dear ones can expect. We are soldiers and can expect to die. That is a risk we take on ourselves when we go forth to battle. We have been looking death in the face from the moment that we raised our hands in anger to defend our rights and our freedom. Who can doubt that our women and children also would fight to the last, even without strength or knowledge of war? If I thought that we could fight on until every one of us was killed, I would say let them buy this victory dearly, drench the summit of the rock in Roman blood!

"But it will not happen thus; large numbers will be captured alive, and the survivors are fated to face many types of obscene and revolting deaths and lives. The girls and even many of the boys may anticipate lives of prostitution. Men and women can expect slow, lingering death in the arena. If you doubt my words, remember that King Agrippa, son of the good king, promoted games in honor of Titus at Caesarea Philippi. This sacrilege was performed with Jewish men and women by a Jewish king on Jewish soil! Comfort not yourselves with false optimism—violation, murder, and prostitution lie ahead for your beloved ones!"

Nahum stood impassively at Eleazar's right hand. He scratched his blond beard as he always did when troubled, and his wide-set gray eyes were clouded with worry. He would be fighting in his position, doing his duty. What could he do to

284

protect his wife and children? He had always been proud of his children's unique beauty; now he shuddered with horror as he considered what might happen to them.

"We are not compelled to allow this to happen," said Eleazar. He spoke quietly, and his listeners were forced to crane forward to hear what he was saying. "There is a way by which we can prevent these terrible and unspeakable things from happening. There has been one thought uppermost in my mind; the thought that it must not happen!"

Joab felt a shiver of recognition as he heard the echo of his own thoughts. Eleazar's words echoed and reechoed in his head. He was still in a state of abject terror. He saw his wife violated, his daughters harlots, their spontaneous laughter trained to please clients, his granddaughter.... Joab felt himself losing control and forced himself to listen to Eleazar's words.

"I was thinking back to my youth yesterday, and I recalled a story told me by my uncle Menahem ben Judah, of Hezekiah's Galilee band, who dwelt in the caves of Arbel where the cliffs are so steep that no one could seek them out. Herod pursued the rebels even after the death of Hezekiah and had his soldiers lowered to the caves in baskets from above. Many rebels were killed and some surrendered. But their old leader, seeing that there was no hope, lined up his family in the mouth of their cave and killed them one by one, leaping to his own death only when all of them had perished."

Rivka grasped the rough flint wall to prevent herself from falling. She wanted to scream, "No! Ten thousand times, no!" Eleazar's suggestion was monstrous! Even a life of slavery and prostitution was life. The soul had a chance to develop even in the worst of conditions. There was a chance for everyone; and even if they were slaughtered, at least they would have avoided the final sacrilege of taking with their own hands that which the Lord had given them. They had no right to abandon hope; abandoning hope was abandoning God. They had no right to carry out this terrible deed! Rivka looked at the faces, lit by torches and the ruddy light from the flame-filled sky. They regarded Eleazar dumbly, hanging on his every word.

They would do it, Rivka was sure; they would carry out this horrible act!

If only Eleazar would shout! Were he to rant and rave, his madness would be evident. His proposal would sound natural coming from the mouth of a hysterical mob orator. There was something insidious about the tone of his voice, the perverted reasoning which led to his insane conclusion. It was then that Rivka realized that she could never oppose her nephew, that no one would listen to her or follow her. As Eleazar continued to speak, she slipped quietly away. No one saw her leave.

"We have been given the opportunity of emulating the brave rebel cave dweller," continued Eleazar. He had raised his voice to add emphasis, but his tone was still quiet. "There is no way out of here; the Roman wall is everywhere and it is guarded. We have until the morning. I have been watching Silva for nearly half a year. I know how his mind works; he will not risk losing men unnecessarily on a night attack.

"You have the choice, my friends. I do not wish to choose for you. So dreadful a decision can only be taken freely by each and every one of you. The choice is between death and death. That is the only choice I am able to offer you."

8

Rivka also knew exactly what she had to do. The realization of her purpose had come to her some time after a similar enlightenment had come to her nephew, but it was no less certain. She knew he was wrong just as surely as he knew he was right. This time she was not going to argue; she was going to take action. She had always lost the arguments before they began. No one had ever really listened to her or attempted to understand what she was trying to say.

But, she reflected, a center of rebel activity was not the appropriate location for preaching Hillel's message of love. Despite her utter rejection of the Sicarii way, she could understand their motivations and the forces that drove them to act as they did. She had, after all, been with the movement longer than anyone else at the fortress. Her husband had been one of its most effective leaders. She had not ceased loving Menahem when she had come to believe in the school of Rabbi Hillel. Followers of Hillel disapproved of rebellion and bloodshed. So they accepted Roman rule passively and condemned violence.

The Sicarii, on the other hand, rejected Roman rule and believed that it should be resisted by force. They were constantly fighting, believing even assassination to be justified in certain circumstances. Yet both movements had their roots in the poor peasantry of Judea, victimized by the Jewish landlords and priests and by the Roman rulers. Both movements represented a rejection of the society based on Jewish aristocracy and Roman might.

It was in the manner of this rejection that the differences between them arose. Whereas the Sicarii were prepared to fight at every opportunity, aiming to kill every Roman soldier, every official, every tax collector, every administrator in Judea, the followers of Hillel wished to withdraw into themselves. The Jew would create an inner Jewish existence that totally dominated his outer life. His freedom was internal, spiritual freedom. What did it matter if the body was in chains, provided the soul remained free? The Sicarii did not accept this. For them life was a single unit—everything that one did or thought was a part of this organic whole.

Despite her views, Rivka was no foreigner in the ranks of the Sicarii. The people at Masada were her people with her background. She felt their anguish, understood their problems, their wishes, and their dreams. Despite her continuous fight to obtain a hearing for her views, and her lack of success, Rivka had never for an instant doubted that her place was at Masada with her husband's community.

It was a fact that some of the community at Masada did listen to Rivka with respect, but her only real success had been with Naomi, the wife of Yoezer. The thin-faced, bitter woman was a natural dissenter and gravitated toward Rivka as the only center of dissent at Masada. It was to Naomi's room, a place of mourning for her dead husband, that Rivka now went. She found the widow sitting at the side of the room by the shrouded body of her husband, rocking backward and forward. Yoezer had died too late to be buried that day; now it was doubtful whether he would ever be buried. Rivka strode into the room, a small, narrow cell in the western casemate.

"Naomi," she called, "Prepare some food and blankets, enough for one night." The woman did not move or respond. "Come now, Naomi, hurry!"

"What has happened?" the woman asked finally.

"Quickly, now," said Rivka. "If we are to save the children we must act at once."

"Save the children?" she asked. "How are we to save the children? The wall burns. Nothing can help us now. There is no way out."

Rivka seized her by the shoulders and shook her. "Listen, Naomi, I promise to explain everything. We will have all the night to talk. There is no time to talk now—we must act!"

"You want me to come with you ... to leave ... him?" She indicated the shrouded figure of her dead husband.

"May his memory be blessed," said the older woman. "We cannot help him now. You must come with me—you and the children!" There was desperation in Rivka's voice. In all her years of bitter dispute at Masada, Naomi had never known Rivka to lose her composure; she had always managed to remain calm and reasonable. But now it seemed as if her self-control was about to disappear. The children, who were used to taking orders from Rivka, were making bundles of food and rolling up the heavy sleeping cloaks and sheepskins.

"Do we not need water?" asked the eldest child, a lanky girl of fifteen. She was as tall as her mother, with the same taut-skinned face, but her expression was more open and intelligent. "We have half a jar of water."

"We do not need water," said Rivka firmly. The eldest child looked surprised, but simply picked up her bundle and the other children picked up theirs. Rivka picked up a cloak and thrust it in Naomi's hands.

"Come, Naomi," she ordered. "You must come now!"

Rivka led them along the casemate until they came to the water gate, which was not guarded. There was no moon and the burning section of wall cast a lurid red light over everything. As the party descended the steep path of the water carriers, they could not help but dislodge some of the scree, which went rattling down the hillside into the valley. They froze, but no one had heard, either from the Roman side or from the fortress. They would remember that nightmare scramble down the dangerous path in the blood red night as long as they lived. In all it took less than five minutes, but it seemed like a lifetime.

With the exception of Rivka, none of them knew where they were going or why. It had all happened too quickly: the Roman attack, the death of their father, the fire. Rivka led them along the narrow ledge to the northernmost cistern, which was already depleted. It contained more than enough water for their needs, and there would be more room for them there than in the fuller cisterns.

They crouched on the steps inside the cistern, gradually accustoming their eyes to the very dim light in the huge cavern. In the daytime, despite the blazing sunlight outside, the light inside the cistern was not strong. Now, with the flames from the fire above providing the only source of light, it was almost impossible to see anything. The walls were indistinct, and they could only just make out the level of the water, glistening blackly some dozen steps below them. They huddled in unnatural positions, the children wrapped in their sheepskins and cloaks. The sweat was starting to dry on their bodies and the cold desert air penetrated the reservoir. The younger children slept, while the older ones held them to prevent their falling down the steps into the water.

"What are we doing in this place?" Naomi asked Rivka.

"For tonight, we are better off here than at the fortress," replied the old woman.

"It is terrible here," exclaimed Naomi. She shivered.

"No. *There* it is terrible!"

"But this is no escape," the younger woman pointed out. "We are no more free of the Romans here than in our rooms above."

289

Rivka ascertained that the children were sleeping and then in a low voice she told the other of Eleazar's speech and of that which they were planning.

"We cannot escape our fate here!" insisted Naomi.

"When this madness is over," answered Rivka, "we can emerge and take whatever life has in store for us. Hope must never die. You and the children must continue to live, even though Yoezer of blessed memory has died. When we come out of this cistern, the Romans may kill us or they may not. Were we to remain in the fortress above, there would be no room for doubt as to our fate. Maybe the Romans will even treat us well."

"And if they do not?"

"If they do not, the Lord God has condemned us and we must suffer. It is our duty to live for as long as we can draw breath. I would gladly submit—even to violation—if I thought it would save these innocent children; but I will not violate myself in the obscene manner designated by Eleazar. There is no action which betrays a greater contempt for the Lord than to take the life that He created and throw it back in His face."

"What will they do to us?" The younger woman was frightened.

"You must put your faith in God," replied Rivka. "You must accept the fate that He has decreed for you." There was a pause in the conversation, the silence broken only by the breathing of the children and the sobs of Naomi.

"Rivka," she said at last. "It would not hurt so much to do as Eleazar says. . . ."

"You are not to think of it!" snapped the old woman, whispering harshly in the dark, echoing chamber. "It is expressly forbidden in our Law: it is a crime against God Himself!"

9

Leah, small and plump, sat hunched up in the corner of her room next to the cooking fire. The cold of the night penetrated the room despite the oven, and she had drawn her cloak tightly around her. Her face bore a somber expression. The red light from the fire outside was visible through the doorway. It was for the children she feared primarily; it was not right that they should have to face the certainty of death and misuse. She had shouted at them hysterically that evening, as they had fought and tumbled in boisterous war games; but now she regretted the shouting as she crouched in the dim red light. She may well not have another chance to shout at them. From where she sat, they looked like shapeless bundles, wrapped up on their sleeping pallets. She ought to be at their side, but a lethargy too strong to overcome kept her by the stove.

She thought of David, the eldest, grown large now, but still vulnerable in a way that only eldest children are vulnerable; of Uri, still too young to understand, his sulky lower lip always ready to protrude as a prelude to tears; of Joseph, the youngest. The three of them possessed the blond hair of their father with the honey-brown skin of their mother. David was tall and thin, his limbs lanky and awkward. The younger ones were stocky and broad, more like their mother in physique. All three boys had a look of their father about them, a good-natured, open-faced look, bright but not scholarly. Nahum was no scholar; nor, it seemed, were they. David and Uri possessed his gray eyes, but the youngest had the sharp brown eyes of his mother. David and Uri still quarreled as they had since they were very young; but they looked after Joseph, and he worshiped them, his fat brown face lighting up whenever he saw one of them.

Even if she had been more optimistic, the expression on her husband's face as he entered the room would have banished all hope from Leah's heart. Nahum's normally happy face wore an expression of tortured bafflement; there was terrible pain in his wide-set gray eyes. It was only when he came and sat by her, and put his arm around her shoulders, that she felt how he was trembling.

"What is it, Nahum? What has happened?" The man was unable to speak. His throat was dry and he found that the words refused to emerge. He brushed away an imaginary obstruction over his head with a nervous movement of his hand. "What is it, Nahum?" the woman persisted.

Once again he could not bring himself to articulate the

words. Leah poured him some wine from a narrow-necked earthenware jar. He tossed back his blond head and drained it in a gulp, but the red liquid dribbled out of the corners of his mouth and down his beard. He wiped his mouth with the back of his hand. He shut his eyes and shook his head, trying to control himself.

"We have made a plan," he said at last. "It is a dreadful plan, but I think it is the only thing we can do.

"We have decided to kill ourselves!"

"I do not understand," said his wife. "What do you mean?"

"I mean that when the Romans enter the fortress tomorrow morning, they will find no one alive."

"But surely we shall not all be killed by the Romans!" said the woman. "There will be some survivors among the women and the children. We knew that the Romans would probably defeat us; there is nothing new in what you say."

"You do not understand," rasped Nahum, his voice hoarse with fear. "We shall be dead before they enter the fortress. I am going to kill you and the children. All the men are going to kill their families; then we shall kill each other!"

"But Nahum, why? What have we done?" Leah rose from her place, backing toward her sleeping children.

"The death will be quick and almost painless," insisted Nahum. Now that he had begun to argue, his nervousness receded and his voice became stronger. "There will be no torture or degradation. The children need never awaken."

"No!" his wife interrupted him. She stretched her arms out as if to protect the children. "We cannot do it; we cannot kill our own flesh and blood."

"Would you rather see them violated, prostituted to uncircumcised soldiers?"

"Why did we bring them into the world?" demanded the distraught woman. Her eyes were red and her plump face was streaked with tears. "Did we have the right to create them?"

"Leah!" Nahum was shocked at the sacrilege. "The Lord God Almighty creates life and no one else!"

"Then why does He not do something to protect His creation?" She was weeping, her short body shaking with sobs. "Look at your children; look at them."

"There is no alternative."

"We can surrender," she said. "We can surrender and beg for mercy."

"The Sicarii beg for mercy?"

"Yes, that is what I said. Beg for mercy. What is so terrible about that? Are my children also Sicarii? Is Joseph an assassin? Why do we have to be different? The Romans hold sway over an empire of hundreds and hundreds of thousands. The others accept their rule. Why do we have to resist?"

"We are the Jews—the chosen people of God!"

"I do not want to be chosen. I want nothing to do with a God who allows innocent children to be slaughtered." She gestured at the sleeping forms.

Nahum held the lamp and advanced to look at his sleeping children. His wife stood aside. They were relaxed and breathing regularly, undisturbed by the bitter quarrel that raged over them. David lay on his stomach, his arms sprawled left and right. His face lay on its side and his slightly open mouth dribbled on his pallet. Uri was curled up in a ball, his face only half visible under the sheepskin which covered him. His features were rather ugly in sleep. Joseph lay on his back with his fat brown arms above his head, his dimpled hands curled loosely into tiny fists. He was snoring gently, the air whistling quietly through his slightly blocked nose. Nahum touched the silk-smooth cheek with his hand.

"I do not want this horrible thing, Leah," he said, "but there is no way out."

"We grew up in a Judea that was not free," replied his wife. "Judea was under the rule of Rome and yet we grew up there. We laughed and played, ate and drank—was it so dreadful?"

"There was no choice; we did what we had to do."

"What did we do all this for?" demanded his wife. Her gesture took in the fortress, the flames, the destruction of war.

"The choice was between a living death or a real one," replied Nahum. "I know: I worked for five years in the copper mines of the Aravah. The horror of that black, diseased place,

293

with the heat and the flies, is far greater than you can possibly imagine. I shall never forget it. All of us were riddled with disease, but the Nabateans still worked us until we died—and most of us died quickly enough. Our eyes were gummed together, our skins were burned and blistered, our bodies bent and lacking moisture. How can I describe the physical shock of emerging from the darkness of the seam into the white, glaring sunlight?

"But even that was nothing compared to the smell of putrefying flesh, of men dead and dying. It is not that the Nabateans were worse than other people; their behavior was the normal behavior of all slave owners.

"When I escaped and managed to struggle northward through the desert, past the Nabatean towns and past the primitive camps of the nomads into Idumea, I decided that a life which could lead to the copper mines of the Aravah was not worth living. Because if you have one place like that, then everything must eventually become like that: selfishness and greed would then rule the entire world. I walked in Idumea, in Judea and Samaria, in the plain and in Galilee, and I saw that I had been right. Everywhere the people were becoming more wretched, while a tiny group was becoming richer and greedier. The small farms were shrinking and the large estates were expanding. Most of the people had less and less to eat, while the landowners and priests grew fatter with luxury; there was no limit to their greed, no boundary to their shame. The whole country was turning into an Aravah copper mine because no one cared for his neighbor, and everyone was concerned to grasp a little bit more for himself. Perhaps the worst thing of all was the way people accepted the situation and believed that as it was, so it would always be, and that nothing could be done to change it.

"Then I met a group of people who truly believed in God and His message. I might have found the Zealots, or bar Giora, or the Sons of Zadok, or John ben Levi's Galileans; but it happened that I found the Sicarii. From the day that I joined them, my entire life was changed, because they gave me something I had never previously possessed: hope. Nothing else was changed; the land was as wretched as before, but we believed that we could do something about it and we were determined to try. It did not matter that we lived in constant danger, that each day might be our last, for within the Sicarii group I found that people were united. They were not incessantly plotting to destroy each other—they lived together in comradeship. So I fought and I ran and I feared, but at last I was alive and there was something for which to live.

"Then we met, Leah, and from that time onward my thoughts were with you. Wherever I was, whatever I was doing, I lived for the moments that we would be together. For a time the fortunes of war seemed to be with us, and I believed that at last we were destroying the old world in order to build a better one. I never understood about the last days or the kingdom of God. What I desired was a world without the Aravah copper mines, a world where my children could grow up without fear and misery. We have failed, but I do not for one moment regret the attempt. I only regret that we did not succeed."

Leah had listened in silence to her husband's long account. It was the longest speech he had ever made.

"I just want my children to be alive," whispered Leah. "Is that so much to ask of God? We have lived our lives through. What right have we to decide that they shall not live theirs?"

"It is not we who decide," protested her husband. "It is God."

"Let us leave it in His hands then. If we carry out this plan, the end is final; if we fight on or surrender, He will decide."

"He has already made His decision," stated Nahum, pulling his cloak tightly about him. He shivered in the chill night air.

Sarah had learned of the decision from bar Nottos before Joab returned. Had she not heard, he would not have had the courage to tell her. As his daughters were still awake when he arrived, he had good reason to evade the issue; but he sat by the table, brooding. He knew that there was no choice, but he knew also that he was personally incapable of carrying out the decision. He was an old man suddenly, the white prominent in the red of his head and beard. He responded in a desultory manner to his daughters' attempts at conversation. Deborah and Rachel were older than Nahum's children and more aware of the situation. They were subdued and rather impatient with each other, but the gaunt, gray-haired Sarah dominated the scene, calming the children and seeing that her husband was not disturbed.

"What have you done to my weaving, Rachel?" demanded her elder sister.

"I never touched it."

"You are a liar!" There was a sharp edge to Deborah's voice. "It does not unravel by itself."

"Quiet, children!" There was a calm authority in Sarah's voice. The normally patient Joab ground his teeth, as the sharp voices grated on his nerves.

When at last Sarah persuaded the children to go to bed, they lay sleepless for a long time with their eyes open, staring silently at the beams of the ceiling.

"The wall is burning, Rachel," whispered Deborah. "You know what that means?"

"The Romans can enter tomorrow."

"That is right—tomorrow or the next day."

"David was saying that there is a secret way out, and that tonight they are going to wake us up at midnight and we are all going to escape," whispered the younger sister excitedly.

"You should have more sense than to believe him," replied Deborah. "You have seen the wall surrounding us—you know that there is no way out."

"I did not say that I believed him," hissed Rachel. "I was just telling you what he said."

"How could it be true?" demanded the elder sister aggressively. She wanted desperately to believe in the story, but she could not. "It is a waste of time even to talk about it!"

"David said that it was through the cisterns," continued Rachel. "He says that there is a tunnel that leads right down into the rock and underneath it. The tunnel continues underground and emerges halfway to Ein Gedi."

"Oh, what nonsense!" exclaimed Deborah. "Do you realize

296

how difficult that would be to make? It would take thousands of years. I do not think it is possible at all."

"David says that Herod made it. He says that Herod escaped down it before he was king and fled across the Sea of Salt to Petra."

Deborah was forced to laugh. "Herod left for Petra before the siege," she pointed out. "His family were besieged, not him. They were only saved by the rain; otherwise, they would have died of thirst. That proves there is no way out. In any case, how could Herod have built anything at Masada before he was king?"

Rachel changed the subject. "What will the Romans do to us, Deborah?"

"Be quiet, Rachel," said her elder sister. "Will you stop talking nonsense?"

"I will not let them do it to me."

"Be quiet, I say!"

"I shall not let them—I shall jump off the wall!"

"Please, Rachel, stop talking nonsense."

"You say everything I say is nonsense," complained the girl. "If I talk about escaping, you say it is stupid, and when I talk about what is going to happen if we do not escape, you say that is stupid also."

"Why not try saying nothing?"

"Deborah," persisted the young one, "would you let the soldiers do it to you?"

"Do what?"

"You know what!"

"Rachel, you must stop this nonsense or I will tell Mother!"

"I do not think I would mind if bar Nottos did it to me. . . ."

"Rachel!" The image was profoundly disturbing to the older sister.

"In fact I think I would like it," she mused.

"Rachel, how dare you speak so sinfully? I will tell our mother."

"You would not dare!" came the confident reply. "How would you tell her?" The question embarrassed the older girl, and she was at a loss for a reply. "What should we do?" persisted Rachel.

"Why don't you ask our mother?"

"I did," replied the girl. "She told me to trust in God." She lay on her pallet, her mind filled with fantasies, some of them not unpleasing. Within a few minutes she was asleep. Deborah rose and went to her mother.

"I am frightened."

"Do not be afraid," her mother comforted her, hugging the child to her, smoothing her russet-colored hair. Her hand continued to stroke the hair and she repeated, "Do not be afraid. You will know what to do. We have come to the time when there is no choice, when we shall do as we have to. Do not fear, my love, the Lord is good and He will decide for you."

"I am frightened, Mother," whimpered the girl. "Dreadfully frightened."

"Have some wine." The young girl's hand shook as she took the cup. She drank and the wine warmed her inside. Sarah added wine from the jar and her daughter drank again. When she had fallen asleep with her head on her mother's lap, Sarah lifted her gently and lowered her onto the pallet by her younger sister. She put another cloak over them and gently kissed their freckled cheeks. Then she stood and faced her husband.

"I know what it is that you have to do," she told him.

"I cannot do it," he said. It was a simple statement of fact. Joab had not moved from the table. He rested his head on his sturdy, freckled forearms.

"You have never failed in anything, Joab," she reassured him.

"This time I shall fail!" He felt chilled right through his body.

"You must do it, Joab." Sarah was surprisingly calm. "There is no alternative. For weeks I have anticipated our defeat with helpless terror; but now we are not helpless and my heart is at rest. It is so simple, Joab."

"I cannot butcher my own wife and children!"

"Would you have the Romans do it for you?" she demanded.

298

Her gaunt face was set and determined. "Think what the soldiers will do when they come in. If your daughters are unlucky
enough to survive their first contact with the soldiers, it will be
a mere beginning. We could never afford to lose this war, but
we have lost it. For the Romans to lose meant a loss of power,
prestige, wealth; for us, defeat is the end. I have known this
for a long time and I feared what would happen; but God is
merciful and He has put this idea into the mind of Eleazar, and
my daughters will die clean and unviolated. All must die
sooner or later. What are a few years against the breadth of
eternity?" She poured out a cup of wine and handed it to Joab.

"Drink now," she urged him, "and we shall do what must be
done."

As soon as Shifra entered the room, she ran to her father. She
threw her arms about him and held him, sobbing. Bar Nottos,
dark and slim, ageless as ever, followed her into the room
carrying the bundle that was their child. Joab, helpless in the
situation, patted his daughter's back, trying to comfort her as
he had so many times before. On this occasion he was at a loss
for words, and it was the younger man who spoke.

"Trapped like animals!" he exclaimed angrily. "I should
have gone with Simon; he did not sit here waiting to be strangled by siege. What did we gain by all this waiting?"

"You should indeed have left with bar Giora," Sarah was
stung to reply. "You should have gone grubbing after glory
with the slave instead of returning here for a love that you only
half gave!"

"Mother, no!" protested Shifra, turning on her mother, red
hair blazing above her pale face.

"He was more suited to be a soldier than a husband," insisted her mother. "Look at him now—is he worrying about
you and his daughter? No, he worries about whether he was
right or wrong six years ago."

"You cannot understand, Mother," said Shifra. "You cannot
possibly understand!" The oil lamp flared and a coil of black
smoke twisted up toward the ceiling. The soft glow picked out
the contours of their tense faces. Shifra was still in her father's

arms as the slender, dark bar Nottos, his baby in his arms, faced the angry, gray-haired Sarah. They spoke in angry whispers.

"Simon knew what he wanted," insisted the young man.

"And Simon ended up at the rear end of a Roman triumph, strangled to death for the edification of the citizens of Rome!" flared Joab suddenly. "We may have failed, but so did he."

"He went out to fight the enemy," insisted the young man. "He did not stay to be trapped by them."

"He defended Jerusalem; we defended Masada," said Joab.

"He took his life in his own hands, whereas we allowed events to dictate to us."

"The end was the same."

"It is not; Simon would never have agreed to this abominable plan!"

"What do you think that we should do?" inquired Joab.

"Fight," replied bar Nottos. "Fight our way out through their lines."

"You talk as if we were an ordinary garrison here," exclaimed Joab angrily. "What of the women and children? What of your own wife and daughter? What are you going to do with them?" Bar Nottos had no answer, so the older man continued with mounting anger and scorn: "Are they to break through with us, or will you leave them behind for the Romans to enjoy? What weapon is your baby, Bathsheba, to use—javelin, bow, *sica?*"

"We should never have allowed ourselves to arrive at this situation, sitting here with our women and children in the midst of a battle."

"It always comes to that in the end," Joab told him. "We are not fighting a war of conquest in a foreign land—we are defending our country. Jerusalem was also full of women and children. Where are we to send them?"

Bar Nottos could make no reply. He hugged his daughter to him, smelling her sour baby smell and kissing her soft face. Shifra detached herself from her father and went to her husband, putting her arm around his shoulders.

"Do not let us quarrel," she said. "There is not so much time left that we should waste it in futile argument."

Joab stood by himself, looking a little ashamed at his out-burst; but he had stopped trembling. The wine had flushed him and his freckles were prominent. Sarah's lean face almost bore a smile—she had reestablished unity and purpose within her family. For a moment an expression of pain appeared, as she saw herself matriarch of a large family, of all those children and grandchildren who would never be born.

"Simon," she called her son-in-law by his first name, "Joab will need your help."

The group of the Sons of Zadok sat on the plastered benches of the schoolroom which they had made their own. The few lamps were unable to light very much of the large hall; but it did not matter to ben Levi. He did not need light in order to visualize every face.

"You will remember," he said, "that the phrase '*the End of Days*' occurs frequently in Scripture and in the writings of the Teacher. It refers to the very last days of the world as we have known it, the prelude to the new world where the kingdom of God will be established. We first hear of this period of time when the pagan prophet Balaam says to King Balak concerning the holy people of God, in the fourth book of Moses. ..."

Jacob had been numbed by shock since the death of the Priest some hours before. It was clear to him that with the Priest dead, nothing further would happen except defeat. All those years of plotting in the community, the Master's plan, the saving of the Priest, and the flight to Masada were wasted. It had all been for nothing. He listened to ben Levi without concentration. Ben Levi had been feverishly active since the Priest's death. Following the general meeting that Eleazar had addressed, he had been lecturing the Sons for more than an hour. His eyes glittered in his finely drawn face and his hands gesticulated wildly. Jacob noticed that all the others present seemed to be mesmerized by ben Levi. Hanan, as usual, wore a tortured expression on his simple face as he endeavored to follow the abstruse reasoning of the Levite.

"As you know, the concept of the final age appears in many later books, and of course it is central to the writings and

301

prophecies of our beloved Teacher. Whereas earlier accounts merely predicted that the kingdom of God would one day be established on earth, the Teacher stated clearly how it was to come about, and he went into considerable detail about the course of the final struggle between the forces of light and darkness. Perhaps when you saw the burning of the Priest, you were filled with dread that this was not the final struggle as we had thought. And yet we know that the sons of light will suffer severe reverses in the initial stage of the conflict, the first seven years. We also know that the new age is an age of rebirth. If something is to be reborn, it must first of all die. This then is the meaning of what has happened: the Messiah of Aaron has died, but he will rise again. We too are to die, and we will arise to participate in the banquet which will initiate the kingdom of God!"

Hanan found it difficult to understand everything that ben Levi said. Despite his years of rigorous training at Sekaka, his mind had remained slow and dull. Obedience he could grasp. He had obeyed the Master and since then he had obeyed the Levite, without always understanding why.

Ben Levi thought of this while he was speaking. He noted Hanan's face even as he spoke, and even as he spoke he planned the deed. He knew that it would be the three of them as in the past: he, ben Levi, the leader, Jacob the organizer, and Hanan the faithful servant.

Eleazar lay with his arms about his wife. Nearby their son lay sleeping. They could hear him breathing softly as they lay in the dark. Eleazar stroked his wife's face, running his fingers over her features, from her chin to her soft mouth, with its small regular teeth, to her nose and eyes. Her eyes were moist and the cheeks were wet.

"You weep, Hagar?" he asked.

"I am content as long as we are together," she replied, "and as long as our son does not suffer. I have always known that this would come to an end. It was clear from the start."

"But you weep."

"I weep for what might have been, for our son who will

302

never know such love. But I am grateful for what we have had, the three of us. It is not given to many to be as happy as we have been."

Eleazar smiled in the dark. "You do not ask for much, Hagar," he said.

"I never had very much," she replied. "We were always poor. Our village was simple and we never knew comfort. The desert was harsh and dry, hot and cold. I neither expected nor craved an easy life."

"I love you, Hagar. In all this time I have loved you more than I can say."

"I love you also, my husband. I love our son, and I do not want him to suffer. I cannot bear the thought of seeing his face crumple in fear; I cannot bear to think of the things that they would do to him."

Eleazar stretched over his wife's prone form and felt his child. He kissed the boy's forehead, cheeks, and eyes. The boy grunted and stretched, turning on his side but not awakening. He shouted something indistinct in his sleep. They laughed.

"I do not mind as long as he does not suffer," said Hagar. "He was known as the laughing baby, here in the fortress."

"He cried sometimes."

"Of course he did."

"I never could bear to see him cry," he recalled. "When he cried it seemed as if the whole world suffered; and when he smiled, the sun would shine."

"You are foolish." Hagar kissed her husband.

"You have been wonderful, Hagar!" he said. "All the time that I have known you, but never more than now!"

"I have done nothing."

"I was afraid to tell you of our plan. I did not dare to think of what you might say. Despite all I have said, had you not agreed, I could not have carried out the deed: I should have been as Joseph the traitor. I have never feared anything save the Lord God Almighty; but I feared you this night."

"Why should you be afraid of me?"

"I was afraid of your fear; I could not bear it. It is so terrible a thing that we must do."

"We dwellers of the desert have never feared death. It is too familiar to us. It has always been near—in the bite of a snake or the sting of a scorpion, in the fury of a flood or the summer drought."

"There is no other way," he said.

"There is no other way. Any other way would be more frightful. If there were some less bestial way out, we would take it. This way means the least suffering. That is why it is . . . not good, but sensible." They lay in silence, warm in their proximity to each other and to their child.

After some moments Hagar spoke again. "Eleazar?"

"What is it, my love?"

"Why did Judah not return to us? Why did he have to die alone in the forest of Jardes?"

Eleazar waited for some minutes before replying. He was thinking of his two brothers in that last scene as they marched off with bar Giora. Judah, tall and terrible, with his cruel, broad face, and Simon, shorter, better natured, but equally determined. The image was engraved on his memory.

Hagar waited for his reply. "Have I angered you?" she asked finally.

"No, it is not that. I am trying to explain it to myself, so that I can answer you. I never understood Judah. How can I tell you what it meant for a descendent of Judah of Galilee, a grandson who bore his name, to desert the Sicarii movement? Such a thing is not done lightly. He had become convinced that I was a traitor to Judea and to God. That is a hard thing to learn about your brother.

"We Jews have thousands of years of history behind us. You have heard of the legend that our family is descended from the line of David the King. We have not been able to prove it one way or the other. In the dark years after the return, only the priestly families were able to keep track of their lineage. Some people have made much of it, but our family always believed that the age of kings ended with the exile. Only evil, illegitimate kings have ruled in Israel since then. The ruler of Judea must be the high priest. The Messiah is to be of the seed of

304

Aaron. The Davidic line at best might lead in war. We have always strived for the legitimacy of the high priesthood, like the Pious Ones before us.

"Our family began anew with Hezekiah. For more than a century since his time, we have been bent on revolt. We carried the torch from generation to generation. All the other rebel movements were plagued with splits and revolts, but one of Hezekiah's seed always led the Sicarii. Hezekiah passed the torch to Judah and Judah bequeathed it to his sons, Jacob and Simon. When his two brothers were crucified, Menahem took up the cause and he left the care of our movement to me. The priestly line was not guarded more closely than ours. Do you see the enormity of Judah's desertion? With that between us, Judah could never return, although he died only a few miles to the north of your father's village. I shall never see the place where he died."

They lay for a long time without speaking. The only sound came from their breathing and the regular breathing of their child, the young Menahem. Trusting her husband, Hagar was relaxed and at peace.

When it was time for him to go and inspect the guard, for even at this time they set a watch, he rose reluctantly from his pallet and stretched.

"What are you thinking?" he asked his wife as she smiled up at him.

"I was thinking that every moment with you and our son is worth a lifetime."

"Even now?"

"Especially now!"

"You are a great source of strength for me."

"Will it hurt very much?" she asked suddenly. "Do not lie to me, my love, please do not lie!"

"It will hurt, but the pain will not last for long."

"And the boy?"

"He will suffer, but only for a moment. He will never know what happened to him. He will feel a sharp pain in his sleep, that is all."

10

Joab and bar Nottos clung tightly to one another as they made their way toward the western palace. The flaming wall lit up their strained faces. From all parts of the fortress men were streaming to the western palace, wishing to arrive there as quickly as possible, for the deed had been done. Sometimes a man fell and cursed in the dark as he picked himself up and pressed on, gasping for breath, stumbling forward in the half-light from the fire. Joab kept his eyes firmly shut, relying on his son-in-law for guidance. He wanted to obliterate the image which was engraved indelibly on his mind.

Sarah had been forced to commit the final act. As the hour of midnight had approached, Joab had been paralyzed. His limbs had refused to respond. His normally bright eyes were dull and he sat as one already dead. It was Sarah who rose finally, her lean face set in determination. She had walked over to her husband, looked into his face, and seen there his misery and impotence. She had not been angry. Joab was one of the bravest men who had ever lived in Judea, but some things were beyond bravery.

Sarah forced herself to see the violation of her daughters by the Roman soldiers. She was not satisfied to think about it; she actually saw it and heard their cries of alarm and terror. She heard their voices begging for mercy, their screams, and the vulgar oaths of the soldiers as they subdued them. She shut her eyes and she could smell their wine-laden, garlic-filled breath. She saw a hairy leg forced between the slim young thighs, the uncircumcised member protruding from the sweat-soaked tunic. When she had seen and smelled and felt everything, she crossed the room and took the razor-sharp *sica* from its sheath on her husband's belt.

She cradled her daughter's head in the crook of her arm; her hand did not tremble. Deborah made no sound at all as the knife cut swiftly through the tendons and cartilage of her soft young throat. The knife traveled no less certainly through the vital arteries in Rachel's neck; but the younger daughter released a choking gasp.

Joab gave a scream of horror as he looked up and saw the gaping red throats of his two daughters. It was not a loud scream. His vocal cords failed him. Sarah, his wife, looked into his eyes. She only looked briefly and then she looked down to her own body. She placed the point of the *sica* under her ribs on the left side of her body, and then with a sudden movement she drove it in. The knife remained fast with half the blade exposed; she had not managed to penetrate fully. She sank to her knees, her eyes fixed pleadingly on her husband. With a gasp of horror, Joab sprang to his feet and drove the dagger in up to the hilt. Sarah's lips drew back in a hideous grimace. Her angular body gave one more convulsive jerk and she was dead.

Simon bar Nottos regarded his sleeping wife in the lamp-light. There had been violence in their love that night, for they knew that never again would they lie together. At last, utterly spent, they had slept an exhausted, fitful sleep. Shortly before midnight, bar Nottos awoke. Shifra had turned away from him, her fine body covered by a single cotton garment, her flaming hair spread out like a fan. Her breasts rose and fell regularly. He lay propped up on one elbow looking at her for a long time in the lamplight, remembering the bitterness of their quarrels and the sweetness of their reconciliations. He drew his *sica* from its sheath, and holding it by the part of the handle nearest the blade, he struck savagely with the hilt at a point behind her ear. She gave a groan but did not wake. Her breathing became fitful and irregular. He rose quickly and cut her throat and, immediately afterward, that of his baby. The violence of the latter stroke—he had wanted to make certain—nearly sev-ered the infant's head from her body. Light-headed with nau-sea, he laid the small body down by that of Shifra. He swayed on his feet and held onto the wall for support. He was still standing in that position when Joab staggered in.

Sick and reeling, their movements like those of drunken men, the two of them now stumbled toward the western pal-ace. The same group of men who had met five hours previously had assembled once again in the courtyard, yet it was as though centuries had passed.

The men had aged, hair had whitened, wrinkles had become more pronounced. Where before there had been spirit and determination, despair was now evident. Nearly all of those now assembled in the torch-lit courtyard had killed often in the past. They were rebels and outlaws and most of them were not squeamish about death, but what they had just experienced was different from all that had gone before. Nahum stood by Eleazar, his great frame shrunken, a mere shadow of the vigorous fighter he had been only five hours earlier. Eleazar himself was so pale that he looked inhuman. His teeth were chattering and he found difficulty in speaking. The wives, the children, the dependents were dead, and there remained only the fighting men. The first stage of Eleazar's plan was complete.

11

There were only ten of them left; they huddled in their cloaks, beyond all reason. The night had been one of multiplying terrors, with every act bringing a new dimension to the dreadful orgy of death. Each hour had magnified the horror and the ghastliness of what they had done. They shivered as they stood by the water gate, lit by the flaring wall to the south, holding their blood-encrusted daggers. Over to the east the sky was turning from black to gray as a preliminary to dawn.

Eleazar could see his companions clearly in the light of the fire. In a fold of his cloak he was holding ten pieces of pottery, ten sherds with ten names. One of the ten must be selected to finish the job. Some of the men were beyond recognition. Joab was half mad, his green-flecked eyes stared wildly, his mouth was incapable of speech. Nahum had folded in on himself as if his broad, powerful frame had started to decompose. Bar Nottos, always so young and boyish, whose smooth skin had possessed that quality of agelessness, looked old and lined with pain. Even Hanan looked moved with horror; it was the first time Eleazar had seen emotion expressed on that broad Idumean face. Jacob was red-eyed and disheveled. Ben Levi's eyes glittered and he muttered to himself, occasionally shouting out a word or phrase. They had no wish to communicate with each other: they had gone too far for human comfort.

When the men had met together in the western palace after the killing of their families, it had been these ten men who had been selected to kill the remaining defenders. It had been a long job, lasting through the rest of the night, for the men had wanted to die in their own homes by their families. Their homes were scattered all along the casemate wall and in every building on the rock from north to south. It had been a dreadful task, for each room contained dead women and children, infants, youths, and old folks. There was death everywhere: everywhere the same sickly-sweet smell of fresh human blood.

And so the ten of them had killed and killed. All through the night the last ten defenders of Masada, who had already killed their own wives and children, were forced to witness the evidence of similar acts as they killed the perpetrators of those acts. As each group of families was finally finished off, their homes were set afire; the thatched roofs caught fire and the beams and supports and doors, until the whole summit of Masada flamed and roared in the night. The ten men ran from room to room, checking for survivors, for wounded, for those not completely dead. They killed and fired, fired and killed, and all was red: red with blood and red with flames, until it seemed as if God Himself was bleeding and drenching Masada in red destruction.

Nahum had killed all through the night alongside his companions. He had killed almost eagerly, as if all the slaughter could wipe out the vision of the earlier killing.

Leah had finally resigned herself to the plan. "So be it," she had said. "It cannot be much worse than a Roman victory, and surrender is out of the question because you are all insane."

They had rested, quietly and without fear, but they had not

309

been able to sleep. Finally, the time had come and Nahum reluctantly made ready to kill his family.

"No, Nahum, no!" Leah had screamed suddenly. "I do not want to die! "

The children had started to stir, and Nahum had rushed toward Leah in an attempt to quiet her, to force his hand over her mouth if necessary. His move was misinterpreted by Leah, who fled from him squealing with fright. He lunged after her savagely, knocking his hip against the corner of their heavy wooden table. He cursed and stumbled after her.

"No, Nahum, please, no!" she had repeated. "I will do anything if only you will let me live!" He had caught up with her finally and struck her savagely with his fist. Her head crashed against the flint wall of the room and she fell. A further blow had caught her as she had fallen. She lay on the ground, her neck twisted awkwardly; she was dead. He had hastened to kill his children while they slept, starting with Joseph, the youngest. Uri had kicked out in his death throes, waking David. Nahum had clamped his large hand over his son's eyes and mouth; but his knife, still wet with the blood of the younger children, had clattered impotently to the floor. There had been no alternative then—he had killed his eldest son with his bare hands.

All night Nahum had killed in a mindless fury, as he went from room to room, from family to family, trying to wipe out the memory of the clumsy, bungled killing of his own family; but it had not helped. Their image had been constantly before him.

Masada was in flames, and to the east the rim of pale gray sky was widening above Moab; the flames roared into the sky to meet the bloodred dawn. Eleazar held up the ten pieces of sherd with the ten names for all of them to see, but their eyes were dull and none of them showed any great interest. He dropped the pieces back into the folds of his cloak. Shutting his eyes, he dipped his hand into the fold. He felt among the pieces for the one he wanted. There could be no mistake: square on two sides with a curved edge joining the angle.

310

Without opening his eyes, he picked up the sherd and handed it to bar Nottos, who stood by him. Bar Nottos read out the name in a low voice:

"Ben Jair," he said.

12

Eleazar had not taken long to finish the task. Even the dispatching of his two faithful companions, Joab and Nahum, had not moved him. He was the only survivor, the only man left alive on the whole of Masada out of a community of nine hundred and sixty men, women, and children.

It was dawn and the Romans would enter at any instant. He had no time to lose. From the remains of the western gate north of the still-smoldering earth and wood wall, he could see the soldiers advancing up the earth ramp to the tower. They would be inside the fortress in a matter of minutes. In the last stages of exhaustion, Eleazar ran for the northern palace. His side hurt dreadfully and he gasped for breath. He was smarting from several burns. The disheveled, dirty, bloodstained figure was not the same man as the white-robed rabbi who had presided over prayers or the lithe guerrilla fighter who had led his men competently into battle. He was smeared with ash and soot, wild-eyed and desperate. He reached the top of the stairway and plunged down, stumbling on the steep steps.

The fire was everywhere; billowing smoke choked him. The northern palace was in flames. As he arrived at the second level the lower staircase was a sheet of fire. He proceeded undeterred into the fire; but at that moment the whole stairway collapsed with a crash and the roof started to fall in. His wife and child were below and he was trapped on the second story of the palace with the Romans behind him and the fire in front.

Hagar had been awake at midnight, when Eleazar had made ready to carry out his duty. He had sat for several minutes watching his sleeping child. Menahem had lain curled up in a ball, his brown face slightly flushed in sleep, his nostrils distended slightly with his breathing, and his full lips parted, revealing the small white teeth. One brown hand, still dimpled, was clenched in a fist. One slim leg protruded from the sheepskin cover, and Eleazar went over and tucked it under the skin. The boy had grunted and turned over and at that moment Eleazar knew that he had never loved anyone or anything as he loved the little brown creature who lay there asleep. He had stooped and kissed the smooth cheek. He turned to his wife, his question in his glance. There had been no need to speak.

"The child first," she had said. "I will stay with you while you do it; but I cannot watch you." He took her in his arms.

"I am sorry, Hagar," he said simply.

"There was nothing else that you could have done." They kissed and then Hagar turned her back on her husband. As if in a dream, Eleazar moved slowly toward his son. He had unsheathed his *sica,* the razor-sharp dagger with the worn bone handle. With a sense of unreality, he had placed the edge against the slim throat of his only son.

He never remembered consciously doing the act. He only remembered the *sica* dripping with blood, his son's head lying at an unnatural angle, and a dark stain spreading over the sheepskin cover. He had turned to Hagar. She had stood there with a faint smile on her delicate lips, her small white teeth shining in the dim light of the oil lamp. She had stood there slender and graceful and youthful, and all at once she had collapsed, sinking softly to the ground. Then Eleazar had seen the hilt of her small dagger protruding from her ribs. She had been dead before he had reached her. He laid the child near her on the floor where she had fallen by the steps leading down to the bath room. They lay there like two sleeping children, her thick brown plait of hair neat and orderly.

The Romans were coming: he could hear the war cries of the Tenth Legion. The sounds were coming nearer. Eleazar ran out onto the terrace of the center level, standing poised on the edge. The sun had risen and he could feel its burning rays. To his right the mountains of Moab were an indistinct blue haze;

312

to his left of the dark brown rocks of Judea were still in shadow. Beyond the blinding white of the salt flats, the Sea of Salt was a golden sheen reflecting the morning sun. Forty feet below, the roof of his home had collapsed, and through the smoke and debris he could distinguish the two bundles that were his wife and child. He stood on the circular parapet and greeted the morning.

His hand felt for his skullcap. Miraculously, it was still in its place. His lips moved in prayer: *"I give thanks to Thee O Lord this day."* He turned and walked back toward the niche in the wall where there was a small basin. Next to the basin was a stone measuring cup that still contained some water. He picked up the cup and poured the water over his hands. *"Blessed art Thou O Lord our God, King of the Universe, who has sanctified us by Thy commandments and ordered us to wash our hands."*

He was back on the parapet; the Romans were very near now, less than a minute away. He unsheathed his *sica*, feeling the blade with his thumb. He placed the point under his ribs on the left side of his body and drove it upward toward his heart. He felt a sharp, burning pain as he swayed forward. His thin, sensitive face grimaced in agony, and then Eleazar the son of Jair, son of Judah, son of Hezekiah, fell through space to crash in a heap of flesh and bones beside the bodies of his wife and child.

FLAVIUS SILVA: MAY 73 C.E.

L. Flavius Silva Nonius Bassus, seventeenth procurator of Judea, stood on the eastern casemate wall of the fortress of Masada and looked down at the Sea of Salt below. It was all over. His campaign was at an end. As far as he could see nothing stirred in the vast expanse of desert, save only the vultures that wheeled above the still-smoking summit. The Judean war was truly finished. Silva had already sent messengers to Caesarea to convey the highly confidential dispatch to Vespasian at Rome. Looking over the bleak wastes, the Roman commander reflected on the stunning events of the morning. The fortress had been burning all night, and in the morning it was still burning in several places, smoldering in others. The fire had spread with a swiftness that had surprised the Romans.

At dawn the procurator had directed the legion to attack, wishing to end the unpleasant task as quickly as possible. With the famous war cries of the Tenth Legion resounding in answer to the trumpets which signaled the advance, the Roman soldiers charged through the breach in the wall. In all his life the commander would never forget how the shouts died suddenly on the lips of his men, soldiers who had made a business of war for two decades. Even they had been silenced by the sight that met their eyes. In the years of his campaigns Silva himself had never seen anything to equal the quiet horror of the corpses neatly laid out in rows wherever he looked. His soldiers had stared and stared, their faces showing their utter bafflement.

Only a short time after they had entered the fortress, a group of two women and five children had emerged from one of the water cisterns below the northwestern summit. They had at once been brought to Silva for questioning. It was to the old woman, clearly the leader of the group, that the procurator addressed his remarks. She had told him the story of what had happened on that last incredible night at Masada. The story was unbelievable, but the evidence was there before his eyes.

317

Finally he had turned to the old woman. "And you?" he had asked her. "Why did you flee?"

The woman had stood before him, proud and dignified, a halo of white hair surrounding her finely drawn features. "It is a sin to take life," she had answered in a deep and impressive voice. "The Lord gives us life, and only He has the right to take it away."

"Are you then afraid to die?"

"All are afraid to die."

"Yet you fought against Rome—you were of the rebels?"

She shook her head. "With them, but not of them," she had replied. "It is a sin to take even the life of a Roman. The struggle with Rome is irrelevant; it is the inner struggle to know God that is important."

"Why is the struggle with Rome irrelevant, woman?" he had asked.

"Your power is great, Roman, but it will pass. No earthly power is eternal; only the power of the Lord God of Israel!" The procurator had been irritated by the old woman's certainty and disdain. He had been prompted to argue with her.

"Even your own Jewish legends say that our power is forever!" he had claimed. "When the king of Babylon dreamed about the statue, he dreamed that the legs of iron would continue: the head of gold—Babylon—was succeeded by the arms, representing the Medes and Persians, who surpassed him. Then Alexander and the Greeks from the west were the body of bronze, which was superseded by the iron kingdom of the Romans, which will endure forever, for iron is the strongest of metals!"

Silva had been proud of himself, proud of his knowledge and of the way his wit had turned the tables on the old lady; but she had simply smiled and replied, "I congratulate you, Roman, on having studied our books and legends; but your teachers were deficient in knowledge, or maybe deliberately misled you through a desire to placate you. You have not completed the legend that you began so succinctly. You may read it all in our book of Daniel." She paused. "However, I will save you the trouble; but first, Roman, look at the view that your eyes can

318

see!" They had been standing by the breach in the western wall above the siege ramp. "This is only a tiny part of a small country, yet in this waste the Lord God first appeared to His people. How long did your soldiers toil in order to change a small part of this valley? How many weeks did thousands of men work to build your wonderful ramp? The Lord God created the heavens and the earth in just six days: do you aspire to compare Rome's power to His?"

Something in her tone had prevented the procurator from replying. He had regarded her silently, waiting for her to continue.

"Now I shall complete the story which you began," she said. "There is not much more to tell: you see, the statue's head was gold, his breast and arms of silver, his belly and his thighs of brass, his legs of iron, and his feet part of iron and part of clay!

"And the fourth kingdom shall be as strong as iron; forasmuch as iron breaketh in pieces and beateth down all things. . . . And as the toes of the feet were part of iron, and part of clay . . . they shall mingle themselves by the seed of men; but they shall not cleave one to another, even as iron doth not mingle with clay. And in the days of those kings shall the God of heaven set up a kingdom, which shall never be destroyed; nor shall the kingdom be left to another people; it shall break in pieces and consume all these kingdoms, but it shall stand for ever."

Silva had stood before the old woman unable to speak. He had looked out over the desert and then looked back at the features of the woman.

Once again the procurator surveyed the land, the terrible, stark Judean desert. Over by the western palace his soldiers were formed up, motionless under the burning sun. The Roman shivered despite the heat; he tore his eyes away from the hypnotic drop to the eastern foot of the rock and walked over toward where his soldiers stood waiting for their orders.

ACKNOWLEDGMENTS

The italicized Bible passages in the text are taken from the Jewish Publication Society translation of the Bible.

The author would like to express his gratitude to the following:

Penguin Books and Geza Vermes for permission to quote from *The Dead Sea Scrolls in English* the passages before Books II, IV, and V and the italicized passages in the text which are not from the Bible.

Penguin Books and G. A. Williamson for permission to quote from *Josephus: The Jewish War* the passages before Books I, III, and V.

While the main source books were the writings of Flavius Josephus, the Dead Sea Scrolls, the Bible, Apocrypha and Mishna, considerable help was afforded by reading the works of the following scholars, who are in no way responsible for the present work:

MOSES ABERBACH	SHMARYAHU GUTTMAN
YOHANAN AHARONI	JOSEPH HALPERN
J. M. ALLEGRO	CECIL ROTH
ELIAS BICKERMAN	EMIL SCHURER
F. M. CROSS	GEZA VERMES
ISIDORE EPSTEIN	G. A. WILLIAMSON
MOSES I. FINLEY	EDMUND WILSON
NELSON GLUECK	YIGAEL YADIN

The author would also like to put on record the help he received from his friend Reuven Sadeh, to whom this work is dedicated. His intimate knowledge of the Judean desert was of great value in preparing the book.

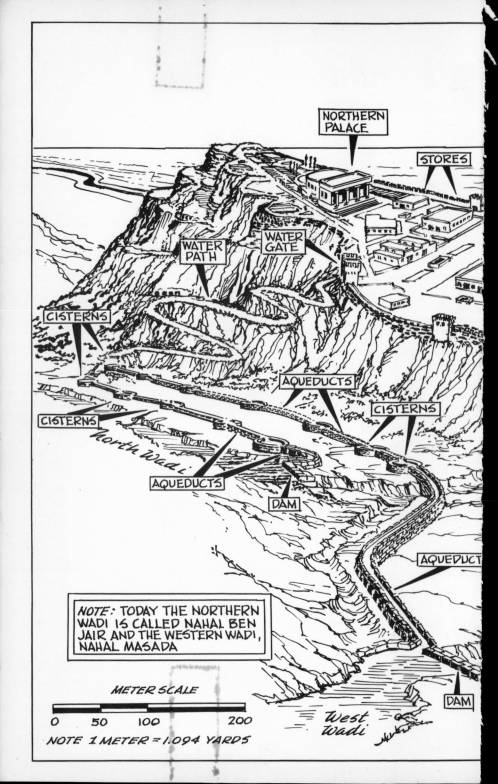

NORTHERN PALACE

STORES

WATER PATH

WATER GATE

CISTERNS

AQUEDUCTS

CISTERNS

CISTERNS

North Wadi

AQUEDUCTS

DAM

AQUEDUCT

NOTE: TODAY THE NORTHERN WADI IS CALLED NAHAL BEN JAIR AND THE WESTERN WADI, NAHAL MASADA

METER SCALE

0   50   100   200

NOTE 1 METER = 1.094 YARDS

West Wadi

DAM